M000306886

Made for
Sex

Books by Joan Elizabeth Lloyd

The Price of Pleasure

Never Enough

Club Fantasy

Night After Night

The Secret Lives of Housewives

Naughtier Bedtime Stories

Hot Summer Nights

Made for Sex

Published by Kensington Publishing Corporation

Made for Sex

JOAN ELIZABETH LLOYD

KENSINGTON BOOKS
http://www.kensingtonbooks.com

KENSINGTON BOOKS are published by

Kensington Publishing Corp.
850 Third Avenue
New York, NY 10022

Copyright © 2007 by Kensington Publishing Corp.
Black Satin copyright © 1995 by Joan Elizabeth Lloyd
The Love Flower copyright © 1998 by Joan Elizabeth Lloyd

All rights reserved. No part of this book may be reproduced in any form or by any means without the prior written consent of the Publisher, excepting brief quotes used in reviews.

All Kensington titles, imprints and distributed lines are available at special quantity discounts for bulk purchases for sales promotion, premiums, fund-raising, educational or institutional use.

Special book excerpts or customized printings can also be created to fit specific needs. For details, write or phone the office of the Kensington Special Sales Manager: Kensington Publishing Corp., 850 Third Avenue, New York, NY 10022. Attn. Special Sales Department. Phone: 1-800-221-2647.

Kensington and the K logo Reg. U.S. Pat. & TM Off.

ISBN-13: 978-0-7582-1277-1
ISBN-10: 0-7582-1277-1

First Kensington Trade Paperback Printing: November 2007
10 9 8 7 6 5 4 3 2 1

Printed in the United States of America

CONTENTS

Black Satin

Chapter

1

"You sent for me, Miss Gilbert?" the man said. Although he looked about forty, paunchy, with a neatly trimmed moustache, he was dressed in a traditional boy's school uniform: short navy pants, white formal shirt, a green-and-navy plaid blazer, and white, knee-length socks. Incongruously, he also wore Gucci loafers with small tassels on the vamp.

"I certainly did, Bobby," Miss Gilbert said. She sat behind an antique desk that she had previously moved to the center of the large, beautifully furnished living room. As arranged, she was dressed in a high-collared, long-sleeved white blouse fastened with a classic cameo at the neck. Her straight black skirt was pulled primly over her knees, covering most of her sheer hose. Her gray hair was swept up and pinned into a bun on the top of her head and her rimless glasses were perched on the end of her nose. She stared at Bobby over the top of her spectacles. "I'm afraid you're in serious trouble."

As Bobby looked at the floor he could see her heavy, black sensible shoes with their thick heels. Although the sound was muffled by the plush carpet, he could see her toe tapping rhythmically. "Yes, ma'am."

"I've seen the results of your exams and they're totally unsatisfactory." Miss Gilbert picked up a ruler from the desk and smacked it into the palm of her hand.

"Yes, ma'am," Bobby said, his knees shaking and a bulge forming in the front of his shorts.

"Do you know what that means?" Again the ruler smacked her hand, her long slender fingers wrapping around the wooden slat.

"Yes, ma'am." Bobby's palms began to sweat and his breathing accelerated.

"Tell me, exactly." She smiled. Smack, smack.

"It means that either you'll tell my parents or. . . ."

"Or what, Bobby?" Smack, smack.

"Twenty?"

"There were three failures," Miss Gilbert said. Her index finger stroked the edge of the ruler slowly.

Bobby's eyes followed the bright red nail back and forth. "Th, th, thirty," he stammered.

"Yes, I'm afraid so." Her finger kept sliding from one end of the ruler to the other. "Thirty." Smack. "It's your choice."

"You can't call my parents," Bobby said. "My father would kill me." Inside he smiled. His father had been dead for almost five years but that didn't matter. This dialogue had been honed over many encounters. Sweat tickled his underarms.

"Then we know what it will be, don't we?"

Silently, Bobby pulled off his jacket and shirt revealing a slightly overweight body and hairless chest. Nervously, he ran his hand through his thick, dark brown hair and wiped a light film of sweat from his face. He dropped his hands to his sides and waited for the instructions he knew would come.

Her voice conversational, Miss Gilbert said, "That's good. Now drop them."

His fingers were barely able to unzip his fly as Bobby opened the uniform pants and let them drop to the floor around his sock-covered ankles.

"What are you waiting for?" Miss Gilbert said.

Trembling, he slipped his fingers into the elastic waistband of his white cotton drawers and started to pull them down. As usual, the task was made more difficult by the size of his erection. He pulled the shorts out over his hard cock and down so they fell and joined his navy blue uniform pants on the floor.

"Well," Miss Gilbert said, rising from her seat behind the large maple desk and staring at his cock. "I can see that dickie is anxious for what is next." She rounded the desk and tapped the end of the ruler against Bobby's hard cock. She reached across the desk and picked up an Ace bandage. She wrapped the wide elastic around Bobby's hard cock, attaching the first turn with a metal clip. Then she wound the stretchy fabric around his hips, then over his now-bulging erection. Around and around, she encased the area from Bobby's waist to his crotch in the stretchy fabric.

Bobby could barely contain his excitement. The first few times they had played out this scenario, he had come inside the elastic before they could get to the best part. By now he had developed some self-control. He bent his arms on the bright green blotter-covered surface and placed his forehead against his crossed wrists, his gold Tourneau watch showing the exact time and date.

"Now, Bobby," Miss Gilbert said, "you know that you must count for me and thank me for not calling your parents." She tapped the ruler against his shins, still covered by the white socks. He moved his legs back and spread them apart.

Swoosh. The first slap of the ruler fell across the elastic over his ass. It didn't really hurt but rather made his cheeks vibrate. "One, Miss Gilbert, and thank you."

Nine more swats fell across his buttocks. Now the entire area covered by the Ace bandage tingled. "Ten, Miss Gilbert, and thank you." He knew what came next, but it didn't make it any easier.

With little warning, the eleventh swat fell across the back of his bare right thigh. Miss Gilbert made sure that it stung and left a slight red mark.

"Eleven," Bobby said, "and thank you, Miss Gilbert." By the twentieth swat, the backs of both well-muscled thighs were bright red and sore.

"I think we'll wait for the last ten for a short while," Miss Gilbert said. She tapped the back of Bobby's neck and he raised his head. She put the ruler on the desk where he couldn't help but stare at it. "Are you very sore?" she asked innocently.

"It's not too bad," Bobby said. His legs were on fire but it wouldn't do to admit it.

"I'll make it better for you," Miss Gilbert said. Carefully, she unwrapped the elastic bandage from around his body and touched the deep indentations it had left. "Poor baby," she said, running a long fingernail over one particularly deep groove on one cheek. Holding the end of the pink stretch material still encasing his cock, she ran the tip of her tongue over the groove in his skin. As she yanked at the end of the material, Bobby's cock pulled toward her. She released the material and it snapped back. Alternately pulling and releasing the bandage, she continued to lick the marks on his ass.

As she straightened and looked toward his cock, she could see drops of sticky fluid oozing from the tip. "Is it hard not to come?" she asked sweetly.

"Oh, yes, Miss Gilbert," Bobby said.

"Well, we can't have you disgracing yourself, can we?"

"No, Miss Gilbert."

Still playing with the end of the elastic, she pulled at his cock and smiled. "You know the penalty for premature ejaculation, don't you?"

"Yes, Miss Gilbert." It happened occasionally. The last time they had been together, he had come like a fountain, spurting semen all over the desk. He had been forced to clean up the mess and had gotten ten extra swats from the ruler. He had come again then, but had been disappointed with his performance, his lack of fortitude. This time, however, he was sure he had enough self-control to finish.

Miss Gilbert unwound the elastic from Bobby's cock, put the roll down, and picked up the ruler. "You've been very good today," she said. "Should we reduce the punishment to twenty-five?"

As much as he might like to decrease his suffering, he wanted to continue to test his endurance. "No, ma'am," he said. "I need to be thoroughly punished."

Swat number twenty-one was a stinger, just hard enough to burn his now-bare ass. "Thank you, Miss Gilbert. That was number twenty-one."

By number twenty-eight, Bobby's ass was as red as the backs of his thighs, but he stayed bent over the desk and took it.

Miss Gilbert knew what was expected now. For swat number twenty-nine she raised her arm as high as it would go and brought the wooden ruler down as hard as she could.

It hurt terribly, but Bobby didn't move. "Twenty-nine and thank you, Miss Gilbert."

She heard Bobby's deep breathing and knew he was trying not to cry out. She raised her arm one last time and administered the final swat as hard as she could.

"Thirty and thank you, Miss Gilbert." Bobby stood up, his hands at his sides, his erection enormous.

"Are you sure you've learned your lesson?"

"Oh yes, Miss Gilbert, and thank you. I'm ready for the rest of my punishment now."

Miss Gilbert went into the bathroom and returned with a large bath towel which she spread over the desk. She tapped the ruler across Bobby's inflamed buttocks and he moved so the fronts of his thighs pressed against the desk. "I'm going to watch you now. That's the rest of your punishment, you know. Show me what a bad boy you are," she said, her voice smooth and soft as cream. "Show me how you rub your dickie when no one's looking. Show me."

Bobby watched Miss Gilbert round the desk and sit down in her chair. He saw her ice-blue eyes riveted on his cock, still striped by the small folds that had been in the elastic. He hesitated. This was still the worst and best part.

"Bobby," Miss Gilbert said, "I want you to play with yourself so I can see. I want to watch everything. Now, wrap your hand around your dickie and rub." When he still hesitated, she picked up the ruler and snapped, "Now!"

His hands shaking, Bobby took his cock in his hands and began to rub.

"Wait," Miss Gilbert said. "I have an idea." She opened the desk drawer and pulled out a tube of lubricating gel. "Hold out your hands."

Slippery stuff. This was new, Bobby thought, a deviation from the ritual. But it was wonderful. She had guessed what he wanted without his having to tell her anything. That was what made her so special. He held his hands out, palm up, in front of him, and Miss Gilbert squeezed a huge glob of slippery goo into one hand. "Now rub," she said.

It feels so cold, he thought as his hands surrounded his hot cock. The moment he touched himself, he was lost. He closed his eyes and slid his fingers up and down his cock.

"Open your eyes you naughty boy," Miss Gilbert snapped. "I want you to see me watching your hands play with your cock." When he didn't obey immediately, she snapped again, "Now! Do it!"

He opened his eyes and looked into her face. Her eyes were riveted on his hands stroking his cock. It was sensational. It only took a moment until spurts of come erupted, falling on the white surface of the towel. His knees almost buckled, but he held on, enjoying the afterglow of one of the best orgasms of his life.

Miss Gilbert sat, unmoving, until Bobby swept up the towel and disappeared into the bathroom. Fifteen minutes later, she was sitting behind the desk reading when Bobby emerged from the bathroom, dressed in a gray pinstriped suit, light blue shirt, and paisley tie. He wore black socks and the Gucci loafers.

Without another word, he checked the time on his gold watch, put a handful of bills on the green blotter, and left the room.

The slam of metal against metal, the impact of her chest against her car's shoulder belt, and Carla's "Oh shit," came almost simultaneously. She shifted the car into park and stared out through the windshield. "Where the hell did he come from? There wasn't anything there a second ago," she said aloud, slumping against the seat. The front bumper of her six-year-old Ford had put a significant dent in the passenger-side rear quarter panel of a classy, gleaming dark blue Cadillac. "Oh God," she moaned. "Oh God, why me?"

Several pedestrians and a bicyclist had stopped to gawk at the tableau. Carla's car was blocking the sidewalk, halfway out of a Kinney underground garage between First and Second Avenues on East 53rd Street, an upscale Manhattan neighborhood. The Cadillac, which had been heading west across 53rd, sat in the road, the front of Carla's car resting against its side.

With a deep sigh, Carla climbed out of her car and watched the driver of the Cadillac emerge. As the woman stood up, Carla stared. The driver was a tall, slender statuesque woman with dark blond hair twisted into a perfect French knot. As the classically beautiful woman stared at her through dark, tortoiseshell sunglasses, Carla self-consciously ran her palms down the thighs of her comfortable, well-washed jeans.

The more Carla studied the woman, the more stunning she looked. The woman removed her designer sunglasses and shaded her eyes from the afternoon sun. She had perfectly arched brows over deep blue eyes, a long slender nose, and coral lips. Carla thought that she looked like Grace Kelly at her best.

Carla ran her fingers through her shoulder-length, brown hair, and tucked an errant strand behind one ear. "I'm terribly sorry," she called as the woman closed the Cadillac's door. "I can't imagine how this happened." Now that's an inane statement, she thought.

Carla had been so happy when her doctor's visit had confirmed that all her worries had been needless. The lump in her breast had turned out to be nothing but a fluid-filled cyst. She had been so relieved after a week of suspense that she had almost run to the garage, bailed her car out, and started for home. Why was she going home? She wasn't really sure. The kids were still at school and her mom and dad were both out for the day. And anyway, she hadn't told her parents or her three boys about the lump. No need to worry anyone, she had reasoned. Unfortunately, that meant that she now had no one with whom to celebrate.

As Carla watched, the blonde walked around the joined vehicles, calmly assessed the situation, and shook her head. God, Carla thought, I had to hit someone like her. The woman wore a classic dark red Donna Karan suit, a matching red-and-white patterned blouse, and perfectly coordinated Robert Clergerie pumps. She adjusted a gold, red, and white Hermes scarf over her shoulder with long, slender, perfectly manicured fingers. "Oh dear," the woman said, her voice soft and well modulated. "I'm so sorry."

"You're sorry?" Carla said.

"Of course," the woman said. "I was going a bit too fast and I wasn't watching where I was going." The woman hesitated, staring. "Wait. It couldn't be." She continued to stare. "Carla?"

"Excuse me?"

"Carla. You're Carla MacKensie."

"Carla Barrett," she answered. "But I was Carla MacKensie before I married. Do we know each other?"

"It's Veronica. Ronnie Browning, now Talmidge."

"Ronnie? It can't be." Carla and Ronnie had been roommates at Michigan State and had graduated together fifteen years before. During their three years together they had shared everything: field hockey, the debate team, the drama club and even, unintentionally, a few boyfriends.

Ronnie's laugh was a full rich sound. "I'd know you anywhere. You haven't changed a bit." She looked down. "I guess I've changed a little since then."

Carla remembered the moderately attractive brunette with wire-rimmed glasses and little makeup whom she had loved like a sister. "Have you ever! You look sensational." She smiled ruefully. "And you're right, I haven't changed. Unfortunately I look pretty much like I did fifteen years ago: medium brown and average, average, average." Carla looked Ronnie over carefully. "What in the world have you been doing for the last fifteen years?"

"More than you can possibly imagine." Ronnie looked at the

two cars and waved her hand. "You know, this seems relatively minor. Listen. Where were you off to?"

"Minor?" There had to be thousands of dollars' worth of damage. You couldn't have an accident that didn't cost thousands these days. "I was going home to Bronxville—where I live now."

"That's silly. Now that we've found each other let's not lose track again. Why don't we park here and have lunch? We can catch up on all those years. And, anyway, I'm starved."

"Weren't you going somewhere?"

"I have an appointment at two," Ronnie said, glancing at her gold Cartier watch, "but that gives us over an hour, and there's a great little Italian place down the block."

When Carla hesitated, Ronnie's voice dropped. "Please. I'd love the company and we have so much to catch up on."

The parking lot attendant ran up waving his hands, trying to clear the entranceway. "You'll have to move these cars," the uniformed man yelled.

Ronnie's voice was soft, yet authoritative. "If you'll wait just a moment, Tom, we'll be out of the way." She turned to Carla and said, "I'm in this neighborhood a lot. I used to park here all the time but I've found a less expensive place around the corner."

As Ronnie returned to her car, Carla climbed into her Ford and backed up. The cars separated and Carla noticed that the damage to the Cadillac was less than she'd expected. Just a nasty dent and some chipped paint. She'd have to examine her car, but since the bumper had been the point of contact she thought it should be okay.

"Over here," Tom said. "Back it right over here." He waved Carla into one parking space and Ronnie drove into the one next to it.

As she climbed out, Ronnie said, "We'll be a few hours, Tom." She leaned into the passenger seat to grab a fashionable bag that Carla knew had to be either a Fendi or a great knockoff and slung the chain strap over her shoulder. Carla reached through the open passenger window of the Ford and grabbed her ersatz leather purse and camel-colored wool jacket. She slipped her arms in the sleeves and buttoned the blazer over her denim-blue-and-white striped shirt.

"Oh, Carla, this is so wonderful," Ronnie said. She looked at the front end of Carla's car. "Not bad," Ronnie said. "Looks like you got out of this little accident with almost no damage at all."

Carla nodded and wrapped her arm around Ronnie's waist. "I'm so glad I ran into you." She laughed. "Literally."

"Me too. This way." Ronnie led Carla under a small awning that proclaimed the restaurant to be The Villa Luigi. As they entered, Carla inhaled the enticing odor of garlic, oregano, and olive oil. They were shown to a quiet table in the back. "Give us a bottle of your Ruffino and some garlic bread," Ronnie told the waitress who seated them. As she left, Ronnie laughed. "Remember the night we got a gallon of jug-red and drank it with an entire package of Oreos with Double Stuff?"

"All I remember is how sick we were the next morning. I had to hold onto the floor to keep from falling off."

"And I puked my guts up for over an hour." The two women laughed. "Tell me what's new with you now," Ronnie said.

Carla took a deep breath. "Well, I was married for almost nine years but Bill was killed in a car accident almost five years ago."

"I'm so sorry."

"Well. . . . Bill wasn't exactly Prince Charming. He drank too much and was not a nice drunk. I had been thinking about a divorce for a year before his death."

"Kids?"

"BJ—that's Bill Junior—is thirteen, Tommy's eleven, and Mike's ten. Three boys. Where did I go wrong?"

"I remember that you wanted ten kids, all girls. And you never wanted to work."

"Never work? God, imagine thinking that being a mommy wasn't work."

"So you're a mommy full time?"

"Fortunately Bill left me pretty well provided for. That, and I sell a little real estate. I got my license about two years ago and I put what I make away for college for the boys. Sometimes I think

I should work more, what with the boys in school all day and my folks right next door, but I can't think of what I could do, college degree or no college degree." Carla put her napkin in her lap. "English literature. A useful degree if ever there was one. Anyway, what about you? Married? Where do you live?"

Ronnie waggled her left hand under Carla's nose. The wide gold band on her third finger flashed. She also wore a thin band of diamonds on her index finger and a heavy free-form gold ring on the middle finger of her other hand. "Jack's an independent geologist who does consulting for a number of oil companies. It's a combination of lots of travel and a house full of computers. He's only home about one week a month." She heaved a sigh. "Unfortunately, no kids. I found out early on that I couldn't have any and neither of us wanted to adopt. We live in Hopewell Junction, in Dutchess County, almost two hours north of here. What were you doing in town, by the way?"

"Doctor's appointment."

Ronnie jumped in. "Nothing serious, I hope."

"Nothing. A lump in my breast that turned out to be a benign cyst."

"I'm glad." She squeezed her friend's hand.

Carla was touched. Ronnie was someone with whom she had always shared everything. It felt good sharing now. "So, Ronnie, I couldn't help noticing the quality of your wardrobe. And the new Cadillac. Jack's obviously doing well."

"Well enough. But the Caddie's mine."

"You work?"

Ronnie smiled in a way that puzzled Carla. "Yes, I work." She paused, then continued. "And I take occasional courses in creative writing at NYU. I've even had a few articles published."

"That's great." The waitress brought their wine and a basket of bread dripping with butter, garlic, and herbs. When she had poured them each a glass and left, the two women picked up their glasses and tapped them together.

"To work in all its forms," Ronnie said mysteriously, then laughed.

Puzzled, Carla drank.

For the next hour, Carla and Ronnie caught up on everything that had happened since they lost touch after graduation when Ronnie traveled in Europe for a year. As the two women finished espressos and the last of the bottle of wine, Ronnie looked at her watch. "I hate to say this, but I have to run. Someone's meeting me at two. But let's get together next week. Noon. Why don't we meet out front and eat somewhere else? And, don't worry about the damage to my car. I'll let my collision coverage take care of it." Ronnie took the check, added a generous tip, and split the amount. After settling up, the two women stood and Ronnie reached out and hugged Carla. "God, I've missed you."

For each of the next three Mondays the two women lunched in the same neighborhood: at a Chinese restaurant specializing in Peking Duck, an Indian hole-in-the-wall that made the best mulligatawny Carla had ever tasted, and today at a sushi bar where Carla sampled raw fish for the first time. Over ginger ice cream and green tea, Ronnie suggested their next meeting place. "I'd like you to see my place," she said. "Let's have lunch chez moi next week."

"In Hopewell Junction? I guess I could. You'll have to give me directions."

"Not Hopewell Junction. Around the corner." With an enigmatic smile, Ronnie gave Carla an address on East 54th.

"I don't get it, Ronnie. You have an apartment right here?" She saw Ronnie nod, then pause. "No wonder you know all the good spots to eat. Have you got a secret life? Tell me everything."

"Next week I promise you'll know all." As Ronnie left for her usual two o'clock meeting, she added, "I'll arrange to have the whole afternoon free. We'll talk."

The address that Ronnie had given Carla led her to a small, three-story brownstone on East 54th. Carla climbed the four steps to the entrance and rang the bell. Ronnie opened the door dressed in a soft gray wool long-sleeved jumpsuit, her dark blond hair loose around her shoulders. A pair of large, free-form silver earrings and a silver herringbone choker were her only jewelry. Carla was glad that she had chosen to forgo her usual jeans and had worn a dark green wool suit with a beige raw silk blouse.

The two women bussed cheeks, and Carla followed Ronnie through a small vestibule and into a beautifully furnished living room.

"Some fantastic place," Carla said as she looked around. Everything was done in black, white, and shades of gray. The sofa was overstuffed, covered in black leather banded with leather straps secured with heavy metal buckles. It was accented with throw pillows in black-and-white stripes and plaids. The two comfortable-looking soft chairs were white jacquard fabric with identical black-and-white pillows. A fluffy white rug covered the center of the floor; Carla could see the original highly polished inlaid wood where the rug ended. The walls were covered with a soft silver-gray silk and the windows were draped in a slightly darker gray damask. End tables of black lacquer held white-based, modern lamps that filled the room with light.

Vases and pots of flowers placed on tables and pedestals around the room provided the only color. Roses, chrysanthemums, and geraniums added their hues to blooming cactuses and unusual blossoms that Carla didn't recognize. Several hanging baskets of living blooms hung from hooks in both the walls and ceiling. One wall was all windows with a decorative but highly functional iron grill outside. The opposite wall contained a long, white, glass-fronted wall unit filled with books of every kind, from popular novels to poetry to volumes on natural sciences and history. The other walls held black-and-white Ansel Adams prints and other, smaller black-and-white photographs by artists Carla didn't know. At one end of the room sat an antique maple desk.

Carla whistled. "Holy cow." Through her real estate wanderings, she had learned enough to appreciate the class and expense of the decorating.

"Just a little hideaway," Ronnie said, laughing.

"Little? Either you inherited a small fortune, your writing is doing extremely well, or Jack indulges you and your 'little hide-away.' "

"Or 'D' none of the above." Ronnie handed Carla a champagne flute and filled it from an already opened bottle of Dom Pérignon. She clinked her glass against her friend's and, with an enigmatic smile, said, "To 'none of the above.' "

They drank. "Okay," Carla said, "give."

"I think we know each other well enough for me to show you my photographs. Sit down." She motioned toward the sofa and Carla picked up a photo album covered in black satin and sat down next to her friend. When she opened the album Carla saw a picture unlike anything she had expected. A statuesque brunette posed, wearing a black leather and chain bathing suit-like outfit. The links draped over her naked breasts, the supple leather caressed her hips and belly. On her hands she wore soft, elbow-length, black leather gloves and her legs were covered with thigh-high patent leather boots with five-inch heels.

The woman's wavy, auburn hair hung softly across her chest with one curl surrounding an erect dark brown nipple. In one hand she had a short, black leather riding crop. Her makeup was heavy, with bright red lipstick and exaggerated eyeshadow and liner. "I don't get it," said Carla.

"Turn the page."

The picture on the following page was of a woman with pale white-blond braids that hung down in front of her dress. She was turned slightly sideways, looking shy and vulnerable and dressed in a puffed-sleeve pink dress, an adult version of the dress a five-year-old girl might wear, with a fluffy full skirt over several petticoats and a wide sash tied into a large bow which peeked out from behind. Her white ankle socks were neatly cuffed and her black patent leather Mary-Janes gleamed. Her face, artfully made up with soft rouge and pale pink lipstick, looked youthful and familiar. As Carla examined the face more carefully, she gasped. "That's you." She flipped the page backward. "So's this."

"Turn the page."

The pictures that followed were all of Ronnie in various costumes: a harem girl with a transparent veil covering the lower half of her face, a prim gray-haired woman in a white high-necked blouse and sensible shoes, a voluptuous female pirate wearing short shorts that showed the half-moons of her ass peeking beneath and a blouse unbuttoned to the waist, and a woman in a black satin teddy standing over a man whose arms and legs were secured to the frame of a brass bed with lengths of heavy-link chain and padlocks.

"Phew. Ronnie, I'm amazed here. Okay, fill me in."

"I call the album Black Satin and it's really a menu. Selected people get to pick their . . . shall we say entrée and I supply the dessert."

"You're trying to tell me that you're a hooker."

"I'm a very selective, high-priced prostitute."

Carla was flabbergasted. She had expected something unusual. After all Ronnie had never been mainstream. But this? What could she say?

Ronnie spoke, her voice a bit tentative. "No condemnation? No 'how could you?' "

"I'm too much in shock to say much of anything. But, of course, your life is your own."

Ronnie smiled. "And it's wonderful. I enjoy every bit of my secret existence."

"What about Jack?"

Ronnie smiled. "I think he knows what's going on. He travels and I know that he entertains himself while he's away, and so do I."

"What about AIDS?"

"I thought about that a lot when all this began. Many of my friends—that's what I call them, my friends—don't want actual intercourse. They want oral sex, toys, and/or mutual masturbation. And those who do want to have intercourse must wear condoms."

"What about oral sex? Isn't that risky?"

"Not as risky as unprotected intercourse, but yes, it is. I thought about it a lot at the beginning, and I decided it was a risk I was willing to take."

"How in the world did you get involved in this?"

Ronnie leaned back and put her feet on the coffee table. "How, indeed."

Chapter

2

"I guess it all started just over three years ago," Ronnie explained. "You have to understand that Jack and I have always had an open relationship. I guess you'd say we were swingers. We both enjoy sex a lot and find that outside activities actually enhance what we have."

"You mean . . . with other people?"

Ronnie chuckled. "Yes, both of us were. And it didn't bother me at all. I loved the idea that someone else was making Jack happy, particularly since he was—and still is—away so much. And back then he'd come home with new ideas, toys, sexy lingerie." When she saw Carla's expression, Ronnie added, "Put your eyebrows down, Carla. You remember I was always the experimenter."

"I remember some of your experiments. Like Oreos and peanut butter. Go on."

"Well, the only strict requirement that Jack and I had, and still have, is that no one has intercourse without a condom. Period."

"Don't you get jealous?"

"I can say truthfully that I'm not jealous. I can't speak for what goes on in Jack's mind, but for me, not a bit. Anyway, because of his traveling, Jack and I spend at least three weeks out of every month apart. We are always very careful with each other's feelings. We talk often, and I'm sure that Jack has no objections to what I'm doing, although he doesn't know all the details. I have no problem with his flirtations. And they're just that, flirtations. Nothing serious, just lust and good sex. For me too."

"If you can really handle it. . . ." Carla paused. "I'm not sure I could."

"I don't actually know of many who can, but Jack and I seem to do okay."

"You were telling me how this thing," Carla waved her hand around the luxurious room, "got started."

"Jack and I were having dinner with a business associate of his, TJ Sorenson of American Oil and Gas Products." Ronnie closed her eyes. "It was Christmastime about three years ago. I remember that there were tiny trees and red candles on the tables."

"What a meal," Jack said, settling back with a cup of espresso. "I've never been here before but you can be sure I'll come here again."

"I discovered Chez Martin several months ago," TJ said, "and I keep hoping that no one else will. I read the restaurant columns and am relieved every time I find other places discussed. So far no reviewer had found Chez Martin. I'm particularly glad I could share it with you. You're two of my favorite people." TJ Sorenson was about fifty, with a head full of white hair and a bushy white moustache, which he stroked with one index finger when he was thinking. An old-time wildcatter, TJ's eyes were the color of cornflowers with deep lines at the corners from squinting in the bright sun for dozens of years. He was a handsome man, with the outdoor look of someone who spent a great deal of time in the sun, wind, and weather. He didn't look old enough to have a grown son, a married daughter, and three grandchildren.

"Thanks so much, TJ," Ronnie said. "I'm so full I could burst." She took a sip of her white crème de menthe on the rocks and gazed at the two men, both looking mildly uncomfortable in double-breasted suits, white shirts, and ties. Although he looks great in his usual jeans and sweatshirt, I love how Jack looks in a suit, Ronnie thought. And the slight gray at the temples of his carefully combed dark brown hair makes him look more like a banker than an oil explorer.

"I'm glad you're so satisfied, because I have an ulterior motive for inviting you tonight." TJ stroked his moustache. "I would like to ask you a favor and I'm not entirely sure how to do it."

"Just ask," Jack said. "You've been so great to me for all these years, I'll be happy to help if I can."

"Well," TJ said, "I need both of you to agree, although it's really Ronnie's favor."

Ronnie's head popped up, her blond hair brushing her shoulders. "Me?"

TJ sighed. "Let me explain. First of all, I hope you don't mind that Jack has told me about your delightfully original relationship."

"Of course not. Jack and I are not ashamed of our lifestyle." Ronnie stroked Jack's hand lovingly. "We love each other and have fun as well." Jack winked one gray eye and nodded.

"You two seem to have figured out something that works for you and you know how much I like you both."

Ronnie rested her elbows on the table and studied the older man. TJ, who had recently been promoted to executive vice president of American Oil, had been Jack's first boss. The two men had hit it off almost immediately, and as TJ climbed the corporate ladder, Jack climbed with him. Several years earlier, when Jack formed his own geology consulting firm, TJ had given him moral support and had seen to it that American Oil put him on retainer. Jack and Ronnie owed him a lot.

In addition to their business relationship, the two men had become friends. In the early days, TJ and Jack had traveled together on oil drilling expeditions, often spending weeks at a time in the field, living in a tent, and actually wielding a pick and shovel. In the years since TJ had become office-bound, Jack and

Ronnie had dined occasionally with TJ and his wife Alice, most recently one evening the previous summer on the Sorensons' new forty-foot sailboat.

When TJ seemed at a loss as to how to continue, Ronnie said, "Whatever is bothering you can't be that terrible. Why don't you just come out with it?"

"Right." He sipped his cognac. "It's my son. You met Tim last summer on the boat. What was your impression of him, Ronnie? As a woman. And be honest."

She remembered TJ's son. He had been on his way somewhere but had paused for a moment to make small talk. She recalled an awkward young man who seemed uncomfortable with her. "He's a nice-looking guy, as I remember," she said, hedging. "How old is he now?"

"He's twenty-four. Tell me what you think of him as a person."

"I hardly spent any time with him," Ronnie said. "But he was charming, seemed to know the right thing to say but I guess he seemed a bit distant, a bit difficult to get to know."

"He's shy with women because he's had a few bad experiences. And now he's much worse. He was engaged, you know."

"No," Ronnie said. "I didn't know. You said *was?*"

"I did. The bitch did a number on him. I think she was more interested in my money than in Tim. Anyway, about a month ago, when he seemed to be losing interest, she lost her temper at our dinner table one evening. There were several other couples, their friends and ours, and Clarisse had been drinking. Something snapped, I've no idea what. But whatever caused it she read him out and, among other things, told him he was a lousy lover. I think her exact phrasing was that he couldn't give a nymphomaniac an orgasm."

"Oh shit," Jack said. "He must have been devastated."

"He was. Fortunately Tim and I have an honest relationship and we've talked at length since then. He doesn't want anything to do with Clarisse, but he admits that she might have a point about his sexual prowess. He told me that he feels inadequate and awkward as a lover. I told him that good sex takes two and that maybe he and Clarisse just weren't compatible, but he's really down on himself. We talked about finding a prostitute to, you know, teach him about women and sex, but he didn't want anything like that. Too impersonal, too clinical."

"Am I starting to see a plan here?" Ronnie asked.

"I hope so," TJ said. "I know and trust both of you and I need someone to teach Tim about women. Ronnie?"

"I'm flattered and I'd like to help. But I won't do anything without his knowledge," Ronnie said.

"Of course not." He looked from Ronnie to Jack. "If you two agree, I'll talk to him. I mentioned you recently and he remembers meeting you last summer. As a matter of fact, I think he was impressed, said you were a knockout, as I recall. I don't know whether that's the good news or the bad."

"I think it would be wonderful for Tim," Jack said, his charming grin revealing even, white teeth. "Ronnie's just the right woman to teach a young man about love and sex. She's terrific." He squeezed his wife's hand.

"So you're both willing?" TJ said.

"If Tim wants to, I'm certainly willing," Ronnie said.

Later that night, Ronnie and Jack lay in bed, naked, propped up on several pillows. "That's quite an assignment," Jack said, "teaching a young man about sex."

"I know," Ronnie said. "It's a bit daunting."

"Nonsense," Jack said. He tangled his fingers in Ronnie's hair. "Any man who looks at your full lips will want to kiss you." He pressed his lips against hers. "He'll want to use his tongue to play with yours." He opened her mouth with his tongue and stroked the inside. "He'll want to touch your face." He ran the pads of his fingers over Ronnie's forehead, cheeks, and nose. "And close your eyes with his lips." He kissed her eyelids.

"Maybe you should teach him," Ronnie said. "You do things so well."

As his hands made her skin burn everywhere they touched, Jack said, his voice hoarse, "Will you tell me every detail? Will you demonstrate to me everything you taught him?" His breathing was rough as his hands found her wet center.

"I may not share exactly what we do because that seems very private. But I'll make up something delicious," Ronnie said, wrapping her legs around her husband's waist. "But for right now, just fuck me good."

They were both so hot that their mating was frantic, tangling their bodies in sheets and pillows. He pounded into her hard and screamed when he came. Her orgasm wasn't far behind.

Tim called Ronnie about a week later. "My dad told me about your conversation," he said without preamble. "I'm really embarrassed about all this."

"I'm a little uncomfortable too, Tim, but I gather that this type of thing is common in Europe. The older woman educating the younger man."

Tim's hollow laugh echoed through the phone. "That doesn't help and anyway, you're not that much older."

Ronnie laughed. "It doesn't help me either, but I'd love to spend time with you, if you'd like. We could talk and do whatever you want, nothing more."

Ronnie heard Tim take a deep breath. "I think I would." He paused. "Maybe we could have dinner at that place Dad took you to. Like next Tuesday evening?"

Ronnie had been dreading a long dinner during which she and Tim would have to make pleasant conversation. It sounded awful. "You know, let's pass on dinner," Ronnie suggested. "Let me meet you at your apartment at about eight. We can talk and see what happens from there."

"I could pick you up." Ronnie could hear the hesitancy in his voice.

"I'd prefer to meet you, if that's okay." No long drive with awkward silences.

"Sure. Ronnie?"

"Yes."

"I'm terrified and mortified."

"Don't be. We'll only do what makes both of us comfortable. Okay?"

"I'll see you Tuesday." Tim gave Ronnie directions to his apartment.

"Okay. I'll see you at eight o'clock. And Tim, wear those tight, over-washed jeans you were wearing that evening last summer. I remember how good they looked on you."

"Yeah," Tim said, his voice a bit lighter. "Sure. I will." He hung up.

Ronnie drove to the apartment complex the following Tuesday and grabbed a heavy camel wool coat from the backseat. She wore a deep red, button front, man-tailored shirt and jeans, with her bare feet stuffed into soft leather loafers. She had on almost no makeup and had pulled her hair into a ponytail. Although she was in her early thirties she looked younger and less threatening. Only her lingerie was intended to tantalize, a dark red demi-bra and matching thong-style panties.

Her palms sweaty, Ronnie parked her car, found her way to Tim's apartment, and rang the bell. It took a moment before she heard footsteps.

"Hi," Tim said as he opened the door. Ronnie was surprised at how much he had changed in the few months since she had last seen him. Although he had been twenty-three that evening on the boat, he had still had some of the gawky teenaged angles and hollows to his body. No more.

"You've grown up," Ronnie said as she looked him over slowly and appraisingly, enjoying the way his body now filled out the navy blue knit shirt he wore. His shoulders were wide and his hips narrow. Lord she loved muscular shoulders and she longed to run her palms over his upper arms, feel them around her. That would have to wait, however. Right now Tim's fists were clenched at his sides and the open ingenuous smile that she knew could warm his ordinary-looking face was hidden beneath his nervousness.

Tim was terrified. When he and his dad discussed Clarisse's ugly comments, and Tim had reluctantly admitted that even before that evening he had begun to doubt himself. He'd been a normal teenaged stud, seducing several members of his high school class, then having several longer-term relationships in college. But with Clarisse it had been different. As the months of their relationship passed, it took longer and longer for him to arouse her. He tried to be considerate and give her the time she needed but after prolonged foreplay, once he finally got inside, he came so quickly that Clarisse complained that Tim always left her unsatisfied. The last few times they had slept together, he'd been unable to get an erection at all. "Don't you have a clue about women?" Clarisse had shrieked late one night. "All you want to do is fuck. Stick it in and to hell with the woman." She'd laughed at him. "Now you can't even get it up." His brain understood what was going on, but his soul had doubts.

The scene at his father's dinner table had been a humiliation for Tim and for several weeks he had gone straight home after work and shut himself in his apartment. After almost a month his father had showed up at his door and sat him down for a serious talk.

At first Tim had been appalled by his dad's suggestion of hiring a prostitute, but when Ronnie's name came up, Tim's interest had been piqued and his body had reacted. Although he'd only met her the one time on the boat, he'd spent many nights fantasizing about her long blond hair and great body. TJ had explained about Jack and Ronnie's unusual relationship, and Tim had agreed to the outlandish plan.

Now Ronnie was here and Tim was panic-stricken. This was all a terrible mistake. As Tim saw the corners of her mouth turn up, he asked, "What are you smiling at?" Her eyes were roaming all over his body, making his skin prickle. Was she going to make fun of him and of this ridiculous idea?

"Nothing. It's just that you've matured and I enjoy looking at you." She would tell him later, in detail, how hunky he'd become. Instinctively Ronnie knew that he wasn't ready.

Tim was nice looking, with sandy brown hair and eyes the color of toast. As Tim nervously ran his long, delicate fingers through his hair, Ronnie thought about how those hands would feel on her skin. Nice, she thought, warming to her task. Very nice. And despite his nervousness, he had a sexy way of looking right into her eyes that made Ronnie tingle. "May I come in?" she said, noticing that he had worn the jeans she'd suggested.

Tim stepped back and let Ronnie brush past him into his apartment. God, he thought, she smells so good. "I'm glad you came." His face reddened and he looked mortified as he realized his accidental double entendre.

"You know, Tim," Ronnie said as Tim shut the door, "we're going to drive each other crazy if we don't relax." She placed a light kiss on his cheek and dropped her coat on a chair.

"Yeah," he said with a sigh. "I've been jumpy as a cat all day." He rubbed his hands down the thighs of his jeans. "I'm not sure this was a good idea."

"It was a wonderful idea and we'll just talk for a while. Nothing you don't want. Okay?"

Tim looked at his shoes, then looked at Ronnie. God, she was so sexy. He nodded.

Suddenly Ronnie was completely comfortable. Tim was a genuinely nice human being. "There's nothing to be jumpy about. Have you got anything to drink? I think we could both use one."

"I've got a bottle of champagne."

"Great. Got any orange juice? We could make mimosas."

"Sure. Good idea. The OJ's in the fridge."

"Any brandy?"

"There might be a bottle in the closet to the right. Why?"

"To make the perfect mimosa," Ronnie said, crossing to the tiny kitchen, "you should add a shot of brandy." Ronnie retrieved a container of juice and rummaged through the liquor closet until she found a bottle of Triple Sec. "This'll do," she said. Returning to the living room, she saw that Tim had half-filled two champagne flutes with champagne. He quickly added an equal amount of juice, then she topped each off with a shot of Triple Sec.

"To the evening," Ronnie said, touching her glass to Tim's.

Tim stared into her eyes over the rim of his glass, unaware of the sensuousness of his gaze. "Yes. To the evening."

Not too fast, Ronnie told herself, tearing her eyes from his face. She wandered. "Nice place," she said. They stood in the large living room which was comfortably furnished with a cream-and-navy rough-textured sofa, a matching lounge chair, and modern wooden coffee and end tables. The walls were covered with photos, mostly landscapes, taken all around the world. One that particularly intrigued her showed a market scene of stalls stacked with merchandise and aisles filled with over-tired tourists. Although the photo was in black and white, it conveyed all the colors of the scene. "Where's this?"

"Cairo," he said. "I was there two years ago with my dad."

"And this?" The picture was of a river with houseboats littering its shores.

"Amsterdam."

"Wow," she said, honestly impressed. "Did you take all these pictures?"

"Yeah. Photography has been a love of mine since I was a kid."

"These are terrific."

"Thanks. I've converted my second bedroom into a darkroom and I do all my own developing and enlarging."

Ronnie walked slowly around the room studying the black-and-white photos. "These are really very good. Do you ever do portraits?"

"Sure." He pulled out an album and proudly showed Ronnie several skillfully taken photographs of women. He pointed to one, a slightly over-made-up woman in her early twenties with an expression that, despite the smile, seemed disapproving. "That's Clarisse, my ex-fiancée. I wanted to mount this photo on cardboard and use it as a dartboard, but it's too good a picture. You know, it's funny. Now that I think about it, this was one of the few times I ever saw her smile when it wasn't for effect."

Ronnie laughed. "From what your father told me, the dartboard idea sounds like a good one."

Tim hesitated, then joined Ronnie's laughter. "You're right.

But it truly is a good picture of her." He studied the photo. "Actually, she's never looked that good."

Ronnie kicked off her shoes, settled onto the sofa, and patted the seat next to her. "Sit here and we'll talk." As he sat down, she asked, "Would you be interested in taking some pictures of me? I'd love to have a good portrait to give Jack for our anniversary."

"Sure. That would be great. I'd really enjoy it."

"Have you ever considered taking portraits professionally? The ones you showed me were really good."

"Do you really think I could do this for money?"

"You never know. Maybe the ones I have in mind will be the start of a new career."

While they made small talk Ronnie felt the alcohol warm her body and knew that it would be easing Tim's fears as well. When there was a lapse in the conversation, she slid down so that her head rested on the back of the sofa. She handed Tim her glass and asked, "Would you like to kiss me?"

Tim put their two glasses on the table and said, "I think I would."

Ronnie wrapped her hand around the back of Tim's neck and gently pulled him toward her. She framed his face with her hands as he touched her lips with his. Gently, teasingly, she moved her mouth over his, nipping his lower lip with her teeth. "Ummm, nice," she purred.

Tim sat back. "This is so awkward. I don't know what to do with my hands. Maybe this isn't such a good idea." He looked away.

"We don't have to do anything you don't want to," Ronnie said, "but I'll be very disappointed."

Suddenly annoyed with the whole thing, he looked at her and snapped, "I don't need charity."

Ronnie stood up, unzipped her jeans, and slid them to her knees. She grabbed Tim's hand and pressed it against the crotch of her panties. "What do you feel? Am I hot and wet for you? Does this feel like charity?"

Her heat warmed his hand and her wetness made his fingers

damp. She wanted him. Really wanted him. He looked into her eyes and saw desire burning there. Oh Lord, don't let me back out, he prayed, both to himself and to Ronnie.

She pulled his hand away from her crotch and held it while she slid her jeans back up and sat back down on the sofa. "I want you," she said softly, her gaze never leaving his eyes, "but I'll stop if you really want me to." She raised his hand to her mouth and placed a kiss on the end of each finger. "Should I stop?"

"No," he moaned.

She flicked her tongue over the tip of his index finger. "Then let's pretend that this is your cock." She drew the tip of his finger into her mouth. "Can you feel it? Does it feel good?"

He certainly could and it was unbelievably erotic. Electricity sparked in his groin, hardening his penis. "It feels very good." The words came out as part breath and part groan.

"Good. Then close your eyes and let me suck you." Tim closed his eyes and let his head fall onto the back of the sofa. It would be all right. Millimeter by millimeter she pulled Tim's index finger into her mouth, licking and nipping at the tip. She moved to the second finger and sucked it, then the third and then the pinkie. She lavished attention on each finger of his other hand in turn, until heat radiated from his body.

"This is how much I want you," she whispered. She took his hand and rubbed the palm against one erect nipple. This was wonderful. She could use his hand to touch herself exactly the way she wanted. She pressed and rubbed, arching her back and reveling in the sensations caused by his hand on her breast. Despite her hunger, however, she went no further, wanting Tim to take some of the initiative.

Soon touching Ronnie's breast through her shirt wasn't enough for Tim. He wanted to kiss her, to touch and taste her. He licked his lips and stared at her mouth. "I want you." Hesitant to do anything to break the mood, yet unable to resist any longer, he leaned forward and brushed Ronnie's lips with his. Suddenly he needed to devour and be devoured. He moved his head so he could delve into her warm mouth. He couldn't get enough of her.

Ronnie had never been kissed so thoroughly. "Oh Tim," she sighed, wrapping her arms around his neck. They kissed for a long time, as Ronnie slowly stretched out on the sofa and pulled him over her so that his body covered hers.

"Too many clothes," Ronnie whispered when they paused for breath. As Ronnie removed her blouse and tossed it on a chair Tim stood up and pulled off his shirt. His body was just as beautiful as Ronnie had anticipated. When he stood and started to unbutton his jeans, Ronnie stopped him. "Not yet." She stood up and moved so close to him that her lace-covered breasts brushed the sparse hair on his chest. Slowly she ran her hands over his well-developed shoulders. "When you opened the door I knew your body would look like this," she murmured. "So beautiful."

"I go to the gym a couple of times a week," he said, breathless. "I lift."

"You certainly do," Ronnie said, sliding her palms over his chest and down his back. "Your body is wonderful."

Tim unhooked Ronnie's bra and freed her breasts. "So is yours."

Ronnie slid Tim's hands down her ribs. "Pick me up," she said. "I want to feel you move."

With Ronnie's palms on his upper arms, Tim tightened his hands on her waist and lifted. "I love the way your muscles move under your skin," she said, kneading Tim's biceps.

"And I love your tits," he said, holding her so her breasts were level with his mouth. He took one nipple and drew it into his mouth.

Her hands roaming over Tim's smooth shoulders and back, Ronnie let her head fall back, exposing her smooth, white throat. Tim took the invitation and lowered her slightly so he could nuzzle her neck. Holding her easily with her feet inches off the floor, Tim licked Ronnie's pulse points and nibbled at the tender spot where her neck joined her shoulder. "You taste so good," he moaned.

He set her down gently and continued kissing her neck and

shoulders. Soon neither of them could stand, so they quickly removed their jeans and underwear and stretched out on the sofa. "This feels so strange," Ronnie said, rubbing her back against the rough texture of the sofa's fabric. "It's actually erotic."

Tim rubbed his arms over the material. "I'll never think about this sofa the same way."

"I want you, you know." Not giving the flash of panic she saw a chance to blossom, Ronnie reached for Tim's already-hard cock. She unwrapped the condom she had dropped on the table earlier and slowly unrolled it onto Tim's hard cock. "Cold?"

"Yes," he said. "And very exciting."

"Let me share it." She rubbed the end of his cold, wet prick over her wet pussy. "Ummm, it is cold. And I'm so hot for you." She positioned his erection between her inner lips and arched her back. His cock drove into her. "Hold still and let me," she said, squeezing her vaginal muscles and watching the pleasure clearly visible on Tim's face.

She turned and pushed him back so his head rested against the back of the sofa and he was half sitting and half lying. "Hold still and just feel." She sat on his lap and impaled herself on his shaft. She used her thighs to raise her body, then drop, over and over, altering the speed and depth to suit her desires.

"Oh Lord," he moaned. "I'm going to shoot."

"Not yet," Ronnie said as orgasm built deep within her. "Hold completely still and feel, but don't come." When she felt him twist, she snapped. "Don't move and don't come!" He opened his eyes and stared at her. Slowly a smile spread over his face and he nodded.

She settled in his lap barely moving, his cock deep inside of her. "I'm going to come and I want you to share it." She took Tim's hand and touched her clit. Waves of pleasure started at her toes and deep in her belly and washed over her body ending in her pussy. "Feel," she yelled.

Her orgasm clutched at his cock, drawing his climax from him. "Yes. Now!" she groaned. "Do it." He thrust upward once, twice, then came, hard. Almost without movement, their mutual orgasms continued for long seconds. Ronnie collapsed pulling Tim with her and they dozed, tangled together.

Later, Tim stretched. "That was amazing."

"It certainly was. You were perfect."

He sighed and smiled. "We were perfect. I never knew making love could be so wonderful. Can we do this again sometime soon?"

"As long as we don't get confused. I enjoy fucking you, and we're friends. But that's all. Jack and I have a special thing and I love him very much."

"I understand. I can keep everything in perspective. Okay?"

"Okay. And you'll take some pictures of me sometime?"

"I'd love to."

An hour later, Ronnie arrived home to find Jack waiting for her. "How did it go, love?" he asked.

"It was fabulous and I think very . . . how should I say it . . . educational. How are you?"

"You know, I'm surprised at how I am. I'm great, and horny as a goat just thinking about you with that boy."

Ronnie grinned. "Well, we could go upstairs and work off that excitement." She walked over to Jack's chair, knelt between his knees, and unbuckled his belt. As she unzipped his fly she brushed his hard cock. "Or maybe we could stay right here." She separated the sides of the fly in his shorts allowing his hard cock to spring forth. "What's your pleasure?"

"You're my pleasure," Jack said softly. "So much pleasure."

Ronnie made a tight ring of her index finger and thumb and slowly slid that ring down the length of Jack's cock. With her fingers tightly encircling the base of her husband's cock, Ronnie licked the tip with the point of her tongue. Then she kissed the tiny hole in the end. "Your cock is so hard—like warm velvet over steel." She sucked the end into her wet mouth and slowly slid the length of it into her throat.

Jack watched his wife's head bob in his lap, unable to control the frantic excitement bubbling inside him. His hips bucked and his hot come tried to rush through the tight ring of her fingers. "Oh babe, let me. I'm so horny."

"Let you come?" she said, letting her breath cool Jack's wet cock. "Release my fingers?"

"Yes."

She sucked in his cock and then pulled back. "Say please."

"Please, babe."

Ronnie released her fingers and took Jack's entire thick cock into her mouth, sucking and flicking her tongue over the tip. Almost immediately hot come filled her mouth. As fast as she swallowed, some thick liquid escaped from the corners of her mouth.

When Ronnie had licked all the stickiness from Jack's cock, she sat back and said, "Now, let's go upstairs and we'll make love nice and slow."

Jack grinned his agreement.

Three days later, Ronnie stormed to the door, waving an envelope, as Jack arrived home. "You'll never believe what came in the mail today."

Jack could tell she was furious. "Calm down, babe, and tell me what happened."

"TJ sent me a check for three hundred dollars and a thank-you note for the evening I spent with Tim."

"So why are you so angry?" Jack said, dropping his briefcase on the hall table.

"I didn't do this to get paid. I feel like a whore."

"But he was going to pay a prostitute anyway. Why shouldn't you take the money?"

Ronnie released her breath. "I am not a whore."

"No one said you were."

"But doesn't this make me one? Sex for money."

"Stop being judgmental," Jack said walking into the kitchen. "You had fun, Tim had fun, and TJ was delighted with the way everything turned out. And Tim's a better person because of your help. Right?"

"Yeah, but. . . ." She was flustered.

"Don't but me. How can this be wrong when no one's been hurt?"

"But I'm not a . . ." Ronnie paused.

"Hooker, call girl, prostitute, whore?" Jack said. "Words. Just words with all kinds of bullshit behind them. Stop using labels and think. Was anyone hurt?"

"No."

"You performed a service, and did it well. Right?"

"Yes."

"So you should be rewarded. Of course, you could send the check back. . . ."

"I could."

"But you don't want to. So the end result is that you had fun and got paid for it. A dream job."

"I guess I never thought of it that way." She dropped into a chair. "God, I did have fun."

"And so did we that night, if you remember." He groaned loudly and pressed a hand against the small of his back. "Our acrobatics almost put me out of commission for good."

Ronnie laughed. "You're right, you know. I am being silly." She stared at the check. "Three hundred dollars for having a good fuck. Seems almost too good to be true."

"So buy yourself something extravagant. Buy some sexy lingerie and gift wrap your gorgeous body for me."

"I could squander this. It's like found money."

"Yes, it is. You know," he paused, "my clients are sometimes out-of-town visitors who need to be entertained. Dinner, a show, intelligent conversation, and afterward . . . well, that's between the client and his date. If you think you'd like to earn some extra money. . . ."

"Prostitution?"

"Fun and games and a little cash on the side. And only if you want to."

"How much cash on the side?" she said, amazed at how excited she suddenly was by the idea.

"I've never been involved directly, but from what I understand they pay anywhere from three hundred to one thousand dollars per evening. For adult entertainment."

Ronnie's eyes widened. "One thousand dollars???"

Jack nodded.

"I'm flabbergasted. For doing what we've been doing anyway. Would you be okay with it, me with other men?"

"Well, if you'll tell me afterward a little about what happens, the idea turns me on."

"I won't violate any confidences, you understand."

"Of course not." He saw the gleam in Ronnie's eye. "Interested?"

"I think I might be."

He took her arm. "This conversation has made me horny. Wanna practice for your new profession? Or I could conduct your preemployment physical."

Ronnie headed for the stairs. "Last one to the bedroom has to sleep in the wet spot."

Chapter

3

"And that was how this began," Ronnie told Carla. "Tim took these pictures of me, you know."

"He really does great work," Carla said.

"He does, doesn't he? He's got a few girlfriends now, and he's marvelous in bed. He loves women, and it shows in his photographs."

"I love happy endings."

"Me too."

"And this works for you, this call girl thing?"

"It does. I make a nice living and I meet fascinating people."

Carla had a thousand questions. "Have you ever had a bad experience? You know, someone who gets abusive and wants something you don't want to do, that sort of thing?"

"No one has ever gotten out of line. I screen my friends very well. They're all recommended by other friends. I never give out my address until I'm satisfied they're safe and I have a private, unlisted phone number. And I never answer that phone. I let the answering machine take a message and I call back or I hear who it is and then pick up. Our first date must begin with dinner somewhere nice. I can size someone up quickly and if I don't get good vibes we part right then."

"Have you ever had an evening go wrong?"

"I've had several men who wanted things I wasn't willing to do," Ronnie answered. When Carla raised an eyebrow, she continued, "One man wanted me to urinate on him as he masturbated and another wanted to give me an enema."

When Carla made an ugly face, Ronnie said, "Don't judge. These activities give them sexual pleasure and that's their business. And some of the things I enjoy would turn others off. But sometimes I have to tell a customer that his fantasy won't work for me." Ronnie's smile was warm. "The urination guy was a really nice man, actually, and he offered me more money. I explained that money wasn't the issue and I suggested that he find someone else. We finished our meal and spent a pleasant hour discussing movies and he paid for dinner. I never saw him again."

"Any others?"

"A man named Harry was recommended by an old friend. We had dinner and talked about his fantasies. He was heavily into control and he wanted to dominate me, run things, and spank me when I was naughty. That would have been very difficult for me, since I'm a dominant personality myself." She laughed. "I never play with anyone when I can't have some fun too."

"Control?"

"Lots of people have fantasies that revolve around power and control. This guy wanted to be in charge of all the action. Actually he had another interesting fantasy. He wanted to have me take a pretend pill that would render me incapable of resisting anything he wanted to do. And there's another man who wanted to tie me to a bed. Not my thing either."

Carla felt a jolt of electricity flow through her body and directly into her pussy. The control fantasies sounded wonderful to her. "From the look on your face," Ronnie said, "I think we've found something you'd enjoy. Should I give you a phone number? He'll pay a thousand dollars for one night."

"Holy.... Not yet," Carla said, realizing that she was more than a little interested in Ronnie's work.

"Hmmm. I don't have to be psychic to guess what you're thinking, darling," Ronnie said, "but you realize that this isn't for everyone. You have to have strong, good feelings about yourself and you have to enjoy sex. The money is just an extra added attraction. In my mind, the fact that the money is secondary is what makes me an entertainer, not a whore."

"Listen," Carla said, glancing at her watch, amazed that it was already after three. "I have to get home and I have a lot of thinking to do. What day next week works for you?"

"I'll be away next week." Ronnie laughed. "A friend has invited me on a cruise. Delicious food, wine, dancing, cavorting under the Caribbean skies, the works." She winked. "And I get twenty-five hundred dollars for little old me."

Carla whistled. "Holy shit."

"Mmmm. And he's a doll. Really an interesting man."

"Why you?" How could she ask what she wanted to know without it sounding like an insult? "I don't mean you're not great, you understand, but why . . . well, you know."

"He's got the funny idea that no 'nice girl' would like the kind of cavorting we do." She settled back. "Actually, the entire cruise is devoted to dominance. It's an annual event and there's a whole group going. We've taken an entire separate area of the ship. I will be his Mistress Ronnie for the week and he'll be my sex slave. I've got a bunch of special toys and outfits for both of us."

"Have you ever done anything like this before?"

"We met two years ago on this very cruise. Another woman and I swapped slaves for an evening and Bob enjoyed being with me so much that we repeated the trip last year and will again next week. We play during the year as well." She flipped to the photo of the gray-haired schoolmarm in the sensible shoes and smiled. "Bobby's a very difficult student."

"I'm speechless." Ronnie shot Carla an understanding glance.

"Let's see. The following week the boys are home from camp and we're going to a lake in the Adirondacks with my folks."

"Then I'm away," Ronnie said. "Jack and I are going to Disney World, of all places, for two weeks in August. I've never been there and despite all the warnings about the heat I'm like a kid looking forward to the rides and the parade of lights. And we'll siesta after lunch, of course. Jack and me, an air-conditioned room, and a king-sized bed."

"You and Jack have a good thing going, don't you?"

"Yeah, we do. It's just this damn *blasted* business of his. He's gone more than he's home. But we have two weeks of sun and fun to look forward to and I, for one, intend to make the best of it."

"It looks like we won't see each other until September."

"I'm afraid so. You know, I'll miss you."

"Me too."

Ronnie checked the tiny date book she kept in her purse. "Okay. How about the day after Labor Day? Lunch here."

"That sounds great." The two women bussed cheeks. "You're quite something," Carla said.

"So are you. And I'm so glad we found each other again."

"Me too," Carla said. "Me too."

During the month that Ronnie was away Carla did a lot of thinking. She was intrigued and titillated by the idea of Ronnie's business and the prospect of joining her was never far from Carla's mind.

With the boys in camp, Carla spent the first week at home, pretty much alone, cleaning and shopping and fantasizing about being tied to a bed with a handsome man standing over her, watching her useless struggles. One morning she lay in bed until after nine, dreaming about being under some man's power, letting him do whatever he wanted without being able to resist him. With that picture in her mind, she slipped her hand between her legs and rubbed her clit until she came.

She spent the second week in the Adirondacks with her three rambunctious boys and her parents. They had a wonderful time together, swimming, horseback riding, playing softball and fris-bee, and eating everything in sight, while blaming their astounding appetites on the mountain air. And every man she encountered became the center of a fantasy in which she was a paid courtesan.

Carla spent the entire vacation in a state of frustrated sexual excitement.

More than once she looked at her three high-spirited sons and thought about their future. All three were exceptionally bright and all would be able to select from the best colleges. The question was would she be able to afford it. There was money set aside, but would it be enough? Or was money merely an excuse to do what excited and intrigued her? What did it matter? She had made up her mind and she knew it.

Trying not to lie too much, she talked to her mother one evening about the possibility of spending more time with her grandchildren. "I've spoken about my old college roommate Ronnie," she told her mother one evening over coffee after their return to Bronxville.

"How in the world did you find Ronnie?"

"I literally ran into her." Carla told her mother the story of her accidental encounter with her old friend, reassuring her that the medical scare had been really nothing.

"And how is Ronnie?" Mrs. MacKensie asked. "I remember the vacation she spent with us. She was such a lovely girl."

"She's hardly a girl now," Carla said. "She's married and she owns her own business."

"Your father and I were always sure she'd go far. She seemed like such an intelligent girl."

Carla smiled to herself. "I wanted to talk to you about that. She wants me to join her business part-time. It'll mean extra money and I could use it for the boys' college fund. The costs are getting astronomical." From upstairs, she could hear the laughter that always accompanied her father's efforts to settle the boys in bed.

"What kind of business?"

"It's a service business of some kind. Public relations. I don't know many of the details but it will involve entertaining clients in the city some evenings."

"That's wonderful, dear," her mother said. "You need some other interests in your life besides your sons."

"It would mean that you would have to stay with the boys more often. A few nights a week and occasional weekends."

"Weekends? How come? Not that I mind, you understand."

"God only knows," she answered, "but Ronnie warned me about some out-of-town stuff. I don't know how often, but from time to time."

"That's great," Mrs. MacKensie said, laughing. "Force me to spend time with the boys. Twist my arm."

Carla laughed as she always did with her mother. "Thanks, Mom."

"And maybe you'll meet someone nice at one of those meetings. Maybe your friend Ronnie knows a nice man for you."

Carla laughed harder. "Mother, please." When her mother raised an eyebrow, Carla said, "Okay. Maybe she does. I'll keep my eyes open."

"And if a date keeps you in the city, like overnight. . . ." She winked. "Just give me a call and I'll see to the boys."

An early September heat wave baked New York City and the humidity that hung over the metropolis caused Carla's short-sleeved rayon blouse to stick to her back. She walked up the brownstone's front steps and rang Ronnie's bell. "Come on in," Ronnie called from inside. "It's open."

Carla walked into the foyer and heard, "Lock it behind you, will you? Then come into the kitchen."

"Sure," Carla called, throwing the dead bolt.

Carla walked to the back of the building and into the large, airy kitchen. Ronnie already had lunch laid out on the table: a green salad, a bowl of crab salad, and a cold pasta with basil. Crisp rolls nestled in a napkin-covered basket and a bottle of white wine stood opened beside two crystal glasses.

"Oh, Carla," Ronnie said, hugging her friend, "I've missed you."

"Me too. How was Disney World?"

"Sensational. The rides were a thrill, the lines were short, and the siestas were . . . athletic." She picked up a small package wrapped in silver paper. "I hope you don't mind, but I bought you a present."

"A present? I didn't think to get you anything, I'm afraid."

"I didn't expect that you had," Ronnie said. "But I saw this and couldn't resist."

Carla tore off the paper and opened the small box. Inside was a pewter figurine of a dragon with his wings spread, his head thrown back as if roaring. He perched on a faceted crystal globe, his talons buried in the transparent ball.

Ronnie watched Carla lift the four-inch-high dragon so that the light turned into rainbows within the crystal. "The dragon is for fantasy," Ronnie said. "And for dreams that can be made to come true."

"You know that I've decided to join you in your business, don't you?"

"I knew a month ago when I watched your eyes light up. Actually, I probably knew when we met again that first afternoon. After all, we were roommates for three years and I knew you very well then." She poured wine into the two glasses and raised hers in toast. "To fantasy. And to making fantasies come true for everyone involved."

"To fantasy," Carla said, sipping the crisp white wine.

Over lunch Carla told Ronnie about her week with her boys and her parents. "How are your folks?" Ronnie asked. "I've always loved your mother. And your dad's a stitch."

"They were always fond of you too. They asked to be remembered to you and want you to come up for dinner sometime."

"I'll do that."

"And how was the cruise?"

"I'd rather tell you about the entire week some other time," she said. "It's a little early in your education for that story."

"Was it that shocking?"

"Not for me. Trust me for a few weeks," Ronnie asked and Carla demurred.

After lunch, Ronnie said "I think it's time for you to have a look around upstairs."

Ronnie and Carla put the dishes in the dishwasher, then climbed the lushly carpeted stairs to the master bedroom. It was softer and more romantic than the downstairs, done in pastel pinks and warm, spring greens. The lounge chair was upholstered in a pink-and-green floral with green piping to match the bedspread and drapes. The oriental carpet contained the same shades of green, and together with half a dozen plants, gave the entire room a warm and comfortable aura. "I entertain in here when romance is at the heart of the encounter," Ronnie said. "I also sleep here sometimes when I'm stuck in the city."

"This is a wonderful room . . . soft and loving somehow."

"That's exactly the way I designed it. We'll need to coordinate, but you're free to use it whenever you want, for whatever you want. I have a cleaning woman who comes regularly so you don't even have to tidy up."

"Are you sure about my using your place . . . this room?"

"Despite the homey feeling, this is my working space, not where I live. Let me show you what I mean." Ronnie opened the door to a huge walk-in closet. "On this side," she said, waving one hand, "are everyday clothes, the usual suits, dresses, blouses, things like that. Shoes are underneath." She looked Carla over. "I would guess we still wear the same size, so take your pick whenever you need something you don't have. I try to keep the two parts of me completely separate so I don't wear my personal clothes during business. You might feel differently."

Carla admired the collection of expensive clothes. She didn't need to examine the labels to know that Ronnie only chose the best. "Isn't this overkill? So many outfits."

With a smile, Ronnie said, "I love clothes and now I can indulge myself. Anyway, I do a lot of entertaining and traveling. It's surprising how many men want a well-dressed, well-educated companion to decorate their arm at a luncheon or business dinner."

"You mean like in *Pretty Woman*?"

"Exactly. Sometimes without any sex at all." She turned and indicated the other side of the closet. "This is the evening stuff."

Carla was stunned at the number of designer dresses: chiffon, lace, sequins, and satin in a variety of colors and textures. Her fingers strained to pull each garment from its hanger and try it on. At the end of the clothes rod hung a deep rose silk jacket, a full-length black satin coat, and two faux furs. "You're ready for anything, aren't you?"

"You have no idea." Ronnie crossed the room and opened the door to a second closet. "Play clothes," she said. Inside hung an assortment of costumes. Carla recognized some of them from the photograph album Ronnie had shown her. The pink little-girl dress and the leather-and-chain outfit hung with a leopard-patterned leotard, three leather dresses with multiple zippers, and several see-through lace bodysuits.

"On each hanger," Ronnie explained, "are all the items necessary for that persona. Besides the clothes and underwear, I have coordinated jewelry, perfume, extra makeup, whatever's needed, all in a plastic bag on the hanger. With one or two there's even a wig, should you care to wear it. I love the wigs; they make me feel like a different person. Feel free to use anything, just put the stuff back in its place. Sometimes I need to dash into the bathroom and change quickly so I like to have everything ready."

Carla whistled, long and low.

Ronnie opened the drawers of the wide dresser and showed Carla dozens of slips, bras both with and without cutouts so nipples could show through, satin and lace panties, silk teddies in a dozen colors, and garter belts with stockings. "Try anything on and wear whatever fits your mood. Or you might want to wear nothing at all under your evening clothes. There are few things more arousing than telling a man that you're not wearing underwear, and then going out for an evening. But everything's replaceable so if anything gets torn or whatever," she winked, "we'll get new."

When Carla looked as though she didn't understand, Ronnie said, "Sometimes a man wants to tear clothes off or cut them off slowly and dramatically."

As Carla gazed into the drawers, she couldn't imagine a piece of lingerie that Ronnie didn't own. She picked up a cellophane package. "Panty hose?"

"Even panty hose," Ronnie said. "I have one friend who loves to pull them off of me, very slowly and lick each part he uncovers. Another friend likes to cut a hole in the crotch and have my legs—in the panty hose—wrapped around him. And, now that I think of it, I had a friend about two years ago who liked to wear them himself. He'd put a pair on before we went to dinner. He claimed they sweetened the anticipation and from the way he attacked me when we got back here, I don't doubt it at all."

Carla tried not to be shocked. She had read about transvestites but she'd never thought to meet one. "Woman's clothes?"

"First of all, he wasn't a transvestite," Ronnie said, as if reading her friend's mind. "Several men I know like to wear satin undies under their business suits. The slippery fabric feels good against the skin and it's a sexy little secret.

"Secondly, don't judge. There's nothing wrong with an activity that consenting adults enjoy in private, or, for that matter, in selected public locations. I learned that first time with Tim that labels are for people with small minds."

"You're right, of course. And I'm not being judgmental, just naive."

"Fair enough."

On the side of the closet opposite Ronnie's costumes were outfits for men: a Robin Hood-style green vest and tights, a black outfit that looked like it was designed for a second-story man, a silver lamé top and pants that had been cut to resemble a knight's armor, and a white shirt and short pants combination. "For a naughty little boy," Ronnie explained. Carla struggled to not let her amazement show.

Eventually they returned to the living room. "I want you to go slowly," Ronnie said when the topic turned to Carla's new career. "I'd like to see you build your sexual and sensual awareness little by little. And I've got just the place to start."

"You have?"

"Um-hmm. Rick. I'm due to call him in," she glanced at her watch, "five minutes."

Carla looked a little flustered. "Now? Oh God. I thought I was ready for this," she said. "Suddenly I'm not so sure."

"Don't worry, I wouldn't do anything for your trial run that you couldn't back out of at any time. Nothing is mandatory. But Rick is the perfect place to start. I call him and we make love over the phone."

"Phone sex? Like 1-900-suck-me-off?"

"Something like that. And don't make fun of it. Talking about sex and describing lovemaking is very erotic, very exciting, and leads to some delicious orgasms." When Carla hesitated, Ronnie said again, "Trust me?"

Carla relaxed. "I do trust you. It's just that phone sex conjures up such awful visions. A sweaty body jerking off while some impersonal bimbo talks and files her nails at the same time."

"It's not like that with me. Not at all."

"Of course not," Carla said.

"Before I call Rick—or Mr. Holloway as I call him on the phone—let me tell you about him. Rick's a happily married man who's involved in some kind of financing business on Wall Street. Like so many of my friends, Rick believes that his wife couldn't be interested in the things we talk about. Every now and then I'm tempted to phone his wife and somehow get her to talk to him. I think he'd be surprised. But, of course, I wouldn't do anything like that. My friend's lives, outside of our relationship, are strictly off-limits. I've never even seen Rick."

"Never?"

"Nope. One of my friends suggested that he call me. He did and we talked in private for an hour. I discovered that he likes to listen to sexy talk, sexy stories, things like that. He'd tried those 900 numbers but never found one he really liked. He has now."

"I assume you get paid."

"Sure. He leaves a message for me once or twice a month. The message tells me what time to call him back. He'll be sure to be in the middle of the office where he's surrounded by people. After we talk, he sends me a check for a hundred and fifty dollars. Now, I'll call first, then I'll tell you to pick up. Yes?"

"I guess. But I don't want to eavesdrop."

"You won't be. Let me take care of everything. I know Rick very well and he'll enjoy this conversation immensely."

While Ronnie dialed Carla settled deeper into an overstuffed chair and tried to prepare herself for what was to come. As hard as she tried, she couldn't imagine what would happen.

"Good afternoon," an efficient-sounding female voice said, "Mr. Holloway's office."

"Mr. Holloway, please," Ronnie said. "Mr. Black's office calling."

"Thank you. One moment please."

Although she was on hold, Ronnie held her hand over the mouthpiece. "Okay, Carla, you can pick up now."

"Are you sure this is okay, Ronnie? After all the man's paying good money for this phone call. He's not doing it to expand my education."

"Not only am I sure it's okay," Ronnie answered as Carla picked up the extension phone and draped her legs over the arm of the chair, "but I'm going to tell him that you're listening."

"You aren't," Carla said.

"I know just what he likes. This plays right into his fantasies. Knowing that you're listening will heat things up for him. You can't imagine how much I enjoy knowing I can make him hot just by talking. He gets hot and so do I. I think you'll find it very erotic also."

"Mr. Holloway here," said a deep, resonant voice. Carla watched Ronnie curl up and tuck her feet under her.

"Mr. Holloway," Ronnie purred into the phone, "this is Mr. Black's office. Can you talk?"

"Of course not," Mr. Holloway answered.

"That's good. How many people are within earshot?"

"About six."

"Can they see you? I mean your entire body," Ronnie said, "not just your head."

"Just the upper levels," he answered.

"Then I want you to move. I want you to be where, when you get all hard and swollen, everyone could see if they knew where to look." When there was no sound at the other end of the phone, she asked, "Have you moved?"

There were shuffling sounds, then he answered, "I have." Carla could hear office noise in the background.

"Good. I have a little surprise for you today."

"You have?"

"Say hello, dear," Ronnie said, waving at Carla.

"Hello, darling," Carla said, dropping her voice a full octave and letting lots of breath escape as she spoke.

"Who's that?" the surprised voice said.

"That's Snow White," Ronnie said. "She's listening to everything we say. And she's never heard anything like this before. She's going to listen as you get excited. You won't be able to hide from her."

"Snow White?" he whispered. "Oh shit." His voice trembled as it resumed its normal timbre. "What's your associate like?"

"Oh, she's beautiful. Would you like to hear about her?"

"That's a fine idea. Let's discuss that."

"Well," Ronnie said, closing her eyes. "She's tiny, only about five feet tall, and she's got wide, sky-blue eyes and lots of long red hair. Her skin is like a soft ripe peach and her mouth is painted with bright red lipstick."

"That's fine," the business-like voice said.

"Her hands are tiny but she has long fingernails. You know how they're painted?"

"Of course."

"Certainly you do. They've been polished so they're shiny and bright red, like her lips. And she's wearing a white dress, cut low across her bosom so the tops of her nipples are just hidden beneath the lacy edging. Her cleavage is so deep and inviting that your hands itch to bury themselves between her large breasts. The dress is tight over her ribs and there's a full skirt with a dozen stiff petticoats. She's wearing very high-heeled sandals that are held to her feet with lots of tiny straps."

"That sounds like a fine arrangement," Mr. Holloway said.

Carla was blushing listening to Ronnie's description. She was also getting very aroused.

"And she's wearing long white gloves," Ronnie continued. "Her fingers aren't covered so you can still see her red fingernails, but white satin starts at her palms and extends up way past her elbows." She paused. "Can you see her?"

"Certainly. I need to know more about how the deal will proceed."

"Well, she's listening to me and getting very excited."

Carla was surprised at how excited she really was becoming as Ronnie described this imaginary Snow White. Her body was responding. She wanted to loosen the jeans that constricted her.

Carla could hear movement at the other end of the phone, together with the clack of keyboards and the occasional jangle of a telephone. "Is that true?" the man's voice said.

"Yes," Carla said, strangely no longer embarrassed. "I'm very excited. My thighs are open and I'm getting wet." Ronnie opened her eyes and nodded her approval.

"Wonderful," Rick said. "It sounds like the arrangement is working well."

In the distance, a woman's voice interrupted. "Mr. Holloway. Can you take Mr. Malone on line two?"

"Not right now," Rick said. "Tell him I'll call back."

"You mean you can't take another call right now?" Ronnie chuckled.

"Not a chance," Mr. Holloway said. "Our business is more important. Where were we?"

"You'll have to refresh my memory," Ronnie teased.

"Shit," the voice whispered. "Okay, we were talking about the irrigation project."

Carla laughed. "Yes we were. I was telling you how wet I am."

"Snow White is just waiting for you, Mr. Holloway. Are you hard enough for her?"

"Certainly. What about the rest?"

"Well, Snow White is wearing pantalets trimmed with white lace. They're getting wet in the crotch as her pussy gets hotter. Should we have her take them off?"

"A fine idea," Mr. Holloway said.

"Take off your pantalets, Snow White," Ronnie said. "Hold the phone so Mr. Holloway can hear your clothes come off."

Carla raised an eyebrow and Ronnie nodded. Carla stood up and pulled off her jeans, holding the phone so the man at the other end could hear the rustle of each leg as she pulled her feet through. "Did you hear that?" Carla said. She heard the man's breathing, then continued, "I'm now naked under my dress, but I'm pulling my skirts down so you can't see or touch . . . yet."

Ronnie made an okay sign with one hand. Carla was continually surprised at how easy and enjoyable this was. And Ronnie got paid for this?

"It's about time you got to the meat of the proposal," the man's voice said.

"Honey," Ronnie said, "it's your meat I'm proposing."

Holloway's deep laugh echoed through the phone line. "I'm not used to this kind of work being amusing. I guess that's why I like doing business with you," he said.

"Does a laugh make your cock any softer?" Ronnie asked.

"Of course not," he answered.

"Good. Now, where were we? Oh yes, Snow White is sitting on her throne, one leg draped over each arm, her skirts pulled down between her spread legs. Can you see her?"

"Uh-huh."

"She reaches down and dips her red-tipped fingers into the sweet valley between her breasts and pulls first one, then the other, out of the bodice of her gown. Her nipples are sensitive and deep pink. She pinches them so they're hard, like large pebbles. She tweaks at one with her nails and rubs the satin palm of her glove over the other. Tiny pains and satiny pleasure. She switches pinching and stroking, going back and forth until her tits are aching."

Carla massaged her breasts, feeling exactly what Ronnie was saying that Snow White felt.

"Is your cock aching too, Mr. Holloway?" Ronnie asked.

"Most assuredly."

"Is anyone looking at you right now?"

"As a matter of fact, yes. Just a moment, please." The two women heard Mr. Holloway shift the phone. "What is it?"

"I need your signature so I can get this into Express Mail by three o'clock."

There was some shuffling, then Mr. Holloway said, "That's done."

"Your poor cock," Ronnie said. "It must be hurting. Your balls too. And you can't do anything about it or everyone will see."

There was a barely audible groan.

"Wonderful," Ronnie purred. "Now, as Snow White sits on her throne, her pussy gets so itchy that she had to reach down and touch it. Can you see her? She's sitting with her legs spread wide apart. She slowly pulls up her skirt and slides her fingers up the inside of her creamy thighs. Do it, Snow White," Ronnie said, looking at Carla. "You know you love to have people watch you."

Carla stroked her pussy through her panties. She was soaking wet. She knew that if she caressed herself just right she would climax immediately but she found that she wanted to wait and continue to amuse Mr. Holloway. And, amazingly enough, she liked the fact that Ronnie was watching her.

"Mr. Holloway?" Carla said softly.

He cleared his throat. "Yes?"

"I'm right here, scratching the insides of my thighs with the tips of my long red nails. Now I'm using one nail and touching my clit, just brushing it, flicking it. It's so good."

"I bet if you play with it, you'll come," Ronnie said. "Right Snow White?"

"Oh yes," Carla groaned. "I want to come."

"That sounds acceptable to me," Mr. Holloway said.

"Stroke your cunt, Snow White," Ronnie said. "Put the phone near your cunt and let Mr. Holloway hear your fingers moving."

Carla held the phone close to her pussy and slid her fingers under the crotch of her panties. She knew just how to touch herself because she'd done it so many times in the past five years.

"Yes," Ronnie said. "I can see you with my eyes and Mr. Holloway can see you in his mind. Rub it harder."

"Yes," Carla whispered, panting. She was so close. Just another moment.

"Rub it faster, Snow White," Ronnie said. "Can you hear her, Mr. Holloway? Hear how close she is to coming? Hear her breathing, how fast it is? She's going to come . . . right now!"

Carla let out a low moan as she spasmed. She held very still and reveled in the waves of pleasure that washed over her body.

"Does your cock hurt, darling?" Ronnie said into the phone as Carla slowly recovered from one of the best orgasms she'd had in a long time.

"I think that will work out nicely," Mr. Holloway said. "I have to go now."

"Are you going into the bathroom to take your big hard cock in your hand and massage and fondle it until you spurt hot come all over?"

"I think that will be enough for now," he said, laughing. "Otherwise it won't go well for any of us."

"Right," Ronnie said, laughing too.

"Thank you, darling," Carla said into the phone, her breathing not yet back to normal. "That was wonderful."

"I'll speak to you soon," Mr. Holloway said. "And thank you for your help in this matter. I'll handle it from here." As he hung up, everyone was laughing.

Chapter

4

"Oh, Lord," Carla said, curling up in her chair. "If that's what it's like all the time, then I'll be both exhausted and delighted." Strange, but she wasn't embarrassed by Ronnie watching as she came.

"It is if you want it to be. You understand most of my rules and know that I stick by them, no matter how much money is involved."

"Spell them out again."

"I never do anything I don't think I'll enjoy and I make it clear to my friends that I always have the right to call things off at any time, as do they. That's part of the reason for having dinner with a new acquaintance before our first encounter. Doing what I do takes trust. Everyone must have the right to say stop and we always agree on a safe word."

"Safe word?"

"I usually use 'popcorn.' At any time, if anyone says that word, everything stops. Immediately. And if I can't trust my friends to obey if I say it, and to say it if they want to stop, it's no deal."

"Why is it important that they say it too? You're the one who needs a way out."

"Not really. Take men who enjoy being dominated. If I can be sure they'll use the safe word, I can do anything that takes my fancy. I describe what I'm going to do if it's the first time and I don't have to worry about going too far. The safe word is there so they can yell, 'Please stop,' and know I won't, but be sure I'll stop when that's what they really want."

"That sounds reasonable," Carla said, still catching her breath after the phone call.

"Also, no heavy drinking, although a glass or two loosens things up. No drugs of any kind and, as you know, I insist that my friends use condoms. He can have seventeen blood tests or whatever, but condoms are mandatory. Period."

Carla nodded. Everything that Ronnie said seemed, if anything, overly cautious.

"You're still interested, aren't you?" Ronnie said.

Carla took a deep breath. "After that phone call," she said, "more than ever. But I'm a little apprehensive about where to start."

"I have a suggestion," Ronnie said, stretching out on the sofa and crossing her long legs at the ankles. "An old friend called me a few weeks ago. His name's Bryce and I've known him for over a year."

Carla had learned in college that Ronnie's particularly delightful, slightly mischievous smile meant that she was deeply involved in hatching an inventive plot. When Ronnie didn't continue, Carla said, "And. . . ."

Ronnie picked up the glass of wine from the table next to her and took a sip. "He's had an ongoing fantasy about wedding nights and seduction. He's heavily into romance, music, wine, all that." Carla could see the dreamy look in Ronnie's eyes. "He's also into a bit of control, which I think you'll find irresistible. And he's dynamite in bed, a deliciously creative man who gets his satisfaction from giving as well as taking pleasure. We've spent some memorable nights together."

"He sounds too good to be true. Is he married? And if he is, why does his wife let him out of her sight?"

"His wife died several years ago and part of the reason he plays with me is that he's surrounded with matchmaking friends who bombard him with suitable women. I think that, when he's with me, he's comfortable. We have wonderful times together, great sex, and there are no strings, no commitments." Ronnie smiled. "I hope you don't mind but we talked about you."

"You knew that I was going to do this, didn't you."

"You're not expert at hiding your feelings, and I know you pretty well."

Carla smiled and pulled on her jeans. "You certainly used to, and after that game we just played with Rick Holloway, you know me even better."

Ronnie laughed. "True. Anyway, I think he'd be a wonderful first time for you. He'd love it and, I can guarantee, so would you."

"It sounds like he's *your* friend."

"He's a special man, but he's just a friend. And I think you'd enjoy being together."

"But. . . ."

"Listen, Carla. I don't know whether you should do this at all. I understand myself and I've been doing what I do for almost four years. I love it."

"I know you do. I've given this entire situation a lot of thought and, well, it titillates me. I've told you that I don't know much about off-center sex, but I know that I want to find out more."

"And, of course, you can call things off at any time and go back to Bronxville and sell real estate," responded Ronnie. Each woman wrinkled her nose.

The phone rang and Ronnie and Carla listened as the answering machine picked up. "This is Black Enterprises. Please leave a message at the sound of the beep, and thanks for calling."

"Hi, Ronnie and Snow White, this is Rick Holloway. You're probably both listening right now so I wanted to tell you that I feel great. I'm in my private office right now and I'm sending you a check for three hundred dollars. I hope to talk to you both again soon. And Ronnie, thanks for knowing exactly what would increase the fun even before I did. Take care." He hung up.

"He really liked it," Carla said, still surprised at the power of the spoken word.

"He sure did. And you had a lot to do with that."

"I thought he usually paid a hundred and fifty dollars. He said he's sending three hundred."

"He's paying double. I guess he's sending half for me and half for Snow White." Ronnie pulled out her wallet and handed Carla three fifty-dollar bills. "That's your share."

Carla stared at the money in her hand. "This has to be immoral, illegal, or fattening. Maybe all three."

"Well, it's certainly not fattening and, as far as I'm concerned, it's not immoral. I don't think you can have a crime without a victim and none of my friends is ever a victim." She sighed. "Actually, some claim that what we do together makes them better lovers at home, either more creative or less demanding. However, it is prostitution and that's illegal . . . but what the hell." She sipped her drink and gave a mock salute. "Anyway, Bryce would love to spend an evening with you—your virgin experience, as it were."

Carla's hands trembled. "Now that I'm actually going to do it, half of me can't wait and half is scared to death."

"That's exactly the fantasy that Bryce wants. He loves the scared little girl and the initiation part of this. And you can say stop at any time. Bryce knows the rules. So, if you're sure. . . ."

Carla took a deep breath. "I am."

"Good. I'll give you his number and you can call him, make your plans. He'll take you to dinner, dancing, then to a hotel room."

"Not here?"

"You know you can use the house anytime, although we'll have to coordinate carefully. But Bryce likes the idea of neutral territory. He's got oodles of money and he can afford the best. By the way, as a present to him, I think we should forgo the fee for this one night."

Carla chuckled. "I'm glad. Somehow it seems more honest for

my first time." As she lifted her wineglass, her hands shook. "I'm nervous."

"Good." Ronnie handed Carla a piece of paper. "Here's his number. Call him right now, while you're in this mood. Use the phone in the spare bedroom."

Carla stood up and looked at the paper in her hand. "Bryce McAndrews—555-6749." She walked into the spare bedroom, picked up the cordless phone, and settled on the bed.

With shaky fingers, she dialed the number.

"Hello."

"Is this Bryce McAndrews?"

"Yes."

"This is Carla."

His voice was suddenly soft and warm. "Ronnie's friend?"

"Yes." She had no idea what to say.

There was a warm laugh and Bryce said, "Are you free Friday evening?"

"Yes." Shit, Carla thought. Why am I so tongue-tied?

"I'll pick you up at Ronnie's place and we'll have dinner at an intimate restaurant I know. They have a small dance combo. I hope you like to dance. Leave everything to me. Just be ready about seven. Okay?"

"Okay." Her voice shook and Bryce was intrigued.

"You have no idea how I'm looking forward to meeting you, Carla."

"Me too," she said softly.

Bryce's laugh was infectious. " 'Til Friday," he said, then he hung up.

"Until Friday," she repeated into the silent phone.

For the next few days, Carla was a wreck. She drove her children to and from Cub Scouts and swimming lessons. She cooked dinner, watched TV, and visited with her parents, all the while quaking inside with a delicious excitement that she was amazed no one noticed.

Thursday, on a whim, she had her nails done. She'd passed Plaza Nails often and had occasionally thought about treating herself to a manicure. Always before, however, the cost had stopped her. If I want to stay home with the boys and not work full time, she had told herself as she walked passed the door toward the supermarket, I've got to be a little careful.

As she drove past the mall on the way to Little League Thursday afternoon she gave in to temptation. It's an investment in my career, she told herself. Anyway, I have Rick's three fifties in my wallet.

So while the boys were at practice, a manicurist named Micki, who didn't stop talking for an hour, lengthened Carla's nails with linen wraps and glue, then polished them in a soft lavender shade called "Lilacs in the Spring." As Carla left, Micki told her to come back in a week for a glue manicure, whatever that was.

"Hey, Mom," said Mike, her youngest son in the car going home. "You've got stuff on your nails."

"I decided to have them polished," she said, glancing at her nails for the dozenth time. "Looks snazzy, no?"

"I guess," Tommy said, "but it'll be hard to make pizza dough." Practicality was Tommy's hallmark. "They'll get all ookey. We are having your pizza tonight, aren't we? You promised."

"Of course. I promised."

Thursday evening after pizza, Carla spent several hours standing in front of her closet debating exactly what to wear. After her call to Bryce, she and Ronnie had rummaged through Ronnie's closet in the brownstone, but nothing in Ronnie's wardrobe made just the right statement. As the boys did their homework and watched TV, Carla put on, then took off at least a dozen combinations, selected then reselected like a schoolgirl preparing for her first date. "I'm an idiot," she muttered, throwing a beige, summer knit dress on top of the growing pile on her bed. She picked up the phone and started to dial Bryce's number to call the whole thing off. "God, this is really stupid." Then she put the phone down. "I can always call it off during dinner."

She hung everything back up, then closed her eyes and pulled a blouse from its hanger, coordinated it with a linen suit and stuffed all three garments in a tote bag to bring with her. Then she sat on the bed, pulled the items back out, folded them neatly, added a pair of low-heeled pumps and put everything back into the bag.

She gazed into the mirror, brushed her shoulder-length hair and shook her head slowly. Should I go down to the city early and have my hair done? she wondered. Somehow that didn't feel right. She had no idea why her nails should look better than her hair but it seemed wrong to have some fancy hairstyle. "Shit," she said aloud, "this is ridiculous. I'll worry myself to death at this rate." She stuffed a strand of hair behind one ear and went to tell the boys that it was bedtime.

The following afternoon Carla packed an overnight bag for each of her boys.

"Are we staying at Gramma's?" her thirteen-year-old asked.

"Yes. For tonight."

"Got a hot date, Mom?" BJ asked as she packed.

"Where did you get that idea?" she asked, taken aback.

BJ put his fingers to his temples and closed his eyes. "I see all and know all," he chanted. When Carla raised an eyebrow he continued, "Well, Mom, new nails, an overnight visit with Gramma and Grampa. I'm not a kid, you know. I watch TV." When she continued to stare at him he continued. "It's okay with me. Mothers need some fun. Oprah and Dr. Phil say so. I'll be nice to Gramma and watch Tommy and Mike."

Her kid was watching talk shows and telling her that mothers needed fun. She playfully swatted his bottom, then stuffed Mike's PJs into his bag.

On her way into the city, Carla stopped at a local mall on a whim and bought a pair of large pearl-drop earrings that matched her outfit perfectly but differed from anything she owned. With the new jewelry in her purse, she arrived at the brownstone at about five. Since Ronnie was in Dutchess County Carla had the place to herself.

She wandered upstairs, filled the oversized tub, poured in a large scoop of bath salts and, while the water ran, put a Sinatra cassette into the tape player. While the crooner's familiar voice filled the room, Carla settled into the deep tub and leaned back, letting the light spicy scent relax her. She spent an hour in the water, adding hot whenever it became too cool. She fantasized about the evening and what Bryce would look like. She pictured him undressing her slowly, touching and stroking her. She could imagine him whispering in her ear, telling her how beautiful she was. She almost felt his hot body entering her and slowly loving her.

When she finally emerged from the tub her skin was soft and deep pink all over, and her nipples and pussy tingled. Part of her wanted to stimulate herself to orgasm, just to take the edge off, but she didn't. The edge fit right in with the fantasy that she and Bryce were creating.

At six-thirty, she put on a white, lacy bra and matching panty, a stylish white garter belt and stockings and a white satin half-slip. Then she slipped into the full-sleeved gold silk blouse and mid-thigh, off-white linen skirt she had brought and slipped her feet into her pumps.

She snapped on the earrings she had bought and looked at herself in Ronnie's mirror. As she had suspected, the earrings set off the blouse perfectly, but felt so alien to her that she pulled them off. After looking at her reflection for a moment she slowly put them back on. In for a penny, she thought, in for a pound.

She sat at Ronnie's dressing table and applied makeup, wishing that she knew enough about cosmetics to be able to do something different with her face. She examined her new long fingernails, then drummed them on the dressing table just to hear them clack. She brushed her brown hair until it shone and pulled it back behind one ear with a gold comb. She stood and stepped back so she could see herself in the full-length mirror. Not bad, she thought, not bad.

Ronnie had told her that if and when Carla wanted, she could have a makeover session with an old friend but Ronnie had also assured her that Bryce would prefer the natural Carla. Ronnie had several spray bottles of scent on her dressing table and Carla selected Opium, dabbing it sparingly on her neck and in her cleavage.

Trying to shake off her nervousness, she looked at herself one last time, grabbed her jacket and carried it downstairs, arriving in the living room just as the doorbell rang.

She took a deep relaxing breath, dropped her jacket on the back of the sofa, and opened the front door.

With a lazy gaze, Bryce looked Carla up and down. "You look splendid."

Carla stared at Bryce and for a moment was unable to move. Carla was dumbstruck. He was gorgeous. Tall and slender, Bryce McAndrews had carefully styled iron gray hair and deep hazel eyes that made Carla shiver as they took in her entire body. His charcoal gray suit was carefully tailored to show off his broad shoulders and flat stomach and his light blue shirt perfectly matched the small design in his Italian silk tie.

Bryce's full lips slowly curved upward indicating that he appreciated what he saw. "I've been looking forward to this evening ever since Ronnie told me about you," he said, "but now that I've seen you. . . . Well let's just say this is going to be some evening."

Carla stepped aside and Bryce walked to the sofa, picked up her jacket, and held it out for her. As she slipped her arms into the sleeves, he leaned down so his lips were beside her ear. "You smell sensational. This was worth waiting for," he whispered. He placed a feather-light kiss in the hollow below her left ear, then stepped back. "Let's go."

His shiny black Porsche occupied a no-parking zone in front of the brownstone. He opened the door for Carla and, as she climbed in, he gazed at her long shapely legs and the shadowy cleavage between her breasts. "Ummm," he murmured. "Nice all over."

During the drive to the West Side, Carla learned that her date had four sons, all grown. She and Bryce talked easily about their children. It was so comfortable and Bryce was so charming that occasionally Carla forgot the purpose of the evening and where they were going to end up.

"It's just like a real first date," Carla said hesitantly as Bryce drove.

He softened his voice. "It certainly is. And I like it like that. Relax and let me make it good for you."

"I'll try," she said, startled that she had voiced her feelings.

"Are you really nervous?"

"Yes," Carla admitted, clasping her hands in her lap to stop them from shaking.

"Good. A little scary expectation is just the right spice. Let me tell you about our evening. We're starting at a little restaurant called the West Side Club. They have great food, a fantastic wine list, and a three-piece combo for dancing. You do dance, don't you?"

"I used to love it," Carla answered honestly, "but I haven't danced in a long time."

"Like good sex, it's something you never forget." Giving her no time for a rejoinder, Bryce deftly pulled the black two-seater into the space in front of a long maroon awning. Immediately a uniformed doorman rushed around to open Carla's door. "Thank you, Marco," Bryce said, "but I'll assist the lady." Marco stepped aside as Bryce rounded the car.

Carla took Bryce's extended hand and, as she climbed out of the car, felt Bryce scratch her palm with one fingernail. Shivers skittered up and down her spine and the area between her legs grew warm. She looked over at her escort but he was busy giving his keys to Marco. Hand in hand, they walked into the depths of the darkened restaurant. "Ah, Mr. McAndrews," the maitre'd said unctuously. "I have your table all ready."

Without a word, they were led to the side of the room. Because of the expert placement of potted plants and lacy screens, each table seemed to be in its own private alcove. Bryce seated her. Almost immediately the waiter brought a cooler with a bottle of white wine already chilling. Proudly he showed Bryce the label.

"I hope you don't mind," Bryce said, "but I made a few

arrangements in advance. Of course, if you'd prefer a mixed drink, or red wine, the waiter can bring you whatever you want."

"White wine will be fine," Carla said.

"Good. This is a Portuguese Vino Verde that I particularly like." The waiter poured a sip for Bryce, who tasted it and nodded. "Don't freeze the poor wine," he said as the waiter poured for Carla. "Take the cooler away and just leave the bottle on the table."

"As you wish, sir," the waiter said.

Carla sipped. "This is excellent," she said. "I've never had a Portuguese wine before. You have great taste."

Bryce gazed into Carla's eyes over the rim of his glass. "If you put yourself into my hands for the rest of the evening, you'll see what good taste I really have."

Bryce ordered dinner for both of them. Through fresh asparagus and thin slices of Smithfield ham, poached salmon with dill sauce and tiny boiled potatoes, they talked about inconsequential things from the music they enjoyed through books and movies to vacations. Since Bryce had traveled extensively both for pleasure and business, he regaled Carla with tales of the sites he'd seen. With Carla's agreement Bryce ordered lemon sherbet and Irish coffee for dessert.

As she finished her sherbet and sipped the heady brew, Carla realized that she hadn't had such an enjoyable evening in many years.

Music began. "Dance with me," Bryce whispered. He took Carla's hand and guided her to the tiny wooden dance floor. He held her gently, his right hand placed correctly in the small of her back. Carla realized immediately that he was a sensational dancer, gliding effortlessly across the small space. Several other couples joined them and, as the floor became more crowded, Bryce held her closer, his mouth against her ear, his left arm pressing lightly against the side of her breast.

"You're so graceful," he said, rubbing his forearm against the side of her bra and the flesh underneath, "like an angel in my arms."

Carla swallowed hard and remained silent. Although she knew that this was to be her initiation into the world of recreational sex, she felt like a woman on her first date with a dangerously attractive man.

"I love holding your body close," Bryce whispered. "Your breasts are so full and your hips fit perfectly against mine." His breath on her ear caused a tingling at the base of her spine. "You're so responsive," he continued, "that I'll bet you're getting hot already."

For some reason, Carla needed to deny what he was saying. It was like a seduction, not an assignation, and somehow it was important not to be easy. When she took a breath to deny her feelings, Bryce interrupted, reading her thoughts. "You can deny it all you want but your body radiates sexual heat." He flicked the tip of his tongue in her ear, then nipped at her earlobe.

She shuddered, telling him about herself as accurately as she could have with words.

"Yes. You want me," he whispered. "But resist as well. It makes it all the sweeter to know that later I will hold you in my arms, naked and open. I'll overcome all your resistance and control your body with your own hunger."

He put his finger under her chin and lifted her face so she had to look into his eyes. "You'll want me so much that you'll beg for it." He tucked her against him and continued dancing, holding her close. No one else on the floor could possibly know about Bryce's erotic whisperings but Carla felt as if everyone was watching her.

They danced for a few more songs. Carla felt Bryce's hand sliding over her silk blouse. "I want your body to know exactly what's to come." His hot breath tickled her ear. "We're going to leave in about fifteen minutes. One or two more dances should be just right."

Carla realized that Bryce's planning and take-charge attitude would turn some women off, but the control that Bryce was exercising was driving her crazy. After the first few years of marriage, she had called most of the sexual shots. Bill would have been content with quickies, but Carla had wanted more. Frequently she would wear an alluring nightgown or a teddy and, when Bill responded, she would tell and show him what she wanted. She had enjoyed the sex, but would have preferred not to be in charge.

"I want you to do something for me," Bryce said a few minutes later. "Go into the ladies' room and take off your bra. I want to dance with you and feel your unrestrained breasts against my chest. I want to be able to look down the front of your blouse and see your nipples. Do it for me, Carla. Do it because I want you to and because it will make you a little less secure."

They walked to their table and Bryce gave Carla a tiny push toward the ladies' room. "Please," he whispered. The wine and the Irish coffee made her brave and daring. Not giving herself time to think, Carla walked to the bathroom, closeted herself in a stall, and removed her bra. She put the bit of silk in her purse and rebuttoned her blouse. She looked down, then smiled and unbuttoned the blouse's top two buttons.

She walked out of the stall and checked her appearance in the large mirror. Nothing showed from the front or side but, as she looked down she could see her full breasts and her hard, erect nipples. She smiled and walked back toward the table, enjoying the sway of her breasts and the brush of her nipples against the silk of her blouse.

"Nice," Bryce said as he watched her approach. He met her on the dance floor and took her in his arms. As they danced, he looked down. "Your breasts are magnificent," he whispered. "Your nipples are a dark, dusky pink. Are they so hard that they hurt?"

Carla had never been asked such sexual questions by a man before. She cleared her throat, unable to speak.

"Tell me. I insist." When she remained silent, he repeated, "I insist. Say to me, 'My nipples are so hard that they hurt.'" He slid his hand into her hair and turned her face up. "Say it, angel."

Certain words were hard for her to say; they always had been, even with her husband. Talking directly about sex and the anatomical parts involved had always been difficult for her. "I do hurt for you," she murmured.

"What hurts?" he said. She was silent. "The word 'nipple' is difficult for you to say, isn't it? I can tell from your body's reaction. Your palm is damp and your hand is shaking." She tried to look down, but his hand remained tangled in her hair. "I don't care whether you want to or not," he said, his lips almost touching hers. "You will do as I say. Say 'My nipples hurt for you.' "

"Oh God. My nipples hurt for you." Carla could barely stand. The thrill and humiliation of saying that word made her knees weak. Fortunately Bryce held her tightly, supporting her.

"Oh yes. I like this. Let's continue this discussion somewhere else." Quickly he paid the check and guided her to the door. They walked a block in silence, the cool air clearing Carla's head a bit. They climbed the stairs to the door of an undistinguished building and Bryce unlocked it. "A very private place," he said as they went inside. "It's owned by good friends of mine who let me use it when they're away, which they are for the entire month of September."

Carla was aware of little as Bryce put her jacket away and guided her to the stairs that led to what she assumed was the master bedroom. They stopped about three-quarters of the way up. "Take off your blouse," Bryce said. "Right here."

She looked at him. Shouldn't he undress her? Removing her own clothes seemed so forward. Remembering why she was here, she realized her feelings were ludicrous, but they were her feelings nonetheless.

"Do it," he said, softly. "Be what they used to call a brazen hussy for me because I tell you to."

Slowly, Carla unbuttoned her blouse and pulled it off. "Yes," he said. "Your tits are magnificent, so hungry for my touch." He saw that the harsh language made Carla's hands shake and he smiled. "Tits. Say that word. Say 'My tits are so hard for you.' " He could see the muscles in her throat working as she swallowed. When she hesitated, he made it sound like an order. "Say it, Carla!"

"My . . . tits. . . . are hard for you."

"That's a good girl," he whispered. He walked down a step so that his mouth was level with her chest. "Hold your beautiful tits so I can suck them. Hold them for me."

It was both scary and liberating for Carla. Bryce was making her do things she wouldn't do herself, and she felt both compelled and freed. She slid her hands beneath her heavy breasts and lifted them so that the swollen nipples were level with Bryce's lips.

"Good girl," he purred. He flicked the tip of his tongue up and down over Carla's left nipple. Then he bit it, gently. "Is that good?"

"Mmmm, yes," she murmured.

He moved from side to side, from nipple to nipple, licking and biting until both breasts were swollen and reaching for his mouth. He turned her, urged her up the stairs and into the large bedroom. He moved to the bedside and turned on a small lamp, bathing the bed with soft light. "Your skin glows," he said.

Carla stood and dropped her blouse, watching Bryce watch her. Suddenly she realized how good it felt to have someone look at her naked body the way Bryce was looking at her. She was a sex object, and glad of it.

Bryce flipped the covers aside, sat on the edge of the bed, and leaned back on his elbows. "Strip for me, slowly."

Carla smiled and slowly unzipped her skirt, a bit less embarrassed knowing how she was pleasing him. She stepped out of her shoes, pulled her skirt and slip down and let them fall around her feet. She stood, wearing only her garter belt and matching stockings and her sheer white panties.

"Take off the panties," Bryce told her, "but leave on the rest. I want to see your pussy-fur surrounded by white lace."

Words like pussy made her tremble as she removed her panties. She stood and watched Bryce's gaze wander slowly over her body. "Nice?" she asked.

"Lovely," he said. "But you're a little too calm. You're getting too comfortable. Let's heat things up a bit. I want you to massage your breasts while I watch. Pinch your nipples."

When she did as he asked without much hesitation, he said, "Exhibiting your body doesn't make you shiver the way I want you to. What seems to tantalize you is saying those words." As he watched her blush he knew he'd found the way to make her hotter. "Say to me, 'My pussy is wet for you.'" When she remained silent he laughed. "You'll need to learn to say those things so I'll have to train you. Walk over here."

Bryce sat up as she walked to the side of the bed. When she started to sit down, he said, "Not yet. I want to make it difficult for you to stand up." She sighed and stood between his knees. "Now," he said, "when you're a good girl and do as I say you'll get your reward." He slid his finger into her wet pussy, touching her erect clit, then pulled his hand back.

"And when I don't?" Carla asked.

"You'll have to just stand there and wait. Understood?"

Carla nodded.

He leaned forward and blew cool breath through her pubic hair. She shivered and he said, "Good. Now say, 'Play with my pussy.'"

"Oh God," she said, feeling her juices soak her crotch. "It's so good when you touch me."

"Like this?" He caressed her clit again.

"Yes."

He pulled his hand back. "Then ask for it."

"Touch me."

"No. Not good enough," he said. "I told you what to say."

"Play with my . . . pussy."

"Good girl." He slid one finger between her swollen lips. He could feel her muscles react to his touch. "Do you want more?"

Her hips were moving involuntarily. "Yes. I want more."

"Then say, 'Put your fingers into my pussy.'"

She was going crazy. She wanted everything. "Put your fingers in my pussy," she said.

When Bryce saw that Carla was shaking so much that she was about to fall, he said, "Lay down and spread your legs so I can see your beautiful pussy."

She stretched out across the bed and parted her legs. "Aren't you going to take your clothes off?" she asked.

"Not yet, angel, not yet. We're not finished with your lessons yet. We have to continue to increase your vocabulary. You've learned to say 'pussy' too easily. Say 'cunt.' Yes. Say 'Finger-fuck my cunt.' "

Oh God, she thought. I can't say those words. She swallowed hard and shook her head.

"Such a bad girl," Bryce said when she remained silent. He leaned over and roughly spread her legs wider. Then he blew a stream of air on to Carla's cunt and watched as her skin quivered. He flicked his practiced tongue over her exposed clit, then blew cool air again. "Say 'Finger-fuck my cunt.' "

It was torture. The alternate warm and cool sensations were driving her wild. She reached toward her pussy but Bryce grabbed her hands and held them at her sides. "Oh no. You can't relieve yourself that easily. Only I can give you what you want and you're going to have to ask for it."

She wanted his fingers inside her. Mindless with desire, she said, "Please. Finger-fuck me. Put your hand inside my cunt. Please."

"Oh yes, baby." He inserted first one then two fingers into her cunt and spread them to fill her. He pulled out, then rammed them inside. With his other hand he rubbed her clit until both of them felt the ripples of Carla's first orgasm.

"Don't stop," she screamed. "Oh God, don't stop."

"I won't, angel," Bryce said, feeling the orgasm roll over her entire body. "Let go. Let it devour you."

"Yes, yes, yes." She spasmed for what seemed long minutes. When she calmed, he stood and pulled off his clothes. His large, fully erect cock stood straight out from his groin. Hungrily she watched his hand stroke the smooth, hard flesh.

"I love the way you watch my hands," he said. "Do you want to touch me?"

"Yes. Let me touch you. Let me take you in my mouth."

"Ahh," he said. "You like sucking cock. Tell me."

"Yes. I want to take you in my mouth." She sat up, watching his cock.

His hand slid over his hard penis, to the tip, then pulling back to the root. "Say, 'I want to suck your cock.' "

Those words again. Carla could feel her body tighten. "I want to . . ."

"Tell me."

"I want to suck your cock."

He leaned over and held his hard cock against her lips. "Open for me, angel," he said. "Suck me into your mouth."

When she pulled him into her mouth he let his head fall back. She was good, giving him exquisite pleasure. Her mouth was slippery and hungry and her tongue slid all over his smooth flesh. She pulled back until the tip of Bryce's cock rested against her lips. "Say 'I want you to suck me'," she said, grinning.

He laughed, then said, "I want to fuck your cunt." He pushed her backward on the bed, slipped on a condom, and drove his large penis into her steaming pussy. Her stocking-covered legs wrapped around his waist and her hips bucked. Over and over he drove hard into her body.

"Yes, angel. Oh yes," he yelled.

"Hard inside me. Don't stop!" she cried.

They came, first Carla, then Bryce. Still entangled, they rested for a few minutes.

"That was unbelievable," Bryce said later. "I'll tell you something you aren't going to believe. It's never been any better."

"Ummm," Carla said. "For me either."

"You're a desirable woman. And from what Ronnie told me, you're going to get to channel your charms into a productive business."

"Yes, I am. And I now know that it's going to be okay. I had almost forgotten how much I love fucking." She laughed. "I can even say 'fucking' now, thanks to you."

"Next time we'll have to find something else to play."

"Next time?"

"Certainly. I'm not letting something as good as you get away. And next time I'll happily pay for your attention."

"You don't have to pay me. This is too much fun."

"If you intend to go into business, your first lesson is not to give it away," Bryce warned. "And I hope you'll enjoy it every time with every man you're with. Especially me."

Chapter

5

Carla and Ronnie had lunch together the following afternoon in Ronnie's living room. "From your contented look," Ronnie said, swallowing a bite of grilled mushroom, "I assume Bryce did right by you."

"He sure did. It was wonderful."

"I'd love to hear all the details," Ronnie said, "But I don't want you to tell me anything that makes you uncomfortable."

With a laugh, Carla said, "That's very funny coming from you and considering the business we have in mind."

"You still have the right to be uncomfortable about things. You give up no rights here."

"I know, and thanks." Carla proceeded to tell Ronnie about the previous evening, chapter and verse.

"This tendency you have to be submissive could be a profitable addition to our business. You know that I tend to be the dominant one and I have many friends who enjoy playing with me. But lots of men like to be the master. Well," Ronnie said, spearing a shrimp with her fork, "we'll figure that out as time goes on. First, I'd like you to think about changing your appearance. Making yourself look more sophisticated. I'd love to get you an appointment with Jean-Claude."

"The Jean-Claude? The one who works with all the stars?"

"That's him. And he's done pretty well for himself since he and I first met," Ronnie said. "He did a makeover for me a long time ago, when he was still a hairdresser named Jimmy and I was still relatively monogamous. He did my hair, taught me how to use makeup, how to select the most becoming clothes, the works. I recommended him to my friends. He'll do wonders for you."

"Am I that bad?"

"You are perfect for the supermarket and the PTA but not quite right for men who want to take you out and show you off. Like last evening. In addition to how it will make you feel, it makes a man feel potent if the woman he's with makes others' heads turn."

"I guess you're right." Carla crossed the room and looked at herself in the antique mirror that hung over the maple desk. She lifted her long brown hair and turned left and right to study her face. As usual she wore only rouge, gray eyeshadow, and lipstick. Her earrings were simple gold hoops. "Do you think Jean-Claude could do something with me?"

"You bet." Ronnie looked sheepish, then said, "As a matter of fact, you're due at his studio in about an hour."

Carla's laughter was immediate. "You were so sure?"

"What woman could resist putting themselves in the hands of a talented, gorgeous Frenchman with the soul of a lover?"

"Does he know about you and this?" Carla said, waving her arm around the lavish room.

"Actually he's a good source of referrals," Ronnie said. "He works around celebrities and he occasionally meets someone who wants discrete company."

"You've entertained celebrities? Here?"

Ronnie sighed. "Russell Street was here just last month."

"I'm impressed," Carla said. "Russell Street."

"Don't get starstruck. Eventually you may entertain someone famous, but what they want as much as anything else is a companion who'll enjoy cavorting without the trophy-collecting mentality that groupies are known for."

"Well," Carla said, "if I'm due at Jean-Claude's, I'd better take a quick shower and wash my hair. Are you coming too?"

"I wouldn't miss it for the world."

Jean-Claude did wonders. He cut Carla's hair short so it formed a soft frame around her face and rinsed in a slight reddish highlight. He and Ronnie spent an hour showing Carla how to put on her makeup and select clothes that would best accentuate her lovely figure. Together they tried earrings and necklaces on Carla to see which complemented the shape of her face and her large brown eyes. Jean-Claude's manicurist redid her nails in a bright shade that Carla thought of as hemorrhage red.

Finally, when she studied herself in the mirror, Carla was thrilled. Her eyes appeared larger and her cheekbones seemed higher. Dangling gold earrings made her neck look longer and the teal scarf Jean-Claude had draped around the collar of her white blouse brought out the pink in her cheeks.

"Remember when we . . . uh . . . ran into each other that morning last summer?" Ronnie said with a wink. "You described yourself as medium brown and average, average, average?"

"I did, didn't I."

"And now?"

Carla gazed at herself in the mirror. "Well, I have to admit that I'm not half bad."

"Not half bad indeed."

When Carla arrived home late that afternoon, her boys just stared. "Hey, Mom, what's with the new hair and stuff?" Tommy asked.

"I had a makeover. My friend Ronnie suggested it. Do you like?"

"Heck no," Tommy said. "You look like a model or something, not like a mom."

"Yeah," her youngest chimed in.

"I think I'll take that as a compliment."

"Cut it out you guys," BJ said. "Mom's looking for a man. It'll be good for her, dating and all." He patted her on the arm and

Carla suddenly realized that her thirteen-year-old son was almost as tall as she was. "It's okay, Mom. If you find a nice man, I'll explain it to these guys."

"Thanks, BJ," she said, completely nonplussed, "but I'm not looking for a man. I just want to look nicer for my business meetings."

"You know as well as I do," BJ said, "that grown-ups need a partner. Hormones and all that."

"Oprah again?"

"Yeah. And we learned about that in sex education."

Carla tried not to laugh.

"Will you still cook and stuff?" Tommy asked, his eleven-year-old mind not yet taking it all in.

"Of course. If you'll let me get into the kitchen we'll do Barrett-burgers for everyone."

Three days after Carla's session with Jean-Claude, Tim Sorenson maneuvered his station wagon into the parking space that appeared unexpectedly when a van pulled out from right in front of Ronnie's door. He sat for a moment, thinking about his assignment: to take photos of Ronnie's friend Carla for an album like Black Satin. Ronnie had told him a lot about the woman he was about to meet and he was confident that he could do a professional job.

Since his first evening with Ronnie, Tim had come a long way. He'd managed to tell his father that his working life wouldn't revolve exclusively around the oil business and, to his dad's credit TJ had taken the news just fine. Although he still worked at American Oil and Gas Products with his father, Tim now also viewed himself as a photographer. His work had appeared in several photography magazines and two of his views of the California coast were appearing more and more frequently in photo stores. Clients wanting Tim to do portraits had to book him three months in advance.

More important, thanks to Ronnie, Tim had discovered the joy of sex, to borrow a famous phrase. His new vibrancy showed in his work. Women seemed more beautiful, men more robust.

His first serious photographic assignment had been the nearly two hundred pictures he'd taken of Ronnie for her album. During that photo session they'd made love in ways Tim hadn't dreamed of and they'd been together several times since. He now considered himself a sexual sophisticate. And he loved it.

He climbed out of the driver's seat and unloaded cases from the back of the wagon, stacking lenses, camera bodies, and video equipment. He also pulled out a nylon bag filled with goodies he'd gathered after his long conversation with Ronnie about Carla. He walked up the steps and rang the doorbell with his elbow.

When Carla answered the door she saw a wholesome, appealing looking young man standing on the stoop, his hands filled with black leather cases. Tim held the handle of a blue nylon gym bag with his teeth, which muffled his words. "Catch the top one," he mumbled. "It's going to fall."

The case toppled from the stack and Carla neatly caught it, tucked it under one arm, and snatched the bag from his teeth. "You certainly come prepared," she said.

"Overprepared, one might say. May I come in? This stuff's heavy."

"Sorry," Carla said, stepping away from the door and holding it open with her foot. "Come on in."

As if familiar with the house, Tim walked directly into the living room, dumped the cases on the leather sofa, and extended one hand. "Hi. I'm Tim, as you already know, and you're Carla."

Carla shook his hand and was charmed by the warmth of both his grip and his open smile. As Tim sat on the sofa and unsnapped his cases, Carla settled next to him and curled her feet underneath her. "Nice to meet you, Tim."

"Me too. I've talked about you with Ronnie and I've got some dynamite ideas about this shoot."

"You and Ronnie talked about me?"

"Sure. She helped me get a handle on what kind of pictures you want. I hope you don't mind."

"I don't. What did she tell you?"

"Just that this is your first venture into this . . . uh, business . . . and that you want shots for your album. I've got ideas about that but, if it's fine with you, I'd like to keep them to myself for the time being. Anyway, what do you think of Ronnie's album?"

"Impressive." Carla thought about the erotic photos of Ronnie and wondered whether she'd be comfortable enough with this stranger to pose like that. She twisted her fingers in her lap. "Ronnie looks so great."

"Yeah, they did turn out well. But I had a good subject." Tim studied his new subject more closely and muttered aloud as he thought. "Great eyes, fabulous cheekbones, great skin so there'll be no problems with close-ups."

Carla squirmed under Tim's scrutiny, glad of the job that Jean-Claude and Ronnie had done with her. She ran her fingers through the cap of soft waves and nervously licked her lips. Tim's smile was warm and understanding and since his manner was both professional and friendly, she began to relax.

"I'm sorry you're nervous," Tim said. "I think you'll find the nervousness wears off quickly once we start."

"I hadn't realized how anxious I was about this. I really don't know exactly what to do."

"Don't worry about that. It's my job. Would you stand up?"

Carla stood, her hands hanging awkwardly at her sides.

"Relax," Tim said. "You're going to be great." Long legs he thought. A great body, magnificent breasts. He decided to take a risk. Either he was going to get terrific, sexual pictures or he was going to blow it before he even took one shot. "I can see your nipples through your shirt," he said softly. "Any man would want to suck them." He watched her body react and knew just how to get the attitude he wanted.

Carla was a bit surprised by the language coming from this stranger, but excited too. Although they shocked her, she realized his raw words also aroused her.

"Can I get you a drink or something?" she asked.

"Actually I'd like to get started, if that's okay. This light is wonderful and I'd like to get a few head shots right here before we do anything else."

Carla used the mirror over the desk to touch up her makeup. "Where would you like to start?"

Tim shoved a chair toward the window, adjusted its position several times and said, "Sit here and let's see." Carla settled into the chair but Tim shook his head and pulled her to her feet. He moved the chair slightly and sat her back down again. "Yeah. That's nice," he said finally.

Heeding Jean-Claude's advice, Carla had selected a simple kelly green tank top and black palazzo pants. She added a gold chain with large open links and oversized gold earrings. As she settled in the chair, she fluffed her short hair and Tim watched the sunlight coming through the window catch the reddish high-lights. She had used three shades of eyeshadow, liner, and mas-cara as Jean-Claude had shown her and, with the addition of rouge and lipstick, she had been pleased with the results.

"You look smashing," Tim said. "Now turn your head this way and tip your head." He spent several more minutes peering through the lens of his camera and adjusting the tilt of Carla's head and the angle of her shoulders. He also set up a video cam-era on a tripod, aimed at her chair.

"Video?"

"Sure. You'd be surprised how many men will enjoy watching you on tape, knowing that you're in the room with them, naked and willing."

"I never considered that but I'm getting an education quickly. Does Ronnie have a video?"

"Several. I'll shut it down if you don't want it."

Carla stared into the video camera's eye and found that being on display was exciting. Go the whole way? she asked herself. Who am I fooling? Damn straight I will. "Leave the camera run-ning. It's fine."

When Tim had her positioned to his satisfaction, he said, "Now close your eyes." When she did, he said, "Picture yourself lying stretched out on your back on a blanket in a secluded clearing in a forest. The sun is beating down and heating your face. Can you feel it?" When she started to nod, he said, "Don't nod, just tell me. Is the bright sun hot on your skin?"

"Yes," Carla said softly, raising her chin to the warmth.

"Now open your eyes." When she did, Tim snapped off several pictures, capturing the soft, dreamy look he'd wanted. "Close them again. You're still lying in that clearing in the forest but now you're naked. You can feel the sun on your entire body, on your shoulders, your belly, your breasts." He paused and watched her face. "Open your eyes." He snapped several more pictures. "God, the camera loves you," he murmured.

"More?" Carla said, her voice husky.

"Close your eyes." She complied and he continued. "A man walks out of the forest. You can't see him because your eyes are closed, but he's tall and very good looking, with a great body and soft hands. He's wearing a pair of faded blue jeans and nothing else. You don't have to open your eyes to know that he's looking at your body, but you're not nervous. The heat of his gaze adds to the heat of the sun. He's staring at your breasts and he can see that your nipples are getting hard. Although you're pretending to be asleep, he knows, Carla. He knows you're excited. He knows that he's making you excited." When Carla opened her eyes, Tim snapped again, then told her to move one arm and retilt her head and took several more shots. With the sound of the clicking in her ears, Carla stretched and extended her arms over her head, making love to the camera.

"Close your eyes. It's important that the man believes you're sleeping, so when he stretches out next to you on the blanket you stay still and keep your body relaxed. He just stares at you for a moment, then brushes his fingers through your pubic hair just touching your love button. You remain motionless, wanting him to continue.

"Although you don't move, he knows how wet you're getting." Tim picked up a different camera and snapped a few shots of Carla with her eyes closed. He didn't know whether it was her expression or the line of her body, but she was radiating sex and he wanted to capture it. "You want to move your hips to deepen his touch, but you don't want him to know how he's affecting you, so you remain absolutely still, pretending that you're still asleep."

Carla was there, in the clearing in the woods. Tim's voice had transported her and she could actually feel the sun on her body, feel fingers probing and exploring the secret places of her body. God, she thought, he's really turning me on. I'm going to explode.

"Keep your eyes closed and pull off your tank top and your bra," Tim said.

Carla removed her clothes without hesitation. She was no longer nervous or embarrassed. Both Tim and the camera seemed erotic and right.

When Carla was naked to the waist, Tim repositioned her in the chair so shafts of sunlight illuminated her shoulders and breasts. Her eyes were still closed as Tim moved back behind his camera lens. "Beautiful. Let your head fall back against the chair." He kept snapping as she moved, each pose a sensual invitation. "Now, he's still touching your clit and you're still pretending to be asleep. His fingers caress each fold and part your lips. You're so wet that his finger slides easily into your body."

Tim watched Carla's body react to his story. He knew that she was having a difficult time holding her hips still and he smiled as he watched her through his lens. "He adds a second finger, then a third, filling you completely." He saw how puckered her nipples were and added this to his story.

"Your nipples are so hard and tight that you think you'll die if his mouth doesn't take them. You slide your hands up your ribs and hold your magnificent tits out for him to suck. Offer them to him, Carla. Don't speak, but offer him your hard, tight nipples."

Carla's body tightened and she did as Tim asked. She flattened her hands against her belly and slid them upward, lifting her full breasts and offering their rosy tips to the camera. When Tim asked her to open her eyes, she still envisioned an attractive man lying next to her on a blanket in the sun.

"So good, Carla," Tim said, trying to resist the lure of his own sensual story. He wanted to take the breasts being offered into his own mouth, but he knew that would come later. For the moment, he kept repositioning her, snapping pictures as the video camera hummed in the background. He finished his second roll of film and changed to a third while Carla stood up and removed the rest of her clothes.

Ronnie had told Tim a lot about Carla and he had come prepared. He took a large piece of satiny soft leather from the nylon bag he'd brought and spread it on the chair. "Sit back down," he said, "and close your eyes again. Feel the leather against your skin." As she moved her naked body against the soft surface, Tim knew he'd been right. Leather would take Carla to the next level of sensuality. "Feel it, smell it. Fill your senses with it. Put your right leg over the arm of the chair and slide your ass forward. . . . Yes, that's right." Her pussy was wide open and shining.

Carla was in a sexual daze. She'd never dreamed that the smell and feel of leather could arouse her so. She felt she was going to climax, but everything about this experience was soft and gentle. She didn't understand it, but then she didn't have to.

"Go with it. Fly with the feelings. The blanket in the forest is made out of leather, soft, black, fine-grained leather. It's becoming warm from the sunshine and the heat of your body, and the man is rubbing a corner of it over your legs, your arms, your belly. There's no sound, except the rustle of his movements. You're unwilling and unable to move. You just lie there in the sun absorbing the sensations. Open your eyes." Carla opened her eyes, and Tim snapped several more pictures.

"He's stroking your clit faster now. It tightens your lower belly." Tim watched Carla's body and saw the tiny movements he'd been waiting for. "Do you want to touch your pussy, Carla? Are you so hot that you want to rub yourself while the man watches, while the camera watches?"

Carla had never wanted anything more in her life. "Yes," she whispered.

"Then do it," Tim said. "Touch your pussy. Make yourself come."

Carla touched herself, one hand on her breast and one in her pussy. She rubbed and probed until the tightness in her breasts and her pussy became almost pain.

"Rub it just right," Tim said. He moved around, snapping pictures of Carla's hand on her breasts, her fingers working in her cunt, her face as she strained in pleasure.

Carla heard the click of the shutter and felt Tim's movements around her. To her surprise, it added a new dimension to her excitement. She opened her eyes and watched the camera as it watched her. She moved so Tim could get a better view.

"You're close now, and you want to come," Tim said, taking the video from the tripod and aiming so it captured Carla's body and hands. "You like the camera watching you. You love it that I'm watching you. I can see everything. I'm going to record you as you come. Anyone who sees the pictures will see you getting off. Tell me when you're going to come. Tell me, Carla."

"Now," she said. "Oh yes. Now! I'm going to come right now! Watch me come." Waves washed over her. She moved her fingers around her pussy touching the right places with exactly the right rhythm. She drew the orgasm from her body, bit by bit, savoring every spasm, making it last as long as she could. Tim alternated between the video and his still cameras, taking dozens of pictures and long moments of tape.

While Carla recovered, Tim fused with his camera equipment. "Unbelievable," Carla said. "I was really nervous about this, but you're amazing. You've come a long way since you and Ronnie met."

Tim chuckled. "She told you about that?"

"I'm sorry. I hope that doesn't embarrass you."

"Not at all. That was the opening to a whole new world. She's wonderful, you know."

"I know." Carla sighed.

Tim handed her a glass of water and she took a long drink as her breathing returned to normal. "If you're recovered, why don't we go upstairs and try on some of the costumes for your album photos." He picked up the piece of leather and threw it over his arm. "And I think you should use a black leather cover on your book. Leather seems to turn you on."

Carla nodded her agreement. "I never realized it, but you're right."

Naked but unembarrassed, Carla climbed the stairs with Tim behind her. "You've got great legs," he said, "and a nice tight little butt. I like the way you walk around nude. You don't parade, yet you don't hide either."

"I used to walk around without clothes a lot but with three inquisitive boys, I don't get much chance to anymore."

Tim squeezed past her and shot a few snaps of her walking up the stairs. "God, you've got a great body," he said. "I love taking pictures of you."

She put her hands behind her head and raised her elbows.

"You've got the most beautiful tits I've ever seen," he said.

In the bedroom, Tim opened a closet and pulled out an evening dress. It was a column of royal blue silk with classic lines and a high neckline in the front. "I've seen Ronnie wear this and I'd like to see you in it," he said. "You should wear primary colors, bright greens and blues. Red would look terrific on you, and black and white of course. Stay away from too much yellow and orange. It won't go with your skin."

"You've got quite an eye," Carla said, selecting a pair of tiny bikini panties from a drawer. "That's exactly what Ronnie and Jean-Claude said."

"I hope you don't mind if I pick out a few things for you," Tim said, flipping through the dresses.

"Not at all." She looked at the high-necked dress hanging on the closet door. "But isn't this a bit tame for our photos?"

"Wait until you see it on."

As Carla reached for a bra, Tim shook his head. "No bra. You don't need it."

"You're the boss," Carla said. She pointed to a large jewelry chest that stood on the makeup table. "What do you suggest with this dress?" While Tim rummaged through the extensive collection of costume jewelry, Carla picked up the hanger and took a better look at the gown. From the front it looked almost demure, but the dress had no back. It was cut low enough to reveal the line between her cheeks. As she slipped it over her head, she said, "I'll have more cleavage in the back than in the front."

"That's the idea. That's the first dress I ever photographed Ronnie in."

"It isn't in the album," Carla pointed out.

"I know. I kept that picture for myself. I have it in my bedroom. I may keep the one I'm about to take too."

"Do you have fantasies about her?" she asked, fluffing her hair.

"Not anymore. I did for a long time after our first meeting. Now we're just good friends. We fuck now and again and I take her to an occasional party, but that's about it." Tim had selected a pair of large silver-and-diamond dangle earrings and he handed them to Carla.

"They look like chandeliers," she said.

"Try them."

Carla stood in front of the mirror and clipped on the oversized earrings. Tim was right again. They accented the dress perfectly. "Change your makeup," he said. "More eyes and a darker lipstick."

Carla quickly adjusted her makeup as Jean-Claude had taught her to and suddenly she was a seductive woman of the evening. "Brilliant," she said.

"Brilliant is right," Tim said. He posed her with her almost-naked back to him, looking seductively over her shoulder. He snapped several pictures. "Now we come to album photos," he said, opening Ronnie's other closet. "Which of these says you?"

"I don't know. Which do you think I should wear?"

"Not my decision. For the album you need pictures of fantasies that you would enjoy acting out with a friend. That's a very personal decision." He reached into the closet and took out the pink little-girl dress. "This fantasy is about the older man who likes to make love to virginal little girls. You wear white socks and Mary-Janes, white cotton undershirts and underpants."

Carla smiled as she put it on. Tim photographed her sitting on the edge of the bed with her hands folded in her lap and knees locked together, looking a bit scared.

"This," he said, holding a short wedding dress and a veil, "is a similar fantasy, deflowering a wedding-night virgin." She dressed and Tim snapped that outfit as well.

They continued for over an hour, with Carla portraying a cheerleader, an aerobics instructor, a bikini-clad nymphet, and a harem girl. When Tim suggested the stern teacher costume, Carla demurred. "I don't think I'm the dominant type."

"Ronnie is," Tim said, "and I have some very sexy shots of her with a whip in her hand and a man wearing nipple clamps licking her pussy."

"I never saw those."

"She has some particular pictures for special friends."

"Should I have a special album? I can't see myself with a whip."

"I know that. But I have a different idea. Come with me into the other room," Tim suggested.

"What other room?"

"Ronnie's playground. She told me she hasn't shown it to you, so let me."

"Should I wear anything special?" Carla asked removing her costume, a nurse's uniform with a starched cap.

"Just your beautiful skin."

Tim opened the door to the other bedroom and let Carla precede him. As she entered the room she gasped. Almost cave-like, it was darkened with wood-paneled walls and heavy velvet drapes. As Carla looked around she saw that the room resembled a dungeon with eyelets, chains, and bondage equipment proudly displayed on every wall. There were three differently shaped wooden benches with hooks and straps attached and two cabinets filled with items Carla didn't recognize. A huge brass bed dominated one end of the room. As shocked as she was, Carla also realized that she could hardly breathe.

Tim walked in behind her and wrapped his long fingers around one wrist, holding her tightly. "Exciting?"

"Yes," she whispered.

"Ronnie thought as much. I took several rolls of film in here with Ronnie dressed all in leather brandishing whips and paddles. But I don't think that's you, is it?"

Carla shook her head. She was picturing herself held down or chained, restrained and helpless with a man standing over her enjoying her vulnerability. Tim took her other wrist and held her arms against her sides. He put his mouth close to her ear. "The word is 'popcorn,'" he breathed, rubbing his fully clothed body against her back. "Say the word and I'll stop whatever I'm doing. And let me give you some advice. Never play in here without a safe word. And never play with anyone you don't trust to honor it. Understand?"

"Ronnie and I discussed that. I understand."

"Say 'popcorn.'"

"Popcorn."

Tim released her hands and moved away. "Now, stand here and look around the room while I get my camera. While I'm gone, picture yourself strapped into each piece of equipment, unable to escape. From now on, don't speak unless I ask you a direct question. And don't move!"

The last was an order, one that Carla had no intention of disobeying. She looked around and studied each device. She imagined herself restrained in a few but she had no idea what many were for or how they worked. She didn't care. Her palms were sweating and she was struggling to get air into her trembling body.

"Good girl," said Tim, reentering the large room. "You're so excited, you're ready to burst. That's very good. Come here." As Carla walked across the thick dark gray carpet her feet sank into its soft lushness. "Give me your arm." Carla held out her arm and Tim fastened on a tight leather wristband. He looped a ring attached to the band over a hook on the wall and took a picture of her hand and arm.

"You know you can unhook yourself any time you want." Tim's voice caused a heat wave to wash over her. "But you want to stay there. You want me to restrain you. That's excellent." He fastened an identical strap around her other wrist and one around each ankle. The rings attached to additional hooks on the wall so her arms were held out from her shoulders and her legs were spread about two feet apart.

As the camera snapped, Carla imagined how she looked, fastened to the wall, controlled and helpless. God she was hot. If she could just touch herself. . . . But she wouldn't move, couldn't move.

Tim walked over and kissed her full mouth. Then he slid his finger across her hip until it was against her clit. "You want to come? Just like that?" He stopped. "No. Not yet. I want to play a while." He put the camera down. "After Ronnie and I had been together a few times, we discovered that we both have a love of dominance. I want to be in control. I want to be able to tease. I want to do anything and everything without any protest. Do you want to play with me?"

Carla nodded. At that moment she wanted to be dominated by him more than she'd ever wanted anything else.

"Do you remember the safe word?" he asked.

"Popcorn," Carla said.

"That's good. Now, a few questions. And I want honest answers. What if I hurt you, just a bit?" He pinched her nipple and twisted it hard.

It was so sudden that Carla cried out.

"Good or bad?"

Carla paused, then admitted, "Good."

Tim grabbed a handful of her hair and dragged her head back. He kissed her mouth, grinding his face against hers. She responded, pressing against him as much as her bound body would allow. "A true playmate," he said, unhooking her limbs from the wall. He pulled her over to a wooden bench, adjusted the length of its legs, and laid a leather spread over it. "This has been a fantasy of mine for a long time, but Ronnie is too dominant herself to really enjoy this. Lie down on your back."

Carla did, feeling and smelling the leather. "Inhale," Tim said. "Smell your own aroma." Carla breathed deeply and knew the scent of her arousal. She was so hot that she doubted it could get any better, but each time Tim spoke, it did.

"Here's something else for you to enjoy." He slipped a leather blindfold over her eyes.

The darkness was total. Being unable to see made her more aware of her other senses. She heard the rustle of Tim's clothes as he moved around the room. She smelled leather and sweat and sex. She rubbed her hands over the leather, appreciating its rich texture.

"Don't move," Tim said. Carla could hear the camera and imagined this scene as it would appear to those thumbing through her own 'special' pictures.

"Now slide up until your head hangs off the end. There's a pillow that will support your neck and let your head hang down gently." She slid along the leather until her neck rested on the pillow and heard snaps as Tim fastened her arms and legs to the bench. "These aren't hooks, they're padlocks," he said. "I want you to struggle to get free."

Carla experienced a moment of panic as she pulled at the locks. She had to test Tim's words. "Popcorn," she said.

Tim fumbled with the first lock until her right arm was free. "Refasten it," she said. "It's all right."

"I was afraid that I'd gone too far," he said. "I was seriously disappointed."

"Don't be. I just needed to be sure."

"Of course you did."

Tim quickly relocked her wrist. "Now struggle. I want to see your body strain, unable to get free."

She pulled at her arms and legs. The bindings didn't hurt at all, but she was, nevertheless, completely helpless.

"Beg me to let you go."

She heard the hum of the video camera. "Please." She knew that she could say popcorn at any time and he would let her go. She could also beg and plead and know he wouldn't release her. Her head angled downward was making her a little light-headed but it was fantastic. "Please let me go. Oh god, please."

"Oh no, baby. Not a chance." Then his hands were on her face, gently feeling around the blindfold. He slipped a finger into her mouth and she sucked as he worked it in and out.

"I want you to understand exactly what I'm going to have you do," Tim said. "This bench is at just the right height." What had to be his naked cock slid over Carla's cheeks. "You're going to suck me good." He withdrew the finger from her mouth and replaced it with his hard erection. Carla gasped as Tim forced his large member into her mouth, but she quickly started sucking as he fucked her mouth. "Too good, too fast," he said, pulling away from her greedy mouth.

She again heard a rustling then a buzzing. "Hear that?" he said. "That's a vibrator and I'm going to make you come with it. I'll be in control of your body. You won't be able to resist. You'll come when I want you to and only when I'm ready."

Carla jumped when she felt the buzz against her nipple. Jolts of magic electricity bounced around inside of her, stabbing her in the breasts, the belly, and in her hungry pussy. She wanted nothing more than for Tim to fuck her, any way he wanted, but she sensed that her resistance was part of his fantasy and she wanted him to have it all. She knew instinctively what to say.

"Oh stop," she said, "please stop. It's torture."

"It's exciting to beg, isn't it? And to know you can't sway me. And I love to hear you plead for mercy, but there will be none." He placed the tip of the vibrator deep in her armpit.

Carla was afraid it would tickle, but it didn't. It just excited her more. "I can't take it. No more, please."

"There's so much more," Tim said. He moved the vibrator until it was rubbing the insides of Carla's thighs. "Want it against your cunt?"

"No. Don't."

"I will. And what's more you want me to. It's so embarrassing to admit that you want me to fuck you with this vibrator, this artificial buzzing cock that can give you such pleasure."

"Oh god, no."

Tim was in heaven. This was his favorite fantasy and it was

better than he had dreamed it would be. And he was taking it as far as it would go. "I think you'd better ask me to fuck you."

"No."

He teased Carla's cunt, touching her swollen lips, then stopping. Sliding the vibrator through her thick wet juices, then moving it back to the inside of her thigh. "I can make you crazy with wanting. Admit that your pussy needs to be fucked. Say it."

"Yes, do it," Carla said, slipping out of character. "Fuck me good."

Tim inserted the penis-shaped vibrator into Carla's pussy and strapped it in place with a piece of leather that was connected to the bench. "Now suck my cock," he said, walking around to the head of the bench and laying his cock against her mouth.

Carla became pure sensation. She sucked and lapped as the buzzing filled her demanding cunt. Tim came quickly, unable to resist the pull of Carla's mouth. She swallowed as he pumped until he thought he would never be able to come again. He pulled his exhausted cock from Carla's mouth, knowing that she hadn't come yet. "Do you want to come now, baby?" he asked.

"Please. Help me."

"Of course," he spoke reassuringly. He knelt between her legs and flicked his tongue back and forth against her clit. "Yes," she screamed. "Don't stop."

He didn't and Carla climaxed, shuddering and bucking against the straps holding her wrists and ankles. Tim pulled the vibrator from her sopping pussy, unfastened the straps and carried her to the bed.

"I've never experienced anything like that before," Carla said.

"It was great for me too," Tim said. "Maybe when I've developed the pictures, we could get together again to look them over . . . and whatever."

"Yes," Carla sighed. "Lots of whatever."

Chapter

6

Carla stretched languidly on her bed and, knowing her friend would still be up, dialed Ronnie's number in Dutchess County from the private phone she'd had installed in her bedroom. It was not quite eleven in the evening and, once the boys were in bed, Carla had soaked in a hot tub for almost an hour. Despite the predictable romance novel she had read, she had been unable to relax. She was confused about the following evening, her first with her new black leather album.

Wrapped in an old velour robe, socks, and a pair of Garfield slippers that her boys had gotten her the previous Christmas, she listened to the phone ring.

"Hello," Ronnie answered.

"Hi, it's me."

"Hi. What's up?"

"Well. . . ." Originally it had felt odd to discuss the business of sex with her three boys sleeping just down the hall, but after a few late-night phone sessions with Ronnie the whole thing felt almost normal. "A man named Max called and I called him back. He says he got my number from you."

"He did. When my friend Bert called and told me he had a friend, I suggested you. You've got to get your feet wet at some point, so to speak. I hope that giving him your number was okay."

"Oh sure it was. He left a message on my answering machine. And now I'm excited, but also nervous. What if I'm not good enough? What if he doesn't get his money's worth?"

"He will. I assume you two talked and you feel comfortable with him."

"Of course. He sounds nice and he's never been with a . . . someone like me before." She giggled into the phone. "I think he's more nervous than I am."

"He probably is. You'd be surprised how anxious some men get. But that can add to the anticipation."

"I know. Part of me is so keyed up I'm ready to come if someone looks at me crooked. But part of me is worried."

"You'll be fine. And if something feels uncomfortable, just tell him. If he's unwilling to do anything else, give him his money back and say good night."

"He says he wants to see my album. He's obviously heard about yours."

Ronnie snuggled deeper under her covers. She had been watching TV in bed, naked, and now she slithered over her satin sheets, feeling the smooth fabric against her skin. Talking about sex always made her horny. "Is your album ready?" she asked.

"I met with Tim yesterday and we looked over the pictures he took. He does marvelous work. Some of those photos made even me hot. I bought an album. It's black leather."

"Great. Satin and leather."

"Max said he's looking forward to a creative evening. How do you broach the subject of fantasy?"

"It's different each time," Ronnie answered. "Some men just want straight fucking and you don't have to use the album at all. Most men who call me, and who will call you, have been referred by someone else, someone who's enjoyed the fantasies that I've created. Let's face it. I'm expensive and you will be too. Someone who just wants a good lay can get that for a lot less money. So our kind of friends, or clients as you call them, want something out of the ordinary, something that they can't get at home. I guess creative is as good a term as any."

Carla shifted the phone to a more comfortable position on her shoulder. "But how, exactly, should I begin things? I can't just say, 'Want to act out a story?' can I?"

"You probably won't have to. Most of the time new friends will know about your album from whomever recommended them. They may even have decided on a fantasy. Some will never have thought about role-playing, and those are the most fun for me. Once you get past a man's initial shyness, play-acting can be the greatest sexual turn-on there is. Gets them outside themselves. They can do anything, be anyone, and no one's judging or censoring."

"You're still not answering my question. How do you start things happening?"

"Okay. Let's take the first man I played with after I put together my album." Ronnie shifted the phone to the other ear, settled back, and stared at the ceiling, remembering Tory Palluso.

Ronnie introduced herself to the maitre d' at La Bon Nuit and he efficiently guided her to a quiet section off to one side of the busy restaurant. As she slalomed between tables of two or four expensively dressed diners, she had a moment to look over Mr. Palluso who, she saw, was sitting on a chair opposite the banquette, hesitantly sipping a glass of red wine.

Tory Palluso was about forty-five, Ronnie guessed, with a receding hairline and wire-rimmed glasses. To his credit, his dark hair wasn't combed over the top to disguise his balding pate, but was neatly trimmed and styled. From several tables away, he didn't appear to be a good-looking man. His granite-hard profile and pointed chin, heavy black eyebrows and matching moustache seemed overwhelming.

As Tory looked up and saw her moving toward him, Ronnie smiled and nodded. He looked straight at her and she was struck by his eyes—so bright blue that if not for his glasses she would have thought he was wearing colored lenses. Both his smile and his unusual eyes made his face surprisingly appealing.

As he watched the beautiful woman making her way to his table Tory thought, She doesn't look like a call girl. But Frank had assured him she was the best. If she was as good in bed as she looked, she was going to make him regret that he only got to New York two or three times a year.

"You're Ronnie," Tory said.

"Tory," Ronnie said, extending her free hand, "I'm so glad to meet you." The maitre d' pulled out the table and Ronnie settled herself on the banquette. She set the package she was carrying down next to her.

"Wine?" he asked. When she nodded, he asked, "Red or white?"

"Red."

"I looked at the wine list and they have a nice Burgundy, if that's okay."

"That will be fine," Ronnie said. She had barely gotten comfortable when the waiter brought the wine. When Tory nodded the waiter opened the bottle and nearly filled her long-stemmed glass. "To an eventful evening," Ronnie said, lifting her glass toward Tory.

"Eventful," Tory said as his glass touched Ronnie's. "A superb way of thinking about things." He sipped. "You're lovely."

Ronnie smiled. She had selected a soft chiffon scoop-necked dress in a shade best described as cantaloupe and worn it with a triple-strand pearl necklace and pearl drop earrings. A matching triple-strand bracelet and a gold watch showed off her long, slender fingers. On a whim she'd had her nails done that afternoon in a frosted shade the exact hue of the dress.

"Thank you," she said softly, and raised an eyebrow. Tory's dark suit was carefully tailored to hide the slight paunch she had noticed as he stood up and he wore a monogrammed white on white shirt and conservative paisley tie. Everything about him bespoke pride in his appearance and money enough to indulge it. "You're not bad yourself."

Through a savory vegetable pâté, a crisp green salad with a peppercorn vinaigrette dressing, veal with capers served with a wine, lemon, and butter sauce, and julienned vegetables, they talked about business, family, and other ordinary things. Over an apple tart with a delicate, thin crust they discussed politics. They agreed more than either had expected.

Over napoleon brandy and espresso, Tory finally broached the reason for their dinner. "We have a mutual friend," he said, suddenly hesitant. "Frank Morrison."

"I know," Ronnie said. "He gave you my phone number."

"Right."

When the silence became awkward, Ronnie said, "Do you want my company for the rest of the evening?"

"I enjoyed our dinner. You're a highly intelligent and knowledgeable woman, for. . . ." He stumbled over the end of the sentence and swallowed hard.

"For a hooker." Ronnie laughed. "Don't be embarrassed. I'm not. I love what I do and I love fulfilling men's fantasies, which, I gather, is what you want."

"My wife is a wonderful lady, don't get me wrong."

Ronnie interrupted. "Why don't we agree not to mention her for the rest of the evening. Tonight is for a little adult entertainment. Maybe, one day, you'll see fit to share some of your desires with her. I'll bet she'll be more receptive than you'd imagine, but that's neither here nor there. Let's discuss you."

"I want something unusual. Frank said you and he played out a fantasy of his. He wouldn't tell me about the specifics. 'Too personal,' he told me. But from the grin on his face, he must have enjoyed it tremendously."

"Do you have a fantasy in mind that you want to act out?"

"Not really. Frank said you'd have suggestions."

"I have something here that may help you decide." The tables on either side of them had long since been vacated, so Ronnie motioned for Tory to sit beside her on the banquette. She picked up the package she had carried into the restaurant and placed it on the table. From a large black-satin drawstring bag, she withdrew a photograph album with a black satin cover and placed it in front of Tory.

She placed her hand on the closed book. "In here are fantasies, scenes that we can play together. Look through the book and I'll describe each fantasy." She handed Tory a flat, black-satin envelope about four inches square, with a black tassel tied to one corner. "When you find something you'd like, put my fee in the envelope and use this bookmark to hold the page. Then we'll go back to my house and play."

Hands trembling with expectation, Tory took the envelope and opened the cover of the album. The first photo was of Ronnie dressed in a black satin bustier with matching garter belt and stockings. "That's Marguerite, the stripper," Ronnie explained as Tory gazed at the first picture. "She'll strip very slowly for you."

He turned to the next photo. Ronnie was dressed all in green. "That's Maid Marian. She's been in love with Robin Hood for months, but they've never had time to be together."

Tory lifted the album page and turned to the next photo. "Nita's a harem girl. You were very brave in battle and saved the sultan's life. He's allowed you to pick one girl from his harem and she's yours for the evening. She's been very well trained in the arts of love."

She continued as Tory turned pages. "That's the Princess Mellisande. She's not allowed to have intercourse until her marriage, but she satisfies herself, and most of the guards in the castle, by masturbating while they watch, then bringing them to climax with her mouth."

The next shot was of Ronnie in her bed, dressed in a nightgown, holding a sheet up against her breasts. "And that's Bethann. She was asleep in her bed when a burglar broke in. At first, he wanted to steal her jewels. Now he just wants her body."

He turned the page again. "That's Miss Gilbert. She's the headmistress at an exclusive boy's school and, if you want to meet her, she'll explain your punishment for being a naughty boy in class."

For picture after picture, Ronnie explained fantasies to Tory. The last dozen photos in the album were explicit pictures of Ronnie, guaranteed to ignite the most selective viewer. Ronnie stood as Tory turned back to the beginning to review the photographs. "I have to use the ladies' room. I'll be a few minutes so look through the book and select. Of course, you could make up your own fantasy or we could just go back to my place and make love."

"Not on your life. I've never had a chance like this."

When Ronnie returned from the ladies' room, Tory had her coat over his arm. He helped her into it, then handed her the book. She opened to the page he had selected and removed the satin envelope. "Nita will please you in every way," she whispered as she slipped the five hundred-dollar bills into her purse.

The ten-minute cab ride was the longest Tory could remember. Ronnie's stocking-covered legs were just inches from his and he longed to run his fingers up the inside of her sweet thighs. He held himself back. This night was going to be something extraordinary. He was going to let Ronnie dictate the speed. And he would savor every minute.

Ronnie had initially been reluctant to use her brownstone, worrying that one of her friends might get out of hand, either during an evening of pleasure, or afterward. But she quickly realized that her customers had more to lose than she did if the police became involved.

The cab let them off in front of her house and they quickly made their way inside, then up to the bedroom. "There's a bottle of champagne in the fridge," she said, pointing to the small wet bar in the corner of the room, "and glasses just above. Pour some for each of us and make yourself comfortable. I'll just be a moment." She took a hanger from the closet and disappeared into the bathroom.

Five minutes later Ronnie emerged from the bathroom. "Sir Knight," she said softly, "I'm Nita. The Sultan has told me of your bravery and I'm honored you picked me for your evening."

Tory just stared. Her halter top was made of light-blue gauze so sheer that it allowed glimpses of her nipples. A veil of the same material covered the lower part of her face. Matching harem pants rode low on her hips, flared at the legs and gathered tightly at the ankles. Through their sheer fabric Tory saw a dark triangle of hair at the junction of her thighs.

Nita's feet were bare, and she wore long earrings and bracelets on her wrists and ankles, all with tiny bells that tinkled as she moved. Her head was bowed and her long blond hair was covered with a soft blue, gauzy veil. A golden chain hung around her bare midriff. Covering her navel was a dark blue jewel.

"I hope I please you," she said softly. "You have only to indicate how I may serve you and your wish will be my command." She crossed to stand in front of him and slid her hands up his silk shirt, sliding his jacket off his wide shoulders.

"Will you dance for me?" he asked.

Ronnie put a tape in the player and the room filled with rhythmic, exotic music. Sinuously, Nita undulated around the room, turning down lamps, and lighting candles and sticks of incense. As she twirled, she removed the veil covering her hair and slid its soft folds across Tory's face. At one point, she stood in front of him, placed the veil over his head and kissed his lips through the sheer fabric, the bells continually tinkling.

When he reached for her, she danced away, trailing the veil over his skin. She held the transparent fabric under her breasts and lifted so the unrestrained twin mounds stood out from her chest and jiggled as she moved, covered only by thin layers of gauze. She thrust her chest into his face but, when he went to kiss one nipple, she danced away.

Near then far, close, yet not quite close enough. The fragrance of her eastern perfume filled Tory's head and he longed to taste her mouth. When next Nita danced close, he grabbed the scarf that covered her face and wrapped it around her body, trapping her swaying bottom.

Nita leaned over and licked Tory's upper lip with the tip of her tongue. Back and forth, her tongue danced over his mouth as her bottom swayed against the imprisoning scarf. Each time he would have pressed his lips tightly against hers, she moved slightly away, allowing only the lightest of touches of mouth against mouth.

"More," he growled. "Kiss me, woman."

Nita's mouth was so close to Tory's that her breath cooled his wet lips. "Your wish," she breathed, "is my command." She pressed her mouth against his and her tongue requested entry. Greedily, he opened his mouth and swirled his tongue against hers. For long moments, their lips and tongues joined in fiery combat, plunging, then drawing back.

While they kissed, Nita opened the buttons of Tory's dress shirt and tugged it from his body. She removed her mouth only long enough to pull his undershirt over his head and finally she ran her hands across his chest so the hair slid between her fingers. She scraped one nail down his skin.

He was on fire, yearning to devour this woman who was his for the evening. When he let go of one end of the scarf she slipped away, teasingly moving around the room. She turned her back, then took off her top. Naked to the waist, Nita held up a scarf and twirled. Tory got quick glimpses of her full breasts, their large darkened nipples standing out from the soft white skin.

Without taking his eyes from her body, Tory stood, removed the rest of his clothes, and tossed them aside. "Your staff is fully ready, my lord," Nita said, staring at his erect cock. "Shall I take it in my mouth and show you how much pleasure I can give you?"

He dropped into the chair. "Oh yes, Nita, but just a little. I will have better uses for my staff."

She knelt on the floor at his feet and brushed her hair across his loins, combing her hair with his cock. The sensation was so exquisite that he was afraid he would come without her ever really touching him. When she finally placed a light kiss against the tip of his erection, it took all his concentration not to climax right then.

Nita flicked her tongue over the end of Tory's cock, licking the sticky pre-come fluid. Then she pursed her lips and sucked his purple cock head into her mouth. She took it in as deeply as she could, then pulled back, her head bobbing up and down in his lap.

"No, not yet," he growled. He stood, put on a condom, grabbed her around the waist, and pulled her harem pants down. He turned her so she was facing away from him, bent her at the waist and plunged his cock into her wet pussy from behind. Over and over he drove into her until he moaned with his release.

Ronnie hadn't actually climaxed, but she was strangely satisfied, sharing Tory's pleasure. She reached between her thighs and cupped his testicles, squeezing and milking all the thick fluid. His body bucked as the last of his orgasm flowed into her.

When Tory collapsed, Ronnie got a warm, wet facecloth from the bathroom and leisurely washed his penis and testicles. She squeezed his cock and satisfied herself that there was, at least for the moment, no arousal left in him. She never left anyone unsatisfied.

He stood up, stretched, and looked at the clock beside the bed. "That was great, but I'm afraid I have to go now," he said.

"You have my number," Ronnie said, "and there are many other pictures in my album."

"I don't get to New York often," he said sadly, buttoning his shirt. "But when I do, you can be sure you'll hear from me."

Ronnie shifted the phone to the other ear. "I see Tory two or three times a year," she said to Carla, "and he's very generous." Carla heard Ronnie's short laugh. "Last time, in addition to paying me, he brought me a magnificent gold bracelet with a tiny bell on it."

"Do you always play the same scene with him?"

"Not always, but we come back to Nita more frequently than any other fantasy."

"Thanks for the story," Carla said. "That makes it much easier for me to deal with Max."

"Well, good luck tomorrow night," Ronnie said. "And most important of all, have fun."

"I will. Believe me, I will."

When she first saw Max, Carla had to smile. He looked like the stereotypical mountain man, about thirty-five, with almost black hair, a rugged build, and a full, bushy beard and moustache.

"You're a great looking woman," he said without preamble. "Nice body, good bones."

"Thank you," Carla said, her nervousness quickly disappearing. "And you're very handsome yourself."

He fluffed the beard that was long enough to cover the first two buttons of his open-necked shirt. "You mean this," he said as she put her napkin in her lap. "I think it's ridiculous that a man spends ten or fifteen minutes each morning scraping a dangerously sharp instrument over his face. When I graduated from high school, I stopped shaving."

"I guess that means that you don't work in the gray flannel world of corporate America."

His laugh was as booming as she had expected. "You're right. I'm a maverick and proud of it. I own my own business, Sheridan Plastics. Hell, I am Sheridan Plastics. Built it myself from the get-go, you might say. Now some guys in pin-striped suits want to buy me out for an amount of money that has more zeros than I had dollars when I started. And I can sell or I can tell them to go to hell. It doesn't matter to me."

"Are you married?"

He saddened. "Unfortunately, just when life was getting good, Marie died. Auto accident. It was real fast so at least she didn't feel anything."

"I'm sorry."

"It was almost eight years ago. Now I just like to have fun. Nothing serious, mind you. Just fun. What do you want for dinner?" Max asked.

"You selected this place and you seem to know your way around. What do you suggest?"

"I love a good steak and this restaurant serves the best in town."

"Sounds great to me," Carla said. Recently her life seemed to be a gustatorial war between nouvelle cuisine and peanut butter and jelly. She looked up as the waiter held his pencil poised. "Sirloin, medium rare with a baked potato and a salad."

"Good choice," Max said to the waiter. "Do that twice. And

let's have a bottle of Chateau Margeaux. I think you have a 1964 hidden away." He turned to Carla. "The Margeaux is a bit light for a steak, but it's excellent."

"Very good, sir," the waiter said.

"You're full of surprises," Carla said. "I would have taken you for a beer type of guy. Or even bourbon."

"I was—still am—but I've learned to appreciate a good wine. I also enjoy ordering the most expensive bottle on the menu."

Carla laughed loudly. She found she really liked this unusual man.

"I understand you have children."

They spent the next hour in pleasant conversation. As the meal neared its end, Carla considered the problem of how to bring up her album but, as Ronnie had predicted, Max saved her the trouble.

"I'd like to see your pictures."

Nonplussed, Carla reached down and opened a black leather attache case that sat near her feet. "How did you know about the album?" she asked as she placed the book on the table.

"I guess that's called Black Leather. Bert told me about Ronnie and her book, Black Satin. I assumed you would have some photos too. That's why I called you. Now, be a good girl and get lost. I want to look at this in private. Oh and take off that bra. I like tits that jiggle."

Carla burst out laughing. "Anything you say." She went into the ladies' room and, inside a stall, took off her bra. She was glad she had worn her teal-blue knit dress and only a half-slip. Max would be happy at the way her breasts bounced. When she arrived back at the table, Max was looking at a picture of a woman in a slinky negligee. "I want to wear something like this," he said, not the least embarrassed. "And I want you to fuck me in the ass with a dildo."

"You certainly know what you want," Carla said, completely surprised by the nature of the request.

"I most certainly do. Can we play?"

"Of course." Ronnie had told her that she had lingerie in

larger sizes and had shown her the love toys. "I can't guarantee that exact outfit, but I'm sure I have something you'll like."

"That's okay. And by the way, you have great tits."

Max dropped a handful of bills on the table and almost dragged Carla to a taxi. In the bedroom of the brownstone, Carla put her coat and Max's away and went through the bureau drawers. She pulled out a black nightgown with a deep vee front and back and thin straps over the shoulders. She placed it across Max's lap. "How about this?"

His huge, calloused hands slid over the delicate fabric. "It's beautiful."

Carla found another, a peach-colored satin lounging set with feathery trim. "Or this?"

Max held the black gown in one hand and the peach in the other, rubbing the slippery material between his fingers. In another drawer Carla found a bright red teddy that had long attached garters and panties to match. As she handed the pieces to Max, she saw his eyes light up. "Do you have stockings?" he asked.

"Of course." Seeing Max's expression she said, "You've obviously selected this one?"

"Definitely." He stood up and quickly removed all his clothes.

Carla tried not to think about how much hair Max had all over his body and how the undies he had selected would look. She was afraid she would giggle. When she looked at his face, however, she quieted. He was mesmerized and his body showed clearly that he was extremely excited. Anything that excites a man like this can't be bad, she thought.

"Will that thing fit around my waist?" Max wondered, pointing to the bustier.

"Well, let's try." Carla stretched the silky red lace teddy around his waist and threaded the laces through their eyelets.

Max let his head fall back and closed his eyes as the silk caressed his skin.

Carla fetched a pair of thigh-high red stockings. "Sit on the edge of the bed and I'll help you put these on." Max sat and

Carla scrunched one nylon on her thumbs. "Raise your foot," she said, kneeling on the rug. Slowly, she took his foot in her hand and slid the nylon up the arch. Inch by inch, the sheer red material covered first his ankle, then his calf, his knee, and his hairy thigh. His cock was rock hard as Carla fastened the stocking to the garters.

Max held his breath and trembled as the second stocking inched up his leg and Carla snapped the garter in place. "Soft," she said, sliding her hand down his nylon-covered leg. "Very smooth."

He lifted her hand from his leg. "Not yet," he said through gritted teeth. "I want to feel the rest of the outfit."

"Of course," Carla said. She slid the bikini panties over his large feet and up to his knees. "Now stand up." Agonizingly slowly, Carla pulled the panties over his engorged cock, then stroked his body through the cloth. Up and down his legs, across his chest, up and down his cock. Her hands were everywhere, their touch muffled by the various fabrics.

Max's breathing was ragged. This was better than it had ever been for him. He stood, his eyes closed, his body quivering, as he tried to retain control. He realized that Carla was no longer touching him. He opened his eyes and saw her, still completely clothed, holding a slender penis-shaped dildo in her hand, stroking its length.

"You know what I'm going to do now, don't you?"

He could no longer remain standing. He collapsed, curled on his side, on the bed. "I know."

Carla sat behind him and applied a generous amount of lubricant on the flesh-colored rod. "You know where you need this?"

"Yes."

She pulled the panties to one side and slid the dildo easily into Max's ass and replaced the nylon. "Now, that's done and held in place firmly. Stand up."

"I don't know whether I can."

"You can and you know it."

Max stood up, almost unable to control his body. It was taking all of his strength not to come. But when she milked his cock with one hand and rotated the end of the dildo with the other he was done. Semen soaked the front of the panties, drenching Carla's hand. It seemed hours and still he came, Carla handling his cock in front and twirling the dildo in back. When his body was empty, Max dropped back onto the bed.

Carla sat beside him until his breathing had almost returned to normal. Then she withdrew the dildo from his body, washed it and put it away in the toy drawer.

"That was marvelous," Max said, turning on his back and watching Carla move around the room. "Just marvelous." He sat up. "Help me off with this stuff."

Carla carefully removed the clothing, then slid a new pair of red satin panties up Max's legs and over his limp penis. "Leave them on under your slacks and think of me as the material rubs your cock."

"Hell, Carla, you'll have me hard all the time."

"That's the idea. Your cock will be hard and you'll remember me."

With a quick laugh, Max pulled on his slacks over the red panties. "I just hope I don't have to pee before I get home. Someone in a men's room might see this red stuff and get the wrong idea."

"Or the right one."

"You're quite something, lady," he boomed. "I'll be calling you. And I've got a lot of friends. I hope you're not overly booked."

"I'll make room. Any friend of yours will become a friend of mine."

As Max left, Carla noticed that he was walking just a bit differently, enjoying the slither of the red silk under his slacks.

About a week later Carla received a note in the mail. "Max told me about you. The plumber will be at your apartment at six o'clock on Tuesday evening the 27th." The note was signed "Gene." The only other thing in the envelope was five hundred dollars in cash. Later, Carla got a phone message from Max saying that a friend of his named Gene would drop her a note soon.

Carla was at the brownstone at six on the selected evening, dressed in a pair of tight, white denim pants and a snug-fitting plum-colored polo shirt that accentuated her bralessness. When the doorbell rang, she opened the front door and faced a muscular, if slightly overweight, man of medium height. He wore a pair of stained coveralls and carried a toolbox. "I'm Gene," he said, "and I'm here to fix your kitchen faucet. Max said your plumbing wasn't usually a problem."

Carla almost giggled. "My plumbing is usually fine," she said. "But that kitchen sink has been giving me a terrible time recently."

"Let's check it out." Gene followed her to the kitchen and proceeded to actually dismantle the faucet while she watched. "Okay, lady," he said, "I'm going to need some help here."

"What can I do?"

"Most things, I'd imagine," he said, grinning. He had disconnected the faucet and fastened a huge pipe wrench around some connection at the back of the sink. "But right now I need you to hold this wrench."

Carla replaced his hairy hands on the wrench with her own. "Now pull hard," he said, "and hold tight. If you let go, we'll have water everywhere."

Knowing nothing about plumbing, Carla had no idea what this man had done, so she pulled on the wrench with both hands. "Don't let go," he warned again. As he stood up, he brushed against Carla's breasts which, since she was bent over the sink, were hanging heavily against her shirt. "Nice melons, lady," he said, squeezing one of the heavy globes.

"Hey," she said, "cut that out."

As she started to straighten, he said, "Don't let go of that pipe or it'll make Old Faithful look like a garden sprinkler."

"Shit," Carla said. She had no idea how much of this was fantasy and how much was reality. Not ready to take a chance with Ronnie's kitchen, she held onto the wrench.

"I'm glad you understand," Gene said. He squeezed her breast, weighing its fullness in his hand. "Nice big tits," he said, nodding. "Fill the hand, and then some. I love titties that are more than a handful."

"Will you let go," Carla snapped.

Gene backed up and, behind her, Carla heard tools banging around in the toolbox. "Here we are," Gene, the plumber, said. Carla heard a loud snipping sound. Suddenly her polo shirt was being cut up the back and across the shoulders. With a yank, she was naked from the waist up. "That's better," Gene said.

"Now wait a minute," Carla said, but Gene silenced her with a pinch of one of her swollen nipples. "Ouch."

"Be a good girl," Gene said, "and don't let go of that pipe." He leaned over and bit her earlobe. "If you say 'Uncle,' I'll stop. Understand?" he whispered. Carla nodded.

With both hands holding the wrench tightly, Carla tried to wiggle away from the plumber's hands, but she had almost no room to maneuver. He pressed his body against her back and his rough palms cupped her heavy breasts and pressed them against her ribs. As he held her, he thrust his lower body against her buttocks, jabbing her with what felt like the largest cock ever.

"That's for later," he said, his laugh warm, moist waves against her ear. Again he backed up and rummaged in his toolbox.

Suddenly Gene draped heavy, cold lengths of chain over her shoulders and wrapped it around her ribs and under her breasts. "That's cold," she shrieked, as he fastened the chain in the back.

"And this is warm," he said, leaning into the sink and sucking one nipple into his mouth.

The contrast between his hot mouth and the cold chains was tantalizing. She started to relax and loosen her grip. "Don't let that go," he said. "I mean it. It'll drown us both."

"Shit," she hissed again.

Gene pulled one nipple while he nursed on the other. He moved around to the other side and exchanged his hand for his mouth. He was rough and both his mouth and hands were painful, hurting yet exciting and soothing all at once. "Am I hurting you?" he asked, pinching her left tit hard.

"Ouch! Yes, you're hurting me." Carla looked down and saw a bright red mark. She knew that she could say 'Uncle,' but she wasn't anywhere near needing to. Quite the contrary. She felt wonderful.

"Good," Gene said, unzipping her jeans and pulling them down. Automatically Carla lifted her bare feet so he could pull the pants off, leaving her dressed only in her panties and several lengths of chain. Gene slid his hand down her belly and into her panties. "You're hot for me," he said, his fingers pulling her wet pubic hair. Carla couldn't deny what was obvious to the touch. "I have just the right tool to use and it's not the one you think."

He pulled something from his toolbox and Carla felt something slender, cylindrical, and cold wiggle into the narrow crevice between her legs. "The right tool for every job," Gene muttered. He slid the dildo deep into Carla's pussy. In and out he fucked her with it, moving the slender object around so it touched every inch of her insides.

Her knees weak, Carla had to be reminded not to let go of the pipe. "Hold on to that wrench, lady. Hold on." He pulled her panties back up to keep the dildo in place while he undressed. Since she couldn't let go of the wrench that held the disconnected pipe, Carla backed up as far as she could and arched her back.

She worried about how to insist on a condom without ruining the fantasy, but, as if he had read her mind, she heard the telltale ripping of the condom wrapper. "Don't you worry about a thing. I wouldn't do any job unprotected."

Gene held his large cock in one hand and moved aside the crotch of Carla's panties with the other. With little warning, he pulled out the dildo and rammed his huge cock into Carla's soggy pussy. He was enormous, stretching Carla's body almost to the point of agony. But not quite. The sensation of being so full drove Carla to climax quickly. With a loud scream she came and soon thereafter Gene spurted come deep into her.

When his breathing was more normal, Gene took the wrench from Carla's hands and disconnected it from the sink. No water spurted out. As she dropped on a kitchen chair, Carla watched Gene efficiently reassemble the faucet.

"Nice plumbing," Gene said, packing his wrenches in the toolbox and gazing at Carla's body. "Very nice plumbing."

"And the tools you used were absolutely perfect for the job," Carla said, still puffing.

"I'll be back if you have any more trouble."

"Any time," Carla said. Gene zipped up the front of his coveralls, picked up his toolbox, and left.

Chapter
7

Over the next few months, Carla and Ronnie established a routine. Carla didn't want to be away from her sons any more than was necessary, so she limited her encounters in the city to Tuesday and Thursday evenings and the occasional daytime frolic that didn't keep her from being home when the boys arrived from school. Ronnie used the brownstone other evenings and occasionally on weekends. Every Monday Ronnie and Carla met for lunch, sharing stories and deepening their friendship.

By Thanksgiving Carla had developed a clientele consisting of about a dozen men who regularly perused her album and played out their fantasies with her. A special favorite, her first customer Bryce McAndrews became a regular visitor to the brownstone on 54th Street. At least twice a month, he and Carla got together, ate at a four-star restaurant, and attended a Broadway show or a concert at Lincoln Center. Once they had spent an hour at a Benjamin Britton concert that they both hated. They left after the first selection, when they discovered their mutual dislike of any music composed in the twentieth century. Most evenings they ended up in the paneled room, although occasionally they parted without making love at all.

One afternoon in mid-December Bryce called and told Carla that he wanted to act out an especially elaborate wish of his.

He'd make all the arrangements for the following Tuesday and he asked her to leave the brownstone at seven-thirty that evening, setting a key beside the front door, then come back at exactly eight o'clock.

Carla left at the appointed time, had a cup of coffee at a little restaurant on Second Avenue, then returned to the house filled with mounting expectation. Bryce seemed to understand her desires more and more and their appetites matched perfectly. She walked into the front hallway and heard his familiar voice. "Up here," he called from the second bedroom.

When Carla walked into the room, the entire atmosphere had changed. Bryce had replaced the dim lighting with strong, 100-watt bulbs and all of the exotic equipment that could be concealed was out of sight. Bryce wore a white lab coat and had a stethoscope draped around his neck. "Thank you for being so prompt, Miss Barrett, and I'm sorry you haven't been well."

It took only an instant for her to slip into the part and only slightly longer for her to be wet and trembling. "It's been a difficult time," Carla said, trying to suppress her growing flush.

"I understand completely." Bryce handed her a light blue paper smock exactly like the one she had worn at her last doctor's appointment. "Step into the bathroom and put this on. I'll be ready for you in a moment."

As she took the smock from him, Carla noticed a narrow, padded table covered with a strip of plain white paper, set up in one corner of the room. Her knees wobbled. Did he know about her "playing doctor" fantasy or was this his own erotic dream? It didn't matter.

In the bathroom it took Carla only a moment to strip off her clothes and put on the smock. "Nothing but the smock," Bryce's voice said through the bathroom door, "and have the opening in the front. I'll need to examine all of you."

Timidly she walked from the bathroom. She realized that the room smelled of antiseptic. "That's a real doctor's examination table," Carla said.

"Of course," Bryce grinned. "And this is a real doctor's office. Now, Miss Barrett, lie down."

She stretched out on the table and the doctor put a pillow under her head. "I hope you're comfortable," he said. "Are you nervous?"

"Maybe a little," Carla said. Barely covered by the scratchy paper gown, she felt exposed, despite the fact that Bryce had seen her nude a dozen times.

The doctor picked up a pencil and pressed the point gently against her upper arm. "There," he said. "I've given you something to relax you. Now let's discuss your symptoms. Any loss of appetite?"

"Unfortunately none that I've noticed."

Bryce ran his hands down her sides. "You've nothing to worry about, Miss Barrett. You have a beautiful body. Any difficulty sleeping?"

They continued bantering for a few moments, then Bryce said, "Are you less anxious? I hope so. That injection I gave you should thoroughly relax you. Your arms should feel very heavy."

The sound of Bryce's voice flowed through Carla's body like warm honey. Although he'd used no real medication on her, she felt almost liquid as she melted into the table. "My arms are very heavy."

"And your legs too. As a matter of fact it's getting very hard to move at all. It's a nice, floaty feeling, but you know you can't move. Close your eyes."

Carla did, slipping further and further into the scenario Bryce was enacting.

"Good girl," he said. He took out some cotton and a bottle of alcohol. He soaked the cotton and pressed it against Carla's upper arm.

The cold was surprising and the smell was enough to transport Carla more deeply into the scene. "That's cold," she whimpered.

"Yes," Bryce purred, "it is. And you want to move away from the cold but you can't. As a matter of fact you can't move at all." He moved the still-wet cotton to the inside of Carla's calf. She wanted to pull away but she couldn't break through the haze of the fantasy. Or she didn't want to.

"You're not frightened, but you can't move. The medicine I gave you is a special blend of exotic drugs. You can see and hear and feel, but you can't move, can't speak, can't resist anything I want to do to you.

"First, your breasts." With almost medical objectivity, he pressed and prodded at her flesh and pulled at the nipples. "Your tits get firm," he said. "Good reaction to stimulus." He used a pair of tweezers to pinch one erect nipple. As Carla's body winced, he said, "That must hurt a bit. It's too bad you can't move. And you can't move, can you?" He used the tweezers to lightly pinch tiny pieces of skin all over her body, nodding as her body reacted. "Very good," he said.

Carla gazed at Bryce but said nothing.

"Next is the temperature test." He reached behind him and picked up a glass full of ice. While Carla watched, he picked up a cube and held it so the icy water dripped on one breast. As the drop trickled down her white skin, he licked up the water with the tip of his tongue. Drip, lick, drip, lick, he alternated ice water and the heat of his tongue. She became accustomed to the routine and closed her eyes. Suddenly the frozen cube pressed firmly against her left nipple. "Owww," she yelled, her body jerking.

"Don't try to move," Bryce said. "It's impossible to overcome the effect of the shot I gave you and it is very harmful to your body when you try to resist. Just hold still and I'll finish the temperature test." He dropped the cube back into the glass and placed the flat of his tongue against her almost-frozen dark-pink bud and held it there as the warmth seeped back into her skin.

"Good," he said as Carla's body relaxed, "you've done very well with this test." He opened the bottom of the gown and slid his fingertips up the inside of Carla's thigh until he reached her cunt. "So wet," he chuckled. "You are excited by these procedures. That's very interesting."

Excited by these procedures? Carla was certainly excited by

these procedures, but it was humiliating to know that Bryce could reach between her legs and tell how aroused she had become.

"Let's see. What else excites you?" he said. "I know. Words excite you. Let's just test to see which ones exactly." Keeping one hand on the springy fur between Carla's legs, Bryce leaned close to her ear and whispered, "How about when I tell you that your pussy hair is so soft? Yes. Your cream is flowing so those words must work." He rubbed the wetness around, stroking her clit. "How about when I say 'Your titties are standing up, waiting for my mouth'?" He sucked her upright nipples and continued to agitate her cunt. "What if I tell you that my balls are heavy and my cock is hard, waiting to slide into your pussy? Soon I'll place the tip of my dick against the opening of your greedy slit and push it in ever so slowly."

Carla was lost in a sensual fog, her eyes closed, giving herself to Bryce, hearing his voice and feeling his fingers between her legs. Tremors began deep in her belly and she knew that his manipulation was going to bring her to orgasm.

"You're close to coming," Bryce said. "But I don't want you to just yet." He stopped and got another ice cube. "Let's cool you down a bit." He maneuvered the frosty cube over Carla's pussy lips.

"Oh God, stop," Carla said, forgetting that she supposedly couldn't speak.

"You know the word to use," Bryce said, removing the ice cube, "if you really want me to stop."

"Yes. I do, Bryce," she said, warmth flowing back into her chilled lips. Then she added, "Doctor, please don't do that."

"It's no use asking me to stop," he continued. "The doctor has to do these sexual tests. It's purely scientific."

He's making me crazy, Carla thought. "Please no more." But she wanted more. As much more as Bryce wanted to give her.

Bryce rubbed the cube lightly over Carla's clit, watching her arousal decrease. "Good girl," he said. "Your reaction to this test is excellent." He pushed the cube into Carla's cunt, then pushed two fingers in after it. "You feel hot and cold at the same time," he said. "The sensations must be driving you crazy."

"Ummm," Carla said. Cold water from the melting ice trickled down Bryce's fingers and ran from her cunt down over her ass.

"Maybe you're getting hot enough for the final test," Bryce said.

Final test?

With two fingers buried deep inside of Carla's pussy, Bryce took his other hand and explored the rim of her tightly puckered hole. Then, with both hands moving he leaned down and flicked his tongue over her clit. Fire blazed to and from all the sensitive places he was touching. Hot and throbbing, Carla released, screaming. Every muscle in her lower body spasmed.

"Your body is clenching my fingers," Bryce said, his face buried in her pubic hair. "Come baby," he purred, his hot breath restoking the fires in her pussy. "Keep coming." He drew his fingers from her cunt and quickly moved around the foot of the table and parted the sides of his lab coat. He wore nothing underneath and his arousal announced itself.

As he stood at the foot of the table his cock was at the height of Carla's pussy. He slipped on a condom, then pulled her legs so she slid down the table. He parted her thighs so her soaked cunt pressed against the tip of his cock.

Her juices were still mixed with melted water from the ice. "Not too fast," he told himself, gritting his teeth against the desire to slam his body into hers. "Make this last." His body shook and sweat ran down his chest as he fought for control. He rubbed his sheathed cock against Carla's overheated flesh, then pressed just the tip into her.

She was more excited than she had ever been, yet, because she had already climaxed once, she was able to experience all the nuances of Bryce's body. She could hold herself at a level just below climax, slipping into the ecstasy whenever she wanted to. He opened her inch by inch with his cock, slowly filling her. Occasionally she squeezed her inner muscles and smiled as Bryce shuddered.

When he was fully inside, Bryce stood still for a moment savoring the sensation of being encased in pulsating velvet while the tip of his cock was slightly cold from the remains of the ice. Carla wrapped her legs around Bryce's waist, then pushed her cunt against him driving Bryce's cock still deeper. He could hold still no longer. With panting breaths he clenched his ass muscles and let his body thrust into the slick heat.

"Oh yes," he cried as hot bursts of semen exploded from his penis. "Oh, Carla, yes." He collapsed, his upper body lying across hers, both breathing hard and trembling. She shuddered as her muscles pulled at him.

Long minutes later they were calmer. "Oh, doctor," Carla said with a giggle, "your tests are so educational."

"Zertainly," Bryce said, imitating a thick German accent. "Ve try to be zo zientific." They lay together until Carla's leg began to fall asleep. She moved slightly and Bryce's satisfied cock slipped from her body. As Bryce stood up, he said, "Okay, last one to the shower has to scrub the other, all over."

They made love again in the shower, steaming water pouring over their soapy bodies as Bryce pounded into Carla's cunt from behind.

When he was dressed, Carla said, "You have no idea how much fun our evenings are for me." She stretched on the bed watching his eyes rake her naked body.

"Me too," Bryce said, kissing her on the tip of her nose.

As usual on their evenings together, Carla had arranged for her parents to stay with the boys so she could sleep in the city. "You could stay here tonight," Carla said, reluctantly. Although Bryce still paid her for their evenings together they were also lovers and she sometimes wanted to spend the night with him. But staying here together felt wrong, somehow. Too comfortable. Too married.

"No, but thanks. We both like things just as they are." He counted out five hundred dollars and put it on the table. "No strings."

Carla smiled. "Right," she said, playfully swatting his now-clothed behind. "Let me know when you want to get together again."

"Will do," Bryce said as he walked toward the bedroom door. "Call you soon."

The Village Tavern, known affectionately in Greenwich Village as the fat-factory, was not one of Carla's usual restaurants. It specialized in mammoth hamburgers, great steaks, forty-five varieties of beer, and desserts covered with real whipped cream. Patrons joked that an ambulance stood by at dinnertime in case of a heart attack.

The two men who sat at the table in the back of the Village Tavern were not Carla's usual type of client. As she studied them she saw that, except for the fact that one man wore rimless glasses, they looked as alike as two men who weren't related could. Both men were of medium height and build with ruddy complexions and weathered skin. Both men appeared to be in their thirties, with well-muscled arms and upper bodies. Their heads were together and they were deep in conversation.

As Carla approached, the darker of the two obviously said something funny and both men roared. "Which is Dean and which is Nicky?" asked Carla, dropping into an empty chair.

Both men looked at Carla, and looked and looked. Carla smiled easily, enjoying their frank admiration of her white cotton man-tailored shirt, western vest, and tight-fitting, stonewashed jeans. She wore a multicolored zuni fetish necklace and matching earrings and had applied little makeup. The two men were silent for a long moment, then spoke simultaneously.

"He's Dean."

"I'm Dean." They laughed together, a warm sound that made Carla imagine how nice it would feel to be so close. "Timmy wasn't kidding when he told me you were a knockout," Dean said. "Until you got here, Nicky and I had been wondering whether this was a dumb idea. Now I think we've done real good."

"Tim told me that you two had some recent good luck," Carla said. Tim Sorenson had called Carla and told her that Dean Gerard and his friend Nicky Romano wanted to employ her for an evening. Except for vouching for Dean's character and setting up the meeting, Tim would tell her nothing else.

"We won fifteen thousand dollars in the lottery. Seventy-five hundred each."

"I've never met a lottery winner before," Carla said. "Congratulations."

"Thanks," Nicky said. The waiter arrived and Dean suggested a German beer that Carla had never heard of. When Carla nodded, Dean held up three fingers and the waiter disappeared.

"Tell me a little about yourselves," Carla said, aware that she was treating them like a pair rather than two individuals.

Dean did the talking. "We both work for the city department of sanitation. Sometimes we toss garbage cans and sometimes one of us drives a truck. In the winter we shovel and plow." No wonder they have such great arms, Carla thought. "We've been doing this for almost fifteen years and we met our first day on the job. Nicky and me are a team."

"Married?"

"Dean is, I'm not," Nicky said. "Not anymore."

"And how do you know Tim?" Carla asked. "He told me almost nothing when he called."

Dean took a breath and pushed his glasses toward the bridge of his nose. "I've known Timmy for many years. We met in a beginner's photography class and we've kept in touch ever since." Dean looked at Carla. "I know, I don't look like a photographer but I've been into picture taking since I was a kid."

The waiter put their beers on the wooden trestle table in front of them and listed the specials of the day.

"I'll have the double lamb chops, medium rare, french fries, and a salad with Roquefort dressing," Carla said. In for a penny. . . .

"A woman after my own heart," Nicky said. "Make that two."

"Three," Dean said and the waiter disappeared. "You know,

this is all a bit strange," he continued, "so let me get to the point and explain what I have in mind. Timmy told me that you're a call girl."

"Dean, that's not a nice thing to say," Nicky said. He turned to Carla. "Sorry, Carla. This is kind of awkward."

"It's okay," Carla said. "I enjoy having sex and fulfilling men's fantasies and I do it for money. I guess that makes me a call girl."

"Fantasies," Dean said. "That's what Timmy said. And I've had a fantasy for as long as I can remember. I want to direct a movie."

"A movie?" Carla said.

"A movie. Just a short thing. Nicky's going to be the male star and we want you to be the girl star."

Carla had a moment to consider the proposal as the waiter arrived with the most enormous chops she had ever seen. When he was gone, Carla took a bite. "Fabulous," she said. "Tell me more about this movie."

"I love to watch X-rated movies and I've always wanted to direct my own," Dean said. "I want to do one that's better than the crap that's out there."

"Don't get us wrong, Carla," Nicky said. "We don't want to sell it or anything. We just want to make it and then watch it ourselves."

"I've never been in a movie," Carla said. "It might be fun. But I don't want to go to my local theater and see my name in lights or my naked body on the screen."

"Of course not. That's not at all what we have in mind," Dean said. "Hey, Nicky, can you picture the guys we know watching you naked?"

Nicky got a strange look on his face but Carla decided to go along with the idea. "If Tim says that you guys can be trusted, it's fine with me."

"That's terrific." They spent the rest of the meal discussing the film's almost meaningless plot.

As the three finished gigantic pieces of apple pie with homemade vanilla ice cream, Dean reached into his pocket and withdrew an envelope. "For your time," he said. "I hope it's right. Timmy told us about your usual fee, but there are two of us and . . . well. . . ."

Carla put the envelope into her purse without looking inside. "I'm sure it's fine," she said. "Now, where to?"

"I've taken a suite in a hotel," Dean said. "Nicky knows where. I've set up lights and some fancy video stuff I rented but let me have one final check and get ready." He glanced at the dinner check and put a few bills on the table. "You two wait here for a few minutes, then follow along. Come into the room together and we'll take it from there."

Nicky raised his hand to his forehead in a mock salute. "You got it, boss, Mr. Director, sir." He turned to Carla. "I hope this works out."

Carla and Nicky talked for ten minutes, then made their way to a suite in the Gramercy Park, an older hotel in the low twenties. As they approached the door, Nicky said, "You know what we're doing?"

"I guess," Carla answered. "It's a little loose."

"We'll fake it." Nicky knocked, then inserted a key in the lock and opened the door. Carla entered and saw the camera, filming their actions. She turned to Nicky, waiting at the door. "I had a nice evening," she said, working herself into the part she was playing. "I enjoyed myself a lot."

"Me too," Nicky said. They were supposed to be coming back from their first date. "Can I come in for a nightcap?"

"I'm kind of tired," Carla said.

"I won't be long. I just don't want the evening to end yet."

Carla and Nicky walked into the sitting room of the two-room suite that Dean had rented. It was done in cream and gold, with accents of light blue and gray. The heavy ivory drapes were tightly drawn and all the lights were lit, supplemented with two bright spotlights aimed at the sofa.

Nicky closed the door and leaned against it. "You know I want you," he said. "Your gorgeous body has been driving me nuts all evening."

Carla's character was supposed to be reluctant, but persuadable. "But we hardly know each other," she said.

"Do you believe in love at first sight?"

Carla laughed. "I believe in lust at first sight."

"Oh sugar," Nicky said. "Let me make love to you."

"Cut," Dean said. "That's great. Let's move to the sofa. Now Nicky, let's say that you and Carla have been making out. Kiss her good, then show me how you get her to start undressing and how you begin touching her."

"This is really weird," Nicky said.

"It's kind of fun," Carla said. "I like being directed, told how to act." She sat on the ivory upholstered couch, ruffled her hair, and extended her arms. "Come here and convince me."

Nicky looked at Dean, shrugged, and sat beside Carla. He kissed her tentatively, brushing his lips against hers. He stroked her hair back from her temples and kissed her forehead. "Hey, Nicky," Dean said. "I don't have endless film. Let's get serious."

"This is making me really uncomfortable," Nicky whispered, his lips against her cheek.

"I understand," Carla answered *soto voce*. "It can be weird having to perform."

"All right," Dean said, "cut. When you whisper I can't hear you. Listen, I gotta take a leak. You two figure out the rest of the show and I'll be right back."

When they were alone, Nicky said, "This seemed to be a terrific idea when Dean dreamed it up. Now, I'm afraid I won't be able to . . . you know. Those guys in the movies are so well hung and seem to get it up whenever. . . ."

"It'll be okay."

"Oh it's not you. I just don't think I can perform on command."

Carla unbuttoned the top button of her shirt, took Nicky's hand and stroked it softly over her breast. "I won't let you embarrass yourself. I promise."

Nicky slid his palm over Carla's erect nipple. "You're very sexy," he said.

"Hey, I've got an idea," Carla said, sitting up. "Let's make Dean tell us exactly what he wants. Move for move. We do nothing unless he tells us to. That sounds extremely sexy to me. And no pressure on either of us."

Nicky took a shaky breath. "You mean that he calls all the shots?" He paused. "Actually, that sounds sexy as hell."

Dean had returned and overheard Nicky's last sentence. "You want me to tell you guys what to do?"

"Right," Carla said. "It's hard to pretend to be part of some story and get turned on at the same time."

"Hummm. Being the director for real. It sounds kinky. The audio will pick up what I say." He paused to think it through. "Telling you to suck and fuck . . . sounds hot."

"Not fucking," Carla corrected. "Making love. Touching, stroking, kissing, licking, you tell us everything. And remember that if we're not hot and ready to fuck when you say so your movie has no final scene and it isn't our responsibility."

"I love a challenge," Dean said. "Okay with you, Nicky?"

"Just so long as you understand that if I don't get hard, it's your fault, not mine."

"Okay. I like this. Let's go into the bedroom." Quickly, Dean moved his lights and video equipment into the bedroom. "Lie on the bed, Carla," he said, "and Nicky beside her." The two did as they were instructed, stretching out on the satin bedspread. "Nicky, kiss Carla on the mouth and slide your hand onto her tit."

Nicky leaned over Carla and gazed into her eyes for a moment. "This really is a turn-on," he said as his lips pressed against hers. He spread his palm over her right breast and kneaded the soft globe. He kissed her mouth, then moved his lips to her ear. "That's right, lick her," Dean said, and Nicky swirled the tip of his tongue into Carla's ear. As he licked, he hummed softly and Carla could feel the vibrations through her entire body.

She twisted, giving Nicky better access to her ear as his hand brushed back and forth against the fabric of the front of her shirt. "Unbutton her blouse," Dean said.

The remaining two buttons came undone easily and Nicky slipped his hand inside. "Pull the blouse open so I can see her undies. I love those shots of breasts in tiny brassieres." Carla was glad she was wearing a pale pink lace demicup bra. They'd have their money's worth and more, as much as she could provide.

Dean moved around the bed, peering through the lens of the camera. "Yes," Dean exclaimed. "Beautiful. You've got such great nipples that I can see them through your bra. Don't you agree Nicky?"

"I certainly do." He rubbed her breasts through the lacy fabric.

"Suck one nipple through the lace and make it hard," Dean said and, as Nicky followed his instructions, Dean rounded the bed and crawled across to get a close-up of Nicky's lips on Carla's erect nipple. When he could resist no longer, Dean put the camera down and sucked Carla's other nipple. Two mouths on her breasts was unbelievably erotic.

A little shaky, Dean returned to his camera. "No, no. Mustn't lose my objectivity," he said. "I want to make this good so I can watch it over and over." He positioned himself at the foot of the bed. "Carla, I think you should take Nicky's shirt off, very slowly. And kiss and lick his chest as you do it."

She opened Nicky's shirt and rubbed her hands over his lightly furred skin. She kissed his flat nipples as she eased his plaid shirt from his shoulders. "And yours too, Carla," Dean said. As Carla shrugged out of her shirt, Dean sighed. "Great boobs. Shit, see how they overflow the cups of that tiny bra?" Carla heard the whine of the zoom lens as Dean came in for a close-up of her right breast.

Suddenly, Dean turned off the camera. "I just realized that we're missing a great opportunity here," he said. "Anyone see a TV?"

Seeing none, Carla said, "There must be one. Maybe it's in that wall unit. Why?"

Without comment, Dean found the large-screen TV and connected some wires from the camera to the back. "Now watch.

Nicky, suck her nipple again." As Dean started the camera, the picture of Nicky's mouth appeared on the screen.

"Oh God," Carla said. "That's wild."

"Right. You get to star in your own X-rated movie and watch it at the same time. Nicky, feel up her breasts so she can watch your hands massage her."

Carla found it amazingly exciting, feeling Nicky's hands on her body and watching it happen on the screen at the same time. "Okay, take the bra off." Nicky unclasped the bra and dropped it on the floor. There, in full color, were her breasts, with Nicky's dark-skinned hands covering them. "Suck and bite them. Lick them until the nipples are real tight."

Nicky's mouth covered Carla's breasts, softly pulling them to tight peaks. Carla watched the TV screen as Dean moved the camera around, getting different angles of Nicky's mouth and Carla's breasts.

"Cut." Carla smiled as she sensed Nicky's reluctance to stop what they were doing.

"Take the rest of your clothes off, Carla," Dean said, "so I can get some shots of your sweet pussy." She pulled off her jeans and panties and stretched out on the bed, with Nicky beside her. "Now, Nicky, get her wet." He turned his back to adjust his video.

Nicky ran his hand up the inside of Carla's thigh and tentatively touched her lips. "She's already soaked," he said, surprised.

"You make me horny," Carla whispered. She reached down and squeezed the ridge of hot flesh that pressed upward against his belly beneath his jeans. She winked. "You seem to be horny too."

Dean turned the camera back on and focused the lens on Carla's breast. "Spread her legs, Nicky. I want to see your hand on her pussy." The camera panned slowly down her ribs and belly until her cunt filled the screen.

Carla turned and looked at the TV. She had never seen herself like this, open and waiting, ready to be filled, with Nicky's dark, blunt fingers playing idly with her pussy hair. It sent a jolt of pleasure shooting into her depths. She saw Nicky's fingers slide toward her swollen lips and, when he touched her, she could both feel it and see it. It was the most intense sensation she could remember.

Without being told, Nicky pulled off his clothes while the camera watched. His erection was rigid and thick, jutting from a nest of black hair in his groin. Carla smiled. Arousal was no longer a worry for him. She reached out and wrapped her hand around the engorged organ and pulled it until Nicky was sitting on the bed beside her. She turned so her ass was in the air and her head was in his lap.

"I'm going to make you come," she said softly. "And you're going to watch. Look at yourself."

Nicky stared at the TV screen and watched Carla's mouth on his cock. He was both feeling and watching a beautiful woman kissing the head of his cock, then pursing her lips and sucking him into her waiting mouth. He closed his eyes and reveled in the sensations.

When Nicky started to lose control, Carla wrapped her fingers around the base of his erection and squeezed his cock and balls tightly, preventing him from climaxing. She wanted Dean to have great pictures, ones that Nicky would be proud of. Higher and higher Carla forced Nicky, her head bobbing in his lap, sucking his cock yet keeping him from coming.

Finally she looked at the camera and said, "Every good porno flick has a come shot and Nicky's going to be the star of this one." She breathed hot air on the end of his cock while she grasped the shaft with one hand and kept the fingers of the other around the base. "Are you going to watch your own climax?" she asked Nicky.

Dean panned to his friend's face and watched as Nicky's eyes opened and stared at the screen. The camera returned to his cock, covered by Carla's hands. "Watch, baby," she said. "Watch your cock as you shoot beautiful come on my tits." She licked the length of his erection, making the hard shaft shiny and wet. She rubbed just a bit more, then, as his semen boiled from his balls, she released her hold on the base of his cock and moved so his come spurted on her breasts. The camera recorded as thick gobs of goo covered her large tits.

"Shit, Nicky," Dean said as semen erupted from Nicky's cock. "I didn't know you were such a stud. Maybe we should show this to the guys." Finally, Nicky collapsed onto the bed, exhausted.

By the time Carla returned from the shower, fully dressed, Dean had returned all the camera equipment to the cases and Nicky was dressed. "We're going to watch the tape," Dean said. "Are you going to stay?"

"No, I don't think so. I already know how it ends."

While Dean fiddled with the VCR, Nicky walked Carla to the door of the suite. "Thanks," he said. "I doubt that Dean will be able to keep that film to himself and now I'll get some kind of reputation with our friends. I hope you don't mind if your face shows a bit."

"Not at all, as long as it's just your friends. After all, a stud like you should be able to show off a little."

As Nicky watched Carla walk toward the elevator, he said, "Hey Carla, thanks again."

Dennis Stanton was an old friend of Ronnie's and they had spent many enjoyable evenings together. Tonight, however, he had something very unusual in mind and since the evening's entertainment wasn't exactly her taste, Ronnie had suggested that he call Carla. When Carla heard about the engagement, and, of course, the fee, she agreed quickly.

A stretch limo arrived in front of the brownstone at exactly eight o'clock. Dennis helped Carla inside. A man of about fifty, Dennis had deep chocolate-brown eyes and dark hair with wings of silver at the temples. He wore a magnificently tailored midnight-blue tuxedo with a matching tie and cummerbund.

"It's nice to meet you," Dennis said softly, sliding the partition window up to prevent the limo driver from overhearing. "It's a short drive to where we're going, so let me get right to the point. Ronnie said she told you what I want."

"She did, but explain again. I want to be sure I understand everything."

"I belong to a sort of unofficial sex club. There are about twenty of us, all men, some married, some not. Once a month we get together and indulge our shared passions. Some men bring women, paid or otherwise, and some don't. The women, of course, must be of a particular type."

"I know. Submissive."

"Exactly. And if you know Ronnie, you know that that's not her."

Carla smiled and nodded. She couldn't picture Ronnie bowing her head and submitting meekly while men used her body. To Carla, however, it sounded irresistible.

"Anyway," Dennis continued, "I've never brought a woman to one of our partices . . . until tonight. If you're willing, of course."

"I am, as long as condoms and safe words are agreed to in advance."

"They are," Dennis said. "No whips or anything like that, except with the permission of the woman involved. The word 'Yellow' is a temporary safe word, in case you want to stop things for a minute, say if you're cold or your foot's asleep. 'Red' is an absolute stop and anyone disregarding it is asked to leave our club and is not allowed back." His soft smile made him look a bit like Cary Grant. "Every member values membership too much to risk banishment so should you say so, everything stops. Is that all right with you?"

Carla took a deep breath and nodded. It was hard to reconcile Dennis's handsome, open expression with the dark nature of the evening's entertainment, but as she thought about the sex party she was about to attend, she shivered.

"Good. From now on you will follow my directions without question. You will keep your eyes downcast and speak only when spoken to. Do you agree?"

Carla started to answer, then decided to begin her part immediately. She looked at the floor of the limo and nodded.

"Good girl," Dennis said. "Are you wearing the clothes I sent you?" When she nodded, he said, "Then take off your dress."

Quickly, Carla pulled off her navy knit dress. Beneath it she wore a tight, crotchless, dark blue satin teddy with openings at the front of each breast so her nipples were exposed. Old-fashioned dark blue-and-white lace garters held up her blue net stockings and she wore very high-heeled blue satin pumps. She placed her dress on the seat beside her, folded her hands in her lap, and stared at Dennis's shoes.

"Very nice," Dennis said, staring at her scantily dressed body. "Your clothes will be here waiting for you when we return." He looked her over carefully then continued, "You really are gorgeous and you seem to have the proper attitude." He pinched one of Carla's nipples hard and, although she winced slightly, she didn't make a sound or look up. "Yes indeed," Dennis said. "I will be proud to present you to my friends."

She knew it was silly but Carla found she was pleased that he thought her worthy of the evening's entertainment. "Now," Dennis said, "a few additions." He buckled a leather cuff with a large metal ring attached around each of Carla's wrists and ankles. A slightly narrower cuff went around her neck and Dennis turned it so the ring was in the back. He attached a short chain to the ring and let it fall, cold and heavy, down her back between her shoulder blades to her waist. "Now," he said, "remember 'Red' is the safe word." He took a small padlock from his pocket, drew her arms behind her back, and locked the rings on her wrist cuffs to the end of the chain. Carla wasn't in any physical discomfort, but, with her arms secured behind her she was awkward and off balance.

"Good," Dennis said, as the car pulled to a stop. He buttoned a long, full-length, royal blue evening cape around Carla's shoulders and, as the chauffeur held the door, they got out. Carla quickly realized that despite her immobilization, to a bystander she looked like any woman might, going to a formal function.

Her head lowered, she moved her eyes from side to side and realized that they were entering the lobby of a very exclusive hotel, although she wasn't sure which one. They entered the 'Penthouses Only' elevator. Dennis said, "Only members and their ladies will be permitted up here. We've taken the entire floor for the evening."

The elevator doors swept open onto a small vestibule. Her eyes on the carpet, Carla followed Dennis through the only open door into a large living room.

"Ah, Dennis," a man said. "I see that you've brought a young lady for us. Wonderful."

Something about the gathering made Carla shiver with expectation. Although she'd read about them in magazines, she'd never believed that clubs like this really existed.

"Gentlemen," a man said, tapping a tiny hammer on a miniature gong, "now that everyone's here, the meeting will come to order. Bring the women forward."

Dennis propelled Carla to the center of the room where she stood, eyes downcast, with two others. One woman was a statuesque blonde with light blue eyes and dark red lips and the other a petite black woman with very short fluffy hair and skin the color of taffy. The women were dressed in capes similar to Carla's, each in a different color. Carla looked around as best she could without raising her eyes and estimated there were about a dozen men, of varying ages and physical types, all in formal attire.

"Do the women know the correct forms of address?" the leader asked. He was of Mediterranean origin, with very dark hair and eyes and olive skin.

"Not mine, sir," Dennis said. "I felt it was your place to instruct her."

"Ladies," the leader said. "For tonight I will be your king and you will address me as 'your majesty' or 'sire.'"

"Yes, your majesty," Carla said. She heard the other women say the same thing.

"All the other men will be addressed as 'my lord.'"

"Yes, sire."

"Obedience is your most important function. You will follow the orders of any man here, without question. The safe words are 'Red' and 'Yellow.' Have these been explained?"

Carla heard voices assuring the leader that the women had been told. "You understand that you must use these words if you feel any discomfort, either physical or mental. I emphasize the word must. If we find that you've been too polite to use the safe words when you should have, then everything will stop and you'll be escorted home. And that would be a shame."

"Yes, sire," Carla said.

"Now, will the gentlemen who brought our gifts for the evening please unwrap them." With a flourish, the capes were pulled from the three women's shoulders. Carla could see that the other women were cuffed and chained the same way she was and dressed in teddies, stockings, and shoes that matched their capes.

The leader started with the blonde, whose cape and teddy were a soft rose. "Vivian," he said, "you're as beautiful as ever." The leader raised his right arm and slapped her hard on her naked ass.

"Thank you, sire," she said, a small smile playing around the corners of her mouth.

"For the two new men here tonight," the leader said, "let me explain that Vivian likes her pleasure a little rough. Sometimes she deliberately disobeys commands and must be disciplined. Those who enjoy that type of play may want to stay with her for the evening."

He moved to the tiny black woman. "Shanna," he said, "we haven't seen you for quite a while. And I see that you've cut your hair."

"Yes, sire. I sincerely hope you approve."

He tangled his fingers in her short fluff, dragged her head back, and kissed her hard. "I do," he said finally. "Down." Shanna clumsily fell to her knees despite her chains and pressed her forehead against the leader's shoe. "As you see, Shanna is very well trained and will gladly do whatever she's told to. We are all happy to have her back with us this evening."

He turned to Dennis. "This one is new. Thank you for bringing her." To Carla he said, "Do you have a name?"

Carla looked at Dennis from the corner of her eye and when he nodded, she said, "Carla."

"Carla what?"

She knew he wasn't asking for her last name. Softly, without lifting her eyes, she said, "Carla, sire."

"Very good. Very good indeed." He turned to the men gathered around. "Blindfold them."

Someone tied a soft cloth firmly around Carla's head. She heard the rustling and shuffling of people moving around, and the hum of lowered voices. Suddenly someone pinched her left nipple, which was proudly standing out through the opening in the front of her teddy. She gasped, but didn't move. "Nice," a voice said. Then several hands slid over her breasts, legs, and buttocks, the sensations heightened by Carla's lack of sight. "Very nice," another voice said.

Carla recognized the leader's voice. "Mark, I assume that you and Harry want to take Shanna." There was a pause, then he continued, "Good. Take her into room two. Paul, take Vivian across the hall."

"Thank you," a man's voice answered.

"I want to break in our newest guest myself," the leader said. "The rest of you," he laughed, "pick your pleasure. You have three lovely ladies from which to choose."

Carla was flattered at having been chosen by the leader. She had no idea how many other men were in the room. Someone thrust one finger between her legs. "She's very wet," a man said.

"Wonderful," the leader said. "She's a lovely piece, Dennis. You've done an excellent job."

"Thank you. Shall I undress her for you?"

The leader must have nodded because someone loosened the laces of the teddy and the garment fell from her body. Hands were everywhere, probing, stroking.

"She has the most fantastic boobs," a voice said. "May I have them?"

"I see no reason why not, Chet. Prepare her." Carla's hands were unlocked and a belt was buckled tightly around her waist. Her wrist cuffs were refastened above her elbows and then attached to rings at the sides of the belt. Her upper arms were now efficiently attached to her sides, leaving her lower arms free. Then she was pressed down until she was lying faceup on a pad on the floor. Someone quickly spread her legs and fastened her ankle cuffs so she was held wide open. Hands checked to be sure that her blindfold was still in place.

"Thank you," the man called Chet said. Chet straddled her waist and squeezed her full breasts. "These are so big and full," he whispered. "I must have them." Hands rubbed something cool and slick all over her chest.

"Chet's in heaven," a voice said.

"If he's not careful he'll come before he's even started," the leader said, laughing.

"A hundred says he'll come in under two minutes." Carla heard a mix of voices.

"Hold them," Chat said, oblivious to what was going on around him. He grabbed Carla's wrists and pressed her hands against the sides of her breasts. "I said hold them!"

Carla had no idea what he wanted, but held her mounds the way Chet's hands showed her. Suddenly, she felt Chet's hard cock thrusting between her tits. He was fucking her breasts, driving his cock so hard that on each stroke it pressed against her chin. Now that she understood, Carla held her breasts tightly together, making a narrow channel for Chet's hard cock. He bucked against her breasts until he screamed and spurts of come covered Carla's chin and chest.

"One minute, forty-two seconds." There was a round of applause.

Almost immediately, Chet was lifted from Carla's body and damp cloths wiped over her chest and face. "You have great tits for fucking," the leader said. "How's your mouth?"

"I hope I am worthy, sire," Carla said, licking her lips.

"Open for me," he roared. When she did, he filled her mouth

with his erection, pressing it all the way into her throat. The velvety length slid in and out of her mouth. She sheathed her teeth with her lips and tightened around his shaft.

"He'll come even faster than Chet," a voice said.

"Squeeze my balls, bitch," the leader snapped, and Carla did as she was instructed, tonguing and sucking until the leader came. She eagerly swallowed every drop.

"My Lord, she's a great little cocksucker," the leader said when he regained his voice. He rubbed her wet pussy. "And she's loving it all." Low voices said things that Carla couldn't quite hear. Then she heard the leader's voice. "Dennis. Since you brought her, you may play first."

Play?

"If you have no objections," Dennis said, releasing her arms, "I'd like to remove her blindfold."

"If you like." When the cloth was removed from her eyes, Carla blinked several times, then glanced around the room from where she lay on the pad. Her ankles were being held open by two men who sat so they had a full view of her wide-open pussy. Another man sat on a chair, intently watching her face. The leader lay near her hip, his head propped on his hand. She couldn't see Dennis until he walked around to her other side, something in his hand.

"Carla, darling," he said. "I have some toys for us to play with." Dennis opened a large black-and-red lacquered box and showed Carla the contents. Inside, a collection of dildos was arranged according to size. The smallest was about as slender as her pinky, the largest almost two inches around. "Let's see how much you can take." He inserted three fingers into her wet pussy, then selected the next to the largest dildo.

It looked too big to ever fit inside her, but as Dennis slid it into her waiting body Carla realized that she was filled completely. "Yes, that's just right."

Carla swallowed hard, trying not to lose control in front of all these men. She saw Dennis select a dildo about the size of his thumb from the other end of the collection. "How's your ass?" he asked.

"Virginal," was the only answer she could think of.

"Fantastic," the leader said. "Dennis, you're a lucky man."

As Dennis spread some lubricant on the dildo two men slid Carla's body forward so her knees were bent. One of the men rubbed cold, slippery gel around her rear hole, then Dennis pushed in the slender dildo until the flange at the base rested against her cheeks. Another man pulled a thin piece of fabric mesh from the belt in the back, and stretched it between her cheeks and across both dildos to anchor them securely in place. The mesh snapped to connectors at the front of the belt.

"How do you feel? Tell us, Carla."

"Strange. Filled, yet empty. Wanting. . . ."

"Ah, Dennis," the leader said. "A gem." There was a round of quiet applause, either for her or for Dennis.

Dennis reached into the box and pulled out a pencil-shaped rod. Suddenly, a humming sound filled the room and, as Carla watched, Dennis knelt on a pillow and inserted the wand through the mesh and into the dildo in her cunt. Shafts of pure pleasure coursed through her body and her hips bucked as much as her shackled ankles would permit. "Ahhh," she cried.

Dennis moved the dildo so the pulses touched every inside part of her. As one dildo pressed against the other, the vibrations flowed from her cunt to her ass. Dennis withdrew the rod, then slid the vibrating tip around her pussy, through her soaked folds. "Watch her," he said, "as I make her come."

"We will," the leader said. "I love it when a woman loses control."

Watch her come? It was humiliating, but erotic. She closed her eyes. "No," Dennis said. "Watch us as we watch you. I command your body and I can make you come whenever I want. All these men will be watching you and they'll know exactly when you lose control."

One man unzipped his pants, took his erect cock in his hand,

and fondled his straining shaft. He caught Carla's eye and grinned, licking his lips.

"Are you ready, gentlemen?" Dennis asked.

"Ready, Dennis."

"Good. Carla, I'm going to make you come now, and you have no choice. We're all going to watch your hips buck and see your face as your climax fills your body. We will all know that you cannot resist."

Oh God, Carla thought. She was so hot that her entire body was quaking. Although it didn't feel right to want to be so controlled, she knew that he was right. She would come and Dennis knew it.

Dennis fitted the vibrator into the dildo in her ass and slowly moved it in deeper. "Now, Carla. Come for us." He rubbed her clit. "Keep your eyes open and watch these men come as they see you lose control."

She couldn't help it. She screamed as one of the strongest orgasms she had ever experienced took over her entire body.

"Oh fuck," a voice yelled. Carla looked up at the man stroking his cock and saw semen spurt from the tip and spatter on his hand and his pants legs.

Dennis turned the vibrator off, but left it inside Carla's body. He pulled down his pants and shorts and threw them on the bed. "Touch your pussy and make your hand wet." Carla did and Dennis took her slippery hand and placed it on his cock. "Hold your hand still so I can fuck it. Do it for me, Carla."

She held his cock in her hand and squeezed. Dennis moved his hips, forcing his erection through her tight fingers. Although she didn't move her hand, she tensed her fingers in rhythm, milking the come from his cock. "Oh that's so good," he said, groaning. "But it's too fast." Carla enjoyed rushing him, forcing him to come as he had forced her. She knew just where to press and squeeze. When he came she could feel the pulses throughout his cock.

The leader reached over, unsnapped the mesh, and pulled the dildos from Carla's passages. "Turn her over," he said, and the men quickly removed her shackles, turned her, then replaced her bindings so that she lay facedown on the pad. The leader placed a pillow under her hips so her rear was in the air, then parted her cheeks with his fingers and rubbed more lubricant around her puckered hole. "So. You have never been fucked in the ass," he said, unrolling first one, then a second condom over his cock. Although he wasn't very large, Carla was afraid.

"No, sire," Carla said, tensing. She had always been a bit leery about anal sex and, so far hadn't been asked for it by any of her clients. Dildos were one thing, but she was unsure that she wanted to go this far. The leader watched her face as she considered.

"I won't come inside of you," he said, gently, "and I'm always very careful."

Although she had climaxed, Carla was still excited and intrigued by the idea of being fucked in a new way. She knew that she could call things off whenever she wanted so she deliberately relaxed her muscles and closed her eyes.

Sensing her agreement, the leader pressed his slick covered cock against her anus. As her body tensed and relaxed, he pushed, slowly forcing his hard penis into her rear passage.

"Oh, sire," she whispered. "That's so strange."

"It is good?"

She hesitated. "Yes, sire."

When he was as deeply inside as he could get, the leader took his index finger and rubbed her clit.

Blazing heat slashed through her body and orgasm took control again, her rear muscles clenching rhythmically on the leader's penis. "Yes! Yes!" Her orgasm went on and on, until she had no more to give.

"Ahhh," the leader said, pushing against her as she came. "Wonderful." He pulled his still-hard cock from her body, peeled off one condom, had his men turn her, and then he plunged his sheathed cock into her pussy, slamming it into her until he suddenly screamed, and spasmed inside her.

Later, when they had all cleaned up and were ready to leave, the leader kissed Carla deeply. "You were a marvelous addition to the evening's entertainment, darling. We'll be sure to let you know when we meet again. Please feel free to join us, whether Dennis can attend or not."

"Thank you, sire," she said, wrapping her dark blue cape around her naked body.

Dennis held her around the waist. "If she can be here, sire, you can be sure I'll bring her."

Carla smiled as she stepped into the limo.

Chapter

8

Ronnie and Carla were in the sunny kitchen of the brown-stone finishing the last of a pint of chocolate-mint frozen yogurt. Falling snow created miniature drifts on the railing outside the living room window.

"Is something bothering you?" Carla asked.

"Jack's home."

"That's great," Carla said. Ronnie's husband had been overseas for the last month. "Isn't it?"

"Oh it's wonderful to see him, if only briefly." Ronnie put her dish on the coffee table and was silent.

"Come on, give," Carla said. "Trouble?"

Ronnie took a deep breath. "No, not really. Not anything I can put my finger on. It's just that, after what you and I do here, sex with Jack seems so ordinary."

"Ordinary?"

"You know. We fuck quickly and hungrily, and then he talks about business: oil, rock formations, three-dimensional computer models, helicopter surveys, whatever. We never talk about us, really. Our lives."

"That's part of the problem of being apart so much. You have so little day-to-day contact that you live in different places. Mentally, I mean. When my folks lived in Florida briefly a few years ago, my mother used to insist that I call at least once a week. She said that when you talk frequently all the everyday stuff is important, but when you only talk occasionally, it's hard to find anything worth mentioning."

"That's true, I guess. It's also the sex."

"No rushing across airports and fucking in the backseat of the car?"

Ronnie's laugh was warm and rich. "Lots of that. We're good together but it's just ordinary, somehow."

"That figures."

"Huh?"

"Of course sex with Jack is ordinary, unless you work hard at it. Everything we do here is exciting, first times with new people, new fantasies, toys, games, whatever. But it's just the same old Jack. Nothing new."

"I guess."

"Have you ever played fantasy games with him?"

Ronnie thought. "Not recently."

"Well, take your own advice. Do what we always suggest that our clients do. Let your mind wander. You're one of the most skilled women I know at reading other men and their sexual desires. Read yours and his, for a change."

"You know, you make a lot of sense."

"Of course I do. I've learned from an expert. Do the two of you have time tonight?"

"Unfortunately, no. Not for a month or so. He's gone again."

Ronnie looked so forlorn that Carla quickly changed the subject. "You know, I've had quite an education over the last three months so now I think it's time for you to tell me about that wild cruise you went on last summer."

Ronnie licked the last of the yogurt from her spoon and dropped it into her bowl. "Yes, I suppose it is. Okay. You make coffee and I'll tell all."

They wandered into the kitchen and Carla got the coffee from the fridge. While she set up the filter, Ronnie started her tale.

"It all began almost four years ago with Bob Skinner. He looked through my album and when he found the picture of me in that stern teacher outfit, he reacted immediately. We came back here and I disciplined naughty little Bobby who couldn't get his lessons right.

"A few weeks later, he selected the photo of me in that leather outfit holding the whip, and said, 'Would you be her for me, ma'am?' In that scenario, he calls me Mistress Ronnie. We've played both those fantasies frequently and he really gets off by being slapped around and made to do things."

"And that's what you did on the cruise?" Carla said, pouring water into the coffeemaker. "Be Mistress Ronnie and whip him?"

"We discovered very early that it's not the pain that turns him on, although Bobby loves it when Miss Gilbert hits him with a ruler. Mostly he loves to feel powerless, to know that he must submit to all of my demands without question. He's hard all the time until I let him come. Some women don't let their subservants come at all, but I make sure that Bobby climaxes every time we're together. Eventually."

"I'm so curious," Carla said, settling at the country kitchen table across from Ronnie, the room filling with the smell of brewing coffee. "Tell me about the cruise. How do they set it up? Aren't there other people on the boat?"

"Two couples started this group," Ronnie explained, "and they set up each cruise. We use the same ship, the *Atlantic Voyager* each year. It's small and they set aside a special area for just us, off-limits to the rest of the passengers: a private dining room, secluded deck space, and so on. And our cabins are in a roped-off area. The crew knows what we do and only those who've agreed to ignore what goes on work in our section." She sighed. "That caused an unusual situation this time, but I'll get to that later."

"How many people go on this cruise?"

"There are usually about thirty couples, most like Bob and me, a dominant mistress and her servant. A few are men with submissive women. We use common sense and rules, like you and I do with our customers. Everyone gives and gets pleasure and that's all that matters to any of us."

Carla nodded. Since she had gotten into power and control fantasies, first with Bryce and then with Dennis and the sex club, she had a much better understanding of the intense eroticism of dominance and submission.

"Some of the couples are into heavier activities than Mistress Ronnie and Bob. Some get into heavy pain and whips, shoe licking, and other things that Bob doesn't enjoy. But each of us knows our partner's tastes and we cater to them, and to ourselves. And we always use safe words."

"Are there many . . . professionals like us there?"

"Some are part-time relationships like Bob and mine, and some are married couples or partners who live together and are into dominant fantasies either full- or part-time. But both partners enjoy their roles and love the chance to submerge themselves in eroticism for a week."

"Okay," Carla said, pouring the steaming coffee into mugs. "Tell me everything."

"When we first arrived, Bob unpacked and put away our clothes while I wandered around our area of the ship. I ran into several women I remembered from the previous year and we sat on deck and discussed a few special activities we had planned. I have to tell you that talking about the upcoming week got me going. I couldn't wait to return to the cabin. When I arrived at our stateroom Bob was prepared."

"Everything's ready, Mistress," Bobby said as Ronnie walked back into the spotless cabin. He had arranged the closets carefully and Ronnie's clothes were all hanging or neatly folded. He had put his few outfits in a bottom drawer. He had set out two lightweight paddles on the small table. Several brown-paper-wrapped packages sat on the dresser where he had been instructed to put them. He had no idea what was inside but knowing Ronnie's creativity, curiosity made his cock hard.

"Very nice," she said and Bobby glowed with pride. "Are you ready as well?" Ronnie asked. She was dressed in a soft pink sleeveless blouse and a full deep blue peasant skirt. She wore high-heeled sandals over her bare feet. Her toenails, like her fingernails, were painted deep red.

"Yes, Mistress," he said, staring at the floor. Ronnie circled Bobby examining his outfit. He had changed since arriving on shipboard and now wore only a pair of extremely tight black spandex shorts that enclosed his erect cock. He had fastened a leather collar around his neck and he wore a green band around his right bicep signifying his servitude. His feet were bare and he stared at his naked toes.

Ronnie patted the giant bulge in the front of his shorts. "My goodness. Have you been thinking about the mysterious packages? Have you been wondering what's inside?"

"Yes, Mistress."

"Well, you'll find out." She patted his groin again. "And you'll be glad."

"Thank you, Mistress. Is there anything you desire of me?"

"Yes. I think I'll let you pleasure me before dinner."

"Thank you, Mistress. How would you like me to do that?"

Ronnie glared at him. "You shouldn't have to ask. You should know how to please me by now." She walked to a small chair and sat down. "After you've done your job, you'll have to be punished for your lapse of understanding."

Bobby knew that there was no way that he could have guessed how to please Mistress Ronnie at that particular moment, but the punishment was part of the excitement. And anticipating the punishment was another. But now he would give his mistress pleasure and there was nothing better than that.

"Down," she said and Bobby got down on his hands and knees and crawled toward her. "I need my feet massaged."

Carefully Bobby removed each of Ronnie's shoes and placed them under the table in the corner of the room. Then he sat at his mistress's feet and pressed his fingers deeply into her arch, which he knew she loved. He massaged each foot and calf, then paid careful attention to each toe until his fingers ached. Slowly Ronnie relaxed. "Mistress, may I go further?" he asked, knowing better than to look her in the eye.

"I think so," she answered, excited by Bobby's submissive behavior. "But first, take off my panties." When he reached for her undies, she added, "With your teeth."

He looked startled, but quickly addressed himself to the task. "Yes, Mistress," Bobby said. He rolled Ronnie's skirt up around her waist and, as he grasped the elastic of her bikini panties with his teeth, he could smell her musky aroma. She wanted him and that made him happy. He jerked at the elastic.

"Ouch!" Ronnie said, slapping him sternly on the shoulder. "Be gentle!"

"I'm sorry, Mistress." He pulled at the waistband gently, shifted to the other side, and pulled again. Ronnie moved her rear so he could slowly maneuver her panties over her hips, down past her knees, and off. Bobby picked up the wisp of dark blue silk with his teeth and placed it neatly on the bed. He gazed at Ronnie's cunt, newly shaved and now exposed for his viewing. There was something demanding about a shaved pussy and it excited Bobby so much that his cock became even more uncomfortable inside the tight shorts. But, of course, he knew that that was not Mistress Ronnie's concern.

Bobby massaged Ronnie's calves and thighs, reveling in both her relaxation and her building sexual excitement. "Mistress may I?" he asked, flexing his cramped fingers.

Ronnie shifted her hips to the edge of the chair and nodded. Bobby stroked the inside of each thigh, approaching but not touching her bare pussy. He brushed his mistress's outer lips with the tip of his finger, then with the tip of his tongue. "Please, Mistress."

"Please what?"

"Mistress, may I lick your clit?"

"All right," she purred.

Bobby knew how to please his mistress. He licked and sucked like a man possessed, his tongue and fingertips everywhere at once. He slid two fingers deep into her pussy and sawed them in and out. When he added a third finger and simultaneously sucked her clit, her muscles spasmed almost immediately. "That's so good," she moaned. "Don't stop."

He smiled. She knew he wouldn't stop until he had given her all the pleasure it was possible to give. He licked and stroked, adjusting his movements to her excitement level. Leaving his fingers quietly inside Ronnie's body, Bobby soothed her until she was calm, and then pulled his hands away.

"May I get you a glass of water?" he asked.

When she nodded, he opened a bottle of spring water he had placed in a bucket and poured her a glass.

"That was very good," Ronnie said, taking a long drink and patting Bobby on the head like a pet. "But there's still the matter of your punishment."

"Yes, Mistress."

"Since your tongue was so talented, you may pick the instrument you prefer."

"Thank you, Mistress," Bobby said, picking up a Ping-Pong paddle and handing it to Ronnie. "My pants, Mistress?"

"You may leave them on," Ronnie said.

Without another word, Bobby lay across his mistress's lap, his spandex-covered bottom ready for Ronnie's skillful application of the paddle. "Since I'm in a very good mood," she said, "I think ten will suffice for the moment."

"Thank you, Mistress."

The first three were light slaps and, with the covering of the tightly stretched shorts, Bobby felt only a general tingle. The next three were heavier, making his body jerk slightly with each one. Swats number seven and eight were harder still, stinging his ass and forcing his hard cock against Ronnie's thighs. Ronnie pulled the spandex down and administered the final two swats with all her strength on his bare cheeks. She pulled the stretchy fabric back up and patted his inflamed bottom.

"Mistress, please," Bobby said, his body quivering.

"Please what?"

"Please, I want to come. I'm so excited."

"Are you my good boy?" Ronnie asked, moving so her thighs rubbed his swollen member.

"Yes, Mistress."

"What if I say no?" She usually denied him any release for several hours. The women liked their slaves to be constantly erect, anxious to please in order to be allowed to climax.

"Oh sweet Jesus," Bobby said, sweat forming on his forehead.

Ronnie reached underneath him and squeezed him tightly. "Is that better?"

"Yes, Mistress," he said, although both of them knew it was not.

"You may come," Ronnie told him.

"My shorts?"

"Too bad. After you spurt they'll be all sticky inside." She smiled. "Of course, for the rest of the day, as you move, you'll be reminded of my generosity."

"Thank you, Mistress."

"Touch it yourself."

Standing in front of Ronnie's chair, Bobby rubbed the length of his rock-hard cock through the tight elastic fabric. When she sensed that he was almost ready to climax, Ronnie picked up the paddle and swatted his ass. He came, screaming.

For the rest of the afternoon, Bobby followed Ronnie around, sitting at her feet as she lounged with other women, fetching drinks and snacks for her and her friends, and watching the way the other women treated their slaves. He was so lucky, he realized, that Mistress Ronnie knew exactly what he liked.

That evening, at dinner, he cut Ronnie's meat and fed her, waiting until she was finished with her meal before he ate anything. The cruise ship staff discretely ignored the goings on, although one busboy stared longingly at Ronnie.

After dinner, three of the women and their slaves put on a show. The men danced, slowly stripping, then one of the men was whipped by the other two under the direction of the women.

Bobby took part in a contest to see which of four naked men could hold out the longest against the sexual teasing of a woman who looked like an in-the-flesh Barbie Doll, with huge breasts and a tiny waist. The woman whose slave lost the contest and spurted semen all over the stage dragged the hapless man back to their cabin for what would undoubtedly be a long lesson in self-control. Ronnie praised Bobby for his ability to restrain himself and, as a reward, let him fuck her with a large dildo.

The following morning, Bobby unwrapped the packages Ronnie had brought. Inside one he found a flanged anal plug and in another a harness to both control his cock and keep the dildo in place. Ronnie lubricated the plug and filled his ass with it. Using the many buckles, she fitted the harness so that it held his balls away from his body, showed off his erect cock and held the dildo deep inside his ass. For the entire afternoon, he wore nothing else so that everyone in their part of the ship could examine his body and discuss his excitement level.

About four days into the cruise, Bobby was feeding Ronnie lunch when she noticed the busboy staring intently at her. He was in his late teens and of medium height with shoulder-length sun-bleached blond hair held with a rubber band at the nape of his neck and pale blue eyes that seldom left her hands. As she thought about it, Ronnie realized that he had been watching her since the week began. As he stared, she quite deliberately poured the contents of her water glass into an empty cup beside her and when Bobby tried to refill it, she waved him away.

"Young man," she said, pointing at the busboy, "I need more water." The other two couples at the table stared at her, obviously curious as to what was going on.

"Certainly," the busboy said, fetching the pitcher. When Bobby looked crestfallen, Ronnie said, "I know you like serving me but don't worry. You'll be rewarded later." She pointed to an area on the floor beside her chair and Bobby sat down.

As the busboy arrived with the water pitcher, Ronnie said, imperiously, "Pour very slowly and don't spill a drop."

"Yes, ma'am."

"You've been watching me," she said as the young man poured the water, his hand unsteady.

"Yes ma'am." The glass was about half full.

"Don't stop pouring," she said, unzipping the front of his black slacks. His hard cock sprung free, sticking out lewdly. She wrapped her hand around it and held tightly. The busboy's hand began trembling so much he spilled water on the table. "You spilled," Ronnie said.

"I'm terribly sorry, ma'am," the young man said.

"What's your name?" Ronnie asked, still holding his erection.

"Mike," he answered, gazing at Ronnie's filled water glass.

"Well, Mike, you've been very careless." Ronnie looked at the other two women and their subservients, all of whom were watching the scene before them intently. "What should we do with careless workers, Mike?"

"They should be punished."

"I agree," Ronnie said. "What are your duties for the rest of the afternoon?"

"I'm off duty at two and I don't have to serve again until dinner."

"Oh, you'll have to serve again before that." Ronnie glanced at her watch. Quarter of two. "Good. Report here to me at two-oh-one sharp."

"B-b-but I have to change out of my uniform. That will take at least five m-m-minutes."

"Two-oh-one. And I don't like to be kept waiting." She gave his hard cock a final squeeze.

Zipping his pants, Mike scurried away.

"May we stay and see the show?" one of the women asked.

"Of course," Ronnie said. The two women moved to the far side of the table, their men at their feet. Ronnie's heart was pounding. She particularly enjoyed the thrill of a first encounter with a man who wanted to be dominated. She looked at Bobby, sitting quietly at her feet. Since he was paying for the week, she had to be sure this was all right with him. "Yes?" she whispered. From the smile on his face, she knew it was fine.

Precisely at two-oh-three, Mike arrived in the small dining room dressed in jeans and a sweatshirt. His breathlessness was a result of either running from the kitchen or his excitement. Ronnie purposefully looked at her watch. "You're two minutes late."

"I did the best I could."

"Let's understand a few things. First, I am Mistress Ronnie and you will always address me that way."

Mike rubbed the palms of his hands down the thighs of his slacks and swallowed hard. "Yes, Mistress Ronnie."

"Good. Second, you will never look me in the eye. Your gaze must never be above my waist." Mike's eyes dropped. "Third, you will never wear anything from the waist up or the ankles down in my presence unless I expressly tell you to." When Mike didn't move, she added, "Is there any problem with that?"

"No, Mistress." As rapidly as he could, he pulled off his sweatshirt, kicked off his shoes, and dragged off his socks.

"I love the look of bare toes. Wiggle yours for me." He did.

"Have you ever been with someone like me before?"

"Yes, Mistress." He hesitated and Ronnie motioned for him to continue. "Her name was Mistress Gail and she was my neighbor for a few months about a year ago. We were together only a couple of times."

"Good enough. Then you understand what is expected." Ronnie reached out and grabbed Mike's crotch. "Why me?"

Mike trembled. "You're very strong, and very beautiful. . . ."

"And . . . ?"

"And you treat your slave the way I'd like to be treated."

Ronnie removed her blouse and Mike stared at her bra, which had zippers up the center of each cup. "Unzip me with your teeth."

Hesitantly, Mike knelt down and took the tab of the left zipper between his front teeth. He pulled gently until one puckered brown nipple poked through the opening. "Bobby," Ronnie said, "the other."

Bob quickly complied. Ronnie placed one hand on the back of each head and forced one mouth to each breast. "Suck," she said, "and maybe I'll reward the one who does the best job." Ronnie leaned back, submerged in the sensation of two mouths on her body. "Nice," she said. "You are each doing a fine job."

Ronnie looked at the two other women who had been intently watching the performance. Each of them had bared her breasts and had her slave servicing her nipples.

"Bobby," Ronnie said, waving the two men away, "you know how I like my pussy licked. Instruct Mike on the proper procedure." She slid forward on the chair until her hips were at its edge. When she parted her thighs, the two men saw that she wore no panties.

As Mike knelt between her spread legs, Bobby said, "See how wet she is. Doesn't she smell fantastic?"

Bobby showed Ronnie's newest servant how to stroke her inner thighs, flick his tongue over her swollen lips, and use his fingers to give her maximum pleasure. "Now," Bobby said, pointing to her clit, "rub her right there, just hard enough to make her feel it."

"Ummm," Ronnie purred. "So good."

To Bobby, this situation was unique, and incredibly erotic. He was not quite a servant, but not a master either. And he was anxious to show the newest slave how to satisfy his mistress.

"You're doing well," Bobby said, slightly jealous of Mike's ability to please. "She likes three fingers in her pussy if she is going to come." He hesitated. "Mistress. May I touch you as well?"

Ronnie nodded and Bobby took one nipple in each hand and pinched the swollen tips. With Bobby's hands on her tits, Mike's tongue lapping her pussy, and his fingers deep inside her cunt, Ronnie came. Her body jerked so hard that the two men had to struggle to stay connected.

"Oh, splendid," Ronnie said when her breathing returned to normal. She smiled at the two other women, each of whom was having her pussy serviced. "Are you very horny?" she asked her slaves.

"Yes, Mistress," they said in unison.

"Then strip. Quickly."

When they were naked, she said, "Face each other." The two men stood, close enough so that their erections were almost touching. "Now, hold each other's cock."

When they hesitated, Ronnie ordered, "Do it now!"

With a groan, each man reached out and wrapped his hand around the other's cock. Ronnie remembered a conversation she had had with Bobby several months earlier when he had admitted to the dark fantasy of holding another man's cock and being held by him as well. She had decided to make it come true for him.

"Mistress, please don't make me do this," Bobby said. His body, however, said that, rather than stopping, he wanted to be forced.

"Quiet," Ronnie snapped, looking at Mike carefully. "And you, Mike?"

He bowed his head and whispered, "I will do whatever gives you pleasure. If it gives you delight to watch me do this, then I can only obey."

"Then, Mike, make Bobby come."

"Please no, Mistress," Bobby said.

Ronnie stared at him and raised an eyebrow.

"I'm sorry, Mistress," Bobby said.

"Good. Now you will both do as I say. Make each other come while I watch."

The two men stood, stroking each other's cock, watching their hands, their breathing hard and ragged. "Concentrate," Ronnie said and the men did.

"Cup each other's balls and fondle them. Use both hands!" As the small group watched, the two men acted out their hidden desire.

It took only moments until each man spurted semen on the other's hand. One of the women cried out her pleasure as her slave drove her to orgasm. The other climaxed silently.

"The rest of the cruise was delightful," Ronnie told Carla, sipping a fresh cup of coffee. "Mike spent each of the remaining afternoons with a different woman."

"How did you know about Bob's desire to touch another man?"

"He'd told me once, when I forced him to reveal his darkest fantasy, and his body language that afternoon was more than eloquent."

"You always seem to know how to find that extra bit of spice. How do you do it?"

"I've no idea. I guess I read my friends well." She tapped her forehead. "And I remember everything."

"I hope, someday, I'll be that good."

"You will," Ronnie said. "You will."

Jeffrey DeLancy III was an extremely dignified looking man in his mid forties with eyes that were almost navy blue and carefully trimmed, salt-and-pepper hair, beard, and moustache. A corporate attorney visiting New York, his three-piece suit was immaculately tailored and he wore a heavy gold ring with three channel-set sapphires on the ring finger of his right hand. When they met, Carla had commented on his well-developed body, and he had told her that he played racquetball and tennis as often as he could.

Now, as Carla returned from the ladies' room, Jeff was staring at the picture of the nightgowned woman clutching her bedclothes to her breast and staring, terrified, at someone just behind the camera. As Carla sat down he slammed shut the book. "Let's go back to your place," he said, picking up his coffee cup, then setting it down without drinking any. "This fantasy business is silly."

"We can go if you like," Carla said, "but I think there's something you want to tell me."

"I don't think so." He signaled the waiter for the dinner check.

"Jeff," Carla said, placing her hand over his, "tell me. That's what I'm here for."

"We both know what you're here for. So let's get to your place and do that."

"You don't have to tell me what's upsetting you," Carla said, "but I doubt that it's as bad as you think it is." Jeff sat silently staring into his coffee. "I saw which picture turned you on. That's Bethann and she was asleep when the burglar broke in. Do you know what he's going to do?"

Jeff's hand trembled under hers as she continued her story. "He's going to hold her down, feel her struggles, force her to bend to his will. She's afraid that she will be unable to fend him off." She was as excited by her recitation as Jeff obviously was.

"You're talking about rape," he said.

"Yes. But this is fantasy rape, not intended to actually hurt or do anything that Bethann's not willing to do."

"Fantasy rape, real rape. It's wrong however you define it."

"You know, nothing that goes on only in your mind is bad."

Jeff slowly raised his eyes and looked at Carla. "I wish I could believe that."

"You've got a fantasy. You want to rape a woman. Well not rape exactly. You don't want to really hurt her, just have her pretend to resist so you can subdue her. Force her. Right?"

The waiter arrived with the check, took Jeff's credit card, and disappeared.

"More people than you might imagine have rape fantasies," Carla continued. "As a matter of fact, I've always wanted to be ravished. Held down so that I couldn't move."

Jeff gazed into Carla's eyes. "You mean that, don't you?"

"I really do. While I was having that picture taken, I was thinking about the man who would tear off Bethann's clothes."

"Will Bethann fight the burglar?" he asked softly.

"She'll fight very hard."

"She'll know that he won't really hurt her, but she'll fight anyway? Struggle and try to get away?"

"Yes," Carla whispered. "Let's just be clear about two things. First, 'popcorn' is the safe word. If either of us says that, everything stops. And second, you'll use a condom even if it's out of character."

Jeff looked into her eyes, believing that this might actually happen. "Popcorn. Everything stops." He pulled out his wallet and slipped five crisp one-hundred-dollar bills into the black leather envelope. "I understand."

They traveled to the brownstone in silence and Carla motioned to Jeff to wait downstairs. She ran to the closet then back downstairs and handed Jeff some loose-fitting black sweatpants and a black turtleneck shirt. "When the light goes out, Bethann will be in bed, asleep. There has never been a burglary here, you know, but Bethann has always been worried."

Carla hurried back upstairs and pulled off her clothes. Knowing that many men have fantasies about ravishing a woman, she and Ronnie had adjusted several pieces of lingerie by clipping a few threads to make them almost fall apart if someone yanked. She slipped on a specially prepared kelly green charmeuse short gown, climbed into bed, pulled the sheets up to her chin, and turned out the light.

Minutes later she saw a dark form slip through the doorway. Light suddenly filled the room and a hand pressed across her mouth, forcing her against the mattress. "Don't scream," the voice hissed. His other arm snaked across her belly, pinning her down. "I just want your jewelry."

She struggled, trying to get free but he was too strong. But she had to be sure he understood the rules. "Popcorn," she mumbled. Reluctantly, he eased the pressure against her mouth and stood up. Carla stared into Jeff's eyes, deep blue against his black turtleneck. "You understand."

He nodded and she smiled. She slid across the bed, away from him. "Don't hurt me," she whimpered. "I'll tell you where all my jewelry is."

He watched her heaving chest. "I've changed my mind," he said in a menacing tone. "I've decided I don't want your jewelry. I want you."

"No, please," Carla said, getting into her part. Even pretending, the danger felt incredibly real and exciting. Her heart pounded as she grabbed the sheet and held it against her breasts.

Jeff crossed the room and theatrically closed the door. "You're not getting away," he said, "but you can try, of course."

"Don't hurt me," Carla said in a tiny voice.

"I won't hurt you unless you resist." He grabbed Carla's wrist and dragged her across the bed. He tangled his hand in her short hair and pulled her head back.

Carla's eyes widened. His hand in her hair hurt, but the discomfort excited her. She tried to twist her head to avoid Jeff's mouth which was slowly descending on her, but his hold in her hair allowed her almost no movement. She used her fists to pound on his chest, but it was like hitting a board. His mouth captured hers and molten heat flowed through her lips. Somehow it wasn't just a kiss, it was possession.

Jeff climbed onto the bed and straddled Carla's hips, effectively pinning her to the bed. He leaned forward, pressing his forearms on hers and holding her head with both hands in her hair. "You're mine," he growled, "whether you want it or not."

"Please, let me go. I won't tell anyone you broke in here." Real tears pooled in the corners of her eyes. "Please."

"Not a chance, lady," Jeff said. His mouth moved over her face, licking her eyelids and nipping at her earlobes. "I can do anything I want and you've got no way to stop me." He grabbed the front of her green nightgown and pulled. The fabric parted easily, leaving Carla naked.

She had to get away. She relaxed for a moment, then with a burst of energy, she arched her back and pulled her arms free. As Carla lay on the bed panting Jeff suddenly needed to get out of his clothes. He pulled the dark turtleneck over his head and tossed it on the floor. His pants and shorts followed and, erect and huge, he climbed back on top of his victim. "You've had enough time to contemplate what's going to happen."

Again Jeff grabbed her wrists and held her arms above her head. He devoured her mouth, forcing his tongue inside to duel with hers, rubbing his naked, lightly furred chest sinuously against her chest. "Nice," he rumbled. He released her wrists and held her head as he kissed her face and neck.

"No," Carla yelled, dragging her fingernails across Jeff's back. "Let me go."

"A regular wildcat," he said. He used the weight of his body to pin Carla to the bed, then slapped her hard across her thigh.

His handprint stung, but it also increased the heat in her groin. It was hard to fight against being raped when being possessed by him was exactly what Carla wanted.

Again and again he slapped her until his hand began to sting. "Had enough?" he asked.

Carla nodded, blinked hard. "Just don't make me ... you know. I'm a nice girl. I've never been with anyone but my husband. Don't force me. Please."

"Ah," Jeff said, "but I will do just that." He slipped on a condom, then held his hard cock at the entrance to Carla's pussy. Sensuously, he rubbed it against her clit. "You say you don't want me," he said. "I'm a rapist, forcing you to accommodate me, but your body is wet. You must be very evil."

"I'm not wet. I don't want you." She struggled, dragging her fingernails down Jeff's back and across one shoulder. Bright red tracks appeared down his skin.

"Your body says different." He guided his turgid erection to her opening and pushed. "And you can't stop me anyway." He pressed his hips forward and drove his cock into her. "You're wet and wide open so I can fuck you." His fantasy was so real that he lost control, pounding into his victim until he arched his back and spurted semen deep inside of her in shuddering pulses. Panting, he collapsed on top of her.

Carla stroked his back and ran her fingers through his hair. "That was so good," she whispered.

"It was unbelievable," he said, his body limp and exhausted. The scratches on his back stung. He rolled to one side and Carla walked, naked, to the bathroom. She returned with some antiseptic and applied some to his back and shoulder.

He looked at the welt on one side of his chest. "I'll enjoy looking at that for days," he said, running one finger over the mark.

"I'm glad. I was afraid of doing damage."

"And I'm really sorry if I hit you too hard."

"You didn't."

Jeff put his clothes on. "Thanks for a fantastic evening," he said. "May I call you again?"

"Of course. Bethann will always be here, as well as any other women you want to be with."

"I'm glad. You'll be hearing from me."

As the winter waned, Carla and Ronnie spent one day every week sharing experiences, since they were the only ones with whom they could discuss their flourishing business. Each Monday Carla packed her boys off to school, tidied the house after the weekend, and then drove into the city. Ronnie discovered R & R's Gourmet Take-out and each week she picked up a luxurious luncheon, usually a pasta salad and one of the unusual breads for which R & R's was famous. When she returned to the brownstone, she selected a bottle of fine wine from the cellar and made sure that it was the proper temperature.

One Monday, after a particularly sumptuous meal of prosciutto and cantaloupe, rottini and mushroom salad, and crusty, hot sesame bread, Carla and Ronnie slipped off their shoes and stretched out at opposite ends of the living room sofa, their bare feet on the coffee table. "That was a particularly good Sauvignon Blanc," Carla said.

"You know, six months ago you wouldn't have known it was a Sauvignon. You've grown, you know."

"I know. Every now and then I say something to my mother and she gives me that look. You know the 'I didn't teach you that so how could you possibly understand it' look."

"Oh yes, I know it well." She sipped her second glass of the full, flavorful wine. "Carla, I have something I'd like to discuss with you."

"Sure, shoot." Carla set her glass down and her body became more alert.

"Occasionally one of my friends makes a request that I'm not sure I can fulfill." She toyed with the stem of her wineglass.

"Are you getting coy with me?" Carla asked.

"No, but this is a bit unusual and it involves you." Heat flushed Ronnie's cheeks.

"You're blushing. I don't believe it."

Ronnie laughed. "Neither do I. Anyway, I've been getting together with one friend every month or so for years. He enjoys selecting erotic stories from magazines, scenes from novels, things like that, reading them to me, then acting them out. He's very creative and I've learned a lot from him and his stories." She sipped her wine.

"You're working up your courage, Ronnie. I can tell. Just remember there's nothing you can ask or tell me that will change our friendship."

"Thanks. He read me a story about two women involved in a torrid love scene. In the story, a man first watches, then joins in their lovemaking."

"Oh," Carla said, suddenly uncomfortable.

"I really didn't know how to broach the subject to you since we've never even mentioned that type of sex. If it turns you off, let's drop it right now."

"You obviously didn't say no to him or we wouldn't be discussing it now."

Ronnie sighed. "No, I didn't."

"Have you ever been with another woman?" Carla asked, in a small voice.

"Yes," Ronnie said. "In college. Although we were roommates, even you didn't know."

"No," Carla said, surprise showing in her voice. "Who?"

"Remember Evelyn Sage?"

"The gorgeous blonde with the tremendous eyes and great skin. She had the most fantastic breasts as I recall. I always wondered whether they were hers or silicone."

Ronnie laughed. "She was fantastic looking all over, wasn't she? They were her own. Anyway, we had been in several of the same classes and we got together to study on occasion. Somewhere during our junior year she casually mentioned to me that she thought I was very attractive and she wondered whether I felt the same way about her. One thing led to another, and another, and another. Anyway, we had been together only a few times when I met Sid."

"I remember him. You and he got pretty heavy for a while."

"We certainly did. He was into skin. Used to love to give me back rubs with scented oils. But while we were dating, I didn't see Evelyn and by the time Sid and I broke up, she was with someone else."

"Did you enjoy it with her?" Carla asked.

"Very much," Ronnie answered. "It was new and different and very sensual. I've been with several women since then, always brief flings. I assume you've never done anything like that."

"Never," Carla said, sipping her wine. "This is hard to admit but I guess I've always been a little curious."

Ronnie looked Carla in the eye. "I'd love to show you but I don't want it to spoil our friendship."

"Would it?" Carla asked, now curious at the prospect.

"I don't know. I hope not. But if anything ever feels wrong, just tell me and I'll stop."

"Isn't that what we tell everyone before we play?"

"I guess so." Ronnie put her glass on the table, then leaned over and whispered in Carla's ear. "It will be wonderful. I've fantasized about you. In my fantasy you're here just like this."

Ronnie's breath on her ear made Carla's heartbeat speed and her breathing deepen. Her doubts dissolved and she relaxed.

"Close your eyes and just feel." Ronnie watched Carla's eyes close. "Good. Like that. Don't move. Just feel." Ronnie touched the tip of her finger to Carla's mouth and saw her lips part. "Your lips are so soft. So moist and smooth." She touched Carla's teeth and brushed her nail against Carla's tongue. "Does that tickle?"

Carla was awash in sensations. Nothing sexual had happened but her body tingled and her pussy was swollen. But she was in no hurry. She pursed her lips around Ronnie's finger and sucked lightly.

"Oh yes," Ronnie whispered in Carla's ear. "Suck my finger."

She allowed Carla to draw her finger into her mouth, then pulled it slowly outward. In and out, mimicking the fucking motion that they had both experienced so often in the past. The rhythm was primitive and deeply sexual. Ronnie pressed the tip of her tongue into Carla's ear, echoing the rhythm the two women had established.

Carla had never imagined that such simple things could be so deeply sensual. She was sucking Ronnie's finger as her friend fucked her ear with her tongue. Suddenly her blouse was in her way. She wanted her breasts free.

Carla reached for her buttons but Ronnie stilled her hand. "Don't move at all. Let me be in charge of everything." With a nip at Carla's earlobe, Ronnie pulled her finger from her friend's amorous mouth and unbuttoned her blouse. "Your nipples are so swollen. Are they uncomfortable under your bra? Do they want to feel my hot mouth?"

"Oh yes," moaned Carla.

Ronnie parted the front of Carla's blouse and stroked her palm over her friend's erect nipples through the satiny fabric. "I can feel how hard they are. Do you like my hand?" When Carla moaned again, Ronnie continued, "It's real, isn't it? You want more, I know that. Your heart is pounding and you can't seem to get air into your lungs."

Ronnie leaned over and took one nipple in her teeth. Although the sensation was diminished somewhat by her bra, the nipping drove Carla wild.

"I like it that this bra fastens in the front," Ronnie said. "I can unfasten it without you moving. And I don't want you to move, even a little." With a deft flick of her fingers, Ronnie unclipped Carla's bra and separated the cups so her breasts were free. "Such beautiful breasts, baby," Ronnie whispered. "I've seen you naked many times, and each time I've imagined how your gorgeous nipples would taste."

Ronnie cupped Carla's large breast, weighing the handful. "Heavy and ripe. And hungry. Flesh can be hungry, you know, needing my touch." She drew her fingers from the outside of the breast in her hand to the pink center, pulling at the nipple. She repeated the motion over and over until Carla thought she would go mad from wanting.

"I want you," Carla said, "and need you."

"You need me to do what? Give you pleasure? I'm doing that. Need me to increase the heat? Oh baby, yes." Ronnie leaned over and licked one erect nipple with the flat of her tongue. Then she drew back and blew on the wet tip. Alternately she wet the tight bud, then cooled it with her breath. "Is that driving you wild?" she asked as Carla's hips began to move.

"You're making me crazy," Carla murmured. "My pussy is going to explode."

"No, it's not and that's the wonderful part. Your pussy will get hotter and hotter but you won't come until we're ready. And it'll be so intense I'll be able to feel it, share it with you." Ronnie quickly pulled off Carla's jeans and panties, then removed her own clothes. "I want to be naked like you are."

Carla reached out to touch Ronnie's naked skin. "Not yet," Ronnie said. "This is for you. I don't want you to do anything at all. Another time you can touch me but this time is just for you." Carla's hand dropped to the sofa. "That's a good girl. Just feel."

Ronnie licked Carla's nipple again, then drew it into her mouth. She sucked hard, causing a tightness to flow from Carla's breast to her pussy. It was as though the sucking made a path through her body and Carla could feel the pull between her legs.

"Is your pussy wet?" Ronnie asked.

"Yes," Carla murmured. "I'm so excited I don't know what to do. I can almost reach my climax, but not quite."

"I can reach it for you," Ronnie whispered. "Now spread your legs so I can see your magnificent pussy. Spread them wide. Put your feet on the edge of the table and open your knees for me."

Carla did what Ronnie's deep throaty voice told her. She opened her body as Ronnie moved so she was on her knees on the carpet between Carla's spread legs.

Ronnie watched Carla's soaked pussy twitch with excitement. How long could she keep her friend on the edge of climax without letting her over the edge? There was so much pleasure she could give. She bent her head to one side and allowed her hair to brush the inside of Carla's thigh. She allowed the strands to slide over Carla's white skin, tickling and stimulating. Ronnie blew a stream of air at the other thigh.

Carla was going crazy. She was sure she would fly apart in a million pieces and she didn't think she would even feel the explosion. "You're torturing me," she whispered, reaching for Ronnie's head to force it between her legs.

"Don't do that, baby," Ronnie said, replacing Carla's hands at her sides. "Hold still and let me show you how good this can be. Be patient."

"It's making me crazy."

"Is it bad?"

Carla hesitated. "No. It's wonderful."

"I promise I won't make you wait too long." She used one finger of each hand to part Carla's outer lips, then slowly explored her folds with her tongue. "You taste delicious," she said, continuing her exploration. Then she found Carla's clit with the tip of her tongue. "You can come soon," she said, flicking her tongue over the swollen bud. "And your climax is going to be so big I'm going to share it with you."

Ronnie took one finger and slid it into Carla's pussy, while she slid her other hand between her own legs, rubbing and circling over her clit. A second finger joined the first in Carla's pussy. As she filled her friend's cunt she flicked her tongue back and forth over her clit as she fingered herself.

"Oh God," Carla screamed. "Oh God."

"Let it come, baby," Ronnie said. "Don't say anything. Concentrate on what I'm doing to your body. Don't move. Hold perfectly still so you can enjoy my fingers and my tongue." She blew hot air over Carla's inner lips. "Yes. Share your climax with me." Her tongue licked and her fingers drove in and out.

Pressure built in Carla's belly. Waves of pleasure began to crest. "Don't stop," Carla cried. "Don't stop." Ronnie continued tonguing her friend's clit. Then she shifted her licking to her inner lips, around her fingers. She used the fingers to spread Carla open, then licked all the flesh her tongue could reach.

And then Carla came. The spasms continued, longer than Carla had thought possible. It was a different kind of orgasm than any she had ever experienced. It wasn't the hard, fast kind she had when she masturbated, nor was it the kind she had with her pussy filled with a man's hard cock. It was deep inside, and wonderfully different.

Ronnie slowed her movements until Carla's body calmed. She collapsed onto the sofa, took Carla's hand and gently guided it to her own hot cunt. "Rub gently, just the way you like to be touched." Carla moved so she could watch her fingers while they explored and massaged Ronnie's hot, wet flesh. Ronnie held Carla's hand and used it to bring her to orgasm. "Like that," she cried, "just like that." Gales of pleasure overpowered her.

The living room was quiet for a time, then Ronnie said, "Oh God. That was amazing."

"It was magic," Carla said. "Different somehow."

"I know," Ronnie said, her breathing calming. "But it doesn't detract, at least for me, from heterosexual sex. I enjoy that as much as I ever did."

"I'm glad you said that," Carla said. "I was afraid that you'd be insulted if I did. This was a treat, but I still like men."

"If the situation arises, would you be interested in doing that while someone watches and participates?"

"Yeah, I think I would. You know how I enjoy being watched. Being the passive one makes me crazy."

"And I enjoy calling the shots. We're made for each other and for this business."

"Well," Carla said, "I guess that's settled." She picked up her wineglass. "To new experiences. Especially ones that pay well."

Ronnie took a big swallow of her wine. "Salute."

Chapter

9

Over the months, Ronnie had visited Carla's house in Bronxville many times. With no family of her own, she had become Aunt Ronnie to the boys, and Carla's parents had taken her into the fold. Every time the subject of their business came up, the two women would sidestep any questions, saying only that they were in the public relations field, working for corporate clients, and doing very well.

One evening, while the boys were in their rooms, ostensibly doing their homework, Ronnie and Carla relaxed in the living room of Carla's modest house. "I envy you," Ronnie said, wistfully. "Sometimes I wish Jack and I had kids."

"Sometimes I wish I could lend them to you for a few months. Did BJ thank you for his birthday present? Ronnie, getting him his own phone was really extravagant. The bills may be exorbitant."

"He did thank me, and the bills won't go over a fixed amount that he and I have already agreed on. And I love doing it for him. By the way, don't tell Mike, but I'm getting him his own TV for his birthday next month."

"You're too much. You miss having your own children, don't you?"

"I do. But I often think that Jack and I wouldn't have made

good parents anyway. We're too self-centered. We enjoy our creature comforts, like quiet and privacy."

"God knows, you get little of either with three growing boys in the house. How is Jack?"

"He's good. He's in the used-to-be Soviet Union, somewhere that ends in 'istan,' I think. I talked to him just a few days ago."

Carla saw the wistful look on Ronnie's face. "You miss him."

"Yeah, I do. I sometimes wish that he'd give up the traveling. Maybe we'd have a real life."

"Would you give up the business if he was home every evening?"

"I don't know. What about you? You and Bryce see a lot of each other. Are you two getting serious?"

"I don't know that either. He was here last weekend."

"No! With your parents and the boys?"

"Yup. We spent the day ice skating with the kids, then had a big family dinner." She laughed. "I thought my parents were going to start making wedding plans right then and there. My mother's talked to me several times since. 'He's well off and he likes the boys,' she keeps saying."

"And. . . ."

"And nothing. He's a nice man and we have great times together." She lowered her voice. "Both in and out of bed. But that's not enough to build a life on."

"Give it time," Ronnie said.

"I have lots of that. And besides, I'm having too much fun in *public relations.*"

A few weeks later Carla and Ronnie double dated for the first time. Glen Hansmann was an executive with a motion picture production company. Ronnie had entertained him several times, to their mutual delight. About a week earlier, Glen had called and left his name on her answering machine.

"Ronnie, babe," he told her when she called back. "I know I've asked you this several times, but any chance of a double date? My friend Vic O'Keefe is in from the West Coast and I'd

love to do dinner with you and a friend. You understand. Some
dinner and entertainment."

"I do have a friend. Her name's Carla and her fee is the same
as mine."

"That's super," Glen said, "and the fee's no problem. Is next
Tuesday evening okay?"

"I don't know whether Carla's available," Ronnie said. "But if
she's around that evening I see no reason why it wouldn't work."

"Good. Check with her and call me back. And if she's anything like you, I can't wait."

Ronnie called Carla immediately and explained the situation.
"How would you feel about a double? I don't know what they'll
want, but I think we're ready for anything. And it's a Tuesday."

"It sounds fine. Hang on and let me check next Tuesday."
Carla flipped pages in her appointment book. "Believe it or not,
next Tuesday is the only night I have free for the next month. It
must be fate."

Glen Hansmann was not at all what Carla had expected. He
was in his late forties, soft spoken and rather sweet, with light
eyes and a dimple in his chin. His shoulder-length dark brown
hair curled just above the collar of his light blue dress shirt. Carla
noticed that his hands were beautiful, long slender fingers with
perfectly manicured nails. Other than a functional wrist watch,
he wore no jewelry.

Vic O'Keefe, on the other hand, was a Hollywood cliché. His
tan was too perfect, accented by the laughter-created crinkles of
lighter skin at the corners of his eyes. He wore a ruby ring on his
right hand and a heavy gold-and-steel Rolex watch on his left
wrist. His voice was too loud, as was his tie, and he spent the first
hour of the evening trying to impress the two women, dropping
names and discussing all the exotic places he had been. At one
point Carla caught Ronnie's eye and their expression spoke volumes about their long evening ahead.

Finally, Glen had had enough. "Vic," he said when the man
paused for breath, "you're not usually like this. Remember that

these girls are ours for the evening. You don't have to impress them." His fingers drummed on the tablecloth.

Vic was quiet for a moment, then looked apologetic. "I'm really sorry. I guess I'm so used to Hollywood types that I'm out of practice with real people. I know the arrangement. It's just that you two are so attractive I forgot."

"That we're bought and paid for?" Ronnie said, a slight edge in her voice. The evening threatened to become a disaster.

With a disarming grin, Vic said, "Open mouth, insert foot, and take a giant step. I'm really not a bad guy, you know." His rueful smile seemed genuine. "How about we just forget my gaucherie and start again." He stood up, walked around the table, and sat down again. "Hi, everyone. My name's Vic."

Slowly a smile spread across Ronnie's face. "Hi. I'm Ronnie."

The remainder of the sumptous meal sped by, fueled by good conversation and easy humor. As the foursome sat over coffee Vic said, "Okay, what's the difference between a tire and three hundred used condoms?"

"I give up," Ronnie said, "what?"

"A tire is a Goodyear. Three hundred used condoms is a great year." Everyone laughed. "You know, I can't remember when I've enjoyed a dinner more," Vic continued, looking at his watch. "And Glen and I have arranged a special surprise that we hope you'll like."

"Absolutely," Glen continued. "We've gotten the private use of the spa, pool, and hot tub at Vic's hotel for the rest of the evening. It usually closes at nine o'clock, but I slipped the concierge a little cash and can pick up the key at the desk."

"Sounds like fun," Ronnie said, checking her watch, "and it's already nine-thirty. We're ready if you are."

The two couples, Ronnie with Vic and Glen with Carla, traveled to Vic's hotel. The three waited while Glen picked up the key to the spa. Together, the four slipped through an unmarked door into a back hallway. Giggling, they followed Glen through another door and found themselves in a workout room filled with exercise equipment. "Nice," Carla said. "This is some facility."

"Let's try some of it out," Vic suggested. Quickly, the men were out of their suits and down to their shorts. "Undies only," Vic called so Ronnie and Carla stripped to their bras and panties. "Have either of you ever done circuit training?" he asked, staring at the two beautiful bodies magnificently displayed in bras and panties.

"I do aerobics, when I have the time," Carla answered.

"And I'm a confirmed couch potato," Ronnie added.

"I can show you how to use this stuff. I work out a lot," Vic said.

Ronnie looked over Vic's well-developed body, his wide shoulders, heavily muscled arms, flat stomach, and tight buns and she smiled. "I'm sure you do."

Carla walked behind Glen and ran her hands over his muscular back. "I'll bet you've seen the inside of a gym too," she whispered against the back of his neck. She smiled as she felt his muscles tense and his back straighten. "From time to time," he said, sucking in his stomach.

Vic tapped the seat of an arm-exercise machine. "Let's see how you'd look on here," he said to Ronnie. She sat on the seat and Vic placed her arms on the padded upper armrests. "Now, press down," he said, "then release very slowly. It works your biceps and triceps." As she pressed, he watched her chest muscles swell, lifting her breasts. As she reached the bottom of the machine's travel, he reached out and brushed his fingers over Ronnie's nipples. Smiling, she released her pressure and allowed the machine to return to its starting position.

Glen showed Carla how to lie on her back on the platform of the leg-press machine. He positioned her feet about twelve inches apart on the footrest and showed her how to use her quadriceps to straighten her legs. Several times he adjusted the weights so it took only a moderate amount of strength to extend her legs. "Now," he said, "try to hold your legs straight." Once she had her legs straight, she locked her knees to hold the foot support as far from her body as she could. Glen slid a stool next to the machine, sat down, and rubbed his fingers against the crotch of her panties.

"Hey," Carla said, giggling, "that makes this much more difficult." With the soft warmth spreading through her body, she had to concentrate on keeping her knees locked.

"Yeah, it certainly does." He placed one hand on each of her thighs, pressing his palms lightly against her skin. "Okay. Now release and press." As Carla relaxed, then extended her legs, Glen felt the tension in her muscles under his hands. Carla's body shone with sweat as she continued to do leg extensions.

Ronnie moved from the arm machine to a device Vic called an adductor. Vic sat her down on the padded seat and, spreading her legs at a forty-five-degree angle, placed her legs in the supports. He fiddled with the weight setting. "Try to close your legs," he said.

Ronnie used all her strength to try to press her thighs together. "Not a chance," she said.

"Good," Vic said. He walked around and knelt between her widely spread legs. He yanked at the tendrils of pussy hair that escaped around the crotch of her panties and heard her gasp. Quickly, he soothed the smarting skin, then pulled her hair again. Ronnie gave up trying to force her thighs together, closed her eyes, and relished the sensations that Vic was causing. "Makes you crazy, doesn't it?"

"God, you know it." Ronnie shuddered.

Vic grinned. "I certainly do." He pressed his mouth against the crotch of her panties and nipped at the flesh and fur beneath. His hot breath warmed her lubricating pussy.

"See what Vic's doing?" Glen said to Carla. She turned and watched Vic's face buried between Ronnie's legs. "Now straighten your legs," Glen said. Carla's thigh muscles were getting tired but she pressed the footplate. Glen cupped one hand against her cunt and tweaked her nipples with the other. Carla wanted to sink into the erotic pleasure, but she had to concentrate to keep her knees locked. "Shit, Vic," Glen said, "I never imagined the uses you can put these machines to."

"Enough for now," Vic said, lifting Ronnie's legs from the adductor machine. "I'm for the hot tub."

Glen helped Carla stand and stretch and after a few minutes' walking, her legs felt stronger again.

The foursome walked into the dimly lit pool and hot tub area. Glen stopped beside the steaming water and wrapped his arms around Carla. While caressing her back, he pressed his lips against hers, flattening her full breasts against his powerful chest.

Vic and Ronnie sat on a bench and Vic caressed Ronnie's face with his fingers and his lips. For long minutes, the two couples kissed, adding fuel to the building sexual fires.

Finally, Vic pulled away from Ronnie and flipped the controls for the air and water jets. "Last one in the hot tub is a rotten egg," he said. Still in their underwear, the four slowly settled into the bubbling water, hands and mouths exploring as they moved.

Glen unfastened Carla's bra and tossed the wet fabric across the tiled room. He bent his head and licked the top of Carla's half-submerged breast. "You taste of chlorine," he said.

Ronnie placed one hand on Vic's shoulder and whispered into his ear. "You do exactly what Glen does. Watch very carefully and imitate him, move for move." She felt his back tighten and then the telltale trembling of his shoulders.

Vic looked at Glen and saw his friend's tongue laving Carla's breast. "It feels weird to watch."

"Do it to me," Ronnie said. Vic removed Ronnie's bra and slid his tongue over her skin.

Glen lifted Carla's breast and his mouth reached for her nipple. Carla deliberately settled more deeply into the water so that, when he attempted to take a rosy crest into his mouth, he got a face full of bubbles. They giggled and wrestled until Glen had his arms wrapped around Carla's ribs and she was floating, her breasts out of the water.

Vic was kissing and nuzzling Ronnie's neck when Ronnie whispered, "Look what they're doing now, Vic. You're really not watching carefully enough." She reached down into the swirling water and squeezed his cock, hard.

"Ow," he cried, his breath caught in his throat. The pain seemed to make his cock harder.

"Then pay more attention."

Quickly, Vic repositioned Ronnie's body and suckled her breast, his breathing fast and ragged. Ronnie smiled, knowing that she had found the best way to give him pleasure.

Still supporting her upper body on one arm, Glen lifted Carla's legs onto the tiled edge of the tub. He bent her body at the hips until a jet of warm water shot directly against her swollen lips. "Oh God," she cried. "That's wonderful."

"I want you to play with the water too," Ronnie said to Vic, "but I want it to spray against your cock. Kneel here." She moved his knees onto the ledge and pressed her hand into the small of his back. His erection was now directly in the stream of another warm-water jet. "Oh shit, baby," he hissed. "I'll come if you keep doing that."

"And if you do," Ronnie said, "we'll just have to start again." She held Vic's body in the water stream until she felt him shudder. She reached around and held his cock as he came in the water, his semen feeling thick and gooey through his cotton shorts.

Carla was about to climax as well. Glen sucked on her breast and rubbed his finger against her rear as the water pulsed against her cunt. It was so quick and so intense that her orgasm took her by surprise.

"Oh baby," Glen purred. "You're hot as a pistol. I want to fuck you good, but I've got no rubbers."

"Sit up here," Carla said, patting the edge of the tub, "and let me take care of you." As he climbed up, she pulled off his shorts so that, when he was seated, his cock stuck straight up from his lap.

"Look at that hard cock," Ronnie whispered into Vic's ear, feeling him getting hard again. "Do you know what she's going to do?"

"Yes," he murmured.

"Well, you're going to watch. Have you ever watched a woman

suck cock in person? So close you can touch her?" Vic shook his head. "Good," Ronnie purred. She and Vic moved beside Carla in the water. "Now watch very carefully," Ronnie said. "Watch her mouth as she gives Glen pleasure."

Carla licked the hollow behind Glen's knee, then kissed and bit the inside of his thighs while Ronnie kept up a running commentary in Vic's ear. "She's licking his leg," Ronnie said, scratching her fingernail up his skin. "Right here."

Carla slipped her hand between Glen's thighs and tickled his heavy balls. Ronnie did the same with Vic, while saying, "I'll bet his balls feel tight and hard. See his cock? It's hard and throbbing." Ronnie pulled Vic's shorts off under the water and placed the wet garment on Glen's knee. "Hey Glen," Ronnie said. "I just want you to know that Vic is naked under the water and I'm holding his cock."

Carla wrapped her hand around Glen's cock. "Like that?" she asked Ronnie.

"Just like that."

"And if I slide my fingers right to the end?" Carla asked Ronnie.

"I'll do the same to Vic's cock under the water."

"And when I squeeze his balls?"

"Yeah," Ronnie sighed.

Glen and Vic groaned simultaneously. Carla stroked the sensitive flesh between Glen's balls and his anus. "His ass is very tight," she said.

"Vic's is too, but I think a finger will fit. The hot water makes it easy." Ronnie rubbed his tight hole, then slipped the tip of her finger inside.

"No," Glen groaned. "It will hurt."

Since she knew that Glen knew the safe word, Carla realized that he didn't really want her to stop. "Yes, it will hurt," Carla whispered, "but it will feel so good." As Carla's finger invaded Glen's ass, she said to Ronnie and Vic, "Look how hard it makes him. His cock is twitching and moving all by itself."

Glen was so excited by Carla's hands and her voice that he

knew he should be ashamed at her vivid descriptions of his body's reactions but he was too far gone to care. Carla kept her finger just inside of him, not moving.

Vic felt Ronnie's finger slide deeper into his rear. "Vic's able to tolerate more of this," Ronnie said, "since he came just a little while ago. I'm sliding my finger farther inside him. I can slide in and out, rubbing the sides of his channel. I'm fucking his ass and he's trembling. His cock is getting very hard again."

Carla looked at Glen's face, knowing it was difficult for him not to come. She flicked her tongue over the tip of his penis, licking the sweet drops of pre-come she found there. "Ummm, he tastes good." She pursed her lips and sucked the end of Glen's cock into her mouth.

"Look, Vic," Ronnie said, her finger still deep inside his ass, "Carla's got Glen's cock in her mouth. Touch her head as she sucks. Do it."

Barely coherent, Vic reached out and cupped the back of Carla's wet head. "Press," Ronnie said. He pressed her head and she sucked Glen's cock deeper into her mouth. "Release," Ronnie said and Vic relaxed his hand, allowing Carla's head to release Glen's cock. "Again," Ronnie said and Vic pressed Carla's head.

Glen watched as Vic pressed Carla's mouth up and down on his cock. It was the most erotic thing he'd ever seen. He held himself as tightly as he could, trying to keep himself from coming too fast but it was impossible. He filled Carla's mouth with his semen.

"Good baby," Ronnie said to Vic. "You did so well that you deserve a reward." With her finger still deep in his ass, she pressed him upward until his hard cock was sticking from the water. "Make it good for him, Carla," she said and Carla squeezed her large breasts around Vic's cock. He climaxed right then, spurting into the air above the water. "Oh fuck," he yelled.

"What about you?" Glen said to Ronnie. "You didn't come. Neither of you did. I mean you two should. . . ."

"Would you like to watch Carla and me?"

Silently, Glen and Vic stared at the two women. Ronnie

climbed out of the tub and sat on the side, her feet in the water. "Come here, baby," she said to Carla.

Eagerly, Carla buried her face in her friend's furry muff and licked and sucked the delicate flesh. "Is she hot?" Vic asked tentatively.

"Oh yes," Carla said. "Feel." She took Vic's finger and held it against Ronnie's pussy. "You too," she told Glen.

The two men fingered Ronnie's pussy until she was ready to come. "You know what she'll enjoy?" Carla said. "She loves having her tits sucked." With Glen's mouth on one breast and Vic's on the other, Carla flicked her tongue over Ronnie's erect clit.

"Do it good!" Ronnie yelled. "Oh yes. Do it so good!" Her entire body contracted as her orgasm roared through every part of her. "Oh yes, it's so good."

Later, the four lay silently on towels on the tile. "I think there are seismographs as far away as California that registered that." Ronnie laughed.

"I've never had a more satisfying experience," Vic whispered.

"Oh yeah," Glen added. Glen and Vic held a quick, whispered conversation. "Look, I think I can convince the folks on the West Coast that Vic has to stay another week. Can we get together over the weekend? The four of us?"

Carla thought about it. She didn't usually spend weekend time away from her children, but BJ and Tommy each had a sleepover and she was sure she could leave Mike with her parents. And she was flattered. Every time a client called her again, she felt wonderful. This was the ultimate compliment, to her and to Ronnie. These two men wanted a repeat performance.

"I think I can arrange it," Carla said.

"Me too," Ronnie agreed.

The following Saturday evening, the four gathered in Vic's room at the hotel. Glen and Vic sat on the sofa in the sitting room of the luxurious suite and Ronnie and Carla each occupied a soft chair. They were all dressed casually, the men in slacks and sport shirts, Ronnie in a soft rose wool skirt, a matching sweater, and high black patent leather boots, Carla in black slacks and a royal blue silk blouse.

"We've already ordered room service for the four of us," Vic said. "Glen and I have talked a lot about this evening and we've got a few exciting ideas."

Carla stretched her long legs in front of her and said, "Like what?"

Glen opened a bottle of champagne and poured four glasses. He handed two to Vic and kept two in his hand. "Vic and I loved the way Ronnie took control that evening. It was erotic, being told what to do, where to look. So, for the moment, we've decided to be in charge. We'll do everything, take care of you for the evening. You just relax and do as you're told." He held a glass near Carla's lips. "Have a sip," he said as he tipped it. As she drank, she saw Vic hold a glass for Ronnie.

As they finished the first glass of champagne, a white-jacketed waiter arrived and wheeled a table to the center of the sitting room, opened leaves on the sides, and arranged plates of food. "The main courses are in the warmer under the table," he said, showing Vic how to open it. "And be careful. The plates will be hot."

Vic added a large tip, signed the check, and closed the door behind the waiter. "We're going to play a game," Glen said. "We're going to make you guess what you're eating." Ronnie and Carla felt blindfolds placed over their eyes. "First course," Glen said.

Glen pressed something cold and smooth against Carla's lips. "Open," he said, "and stick out your tongue." He placed a round object on Carla's tongue and she drew it into her mouth. "A grape," she said.

From across the room she heard Ronnie say, "A piece of cheese."

"Good. Both right." Carla ate several more cold grapes, followed by some of the cheese that Ronnie had been enjoying.

Carla felt something spread on her lips and when she licked off the creamy substance she knew immediately. "Blue cheese dressing."

"Mine's Italian," Ronnie said.

Carla chewed crunchy bits of lettuce, cold, crisp slices of cucumber, and tomato wedges, all coated with dressing. Then Glen whispered, "My finger's are all gooey. Lick them off, will you?"

As Glen placed one finger at a time against Carla's mouth, she used her rough tongue to lick off the dressing. She drew each of his fingers into her mouth to suck off the last bits, then Glen wiped her mouth with a soft napkin. "Thirsty?"

"Yes," she said. Glen held the champagne against Carla's lips and she drank.

"I hope you like oysters," he said, pressing the slippery morsel against her lips.

"Love them," Carla said, as the slippery bite entered her mouth. It was not in the least sexual, but the entire experience was sensual and being blindfolded enhanced the sensations.

"Want a drink?" Glen asked.

"Yes," she said. She felt Glen's lips, wet and cold, press against her mouth. A trickle of cool liquid flowed from his lips onto hers. Drinking from his mouth made the champagne extra bubbly and it tickled her tongue.

"More?"

"Ummm, yes," she said and they shared a few more swallows.

Vic and Glen fed the two women the main course, sole almondine, tiny roasted potatoes, and petit pois with pearl onions.

"What's for dessert?" Ronnie asked, her voice sensual and hoarse.

Vic took some chocolate mousse in his fingers and pressed it against Ronnie's mouth. Slowly she sucked each finger, and heard Carla doing the same thing.

"What about you?" Ronnie asked. "Did you get some dessert?" She pulled off her blindfold, scooped up a handful of mousse and held it for Vic. He smiled at her and ate from her palm, licking up the last of the chocolate. "That was nice," she said, "but you missed a spot." He licked the mousse from her thumb.

Glen removed Carla's blindfold and she offered him some mousse from her fingers. When the mousse was gone, the two women went into the bathroom to wash up while Glen and Vic put the table outside the door.

Carla ran a comb through her hair as Ronnie freshened her lipstick. "You know, Carla," Ronnie said, "they're waiting for something."

"I agree. You're always so quick about these things. Do you know what they want?"

"I think they want me to take over as I did last time. Is that okay with you?"

"Sure. If you don't know what turns me on by now, no one does."

"Have you ever gotten into pain as pleasure?"

"Once or twice," Carla said. "I've been slapped a few times, once until I had to tell the guy to stop."

"Bad?"

"Not really," Carla said. "As a matter of fact, until it got to be too much, it was very erotic."

"Great. Are you willing to give it a try if things go the way I think they will?"

"Sure. Are you certain that this is what they have in mind?"

"I'm not, completely, but I've developed a sixth sense over the years. I'll go slowly and read the signs. Just remember the safe word."

Carla nodded. "I'll use it if I need to."

They went back into the living room. "Carla, pour everyone another glass of champagne," Ronnie said. "You two," she said to the men, "sit down."

The two men dropped into chairs while Carla poured wine. "You've called the shots so far," Ronnie said. "Now it's my turn." When neither man answered, Ronnie knew she had been right. "Each of you close your eyes. Picture the rest of the evening. Play it in your mind like a movie—picture it exactly as you wish it would happen. Now, Glen, you first. Tell me precisely what you see." When Glen hesitated Ronnie said, "Do it now."

"This is very difficult."

Carla walked behind Glen's chair, cradled the back of his head in the valley between her breasts, and glided her hands down the front of his shirt. "I know it is, baby," she murmured. "Tell me. Are we making love? Are we fucking good?"

"Yes, but before. . . ."

"Tell me, baby." She bent over his shoulder and placed her ear next to his lips. "Whisper it to me."

"Ronnie's making me do things to you." The words exploded from his mouth and his body shook.

"What things? Tell me, baby," Carla whispered.

When he was silent, Ronnie said, "You must tell us, Glen. Do it."

"Oh Carla. Ronnie's forcing me to spank you. And she's forcing Vic to watch everything."

Ronnie knelt in front of Vic, whose eyes were still closed as he fantasized about the evening. She placed her hands on his thighs. His body would tell her even if his words didn't. "What do you see, Vic? What are you doing?" When he was silent, Ronnie continued. "You must tell me." She had heard what Glen said. "Am I making you watch? Are you getting hard?" When he remained silent, she continued, "Am I spanking you, too?"

"No," he whispered.

Ronnie knew there was something else, but Vic was unable to tell her what it was. "Vic, put your mouth close to my ear. Now, whisper. Say, 'Please don't make me . . .' and end the sentence."

She felt him shudder as he whispered. Now she knew. "It's all right, baby," she said. "I'll make it all right."

Carla stared at her friend. She had no idea how Ronnie sensed the things she did, and got men to admit to their darkest sexual fantasies, but she felt the level of tension in the room increase moment by moment.

Ronnie stalked to the closet. She took out a wooden coat hanger and slapped it on her high boot. She pulled off her sweater and skirt and revealed a tight black satin teddy and black stockings. She settled comfortably on the couch, one ankle resting on the opposite knee. She slapped the hanger against the leather as she spoke. "Glen and Vic, shirts, shoes, and socks off. Now." The two men hurried to comply.

Ronnie's boots, Carla realized, hadn't been an accident nor had the underwear. Somehow Ronnie had known. "Vic, sit here," Ronnie said, indicating the spot on the sofa next to her, "and Glen, close your eyes and stand facing Carla. Now, touch Carla's face. Describe it to me. Tell me how it feels and smells and tastes."

Glen gazed into Carla's eyes, then closed his eyes and touched her face. "Her skin is so smooth. She smells of perfume, exotic and eastern." He licked her cheek. "Her skin tastes of salt and spice." He ran a fingertip over her lips. "Her lips are soft and warm."

"Now, Glen, open your eyes and undress Carla. Do it slowly and describe her body for us as you do. Blouse first."

Glen slowly unbuttoned Carla's blouse and slipped it from her arms. "Her skin is smooth and pale. There are no marks from the sun anywhere, just white skin." He touched his tongue to the pulse of her neck. "Her neck is slender and she tastes and feels smooth under my tongue."

"Do you want to take her bra off? Taste and feel her tits?"

"Yes," Glen whispered.

"Then do it."

Glen unfastened Carla's bra and took it off. "Her breasts are gorgeous. I saw her body last week, but I never realized how beautiful her tits were." He filled a palm with one large breast and lifted. "They're heavy and fill my hand. Her nipples are delectable," he grazed her areola with his tongue, "and so soft."

"Do they get hard if you suck them?" Ronnie asked, idly rubbing her hand over Vic's chest.

Glen drew one tight tip into his mouth and pulled. "Yes. Hard and warm."

"Use your champagne to flavor them," Ronnie said.

Glen smiled and picked up his glass. He slowly trickled cool liquid down one breast, then licked it off her erect nipple. "Vic," Ronnie said, "the other one."

Vic jumped up, dribbled champagne down Carla's other breast, and sucked it off. Carla's breath caught in her throat and her knees wobbled. Pleasure knifed through her.

"Vic," Ronnie said, tapping the sofa with the coat hanger, "over here." Again he sat beside her. "That's good," Ronnie said. "Now Glen, pull off her slacks and panties."

Glen unzipped Carla's pants and pulled both slacks and undies off in one motion. "Tell us about her body, Glen," Ronnie said.

"Her stomach is flat and her belly button is very deep." He flicked his tongue into her navel. "Tastes smoky. And I can smell the aroma of her cunt."

"Feel her pussy. Is she ready for fucking?"

Glen ran his fingers through her pubic hair. "Yes, she's steaming."

"That means we're ready for the next part." Ronnie got up and turned one of the chairs from the dinner table to face the group. "Sit there, Glen. And Carla, you know what you must do. As they say, assume the position."

Glen sat on the chair and Carla lay across his thighs. He stroked the gorgeous globes laying so invitingly across his lap, delightfully crushing his erection. "Spank her on one cheek, hard." Glen raised his hand and brought it down on Carla's bottom.

"Again." He did. "Again."

After a few minutes, Carla whispered, "Popcorn."

"Oh, poor Carla," Ronnie said. "Her poor ass is so sore. Glen, make it feel better."

Glen stroked Carla's flaming bottom, caressing each cheek softly. "Does she feel good?" Ronnie asked.

"Yes, very soft and very hot."

"Does her hot bottom make you hot as well?"

"Absolutely," he said. "I want to fuck her."

"Not yet!" She reached down and held Glen's cock. "Neither Carla nor I have climaxed yet. Lie on the floor."

When Glen was stretched out on the carpet, Carla impaled herself on his erection and Ronnie crouched over his face. As his cock serviced one woman, his mouth serviced the other. Vic squeezed Ronnie's breast in one hand and fingered Carla's clit with the other and the two women climaxed almost simultaneously, then Glen screamed and came.

"You've been so patient," Ronnie said to Vic. "Now you get your reward." She snapped her fingers and Vic stretched out on the sofa. Carla licked one side of his fully erect penis and Ronnie licked the other. The two women licked in perfect unison, until thick come spurted from Vic's member.

Vic looked at Ronnie and smiled. "Holy shit."

"Precisely," Glen said.

Later, as Ronnie and Carla were leaving, Vic and Glen stood at the door. "Next time I'm in town?" Vic said.

"Love to," Carla said.

"Just give me a call," Ronnie said. "You both know the number."

Chapter
10

"I got a catalog in the mail a few weeks ago," Bryce said to Carla as they entered the paneled room one evening in early spring. "And I did some shopping." He put a large cardboard box down on a wooden bench.

From the expectancy in his voice, Carla assumed that he wasn't talking about new shirts or remaindered books. "And . . . ?"

"And I bought us a few new toys. I know Ronnie has a bunch of stuff here, but I wanted some things of our own. Why don't you get undressed?" As Carla took off her clothes, Bryce opened the box and pulled out his first purchase, two pairs of handcuffs. "Come here." He kissed Carla firmly, cupping her firm buttocks and squeezing her cheeks. He nibbled on her neck, then fastened one cuff to each wrist. "Now let's see. . . ."

Carla had a general idea of what was to come. She and Bryce had played here often and several of their fantasies had become regular games. They had learned to easily communicate their desires. Often an evening started with one fantasy and veered off in another direction midway through. But, no matter what scene they enacted, they always ended up truly satisfied.

Bryce backed Carla against a wall and fastened the cuffs so her wide-spread arms were stretched over her head. "Nice. I love to see you like that, exposed and vulnerable." He took a sip of his wine. "Tonight, you need to learn a new sexual lesson."

"And what might that be?" Carla asked, her body already wet and hot, ready for whatever Bryce wanted to teach her.

"Patience," he said.

"What's that supposed to mean?"

"Tonight I'm going to see how far I can push you. It's a game that we're both going to win. As they say so dramatically in those romance novels you're so fond of, 'I'm going to make you beg for me.'"

"I'll beg right now. I want you and you know it. And you want me too."

"Of course I do, but tonight is a contest. I want to make you want me like you've never wanted anything before. I want to push your need as high as it will go, tear it down, and push it higher still."

"This isn't supposed to be an endurance contest," Carla said.

"An endurance contest might be fun." Bryce took out his wallet, counted out ten one-hundred-dollar bills and placed them on the bed. He pulled a timer from the bag and set it for fifteen minutes. "I'm putting this right here," he said as he set the timer on a bench. "If you can hold out until it goes off, the money is yours."

"This is nuts," Carla said, intrigued. "You already paid me for the evening."

"I know that, but this is a wager. I'll bet you that I can make you so hot that you'll say, 'Fuck me,' before the timer goes off. Of course, if you should climax you lose."

"Why are you doing this?" Carla asked, truly puzzled.

"I love making love with you," Bryce said, "but I've always felt that you're so busy giving me pleasure that you never reach your own limit. I want to extend you, push you to the ultimate." He grinned at the beautiful woman spread-eagled against the wall. "Is it a bet?"

"Let's get this straight. If I can keep from asking you to fuck me until that thing bings, I win a thousand dollars?"

"Yup."

"And if I fail?"

"You get the best damn fuck you've ever had."

"That sounds too good to pass up."

Bryce slid his hand up the inside of Carla's thigh, past the top of her stocking, and brushed the crotch of her panties. "You're soaked already," he said, rubbing her crotch lightly. "Want me to fuck you right now?"

"I can wait," Carla said, feeling the electricity that always jolted her body when Bryce touched her. She liked Bryce a lot and would have dated him without the money, but he always insisted on paying. He tried to explain that it made it easier for him. And whether or not she truly understood his reasons, she knew that he could afford their frequent rendezvous and Carla enjoyed watching the boys' college fund grow.

Bryce pressed his fully clothed body against Carla, entwined his hands in hers, and placed his mouth against her ear. He traced the tip of his tongue across her sensitive skin and whispered, "Remember, just say 'Fuck me' whenever you're ready." He bit the tip of her earlobe, then kissed a fiery path along her jaw and down the pulse in her neck.

"You'll have to do better than that."

"If that's a dare," he said, "I'll take you up on it." He opened the box and pulled out a jar. "This is called Slippery Stuff," he said, opening the jar and tasting a bit. "Strawberry." He rubbed some of the goo on Carla's nipples, then withdrew another package from the box. "These are nipple suction cups. I thought about getting clips, but I know you don't enjoy real pain and those things hurt. But these, well according to the package," he said, reading the cardboard, "these are supposed to 'create the erotic sensation of love-sucking.' Let's see."

"That's not fair," Carla said, heat rising through her belly.

"It's my game and I decide what's fair." He held the silver-dollar-sized suction cups where she could see them, then attached one to each already-erect nipple. "Are they right? Do they feel like my mouth?"

"Not really," Carla said, "but they're exciting just the same."

Bryce's fingers danced over her breasts as the suction cups enhanced the sensation. "They make your skin blush," he said. "Want to stop?"

Carla's hips moved of their own volition, but she said, "Not a chance."

"Good." He pulled another cardboard-and-plastic-wrapped package from the box. "Here we have a pair of 'Vibrating Ben-Wa Balls.' It says, 'Guaranteed to give maximum vaginal or anal pleasure.' You'll be happy to know that I even thought to bring batteries." Agonizingly slowly, Bryce put batteries into the control pack, then inserted the one-inch balls deep into Carla's vagina. "Now, let's see how this works." He pushed the slider so the balls hummed.

Vibrations filled her body. "Shit, Bryce," Carla said. "Oh God."

"One more thing," Bryce said, pulling another toy from the box. "An anal plug." As he unwrapped the plastic, he continued. "We've played with these before, but this is our very own, just made for your sweet little ass." He held the almost-two-inch-wide dildo in front of Carla's face. "See how big it is?" He rubbed the thick phallus through the over-sensitive valley between her breasts.

"That won't fit inside of me," Carla said, squirming. The vibrations still filled her cunt and the suction on her nipples made them almost unbearably sensitive.

"Let's see," he said. "Make it wet." He pressed the tip against Carla's lips. "Open," he snapped. Carla took the thick plastic cock into her mouth and slid her tongue over the plastic.

"Good," Bryce said. "I wonder how this will feel pressing against those vibrating balls in your pussy." It took only a little pressure to insert the dildo into Carla's rear.

"Oh God," Carla screamed. "Too much."

"Don't forget that if you come, you lose."

Carla gritted her teeth, trying to think about cold showers or trips to the dentist. It didn't help.

Suddenly, the timer sounded and Carla sighed.

"Good girl," Bryce said. "You win. Now, how about double or nothing for another fifteen minutes."

Carla's eyes were glazed and she was unsure whether she could last much longer. "Done," she said, deciding she could hold out, or at least try.

"Wonderful." He stood up and took a video tape from his jacket pocket. "This toy's a little unusual. Do you remember two men with whom you made a movie several months ago? Dean and Nicky."

"I remember," she hissed through gritted teeth. She was on fire and it took all of her concentration not to surrender to the pleasure.

"Well, when you told me about it I was curious. I called Tim who put me in touch with Dean and he made me a copy." He brandished the unmarked video cassette. "Now I want to watch it."

He turned on the TV and slipped the tape into the VCR. Familiar images appeared on the screen. For several minutes Bryce rubbed his hands over her body while, on the screen, Nicky kissed her as she lay on the couch of the hotel suite. As the scene changed to the bedroom, Bryce's hands became more demanding. Suddenly, almost angrily, Bryce removed the toys from her body, unfastened her wrists, and almost dragged her to the bed.

Bryce pulled down his jeans and briefs and forced his cock into her mouth. "Do me just the way you did him. Hold my cock with your free hand just like that."

Carla squeezed the base of Bryce's cock and his sac the way she had Nicky's, effectively keeping him from climaxing. Watching the TV screen, she sucked his erection. "Now," he cried and she released her hand so his hot semen could fill her mouth. As he came, the film ended.

Moments later, the timer sounded again. "You win," Bryce said, burying his face in her muff. "Come for me, baby." He licked her clit and fucked her cunt with his fingers until she, too, came.

Although her orgasm was wonderful, Carla was disappointed

that Bryce has given up the game so easily. As he lay silently beside her she knew that something was wrong. "Tell me," she said softly, wrapping her arms around his waist and placing her head on his shoulder.

"Nothing."

"Bryce, that's not fair. If there's something you don't want to talk about, that's fine, just say so. But don't insult me by saying that nothing's wrong."

Bryce sighed and stroked her hair. A few moments later he said, "Seeing you like that bothered me in a way I didn't expect."

"I'm sorry that it upset you."

"I guess I care about you more than I thought I did. It surprises and scares me." When Carla remained silent he continued, "Would you consider giving this all up?"

"What?"

"I suddenly realize that you mean more to me than I thought and I'm suddenly very bothered by the thought of you with other men."

"But. . . ."

Bryce placed a finger across her lips. "Let me finish. I've spent a few days with your parents and your boys and I like all of them very much. If everything works out, eventually we could get married. You know that I'm very well-off, financially, and I'd make sure your boys' college was provided for. You wouldn't need to do this to earn money."

"But that's not the reason I do this," Carla said. "Sure, the money's nice, but I really enjoy giving pleasure and discovering new games in bed. And when the men that I'm with discover that their darkest fantasy isn't really so terrible, well, it makes me feel so valuable."

"We have fun together and there's nothing we couldn't do together, in or out of bed."

Carla patted Bryce's hand. "I know that, but this is what I want to do right now."

"But I love you. I want you to be part of my life forever."

"Love?"

"Of course. I guess I didn't realize it until now." He kissed her. "I love you," he whispered against her lips. "I guess it just takes a jolt like that movie to make me realize it."

"Oh Bryce," Carla said, pressing her lips against his. "I love you." But I love this too, she said to herself.

"Think about it. Please."

The following Monday morning, Carla and Ronnie sat across from each other in the living room of the brownstone. "Bryce proposed last Thursday," Carla said.

"That's great." Ronnie jumped up, wrapped her arms around her friend, and squeezed Carla. "What did you tell him? Should I break out the champagne?"

Carla sighed. "I told him that I loved him, but now I don't know. I think I said it because he did. Of course I'm very fond of him, but I don't know whether it's love. His offer is tempting: security, affection, and good sex. But although he told me he does, I don't think he loves me, at least not yet."

"What makes you think that?"

"Well, for one thing, we haven't spoken since last Thursday. You'd think that he'd have called over the weekend. I think the 'I love you' was sort of an afterthought, that his sudden decision to get serious is about me and this business. I think the thought of me with other men bothers him a lot."

"If he loves you, it would."

"Jealousy and possessiveness aren't love. Jack loves you and he understands. I think what Bryce is saying is 'I want you to love me so much that you'll give up fucking other men for money.'" Carla told Ronnie about the video that precipitated Bryce's proposal. "Bryce is a wonderful man, but the more I think about it, the more I realize that I'm not in love with him. Maybe some time in the future, but not now. And I enjoy what you and I do."

"I know."

"It's a tough decision."

"I don't think it would be a difficult choice if you really loved him."

"You may be right."

"I've got a similar problem," Ronnie said. "Jack's home."

"Great. For how long this time?"

"He's back for good. He got in late Saturday night, so excited and he wanted to surprise me. He's gotten an offer from a computer software house to develop a program about geological formations, three-dimensional modeling. He got a small advance and will get a nice royalty deal when it sells. His old boss, TJ Sorenson, has wanted him to come back here for a long time but there wasn't enough work to offer him a full-time position. Now Jack's sure that he can arrange a three-day-a-week slot with TJ, and spend the rest of his time at the computer."

"Ronnie, that's great!"

"I guess."

"What does that mean?"

"I've made a life for myself here, with our business and all. I don't know if Jack will want me to stay at home all the time and I don't know whether I want to give this up. And I sometimes wonder if Jack and I have enough for a full-time life. It was always easy to believe that we still had something between us when he was gone most of the time."

"You've told me often enough that your sex life wasn't very adventurous."

"Yeah. Hot and hormonal, but predictable. We fucked like bunnies all day yesterday, but I've come to enjoy the creative side of our work."

"Does he know the details of what you do? The fantasies and all? Have you ever showed him Black Satin?"

Ronnie shook her head.

"Maybe he'd be interested in meeting one of your characters."

"You think? It's silly but it's easier to share that side of me with a stranger than with my own husband."

"From all you've told me about Jack, he may be no different

from some of our clients. He may have fantasies in his mind that he can't share with you. Maybe you should give him the chance."

"And maybe you should do some thinking about Bryce. I've known him for years and he's a very special person."

"You're changing the subject."

"I know but the comment's still relevant."

"I've got a date with a new guy tomorrow night. I somehow think that it will help me clarify things. And you need to have a good heart-to-heart with Jack."

Since Carla enjoyed making a bit of an entrance, she usually arrived slightly late for dinner with a client. So it surprised her when she was seated at a table in Vinnie's Waterfront Cafe, a well-reviewed yet inconspicuous seafood restaurant overlooking the Hudson River and her client wasn't there waiting for her. She placed the leather case that contained her album on the floor beside her feet and ordered a glass of club soda with a piece of lime. As she sipped, she gazed out through the wide expanse of glass at the river with the lights of the boats making patterns on the rippled surface.

Almost fifteen minutes later, Carla glanced up and saw a man weaving his way toward her. Gil, he'd said his name was. Just Gil. He had refused to tell her his last name and that was all right with her. He had been recommended by a client she'd been with many times.

As he approached, she realized that he was unusually tall and incredibly thin. He really does look like a bean pole, she thought. He's maybe six-six and he couldn't weigh more than one fifty. Carla extended her hand. "Gil," she said as she took his tentatively offered hand, "I'm Carla."

"Nice to meet you," he said. He sat down quickly and took a long swallow of the glass of water already waiting at his place. "Sorry I was late. Unavoidable."

Carla watched her newest client intently. His hands were never still. He put his glass down and fiddled with his napkin.

When it was neatly in his lap, he picked up his fork and twirled it in his long slender fingers. "You sounded nice on the phone," he said, his words quick and clipped, "but I'd like to make this perfectly clear. I don't want to talk about my wife or my marriage. I won't talk about my job and I've given you a phony name so you won't be able to trace me."

Carla tried to keep her smile warm yet impersonal. If she had any desire to find out who he was, her friend Ed, who had vouched for him, would tell her anything she needed to know. But why should she? A man's personal life was his concern. "I have no intention of trying to find out who you are, Gil. I'm here because you called me."

"Yes, yes I did," he said, putting his fork down and picking up his water glass. His nails were bitten down to the quick and his cuticles were chewed and scabbed over in a few spots. He wore a casual shirt and tan slacks, an outfit that unfortunately made his almost emaciated body look even thinner. "As I told you on the phone, I have these needs that no one would understand so I decided to hire a hooker." He looked at Carla, stylishly dressed in a pair of black wool slacks and a long-sleeved, kelly green silk blouse, and his mouth tightened. "I'm sorry. You're not really a hooker."

"I am a hooker and I enjoy it. Do you know where the word hooker comes from?" When he was silent she continued. "During the Civil War a general named Hooker brought women along with his army to keep the troops happy between battles. Hooker's Women, they were called. That's what I do, after all. Keep the troops happy. And what's wrong with that? Sex is fun."

The corners of Gil's mouth turned up for a moment, then his lips returned to their original thin line. "I don't want to talk about sex either. That is, not yet."

"That's fine. Tell me what you like to do in your spare time. Do you like sports?"

"You mean do I like basketball," he snapped. "A tall guy like me has to like basketball, right?"

"Ouch," she said softly and Gil had the good grace to look chagrined. "I thought no such thing. I'm just trying to make small talk. Wow, you've got quite a chip on your shoulder."

Gil's shoulders slumped. "I guess you're right. I'm sorry."

The waiter interrupted. "May I get you a drink?"

"Sure. What have you got on tap?"

The waiter listed several brands and Gil and Carla each ordered a Sam Adams.

"I'm sorry," Gil said as the waiter disappeared, "about my remark before. You hit a sore point and I'm very strung out."

"I wouldn't have noticed," Carla said, taking his dinner knife from Gil's hands and placing it back on the table. "Want to talk about it?" Carla had realized long before that part of her job was being a counselor, friend, and confidante. So many of her clients had problems and no one to talk to about them.

"They used to call me Zip in school."

"Zip?"

"I was already over six feet tall in junior high and I weighed under a hundred pounds. The kids used to tease, 'Stick your tongue out and you'll look like a zipper.' Thus the nickname Zip. I lifted weights but it didn't help."

"You are what you are."

The waiter arrived with their beers and they each took a long drink. "I understand you're a college graduate," Gil said.

"Unusual for a hooker. Right?" Carla winked and Gil smiled ruefully. "Touché," he said.

"I went to Michigan State and majored in English Literature. You?"

They spent the meal talking and quickly discovered that they had similar taste in movies and books. They had both vacationed in St. Martin and both lamented the commercialism of what had once been a quiet island with great French and native island food. They also shared the same taste in restaurants and each had a quiet little out-of-the-way spot to recommend. They had completely different opinions of the currrent administration and argued hotly over a recent cabinet appointment.

Over coffee, Carla decided it was time to get to the reason for the dinner. "Not that I'm not enjoying our dinner," Carla said, "but maybe it's time to get slightly more serious. What led you to call me?"

Gil picked up a sugar packet and turned it over and over in his long fingers. "I have needs. You understand. I have things that pound on my brain, fantasies that I have when I'm with my wife. You know, in bed. It's gotten so I never really make love to her but always pretend she's someone else or that I'm someone else."

"She wouldn't be interested in playing out these fantasies with you?"

"Of course not. We've been married for twenty-four years. She's not that kind of woman."

Carla let that remark pass. "What kind of fantasies?"

He jumped up as the packet in his fingers burst open and sugar poured into Gil's lap. When he was seated again, he said, "I was talking to Ed, you know, like guys talk, and he told me about you. That you fulfill fantasies. That's what I need. Someone like you."

"I'm happy to oblige," she said, "but you'd be surprised what your wife might enjoy if you gave her the chance."

"Don't talk to me about my wife," Gil snapped. "I know her better than you do."

So many men came to her with the same story. And so many of them were wrong. Carla's sigh was inaudible. It wasn't her job to educate her clients, just to please them. "I won't say another word about your wife," Carla said.

His gaze was fixed on the corner of her leather case. "You have a book. Ed told me about it."

Carla pulled her album from its case and handed it to Gil. "Ed probably told you how this works. There's an envelope inside." When he nodded, she rose and picked up her pocketbook. "I'll freshen up and be back in a few minutes."

Gil opened the cover.

When Carla returned from the ladies' room Gil was staring at one of the pictures. She glanced over his shoulder as she took her seat. "Gil?" He was a million miles away. "Gil?" she said again. His eyes cleared and she caught his eye. "That's Sally. She's twelve and she really likes candy." She could see Gil's Adam's apple bobbing up and down.

Suddenly, Carla knew exactly what he wanted and although she'd never been Sally before, she could think of several ways to enhance the experience. She could see his fantasy playing, like a movie, behind her eyes. "I know where she lives."

Gil held the book with one hand and his fingers fiddled with the tassel of the now-filled black satin bookmark. He suddenly pulled out a credit card and dropped it onto the dinner check. The waiter whisked it away and returned with the receipt which Gil signed, his finger still in the album marking Sally's photograph.

It took the cab almost fifteen minutes to arrive at the brownstone. Carla showed Gil into the living room, then disappeared upstairs.

Ten long minutes later Gil stood in the center of the room. "Gil," Carla said as she walked down the stairs.

He turned and stared at the little girl in the pink party dress who walked toward him. Her face was freshly washed and she wore no makeup or jewelry. "Hi," the girl said, hugging a large doll under one arm. "My name's Sally. My mommy says that I should always call my elders by their last name. May I call you Mr. Smith?"

Gil could only nod, his hands still for the moment.

"Can I have that?" Sally said, taking the book from Gil's tight fingers. "Thanks," she said, her voice slightly higher pitched than usual. She placed the book on the desk at the side of the room. "Do you like my new shoes?" She stuck out one foot then polished the shiny tip by rubbing it up and down Gil's trouser leg. "My mommy lets me wear them on special occasions."

Gil cleared his throat. "They're very nice," he said, dropping onto the sofa.

"Wanna play a game, Mr. Smith?" she asked. "We could play

with my doll." She bent over and put the doll on the sofa beside Gil. As she bent, her short skirt allowed a clear view of her white cotton underpants.

This is a grown woman, a prostitute, Gil told himself. But oh Lord she even smells of baby soap. He rubbed his sweating palms on his trouser legs. "I'd love to play a game." He saw the candy dish on the end table next to him. "There's some candy here," he said, trying to say the right thing to make this fantasy go on and on. "Would you like some?"

"My mommy only lets me have candy on special occasions. Is this a special occasion?"

"It certainly is," Gil said, slowly slipping into the fantasy. She was a hooker, but she was a little girl and he wanted her as he'd wanted nothing else in his life. "If I give you a piece of candy will you do something that will make me happy too?"

"Okay, Mr. Smith," Sally said. Gil handed her the dish and she selected a Hershey's Kiss. Slowly she removed the silver paper while Gil watched her every move. Reflexively he wet his lips as Sally stuck out her pink tongue and licked the surface of the chocolate.

As she watched his eyes on her hands and tongue Carla was happy that she'd taken an extra minute to remove her nail polish. He wouldn't realize how much thought had gone into creating Sally but he would get tremendous pleasure out of playing with her. "Thanks for the chocolate," she said, popping the morsel into her mouth, but deliberately leaving a chocolate stain at the corner. She slowly licked her lips, missing the stain.

"You've got some chocolate on your mouth," Gil said. "Come here." He took her arm and used his handkerchief to wipe the brown goo from her mouth. He pulled her close and placed a feather-light kiss on her lips.

"I can do a dance for you," Sally said, bouncing up from the couch. Anticipation was the best part of the game.

"That would be nice," Gil said, disappointed that she had moved away.

Sally put a tape in the player and whirled around the living room, flipping her skirt so Gil could catch glimpses of her undies. "Sometimes," she giggled, "I do this without my panties. The wind feels funny when I twirl. Wanna see?"

Gil could only nod, his fingers playing with a fold in the sofa's leather. Quickly Sally pulled off her panties and twirled. In her ten minutes upstairs, Carla had run an electric razor over her groin and now her crotch was clean as a baby's. "Wheee," she said, landing on the couch as if dizzy. "It's all tickly." Since Gil was silent, Carla continued to lead him through the fantasy. "If you give me another candy, I'll let you touch where it's tickly."

A bit dazed, Gil handed Carla the dish and she selected a caramel. She unwrapped it and popped it into her mouth. As he watched, she chewed the sticky candy slowly, moving it around her mouth with her tongue. She inserted a finger into her mouth and pulled a glob of candy free. "Now I'm all sticky," she said. "Wanna lick?" She pointed her finger at his mouth and reflexively he opened and sucked her finger inside. She pulled just hard enough to create suction, then allowed him to draw her finger back in.

He flicked his tongue around her nail, sucking at the sweetness. "Wanna touch my tickly part?" she asked as she withdrew her finger.

"Yes," he groaned. She lifted her skirt, took his hand and brushed his fingertips over her freshly shaved and lotioned flesh. "Oh Jesus," he moaned, rubbing his palm over her now-hairless mound.

"You moaned, Mr. Smith. That's too bad. You must be hurting." She patted the bulge in his pants. "When I hurt, Mommy takes all my clothes off and puts me to bed. Like this." She whisked her dress off over her head and pulled off her shoes and socks. She stood before Gil dressed only in a white cotton undershirt, stretched to its limit by her large, unrestrained breasts. "You should take your clothes off if you're sick."

He stood and removed his shirt, folding it carefully and placing it on a chair. He pulled off his slacks and straightened the creases with quick, efficient motions. His shoes and socks followed, then his underwear until all his clothing was folded and stacked in a neat pile. He stood in the middle of the living room, naked, with his long, slender erection poking straight out from his body like a large thorn on a long, skinny branch. His fingers stretched across his flat abdomen, twisting and untwisting.

"Wow," Sally said, "you look different from me. You've got that thing sticking out. Can I touch it?" Without waiting for Gil to answer she cupped his prick and slid it through her hands. "It's very long and very hard," she said. She touched, examined, and stroked his cock and balls as though she'd never held one before. "What does it do, Mr. Smith?" she asked, her voice high pitched and a wide-eyed innocent expression on her face.

He pulled back, unsure of his ability to control his body for long. "I'll show you, if you want."

"Can I have candy when you're done?"

"Of course," he said, barely able to keep the quaking from his voice. He sat on the sofa and pulled the little girl so she stood between his knees. "But first I have to make you ready." The insides of her thighs were like the softest silk as his fingers tickled their way from her knee to her smooth, hairless crotch. She was already wet and his cock and balls were on fire with his need for her.

"Come here." He pulled her so that she was kneeling astride his lap, straddling his cock. "Sit down right here and you'll understand."

She opened a foil package she'd taken from the end table and unrolled the condom over Gil's cock. "A little girl is always prepared." Without any delay, she sat on his erect cock. "That way? Is this what that's for?"

Gil rubbed the sides of the cotton undershirt. Avoiding her large breasts, which would have ruined the fantasy, he bucked and arched as she bounced in his lap. "God, yes," he cried as an orgasm deeper than any he ever remembered overtook him. "Sally!"

Ten minutes later they were still in the same position and his hands had been quiet for the entire time. "Can I see you again?" he whispered.

"You have my number," Carla whispered, rising and handing Gil a wad of tissues. "Call me anytime."

He dressed quickly and, reliving the evening over and over, he left. Carla gathered her props and walked upstairs, considering. She was pleased at how deeply Gil had gotten into his fantasy. She had given him a wonderful evening and had earned five hundred dollars as well. It's amazing, she thought. I become part of almost every fantasy I play and so far I've enjoyed them all. She pulled off the white cotton undershirt and threw it and the rest of Sally's clothes into the hamper.

In the bathtub, she held the massager hose and played the spray over her freshly shaved pussy, thinking about Sally and Gil. It took only a few moments for her to climax. Bathed and relaxed, Carla climbed into bed.

Ronnie had always called her customers friends and now Carla realized why. These men were her friends, if only for one evening. She liked all the men she had been with and got tremendous pleasure out of satisfying them and, in doing that, satisfying herself.

No, she thought, a smile lighting her face. Although I like Bryce a lot and his offer is flattering, I don't want to give up the pleasures that I've found with my friends. At least not yet.

If Bryce could continue their relationship as it had been, that would be wonderful. And if he couldn't, then they would have to go their separate ways. She would miss him dreadfully, but not enough to make her give all this up.

She snuggled down, pulled the satin comforter up around her ears, and quickly fell asleep.

In Hopewell Junction, Ronnie sat in her living room with Jack, sipping a glass of diet Pepsi. She had just finished telling her husband about the lifestyle she, and now Carla, had established. "I enjoy helping my friends understand that their fantasies are not very different from the dreams that we all have at one time or another."

"I know what you were involved in, of course," Jack said, "but I had no real idea how much there was for men to experience."

"It's fun, Jack," Ronnie said, "and men pay me a great deal of money to share their fantasies with me."

"Are you going to continue in the business?"

"How do you feel about it?"

"Now that I'm going to be in New York full time," Jack said, "I guess I'd be upset if you spent time with other men. Of course, I'd love to meet Carla. You two seem to have become such good friends."

"We certainly have. But if I gave up the business, what would I do all day to keep from being bored crazy?"

"I was thinking about the amount of writing that is connected with my job. There are going to be manuals and guides and scads of documentation. I'll hate that part and you'd be so good at it."

"But what do I know about geological models?"

"Hey, babe. You've got a college degree in writing and you're very bright. I'll teach you how the model works and you can explain it on paper to the users. I know you—you'd pick up what you needed to know very quickly."

"You really think so?"

"I'd like you to give it a try."

Ronnie winked at her husband. "I think I'd like that."

"And you'd give up the business?"

"Only if I can play with you."

"Play with me?"

"Men have been paying me a lot of money to play fantasy games. Wouldn't you like that? Some different ideas to spice up our sex life."

"I guess we've never done much off-center stuff. But it's always been good just the way it is."

"I know that. But variety is wonderful. Don't you have a fantasy that you'd like to act out with me?"

"I don't know. Like what?"

Ronnie reached into a paper bag she had put beside the couch and pulled out the black satin album. She slid over next to Jack, placed the book on his lap, and opened the front cover.

"Is that you?" Jack said. He turned the page. "That is you. Holy shit."

Ronnie smiled and cuddled against her husband. "That's Marguerite, the stripper." He turned the page. "And that's Nita, the harem girl, and on the next page is Miss Gilbert, who enjoys disciplining naughty students. And there are many more. Wanna play?"

"Holy shit," Jack said, turning another page. "Holy shit."

The Love Flower

Chapter

1

THE ROOM KEY

by Nichole St. Michelle

The party had been to honor his boss with a sales award and Rick had spent the evening talking with several witty, intelligent and engaging women. He had enough fodder for his fantasies to last for months. It was almost midnight when he finally walked into the elevator at the hotel, opened his tie and collar button and pulled the top stud from his shirt-front. As he dropped the stud into the pocket of his jacket, it clinked. He reached down and, in his right hand jacket pocket, he found a room key and a short note.

"I found you intriguing and exciting and thought you might enjoy a trip to my room. I'll be waiting for you. Room 207. If there's a red ribbon around the door handle, remove it and come in. If the ribbon's gone, then you're too late and I'll be very disappointed."

No signature. No clue that would help him decide which of the women he had met that evening might be waiting for him. Nothing. As the elevator slowly rose, he pondered.

This is ridiculous. Things like this don't happen to middle-aged salesmen on a business trip to Palm Springs.

Rick wandered off the elevator at the third floor and walked toward his room, the woman's key and note still in his hand. He couldn't. He really couldn't. This was silly. It was probably some kind of weird practical joke. If he used the key he would discover some guy with a camera taking shots of dumb Midwesterners who were stupid enough to fall for this ploy.

Or worse, he would be knocked on the head and awake to find his wallet missing. Nah. He couldn't.

He looked at the key. Nondescript. Warm from the heat of his palm. Shaking his head, he returned to the elevator and pressed the second floor button. With resolute steps he walked toward 207, relieved to see the ribbon around the handle. She hadn't gone to sleep yet, he thought, and was amazed at his delight. He wanted this, bizarre though it might be. He untied the ribbon, stuffed it into his pocket and used the key to open the door.

The room was extremely dark, the light from behind him illuminating only a sofa and coffee table.

"Close it behind you," a female voice said.

"What is this all about?" Rick asked.

"Close the door and I'll explain." The voice was soft, melodious and totally nonthreatening. He closed the door behind him and the room was thrown into complete darkness.

"Okay," he said, trying not to sound like a private detective from a cheap novel, "explain."

"I watched you all evening and liked what I saw. You look like a man who would enjoy taking a chance, so I slipped that key into your pocket. Was I right? Do you enjoy taking a chance?"

Despite his scepticism, Rick found himself smiling. Audacious. Ridiculous. Nervy. And, he had to admit, fun. He chuckled. "Ten minutes ago I wouldn't have characterized myself as someone who takes chances, but I'm here, so I guess I am."

"I want this to be totally anonymous, so I'll call you John and you can call me Mary. If it's all wonderful and we want to exchange true identities later, great. If not, you can leave with neither of us the wiser. Is that all right with you?"

Rick's grin widened. This was so outrageous. "It's great."

"Tell me about you," Mary said. "Are you married? Attached?"

"Hey, you're the one who said no details, no identities so let's just leave it at that."

"Wonderful. I was hoping you'd say that. Come sit beside me."

"I can't see my way around," Rick said. "Where are you?"

"I've moved to the sofa you saw when you first arrived. Take five small steps forward and feel for the coffee table. Move around it to your left and sit down. I'll be beside you.

Slowly Rick moved forward, and cracked his shin on the table. "Ow. It's only three steps."

Mary's laugh was throaty and warm. "Oh John, I'm so sorry." He felt a hand on his hip, guiding him around the low table, and he dropped with a thud onto the sofa. The hand slipped down past his right knee and stroked his shin. "I'm really sorry about that."

Enjoying the stroking, he waited a moment, then said, "It was the other leg."

With more warm giggles, the hand moved to the other knee, then rubbed his left shin gently. "Better?" Mary said.

"Much."

The hand slid up his leg and caressed his knee. "And this?"

"Oh, that's making everything much better." Better? His cock had swelled until it was uncomfortable beneath his black tuxedo pants. The hand was rubbing his thigh, digging long nails into the flesh at the inside. He reached out, found the arm and slid his hand up to the shoulder. He encountered no clothing or jewelry. In silence, he rubbed across her shoulder to her neck. Cupping the back of Mary's head, he found her lips with his.

She leaned into the kiss, her tongue meeting his, thrusting, wanting, taking. It was like no kiss he had experienced. Brazen. Bold. It invited him to take more and he did. He tangled his fingers in short, wavy hair and moved his lips to her eyes, her cheeks, her throat, while her hands wrestled with his shirt studs. Finally, as he bit her earlobe, the studs were gone and Mary opened his shirt and scratched her nails down his bare chest. "Nice," she purred. "Such soft hair." She yanked.

"Ouch," Rick yelled.

"That really doesn't hurt," Mary said. "You feel like it should, but it's just very exciting. Isn't it, John? Tell me."

Rick had to agree that his 'ouch' had been based on expectations, not reality. She was still pulling on a handful of chest hair and, rather than hurting, it was very erotic. "Two can play at that," he said, grabbing a handful of her short hair.

"Yes," she purred, "we can." Suddenly the play got a bit rougher. It took only a moment for Rick to realize that Mary was naked. His hands rubbed over naked breasts, buttocks and thighs. They grabbed and took, rolling around on the sofa until they were panting, from both exertion and excitement.

"God, you're a sexy man," Mary said. Rick felt her hands reaching for the waistband of his pants as he caressed her ribs. As she unbuttoned and unzipped, Rick fondled her breasts and pinched her nipples. He dipped his head and found a swollen bud with his mouth, nipping at the turgid tip with his teeth. As he sucked, hard, he felt her sharp intake of breath, then her hand grasped the back of his neck, forcing his mouth even more tightly against her breast. "Umm," she growled. "Yes. Do it!"

Rick's hand slid down Mary's belly and found her mound,

hot, pressing against his questing fingers. He explored the folds and crevices, sliding easily over the wet slippery skin. "So hungry," he said, finding her clit with his thumb.

"Yes," she said, arching her back and pressing against his mouth and his hand. "Hungry for you."

For long moments, he sucked and stroked, bit and invaded. Fingers filled her channel as her hands pulled off his pants and shorts. He released her long enough to pull off his socks and find his wallet. He unrolled a condom over his cock and, with her hands grasping his buttocks, filled her with his hard penis. It was more like two animals mating than two people making love. Hard, hot, driving, Rick found he had never felt more like an animal with a woman.

She held his ass and pounded her pussy upward onto his cock. Who was fucking whom? It was impossible to tell. Two people were taking pleasure. Taking and taking, while giving to each other as well.

Buried inside of her, his cock pulsed and drove. His mouth found her nipple and his finger found her clit. He could make her come. He *would* make her come. He would make her scream out her release before he came. He rubbed and sucked as she drove his cock into her. "Yes," she yelled. "Yessssss."

Although he couldn't feel her orgasm through the violence of their movements, he knew, and he came, roaring, "Oh, God, good."

Panting, they lay together on the sofa, sweat trickling down his back and covering her chest under his hands. It was long minutes until she stirred. "I knew you'd be wonderful," she purred softly.

"How did you know?"

"I just did," Mary whispered. "But it's time to go now."

"Go?" Rick said, totally puzzled. "I thought you said it was wonderful."

"It was, but now it's over."

"But you said that if we hit it off, we wouldn't have to remain anonymous. You know who I am, but I know nothing about you."

Mary slithered from beneath Rick's body. "John, I know as little about you as you know about me."

He heard the sounds of clothing rustling. She was dressing. He was exhausted and wanted nothing more than to curl up next to Mary in a big bed, doze and make love all night. Now she was leaving. "But . . ."

"No buts," she said. The door opened a crack and Rick closed his eyes against the sudden light. "This isn't my room. I just took it for this. And I put the key into the pockets of about a dozen men so I don't even know which one you are. The ribbon was to assure that only the first man to arrive would get in. You were very prompt."

"So you don't know who I am and I don't know who you are." His eyes were slowly becoming adjusted to the light so he squinted and made out the silhouette of a woman in a long dress standing beside the door.

"No, and I don't want to. Totally anonymous sex has always been a fantasy of mine, so it will stay anonymous. Good night, John."

Rick smiled. Making love to a fantastic yet nameless and faceless woman had always been a fantasy of his as well. She had arranged it and it had been wonderful. He would return home tomorrow with a magic memory, untarnished by any trace of reality. "Yeah," he said. "Good night, Mary."

The woman left, closing the door behind her. Rick fumbled, found a lamp and flipped on the light. He blinked and, when his eyes adjusted, he gazed around the small sitting room, memorizing the furniture, the colors, the smells. Slowly he gathered his clothes and dressed. Unable to find his tie, he searched for several minutes. Unsuccessful in his search, he realized that she must have kept it. He had thought that he had seen something hanging from her hand as she left. And on the coffee table was a sheer light blue scarf. It was hers and she had left it for him. He pressed it against his nose, inhaling her fragrance.

With a sigh, he tucked the scarf into his pocket with the red ribbon, his souvenirs of an amazing evening. Then he turned off the lights, and left.

Fran Caputo sat back on her chair and reflexively tightened the scrunchy on her ponytail. Rotating her shoulders to relieve the tension, she clicked the mouse-pointer on the spellcheck icon and worked her way through the story, fixing typos and correcting her usually atrocious spelling. When she reached the end of the document, she clicked on the print icon and, while the printer turned out its pages, went into her tiny kitchen and poured herself a Caffeine-Free Diet Pepsi. Slugging down the entire glass, she realized it was long past dinnertime and she was ravenous. Quickly she slathered peanut butter on one slice of white bread, topped it with another and took a healthy bite.

She looked at the clock on the front of the microwave oven. 8:26. I have to stop doing this, she thought. I get a story banging around inside my head and I can't rest until it's on paper. She re-filled her glass, wandered back to the spare bedroom she had set up as her office and picked the pages off the printer tray. As she rearranged them with the title page on top she reread the beginning. *The Room Key* by Nichole St. Michelle. "Nicki," she said out loud, "you do write the most delicious stuff. You devil you."

Grinning, she stuffed the sandwich into her mouth and washed it down with the second glass of Pepsi. Finished, she dropped the pack of pages onto her desk chair. Tomorrow she would do some final editing, although her writing seldom needed much, then go through the list of erotic publications to which she had become a semi-regular contributor and decide who would get the first chance at *The Room Key*. The money was small but nice and it was a thrill to have her efforts rewarded. She had to be constantly reminded that she could write a good erotic tale.

She rubbed the back of her neck. Where had the evening

gone? It had been partly gone before she had left work. Jenny, who was supposed to relieve her, had been almost an hour late for her shift at the video store again. She had called, of course. "Hon," she had said, "cover for me until I get there. Brad got the afternoon off and we, well, you know. Well, maybe you don't, but you understand. Please, hon?"

Jenny's husband drove a long-haul truck and it seemed that whenever they had a moment they were in bed together. Had her own short-lived marriage ever been like that? Fran wondered. Not really. Sex had been something they did sometimes. They did it because it was Tuesday night and they hadn't done it in a while. Eric would grab her breast, fondle her for a while, rub her crotch and, when she got damp, stuff his cock into her. Sometimes she really enjoyed it and a few times, when Eric climaxed, she had found herself disappointed that things were over. At other times, she merely endured and masturbated in private.

"But Jenny," Fran had said into the phone, "it's already past four."

"I'll be there by five," Jenny had said. "Be a good guy." And the phone had gone dead.

"One of these days," she had muttered, but she knew that she'd probably never say anything. She had sighed and worked until Jenny had arrived at almost five-thirty.

Fran turned off her computer and walked into her bedroom. Why was she lamenting the passing of an evening? It wasn't as if she had anywhere to go or anything to do except look forward to *Designing Women* reruns. She should call her mother or her sister, but, as she stretched out on the bed, she couldn't work up the enthusiasm. It wasn't as if she could tell them what she had just accomplished. They'd be horrified.

She was startled when the phone rang. "Hello," she said into the receiver, hoping it was a wrong number so she could click on the TV and become a vegetable.

"Hi, Fran. It's Eileen."

Fran grinned. She was always glad to hear from Eileen Brent, her literary agent and friend. "Hi. I haven't heard from you in weeks. What's up?"

"What's up is something really great. I didn't want to call you at work because I know how secretive you are and your whooping and yelling would have led to questions."

"Whooping and yelling?"

"You've been nominated for the Madison Prize."

"You're kidding." The Madison Prize was one of the most prestigious awards for writers of romance novels. Although there was no actual money involved, receiving the Madison Prize meant increased sales plus better up-front money, promotion and placement for ensuing books.

"I'm not kidding, babe. *The Love Flower* is up for novel of the year."

"You're for real?"

"For real. You've got some stiff competition, but I think you've got a shot. You know I've loved that book from the beginning."

"But how can they even consider it? It's much too spicy for those eggheads up there. It's erotica. Pure and simple."

"It's a good novel and it's a love story so it's considered a romance novel, erotic or not. I think the publisher pushed for it, too. Sandy told me, in confidence, that they really wanted to see this book do well, and this is one very good way." Sandy McFadden was Fran's editor at Majestic Books. "I understand that she's got some pull with one of the judges."

"Is this fixed?" Fran said, horrified.

"Of course not," Eileen said quickly. "Sandy only got your book noticed. The judges read it and the book did the rest. It's not only good publicity for you, it's good for Majestic to have a nominee as well."

"Wow," Fran said, sitting down, then flopping back onto her pillows and propping her feet on the patchwork quilt on her bed. "Wow!"

"Yes. Wow and double wow. You'll have to be in New York for the dinner, you know. And because it's hooked up with the Madison Romance Writers' Conference, there will be a cocktail party Friday evening, some 'meet the authors' things and general being-seen beforehand."

"I'll have to be there?" How could she? She was Fran Caputo. It was Nichole St. Michelle who was nominated. Sophisticated, worldly Nicki. Not small-town Fran. And how could she face people who had read the erotica she had written. She flushed at the thought.

"Yes, my dear. You and Sandy can have quite an effect on the book's sales. People get all excited about buying a book written by someone they've actually met 'up close and personal.' And you'll have a book signing, too."

"But I can't," Fran said quickly.

"You can and you really should. No one can force you, but you really can't let Sandy go through all this and not cooperate. Take a couple of weeks off, come to the city and we'll get you all set up. And it's a great opportunity to get known at Majestic."

"Look, Eileen, this isn't the Oscars, after all. It's only the Madison Prize." She giggled. "Did you hear what I just said? *Only the Madison Prize.*"

Eileen's rich laughter filled the phone. "That's like saying it's *only* a best-seller. This could do that, you know."

Fran scrubbed her hands over her unmade-up face. "But Eileen, really. I can't take that time off from work. And what if anyone found out?"

Fran had worked for Manhattan Videos for almost seven years, ever since she moved to Omaha after she and Eric split. Almost four years ago she had, for a lark, written an explicitly sexy short story and submitted it to a pulp magazine. Buoyed by the magazine's rapid acceptance of the manuscript and the small check that came with it, she wrote more and more erotic short stories until finally she had written *The Love Flower*, a full-length erotic novel. Through a series of query letters, she had become connected with Eileen Brent's agency and, over the last year and a half, they had become fast friends, despite the fact that they had never met face-to-face.

No one knew that she was Nichole St. Michelle. Not her parents in Colorado or her sister and brother-in-law in Southern California. No one. And she wanted to keep it that way. After all, her mother hadn't brought her up to write slutty stuff like *The Love Flower.*

As Fran thought about going to New York, she had very mixed feelings. She would love to see the book do well, maybe make enough money for her to leave her job and write full-time. An author. A real author. It had always sounded like such a dream, but now, with this nomination and the recognition that she really could write, it just might be possible.

But it wasn't really Fran Caputo who was nominated, she reminded herself. It was Nichole St. Michelle.

"You can do this, Fran," Eileen said. "I mean Nichole can do this."

Eileen knew more about Fran's life than anyone, and Fran was tempted. She lifted her head and pulled the scrunchy from her ponytail, allowing her gray-streaked brown hair to fly free. Rubbing her scalp, she said, "Maybe Nichole can, but where she goes I go, and *I* can't."

"Fran, look," Eileen said. "You have vacation time coming to you. You've told me over and over that you haven't taken time off since Eric. At two weeks per year, you should have about fourteen weeks saved up."

"Actually you can only keep three weeks from previous years."

"Okay, so you have this year's two and three from past years. That's a lot of weeks."

"But Nichole's bio says she's a free-living swinging divorcée. That's nowhere near what I am."

"So come here and take a week or two to become used to living as Nichole."

"Living as Nichole? As a swinger? Not on your life."

"Why not? You're over thirty, single and smart enough to know which chances to take and which not. We'll get you out of those sneakers and jeans and into some real city clothes. A few dinners and whathaveyou and you're set."

Fran giggled. "It's not the dinners, it's the whathaveyous that scare the shit out of me."

"And well they should. But isn't it about time you practiced what you write about? I can't understand how you can be as naive as you claim to be and still write the steamy sex scenes you write."

"I am not naive."

"You told me you have a hard time just going into the back room and rearranging the XXX-rated videos. Ever watch one?"

"No."

"So where do you get the ideas for those hot love scenes. Are there men in your past I don't know about?"

"Not even one besides Eric, and sex with him wasn't the stuff steamy sex is made of. Actually, it's just a good imagination, lots of reading and midnight masturbation." Fran swallowed hard. Had she really just said that? To Eileen, whom she had never really met?

Through the phone Fran could hear Eileen's sudden burst of laughter. "You're a riot. Listen. Think about it and call me in a day or two. The dinner is the first Saturday in May so you have a few weeks to consider it."

Fran looked out of her window at the black March sky and her snow-covered windowsill. She would think about it, she realized. She really would. But she couldn't. She really couldn't.

In the living room of her five-bedroom colonial in Commack, Long Island, Diane Barklay was stretched out on the bed beside her husband Zack. "Being nominated is a great honor," Zack was saying.

"Honor, shmonor," Diane replied. "I was nominated once already. This time I have to win." She knew Zack could feel her whole body stiffen, but he must understand how important this was. "No one's ever been nominated a second time and not won."

Diane gazed at the framed covers of her six romance novels. From *Magic Love* to *Addie's Travels*, they traced her last five years. She also had a framed copy of the certificate that *Lovers in the*

Spring had earned when it had been nominated for the Madison Prize two years earlier. "It's an honor just to be nominated," her editor had said at the time. "There are tens of thousands of romances published each year and only the top five get nominated for novel of the year." But she had lost. Nominated isn't winning and despite what all her friends had said at the time winning had been, and still was, the only thing that mattered.

Diane stared at the spectacular cover the art department had come up with for *Addie's Travels*. A great cover. Violets that symbolized Addle's search for the perfect lover. And a perfect diamond, from the mine that Trask owned, the diamond that brought them together. It was a great story, Diane knew, but that wonderful cover was part of the reason that *Addie's Travels* had been nominated for the Madison Prize this year.

"Then I'm sure it's in the bag for you," Zack said, his hand slowly stroking his wife's arm. "Who else was nominated?"

"Well, there's Virginia Cortez for *Come to Papa*, Mary Kate Allonzo for *Miranda*, Paul Ng for *The Joys of Paris* and Nichole St. Michelle for *The Love Flower*."

"Well, I'm sure those are all worthy competitors, but *Addie's Travels* will win hands down. It's got everything a good romance needs."

Diane smiled and willed her body to relax. "It's really a good book, isn't it?"

"Of course it is," Zack said, still stroking Diane's upper arm. "You've probably read the other nominees. Is there any real competition?"

Diane grinned. "I guess I do read a lot of romances and yes, I have read them all. They are all good books, of course, except for *The Love Flower*. It's just a sexy piece of trash. Lots of steamy love scenes and very little story."

"Who's the writer?"

"Her name's Nichole St. Michelle and this is her first novel." She frowned. "Her first novel and she gets nominated."

"Nichole St. Michelle. Have I ever heard of her?"

"Probably not. She's supposed to be very French for an American. There was an article about her in one of my romance magazines. Wait a minute."

Diane knelt beside a bookshelf filled with magazines and rummaged through the stack. "November. I think it was in November. Why can't I find November?" She located the missing issue and crawled back onto the bed. She thumbed through the magazine until she found the full-page photo of the cover of *The Love Flower*. Grudgingly she had to admit that it was an adequate cover. The love flower was a blood-red orchid and the outlines of the graceful hands of the hero and heroine reached for the flower from opposite sides, their fingers not quite touching.

She turned her attention to the biography of Nichole St. Michelle on the lower half of the facing page and read aloud. " 'Nichole St. Michelle, brilliant new author of *The Love Flower*, is a free spirit. At thirty-two she is eight years divorced and, with no children and few encumbrances, Nicki, as her friends call her, lives a life of freedom and indulgence. Left a substantial sum by wealthy relatives, Nicki is free to travel the world, being wined and dined by the influential and the infamous. This writer has it on good authority that Nichole hasn't done *all* the naughty, sexy things she writes about in her hot first novel, but I'm told she has experienced most of the erotic games that her characters play. When I tried to get an interview, I was told that Ms. St. Michelle was traveling in southern France and was unavailable for comment.' "

Diane closed the magazine. "She's a personality and I'm just a housewife. She'll come to New York, dazzle all the judges and I won't stand a chance." Tears pooled in the corners of her eyes.

Zack enfolded his wife in his arms. "It's all right. I know you'll win. We'll do whatever it takes to make sure you win. It'll be fine."

"Don't patronize me, Zack. It won't necessarily be fine. She might win. Any of the others might, too. And I can't lose again. I just can't."

Fran lay on her bed in silence for a long time after she hung up with Eileen. Despite what she had said about it being just erotica, she knew that *The Love Flower* was a good book. She had worked on it for a year, honing the characters and the plot. The sex scenes were very hot, but so was the plot, which centered around a young woman's coming of age, emotionally and sexually, under the tutelage first of the elders of the tribe and later of a sailor from a visiting schooner. The sex scenes were an integral part of the book. Fran smiled. Well, not entirely. She had enjoyed writing the hot parts almost more than the rest and they seemed to flow from her fingers. The scene where Rhona was first initiated into the rites of womanhood by the priest of a neighboring tribe had taken her only about two hours to put down on paper and she had enjoyed every minute of it. She loved that scene.

Rhona walked into the hut and stood silently as she had been told to do. A priest would come to her on this, the tenth day after her first woman's flow after her sixteenth birthday. They would be together in this hut for an entire week. A high priest had done so with all the women of 'the people' since the gods created the tribe at the beginning of time. This hut had been erected on the first day of the planting and would be torn down the following year, making way for a new hut that would stand on the same spot, far from the village, as such huts had done for thousands of years. It comforted her to think of the continuity of it all, the joining of the women of the tribe through the ages.

And she thought about Aramu, the high priest. He was a wonderful man and had been like a father to her since her real father had been killed when his canoe overturned so many years ago. He would teach her everything she needed to know. He would be gentle and kind. He would be her friend in this as in everything else. It would be all right.

It comforted her to think of all that on this, the most important night of her adult life. Well, adult as of tonight. Rhona had left her long coal-black hair loose, so it hung down her back until it brushed the swell of her buttocks beneath her newly made, soft, flowered sarong. She brushed it

behind her shoulders with her long slender fingers and, as
her eyes adjusted to the dim lighting, she looked around
the hut. Her deep brown eyes widened. The walls were
covered with unusual pictures, pictures of men and women
engaged in the most private of activities. She had known
there would be drawings and her mother had encouraged
her to study them. As a matter of fact it had been the only
thing her mother had told her about the ceremony. "The
drawings will teach you much." Once, Rhona knew, the pictures had been painted on the hides of the small animals
that made their homes on the interior of the island. Now
they were carefully drawn on paper brought by the trading
ships that stopped at their tiny port.

She walked over and looked more carefully at one of the
pictures. A man with a fully erect phallus approached a woman
with large breasts, her arms outstretched to him. Rhona
knew that it was a natural thing to happen between men
and women, but to her it was new, and exciting, and a bit
frightening.

"Don't be frightened, my little one," a voice said from
behind her.

"I'm not," she said, her tone belying her words. "I was
just looking at the pictures."

"Here," the man said, placing his hands on her shoulders
from behind her and turning her to one side. "Look at that
one."

The picture she stared at was of a man with a phallus
even larger than the first, and the woman was crouched in
front of him, her hands touching it, her mouth open.

Rhona felt the hands turn her in another direction. This
picture was of a woman on her hands and knees, the large-
phallused man behind her, poised to drive his shaft into the
woman's body. "There are so many ways to love, and eventually you will learn them all."

A shiver ran through Rhona's body. The man's voice was
soft, warm, almost hypnotic. This was good, and natural, she

told herself. Good and natural. She felt the man's breath on the back of her neck and she shivered again. Anticipation? Excitement? Terror? Was this Aramu?

"It's all right," he whispered. "When we are finished, you will have learned how wonderful it can be between a man and a woman."

She felt the hands turn her so she was now facing the man with the wonderful voice. "You're not Aramu," she said, gazing on a face she had never seen before.

"No, I am Chitan. I come from a village far away. It would be awkward for a woman to be initiated by someone she's seen every day, and will see every day from now on."

A small smile crossed Rhona's face as she thought about Aramu. She had wondered as she looked at him over the past weeks, how she would react afterwards to his knowledge of her that way. Now she wouldn't have to worry. "No one told me."

"I know. Nothing that goes on here will ever leave this room. It will be an entirely private ceremony between you and me and the gods."

"I understand. I asked my mother and my older sisters, but they would tell me nothing. Except about the pictures. My mother said I should look at the pictures." She realized that she was babbling and quickly shut her mouth.

"No one should be told in advance as it is different for everyone." He took her hand and led her to a couch, covered with soft hides. "Sit here beside me and try to relax. This will be wonderful. I will see to that."

She sat on the edge of the platform, her hands clasped in her lap, her knees pressed tightly together. "I am ready."

"No, you're not," Chitan said. "But you will be." He crossed to a small table and poured her a small cup of red liquid. "Just a small amount will help you relax." He took one of her hands and placed the cup in it. "Just sip. Taking the juice too quickly, or drinking too much, will make you too anxious."

Rhona touched the cup to her lips and took a small sip of the sweet liquid. As she swallowed, she felt heat flow down her throat and through her chest to her belly. "It's very good," she said.

"Another sip, love."

A second and third sip followed the first, each causing more warmth to spread throughout her. Strange, she thought. It goes down my throat, but it makes my breasts warm. Odd.

Chitan took the cup from her hands and placed it on the low table. "Are you too shy to let me see you?" he asked.

Rhona lowered her head. "No," she said. "Yes," she whispered. The priest smiled and she felt a bit more comfortable. Then he took her hands and, still sitting himself, guided her to a standing position in front of him. She looked down at the knot that held the wide piece of brightly colored cloth closed. The knot was so large, tied as tightly as the woman who dressed her could make it. "Make him work for it," she had said, then laughed at her joke, a joke that Rhona didn't really understand.

But the priest's hands made quick work of the knot and soon the sides parted and the flowered material slipped to the floor.

"Oh yes," Chitan whispered. "I knew you were beautiful, but in your natural state, as the gods made you, you are truly lovely." She watched his eyes darken as they roamed over her body. "You are truly a woman, long beautiful legs, large full breasts. Your nipples are smokey, and growing hard as you hear how wonderful you are."

Her breasts were feeling heavy and swollen as she watched his eyes and listened to his description of her.

"Your arms are well formed and your waist is so slender that I could almost span it with my hands. Your belly is flat and your woman's place is dark and secret." He reached out and ran one finger down her belly and into the dark curly hair. "I will learn its secrets tonight."

She trembled, and he withdrew his finger. No one had ever touched her so intimately. She had heard that there were some women who had already known a man's touch before the ceremony, some had even felt a phallus inside of them, but she had not. No man had touched her, no one had even held her.

"Oh, my sweet, you are truly innocent. Wonderful." Gently he pulled her down onto the platform. "Just lie there and let me gaze at you. Let me touch you." He held one hand in his large one. "I will enjoy touching you so much." His hand was soft, not callused like the men of the village. Priests had soft hands as a sign of their office. They didn't do manual labor.

He placed his large hand flat on Rhona's belly and just left it there. Then he leaned over on his elbow and softly touched his lips to her face. Small kisses as soft as the wings of a butterfly dotted her cheeks, her brow, her chin and jaw. Rhona closed her eyes and allowed the moment to carry her along. When his lips touched hers it felt natural for her to open her mouth and invite his tongue inside. She heard him groan as the kiss deepened, and she was thrilled that he seemed to be enjoying what they were doing.

They kissed for a long time, then Chitan's lips moved along Rhona's jaw and down her throat to the tender place where her neck met her shoulder. He kissed her there, then licked the spot, then bit her gently. Strange, she thought, trying to sort out every experience, he kisses and bites me on my neck, but I feel it in my breasts and between my legs. Very strange. Very nice.

His mouth moved, kissing along the top of her shoulder and down her arm. He licked and nibbled at the insides of her elbow and wrist. His soft warm hand was still splayed on her belly, but now he began to softly knead her flesh. His hand slid upwards until his fingers surrounded her breast. He separated his fingers and each took a path from her chest toward her nipple, not yet touching the erect area that now longed for his touch. Again and again he teased her soft skin until she was arching her back each time the fingers moved.

"Yes, little one. You are so responsive. You want it now, don't you?"

She hesitated, then said, "Yes."

Her eyes were closed, but she could hear his sigh and feel him move beside her. Nothing she had thought about this moment had prepared her for the feel of his mouth on her nipple. It was as though there was a direct path from the spot his lips touched to her woman's place between her legs. It felt like warm honey flowed through her body and moistened the deepest parts of her. She moved her hips and felt the slippery wetness flowing from her body.

His mouth moved from one breast to the other and she realized that she wanted. This must be why the gods made my breasts this way, so I would want whatever is to come. "May I?" she said, not knowing exactly what she wanted to do.

Chitan lifted his head. "You may do anything that gives you pleasure, little one."

She didn't know exactly, but she reached up and tangled her fingers in the priest's straight black hair and pulled him to her breast. "Oh, little one, you are wonderful," he said as he returned his mouth to her swollen nipple.

Unable to lie still, Rhona moved her hips, enjoying both the feel of Chitan's mouth and the rubbing of her thighs. Then the priest's hand slowly slid down her belly and through the thick thatch of hair. When one finger again found its way to her center, she almost cried out.

"You are so wet," he whispered, "and ready for loving. Seldom has any woman been so quick to prepare." He paused. "You know what we are going to do, don't you?"

"Yes," she whispered. "I have seen animals do it and, of course, I listen to my parents grunting and laughing at night sometimes."

"I must tell you that the first time a man comes into you there will be some pain."

"Oh," she said.

"But it will be brief and it will be followed by so much pleasure that it will be worth it a thousand times." He slid one finger into her body, then a second. "You are small and so tight. That pleases me."

She said nothing. "None of the boys of the village have convinced you to allow them to do this," he said. "Why not?"

"Because the deflowering ceremony is the most beautiful day in a woman's life and I didn't want to spoil it." His fingers were sliding in and out of her body, making her need and want. "Will you do that now?"

"Do you want me to?"

"Oh yes," she sighed.

He knelt over her. "Open your eyes, little one, and watch as I give you pleasure, and you give it right back to me."

She opened her eyes. Chitan opened his waist sash and allowed his single garment to unwind from his loins. His hard, lean body glistened in the dim light from the lamps. His chest was smooth, his arms strong, his belly flat. Then she saw it, a phallus as large as the ones in the picture. She had peeked at a few boys and they had staffs that were small and soft. This was hard as the branch of a tree. Could this happen? Could this really fit inside of her body?

"Yes, little one, it will fit." He crouched and touched the tip of his swollen rod to the wetness. He grasped her hips and held her tightly and he plunged into her in one swift, sure movement.

Although she had been warned, the pain was startling. It seared through her deepest inside and she let out a small cry. He held still inside her and slowly the heat she had felt before built again, replacing the pain. "Is it easing, little one?" he asked.

"Oh yes," she said and realized that she felt little pain now. He pulled back and slowly pressed himself into her again and again. She was breathless, almost unable to think. He moved and moved and moved. Then his fingers found a special place between her legs that made her weak and strong at the same time. He held his body still and rubbed at the hard spot. He gathered wetness from his staff and again rubbed over her hard nub. She felt herself gathering, like the clouds before a storm. Gathering and growing, boiling and churning. Her body reached for something but she didn't know what it was.

It was colors, or tastes, or feelings. It was all that and more and she stretched and yearned. And then it happened. She broke into a thousand pieces, then rejoined. Again and again, in great pulses she flew apart and reassembled. She heard moaning and realized it was her own voice. She calmed just a bit, reveling in the sensations.

Then Chitan screamed and thrust once more. Some instinct made her keep her body still as she felt his staff pulse and throb within her. His loins pressed and relaxed, over and over. Then, still inside her, he collapsed on the platform beside her.

They lay in silence for a long while. She was incapable of coherent thought so she just felt. Her breasts were a bit sore, as was the passage between her legs. But she felt wonderful. Exquisite. Happy. Dazzlingly happy.

Later, Chitan rose and fetched a pan of warm water. Slowly and carefully he bathed the blood from between Rhona's legs. They sipped some fruit juice together in silence. Then Rhona looked at the picture of the woman about to receive the man's phallus in her mouth. "Can I do that?" she asked.

Chitan grinned at her. "Before you leave here we can try anything in those pictures and anything else you would like. And I will teach you special things you can do to increase your pleasure and mine."

Rhona sighed. It was going to be a wonderful week.

Chapter
2

For the next few days Fran worked at the video store but her mind wasn't in it. Several times Albert, her boss and friend, caught her daydreaming. But, since even he had no idea of her other existence, she wasn't able to tell him about her internal debate.

When Eileen called four nights later, Fran was still vacillating. "Listen," Eileen said, "I've been doing a bit of snooping about that week before the dinner and here's the deal. On Friday night there are parties thrown by the publishers involved. They will be held in the hotel where the conference is held and they're traditionally based on the five books nominated. You're supposed to dress appropriately for the period and characters."

As Eileen talked, Fran pictured herself in a sarong. Not a chance.

"The parties are to hype the books. Lots of press and lots of cover models, both male and female. I went two years ago when Tammy Matterhorn's *Yellow Satin* was nominated. What a sight. Those cover-guy hunks all over the place in period costumes, or parts of them, with their chests bare." She giggled. "Anyway, on Saturday you'll spend the afternoon signing books and generally being charming."

"Is that when they choose Miss Congeniality?" Fran asked, a nasty edge to her voice.

"Easy, Cinderella. It's where fans get to know the authors as real people. You know, what's your favorite color, what do you have in the works, like that. Last year, there was someone there from Home Box Office who, it's said, made the deal to option *The Harrington Women* for a Sunday afternoon movie. You know, the ones they do for football widows."

"Really? They decided on a movie right there?"

"It wasn't just there, but it did happen, partly because of the impression the author made. You know, easy to work with, flexible. She actually worked with the guy who wrote the screenplay. Made a bundle I gather."

"Hmmm." There was real money to be made with the Madison Prize thing, Fran realized. This all added more pressure. She'd have to make a decision. "And *The Harrington Women* didn't even win."

"Right you are. There'll be a lot going on beneath the surface. By the way, are you working on a proposal for another book? You've had quite a long time to think about it."

"I've got several things in the works." Fran had nothing. She had thought herself into exhaustion, but she didn't have an idea large enough for a novel. But she couldn't tell Eileen that she might turn out to be a one-novel author.

"I don't mean to press you, but this would be the ideal time to hit Majestic with a proposal. They are certainly going to be receptive."

"I know. Nicki's working on it." She realized she sounded a bit impatient, but Eileen was beginning to push her. She knew she could write short stories, but the novel thing had been a fluke. She couldn't ever do it again. But with all the publicity that would go into this prize thing, she really could get a good deal. "I'm sorry I'm so snappy. I'm just really hung up on this 'being Nicki' thing."

"You would only have to be a good actor for a few days. You don't have to be Nicki, just play the part in public." There was a short hesitation, then Eileen added, softly, "And there's a whole world for her to explore."

"Museums, the World Trade Center, Broadway."

"Romance. Men. Sex."

"Yes, and sexy men, too," Fran said. She sighed and suddenly said, "I'll do it. I'll talk a good game, be Nicki when I have to and enjoy the hell out of it all." She wondered where those words had come from, but having said them, she felt as though a large weight had been lifted from her.

"Good girl," Eileen said, sounding truly delighted. "Listen. Since you're going to fly here anyway, why don't you take a few weeks. Just yesterday I was talking to a friend of mine who's going to be in Europe on vacation for more than a month. She'd be delighted to let you use her apartment while she's gone. It's in the east Fifties, in a great neighborhood and you'll love it. You'll have time to explore the city and get the feel of the 'good life' that Nicki lives. I won't have much time to spend with you, but I've got a dear friend who has a place just a block away. She's often free during the day and I know you two will hit it off. And she'll be able to guide you with some of the Nicki stuff. You know, ordering in fancy restaurants, wines, all the places you've been. And you'll need Nicki clothes. I know Carla can help you there, too. That's my friend. Carla Barrett. You'll really like her."

Fran sighed again. She felt she was being steamrollered, but she found she didn't really object. It would do her good. She pulled a small calendar out of her purse. "Okay, the prize dinner and presentation ceremony is the 19th of April. Maybe I could get to New York around the 29th of March. That's a Saturday. That would give me three weeks. How would that work?"

"Great." Fran could hear the lift in Eileen's voice. "You will just love it here. New York is the only place to be. For me it beats April in Paris any day."

"And for Nicki?" Fran put on a broad, very phoney-sounding French accent. "Nicki says that eet is Paree or nothing." Both women laughed, but beneath the laughter Fran was both exhilarated and terrified. "I will be there," she said. "I will. And I'll get to meet you face-to-face. And Sandy, too."

"You know," Eileen said, "that amazes me. I feel like we've

known each other for a lifetime, but I've never actually seen you." She hesitated. "Or Nicki."

The two women talked for a while longer, and at several junctures Fran had the urge to tell Eileen that it had all been a mistake and that she was going to stay in Omaha. But she didn't.

After she hung up, Fran lay on the bed and considered what she had gotten herself into. She wanted to do it. She wanted to have people tell her how wonderful her writing was, how much they had enjoyed the book. She wanted that kind of reinforcement. And New York. She had always wanted to see it. Not the cliché tall buildings or the hustle and bustle, but the real New York. Rich people eating at Le Cirque, dancing at the Rainbow Room. Educated people visiting the Metropolitan Museum of Art and Lincoln Center. Refined people always knowing which fork to use and what clever remark to make. Not small town, small person, small Fran Caputo. She'd never fit in. She could never be Nicki. But she could give it a shot. After all, what did she have to lose?

Slowly Fran got up and wandered into the bathroom. She closed the door and faced the mirror on the back of it. She pulled off her sweatshirt and sweatpants, socks and then removed her underpants. Damn it, she thought, looking at her small breasts, I don't even need a bra.

She gazed at herself and tried to be objective. Okay, good points. Slender. Skinny, she muttered. No. Wrong attitude. Slender. Perky breasts. Right. Tiny breasts. All the characters in her stories had large, voluptuous breasts. And legs. They all had long, sexy legs. Fran looked at her legs. She was short. She sighed and cocked her head to one side. "What do you want to be when you grow up?" her parents' friends used to ask her. "Willowy," she would answer, and everyone would laugh.

But that's what I want more than anything. That's what Nicki is, at least in my mind. Tall, slender, graceful. She enters a room and everyone stops to look. Long arms with pianist hands. Long fingers with perfectly oval nails. Coral nail polish that perfectly matches her coral lipstick which blends correctly with the shades of her outfit, all coordinating with her shoes, bag, hose and underwear. All put together to complement her tall, slender body.

I'll never be that Nicki, Fran thought. I can't grow eight inches in a few weeks. I can't have my breasts enlarged. She ran her hands over her small tight mounds and large dusky nipples, then shook her head.

But no one knows what Nicki looks like, she answered herself. Maybe Nicki's short. Maybe she's flat-chested. "Well, she'd better be," Fran said aloud. "Because this is Nicki, for good or bad."

Fran shifted her attention to her face. She turned and looked deeply into the mirror over the sink. Not too bad, she thought, again trying to be objective. Good deep blue eyes, nice skin, good features. But they just aren't quite there. This face has nice parts, but when you put them all together, they are just average. She remembered the way she had described a character in a story she had written. "She had average features. Taken individually they were nothing special, but when combined in that heart-shaped face, they became glorious."

"Well," she said to her reflection, "your face is just the opposite. Good features put together to look ordinary."

She pulled on her sweatshirt, threw her dirty underpants and socks in the hamper and flipped off the light. In the bedroom she turned on the TV and tried not to think about the weeks to come.

Time sped by. Several times Fran picked up the phone to call Eileen, but each time she put the instrument back in its holder. All she could do was the best she could do, and if she didn't pull it off, she would really be no worse off than she was now. And she would have had an amazing adventure.

During her weekly Sunday afternoon phone call with her mother she casually mentioned that she was taking a few weeks off to go to New York.

"New York," her mother said from Denver, "how exciting. What made you decide to do it? I've been after you for a long while to have some fun, but this is so sudden."

"Actually a friend invited me."

Her mother's voice brightened. "A male friend?"

"No, Mom, a girl I knew in school." She had thought out her story over the past several weeks. "We got back in touch through the high school alumni group and we've been e-mailing each other almost every day. She's got a friend with an empty apartment I can use and, well, I just decided to do it."

"Good for you," Fran's mother said. "And maybe you'll meet someone nice."

"Oh Mom," Fran groaned.

"You know, Eric's been gone for a long time. It's time to get out, meet new people."

Little does Mom know, Fran thought, that one of the new people I'll be meeting will be Nicki.

And so it was that the 29th of March found Fran disembarking from a flight to LaGuardia Airport and walking down the long corridor toward the security checkpoint, beyond which Eileen would be waiting. She shifted her small suitcase to her other hand, adjusted her backpack and hustled across the carpet. She surveyed the crowd and saw a woman waving frantically, holding a copy of *The Love Flower* in her hand. Grinning, Fran broke into a trot and, when she reached Eileen, they embraced like long-lost sisters. "I don't believe you're really here," Eileen said as they separated. "Let me look at you."

"Not too much to look at," Fran said. "Just a short drink of water, as my father used to say."

"Hey, I was afraid we'd have to pull this off with a four hundred pound, dumpy, ugly woman. You're wonderful. And with a bit of help and support, you'll be just great."

Fran didn't for a moment buy the line Eileen was feeding her, but she loved to hear it.

Eileen scooped up Fran's suitcase. "You've got more luggage, I assume," she said.

Fran shifted her backpack from one shoulder to the other. "I brought everything I thought might be useful, but one look at you and I realize how Omaha my wardrobe is."

"Oh come now," Eileen said.

Fran looked more carefully at her friend. Eileen was of medium height, but still at least four inches taller than she was, wearing a plum-colored wool pantsuit with a coordinated plum and emerald blouse and a black wool coat. A redhead, Eileen wasn't exactly pretty, but she was a handsome woman who made a statement by just standing there. *She* could be Nicki. Oh God, Fran thought, thinking of her lime-green man-tailored shirt and jeans, with the brown wool blazer and trench coat. I just reek of Omaha. This will never work.

"Listen," Eileen said as she guided Fran toward the baggage carousel, "let's get a few things straight here. You look at me as though I'm some sort of New York model. Just for your information, I'm almost twenty pounds over the maximum healthy weight for my height."

"No, you aren't," Fran said, glancing sideways at Eileen who nodded ruefully.

"I select my clothes very carefully to cover up my thunder thighs and gigantic butt."

Fran stopped in the middle of the crush of people and looked more carefully. When she knew what to look for, she realized that Eileen was, indeed, larger than she should have been around the hips and thighs.

"And," Eileen continued, "I have my hair carefully styled and I've taken classes with a makeup artist who does the faces of all the gorgeous women in *Search for Happiness*. I wear large, but non-dangly earrings so the effect of my short neck is minimized. I'm an illusion. And eventually you will be too. Not all illusion, since you've got a lot to work with, but you'll be so much more than you are now." Eileen laughed. "I've dug myself into this. Help, get me out. I don't mean that you're not attractive now. . . ."

Fran looked, really looked at Eileen and smiled inwardly. Everything her friend had said about her body was true. Maybe, just maybe there was a small chance, a very small chance, that she could pull this off. She shifted her backpack and linked her arm in Eileen's. "I think I love you," she said.

Later, they sat across a tiny table in a small Italian restaurant in the east Fifties. They had spent the better part of two hours talking about everything and nothing, but the subject of her visit, even the name Nichole St. Michelle, had not come up so far.

Eileen finished telling her the latest publishing joke, then said, finally, "Okay, it's time to do a bit of semi-serious planning. The apartment is only a few blocks from here. You can take a few days to get used to the city, visit the museums and such, or we can get this Nicki thing started now. What's your pleasure? But just remember that we have only three weeks to create Nicki. Actually two, since I told Sandy you'd be arriving on the 12th. She wants to see you as soon as you're settled, which will mean lunch probably that Monday."

"I hate deceiving her."

"I know, but it's all an illusion. Let's talk about how you'll present yourself when we get closer to the date. So what's it going to be?"

"You know I'd love to crawl into the apartment and curl into a little ball, but I can't." She took a deep breath. "If I'm going to do this, let's get this show on the road."

"Good girl." Eileen squeezed Fran's hand and stood up. She looked at her watch. "I told Carla I'd probably be calling around two o'clock and it's just two-fifteen." She grinned. "I'm not half bad. I'll be right back." Eileen walked quickly toward the front of the restaurant, fumbling in her purse. As she reached the coat check, she brandished a coin and grinned back at Fran.

As she waited, Fran thought, I think I can, I think I can, I think I can.

Eileen arrived back at the table and said, "She's on her way over. You'll love Carla. She's actually got some time free and she's anxious to give you a hand with everything."

"Tell me about her. Is she an old friend of yours?"

"I've known Carla for about two years, since she sort of moved into a brownstone next door to my building. We started running into each other at the cleaners, the supermarket and we just got to talking. She's actually from Bronxville, widowed with three great kids, all boys. I took a day off last fall and we all went to the Big Apple Circus together. I thought the kids would be jaded, there's so much on TV and all, but we were all delighted, dazzled and amazed."

"Does she have a husband?"

"Not anymore. He died several years ago."

"Oh. That's too bad. What does she do for a living? Or is she wealthy?" Inwardly, Fran winced. Am I going to be tutored by some rich New York socialite who's deigning to educate some small-town hick? I don't think so. She brought her mind back to Eileen. "I mean it must be tough raising three boys and having two homes."

"It's a long story and I'll let Carla tell you all about it. Oh, and wait until you see her brownstone. It's got all sorts of unusual amenities."

They chatted for a few minutes and then Fran noticed that Eileen's attention had strayed toward the front door. Just inside, handing a camel colored coat to the coat check woman, stood a statuesque woman in her late thirties. She was immaculately dressed, wearing a pair of pale beige wool slacks and a soft deep-gold blouse with a medium-brown wool vest. She wore heavy gold earrings and a matching neck chain. She might be a bit over-done for midafternoon, Fran thought, but it's so put-together. I know I'm going to hate her and then how do I get out of spending time with her. Eileen's already set all this up. I feel like I've just seen my blind date and I can't stand him.

Eileen waved and the woman walked over and took the third seat at their table. She hugged Eileen warmly, then turned to Fran. "You must be Nicki. I'm Carla Barrett. I read your book and, well, wow. I'm a devoted fan." Her smile was wide and warm and Fran couldn't help but be warmed by it. "I can't put two coherent English sentences together without them sounding like a breakfast cereal commercial."

"Actually my name's Fran Caputo. Nicki's an alter ego and not really me at all."

"I know that," Carla said, "but Nicki's the woman who's going to win The Madison Prize."

Eileen added, "And Carla's just the person to help you become Nicki. I can guarantee it."

"Look," Carla said. "This is really awkward for both of us. So let's just chat for a while, and I'll tell you what I think I can do to help. If you think you want to let me, that's great. If not, well, I'll understand. I don't want you to feel pressured in any way."

Fran felt herself relax. She had a way out. But did she want to take it? This woman wasn't at all what she had expected.

Eileen leaned forward. "Carla, how are the boys?" To Fran she added, "They're all teenagers."

"They're teenaged boys." She shook her head. "BJ's fifteen now and so damn precocious I can't stand it. Since he started high school he's got girls calling him at all hours. He has his own phone so at least I have some peace."

"And Tommy?"

"Please," Carla said, rolling her eyes, "it's Tom. Tommy is for children and, at thirteen, he's all grown up. At least according to him. He'll be in high school next fall and he's already impossible. Thank heavens for Mike. At twelve he's my baby, and he never changes. He's still a jock. Softball, tennis, swimming. Even though my mother does a lot of the chauffeuring, it still seems I am in the car from the time school is out to dinnertime and often after. I never thought I'd say this, but I can't wait until BJ can drive and help out. Fortunately my darlings are all otherwise occupied for the day."

"Do they look like you?" Fran asked, thinking about how handsome they must be.

"BJ does, but Mike and Tom look more like their father."

"I gather you're a widow," Fran said. "It must be difficult."

"Sometimes is it, but my folks help out a lot. My husband's been gone for a lot of years and I've gotten very used to being the boys' only parent."

"I'm sorry."

"I'm not," Carla said. "My husband was not a very nice man

and it was actually a relief when he was killed in an accident." She waved a carefully manicured hand. "Past history."

"It must be nice to have a place in the city. You can see shows and visit friends."

Carla giggled and looked at Eileen. "How much have you told her?"

"Actually, nothing. I thought your lifestyle was yours to tell." Eileen stood up. "Listen ladies, I have things to do and places to go. Why don't you get to know each other and then I'll meet you two at your place, Carla, at say . . ." She looked at her watch. ". . . six-thirty? Then maybe the three of us can have dinner and afterward I can show Fran the apartment. Or do you have plans Carla?"

Carla winked. Some secret joke? Fran wondered. Carla said, "Actually I do have plans for the evening, but before then I would love to have some time to get to know Fran. Why don't I take her over to my place and explain a few things? Six-thirty works well since I have to be uptown around eight."

Fran felt a bit pressured again, but brushed the feeling away. Somehow she knew that she could tell Carla that she didn't want to spend time with her and Carla wouldn't be insulted.

"That okay with you, Fran?" Carla asked.

Carla was a nice enough person and what harm could a little chatting do? "Of course." To Eileen she said, "You go and do your errands and we'll see you at six-thirty. I suspect we'll have a much better idea of future plans by then."

"Okay, I'll see you a bit later," Eileen said, blew the two women a kiss and hustled off. A kiss into the air. That's so New York, Fran thought.

As Fran fought down a moment of panic Carla waved at the waiter and ordered a cup of coffee and a piece of extremely gooey pastry. "Have something," she said.

"I'm still on Omaha time and I was up at six to make an eight-thirty flight. I think I left my stomach somewhere over Pennsylvania."

"More coffee then?"

"It's tea, and yes, I'll take some hot water." Fran reached into an outside compartment of her backpack and pulled out a plastic bag filled with tea bags. When she saw Carla looking at her, she said, "I carry my own herb tea. I can't have caffeine. It gives me migraines."

"Nasty. But you seem well prepared. That sounds like a wonderful little affectation for Nicki." Carla cocked her head to one side. "I cannot abide caffeine," she said in a deliberately lowered voice. "It does such terrible things to the system."

The two women laughed while the waiter served them. As Carla buried her fork in a mountain of whipped cream, she looked seriously at Fran. "Tell me a little about yourself. Eileen tells me you are divorced."

"Eric and I split several years ago. I'm not sure whether it was over or whether it never really started. We had known each other since high school and drifted into marriage because everyone, including us, expected us to."

"Kids?"

"No, thank heavens."

"Hey, don't put kids down. I love mine."

"I'd like to have a husband and kids someday. I'm just glad, since the marriage didn't work out, that there were no children to be tossed around and used as weapons. This way Eric and I have no ties. I got the toaster oven and the microwave, he got the canoe. And that was that."

"I gather it wasn't a particularly good marriage."

Fran thought for a moment. "No," she admitted. "But it wasn't really bad either. It just was."

"And your sex life? That, at least, must have been great, judging from your writing."

"Actually, no. It wasn't. The increasingly infrequent roll over, fondle here and there, and then do it."

"Other men?"

"Nope. Eric was my one and only."

Carla looked startled. "You're kidding. I've read *The Love Flower* and I just assumed that you wrote from experience."

"It comes from reading quantities of romance novels, and erotic stories and learning at a distance. Sort of vicarious orgasm."

Carla laughed. "This makes things a bit more awkward. Eileen didn't tell you about me at all?"

"Only that you were a friend she had met in the neighborhood."

"There's lots more to the story." Carla put a mouthful of cake and cream into her mouth and closed her eyes. "I don't normally eat things like this," she said, her mouth full, "but I'm treating myself today. Tomorrow, the gym."

"You look like you don't have to diet."

"Sweetie, only women who are wonderfully slender like you can think like that. I'll bet you never had to lose a pound in your life. I envy you."

"I guess I never have had to lose weight," Fran said, not having ever considered her tiny body an advantage. "I've always wanted to gain, particularly in certain places." She glanced down the front of her green shirt.

"You mean the bosom? I'd love to lose a bit there. I wonder whether there's some way I could give you some."

"You have a great shape," Fran said seriously. "I always wanted to be, well, let's just say, well endowed."

"You mean like Rhona? She was really built."

Fran smiled. "I guess my characters look the way I wish I looked."

"The grass is always greener," Carla said, putting another mouthful of rich cake into her mouth. While Carla chewed, Fran dunked her tea bag in the pot of hot water the waiter had brought and added a packetful of sugar.

"Oh Lord, this is wonderful," Carla said. "Okay. I've been putting this off long enough." She put her fork down and leaned a bit closer to Fran. "I have to tell you why Eileen thought I'd be right for this project. You see, Fran, I'm a prostitute."

The teapot Fran had been holding stopped in midair, halfway to her cup. Unable to speak, she just stared.

"Pour your tea," Carla said, "and I'll explain."

Fran poured the tea, knowing there was no way this woman could ever explain.

"I'm a very high-priced, well, let's call me a lady-of-the-evening. I entertain men for a living, and a very nice living it is."

"You're kidding. You've got to be kidding. I mean you have kids. You're so . . ."

"Normal?"

Fran looked down as she put the teapot back on the table. "Well," she said, "yes. I don't understand. I've read about the Mayflower Madam and Heidi Fleiss, but, well, that's another world and it's not populated with real people."

"I'm a real person," Carla said, "and I earn a great deal of money being a living fantasy for special men. All my customers come highly recommended, friends of friends. They're out-of-town businessmen, people who believe their wives wouldn't be interested in the activities they enjoy and people without partners who want to have a good time."

Fran took a deep breath. This beautiful, statuesque woman was a hooker. It was almost too much to take in. "How? Why?"

"How? I'll show you at my place. Why? Why not? I love making love, in all ways, shapes and forms, so why shouldn't I get paid for it? I please men in ways they've not been pleased before, so no one gets hurt."

"Their wives. They get hurt."

"I always counsel my 'friends' to discuss their desires with their wives, but so many men are in humdrum relationships and don't think there's any chance of communicating with their wives about anything. So if it weren't me, it would be someone else. And I know that with me they will have a good time, get their money's worth and it won't get serious."

"But what about AIDS? In my stories, the men who fool around wear condoms, and in *The Love Flower* sexually transmitted diseases didn't exist."

"Or they were just ignored. But my friends always wear condoms and I'm very careful about new people for lots of reasons."

"Isn't what you do illegal? Don't you worry about the police?"

"Occasionally I think about it, but I don't worry. The contributions the men make are voluntary. I don't 'charge for services,' but I request a token of affection. So, in my mind at least, I don't solicit."

"But what if they don't pay?"

"If they don't pay, they don't get to come back. And all my friends want to come back, so it's very seldom that I'm not paid. And if they don't pay, oh well. I make enough that the occasional deadbeat isn't a problem."

"Amazing."

Carla nodded, then scraped the last bite of cake from the plate and sensuously sucked the final remnants from her fork. She sipped her coffee, then said, "Why don't we wander over to my brownstone and I'll tell you more when we get there?"

Efficiently, with only a token protest from Fran, Carla paid the check and the two women walked to the front of the restaurant. Carla got her coat and Fran retrieved her trench coat and suitcases. "I'll take the big one if you can manage your backpack and the small one," Carla said, taking charge of Fran's larger piece. "My place is only two blocks away, and we can grab a cab if you want."

Fran formed a mental picture of this impeccable woman hefting her Kmart suitcase. "I can get all this stuff. I managed to get to the airport."

"Not a chance." Carla lifted the suitcase while Fran shouldered her backpack and took the smaller one. "Do you always use a backpack instead of a purse?"

"No, but I thought it would be easier for traveling. You see I brought my laptop computer so I could write while I'm here." The two women stepped out of the restaurant into a raw, cold, blustery March day, so, with necks withdrawn beneath collars, they walked the two blocks to Carla's place in a companionable silence.

Fran was a bit winded by the time they reached the brownstone on East 54th Street. The building was three stories tall, well kept, with a small patch of grass in front. Carla opened the front door and, still toting the suitcase, guided Fran into the living room.

"Wow, this is really gorgeous," Fran said, looking around. The room was done in white, black and gray, with black and white geometric pillows everywhere. The walls were covered with something soft-looking and gray. Without a thought Fran set her suitcase down, walked over and ran her hand over the wall covering. Silk. This place must have cost a fortune, she thought.

To keep the room from looking sterile, there were plants on almost every horizontal surface. Ferns, ivies and several large ficuses, mixed with vases of freshly cut blooms in all colors. "This is really lovely," she said.

"You look the way I must have the first time I saw this room. Actually I had nothing to do with it. A friend of mine had it all done before I ever visited." Carla took Fran's coat and motioned toward the black leather sofa. "Sit and relax." She quickly hung up the two coats and returned to the living room. "I'm sure you've got a million questions and I'll answer them all in due course." As Fran kicked off her shoes, Carla asked, "How about a glass of white wine? I'm going to pour myself one."

Wine? In the middle of the afternoon? Why not? "Sure. That would be fine." Fran tucked her feet beneath her and realized that, for some reason, she felt at home here.

Carla reached into a small refrigerator almost hidden in the corner and brought out a green bottle. She quickly and efficiently used a corkscrew to remove the cork and poured two glasses. "This is a nice Chardonnay. Good for drinking alone, but a bit much, in my opinion, for having with food." She handed Fran the glass. When Fran took it Carla said, "If you don't mind a suggestion, Nicki would know to hold the glass by the stem, not by the bowl."

Fran shifted her grip. "Okay. I'll bite. Why?"

"A few reasons. Most important, a white wine is served chilled because the flavors are meant to be consumed cool. If you hold the glass by the bowl, you warm the wine and it doesn't taste as good. Also, wine is meant to be enjoyed using all the senses. If you get finger marks all over the glass, the wine won't look as good."

"Sounds reasonable." She sipped the wine and found she really liked the taste.

"You didn't come here for lessons in wine. Yet. That all comes later. Right now, you want to know who I am and what this is all about. Let me start from the beginning.

"About two and a half years ago I ran into my old college roommate. Actually ran into is the right expression. I smashed into the side of her car. But, to make a long story short, ultimately she explained that she was a very high-priced call girl. I was widowed, just above the poverty line and I did, and still do, enjoy sex a lot. So Ronnie, that's her name, convinced me to play. Gradually she introduced me to the world of sensuality and, as they say, the rest is history."

Although she didn't, Fran wanted to seem to understand. "Where's Ronnie now?"

"She's on a large yacht, moored somewhere in the Mediterranean for a month with an Arab prince. She was married but it didn't work out."

"Is she being paid for her visit on the yacht?"

Carla looked startled. "Of course."

Fran took another sip of her wine. "Oh."

"I know," Carla said, grinning, "your mind is blown. Actually I don't blame you. It took me a lot of time and soul searching to decide to join her in this business. But I haven't been sorry for a moment. I make my own hours and set my own rules. I have lots of time and money to indulge my children and, of course, myself."

"So you do it for the money," Fran said, struggling to comprehend.

"I do it for the money and because I thoroughly enjoy it."

"You enjoy having sex with strange men, doing kinky, perverted things." The words were out before Fran could censor them.

Not looking as annoyed as Fran thought she should be after

that thoughtless remark, Carla said, "Hey slow down. Let's understand a few things here. Kinky and perverted are in the mind of the beholder. One man's perversion is another's normal activity. I don't judge another's actions. My only rule is that I won't do anything that doesn't turn me on. But most things *do* turn me on. Okay, I can't get into toilet sports or pain." Carla looked away for a moment. "Actually I can't even say that anymore either. But that's a story for another time."

"That's a lot to digest," Fran said, putting her wineglass on a black lacquer end table. "I guess my Omaha is showing."

"Not at all. It was a lot for me to digest when I first learned about Ronnie. Now it seems so normal."

"Does your family know?"

"My folks do. They finally asked a few blunt questions and I decided to stop dancing around the topic. They surprised me. They aren't big fans of my occupation, but they see that I'm happy and healthy and that the boys are great so they don't complain."

"Didn't they ask you to stop?"

"Once very briefly. But now they treat me like a grown-up able to make my own decisions."

A quick picture of her mother flashed through Fran's mind. Never. She couldn't even tell her about *The Love Flower.* "So how does this all work? I'm just so curious. Do men come here? Do you go to hotel rooms?"

"No one comes here until I know them and have spent at least one evening with them. I'm sure you can see why. I don't want anyone to know where I live until I'm sure about them."

"I guess I understand."

"You don't have to understand my 'profession.' But what I do with men and the knowledge I have about everything from cigars and wine to how to dress and how to flirt will make Nicki what you want her to be."

"Eileen told you everything?"

"She told me about you and Nichole St. Michelle and the Madison Prize and the weekend. Congratulations, by the way.

She tells me that it's a great honor to be nominated. Eileen also said you want to be able to act like Nicki would. Right?"

"Right. Act like Nicki." She swallowed. A small voice was whispering in her ear, telling her that that wasn't completely true. She had listened to Carla and the lifestyle excited her. God, she thought, wouldn't it be nice to *be* Nicki, free with men and sex. Her ex-husband had always told her she was a dud in bed, but maybe Carla could teach her. As quickly as that idea crept into her mind, Fran squashed it. It was one thing to write about hot sex, it was another to live it.

"Having second thoughts? We don't have to do this at all. I'm sure that Eileen can help you with a wardrobe and some makeup lessons." Carla patted Fran's hand. "You don't have to deal with me or my life. Later, when Eileen arrives, you two can have dinner and she'll get you settled into her friend's apartment and that will be that."

As Fran hesitated, Carla stood up. "Don't be embarrassed. The things I've told you about aren't everyone's taste." Carla walked toward the windows. "It's really okay."

Fran stood and walked up behind Carla. "If you must know, what scares me is that I'm too intrigued. This is so far out of my league, but I'll admit that it titillates me. I write about steamy sex, and I'm good at that, the writing that is. But most of it is soft, warm and completely heterosexual and vanilla. And even that's mostly from my imagination. I never thought I'd meet someone who lives in an atmosphere like this. It's exciting and scary and I don't know exactly how to react.

"I always thought of hookers wearing spandex and supporting a drug habit. Or maybe in an evening gown entertaining rock stars. I just never thought of a real person being a prostitute."

Carla turned and smiled. "Thanks for being so honest. Actually, when Ronnie told me what she did for a living, I had pretty much the same feelings. And if you're anything like I was, you're curious as hell and that scares the daylights out of you."

"I really am both intrigued and terrified. I feel like I'm visiting my first bakery and all I can do is look at all the pastry. I want to know how it all tastes, but I don't want to do the tasting, so I can learn from you."

The two women crossed the room and resumed their seats on the sofa. "Okay, ask me questions and I'll answer them as honestly as I can."

"How does it work? What exactly do the men want? Are they all into tit-fucking, anal sex and blow jobs." To Carla's startled expression, Fran quickly added, "Sorry. Pardon the language but I do write about this stuff and I read lots of stories from the Internet. Words aren't the problem."

"Obviously," Carla said. "The men I entertain want all of that and lots more."

"So how do you know what they want? Do they tell you?"

"Here. Let me show you what makes Ronnie and me so unusual." Carla rose and opened a drawer in an antique rolltop desk that sat in the corner of the room. It should look out of place, Fran thought, in a black and white, leather and lacquer room, but it doesn't. Carla returned with a large photo album with a soft rose suede cover. "I've replaced the pictures and the whole album several times. I've given away a few of the old ones to really good customers who like to look at the photos between times." She placed the album on Fran's lap. "Open it and have a look."

Fran opened the cover and gazed at the first picture, an eight by ten of a woman in full Egyptian garb, diaphanous gown, thick black wig and stark black and red makeup. The gown was just transparent enough for Fran to be able to see the shadows of the woman's dark nipples and triangle of dark hair at the apex of her thighs.

She turned the page. The next photograph was of a woman in a shiny red bodysuit, which covered her from neck to wrists and ankles. It was so tight and sexy that it was as though she were naked. She brandished a pair of handcuffs and a small riding crop. In the background Fran could make out a set of wooden stocks. The woman smiled but it was a slightly malevolent smile.

Fran turned another page. It was, in its own way, a mirror

image of the last. A naked woman was kneeling, imprisoned in the stocks Fran had noticed in the previous picture. Her wrists and neck were trapped by the wooden frame which was held closed with a large shiny padlock. Her legs were spread and held parted by a wide wooden bar which was locked to each ankle. Her face was turned toward the camera and her expression was a mixture of terror and excitement. Her eyes were closed and her tongue just extended between her lips.

"My Lord," Fran whispered, "that's you." She continued to turn pages. There were photos of Carla with various toys, with parts of men's anatomy in every possible orifice. One had her sitting on a man's face, another of her straddling a man's loins, obviously pleasuring herself with his cock. Fran kept turning the pages. There were a few photos of two women pleasuring each other, and several of Carla with two or three men. The last photo in the book was of Carla lying on a large white-fur-covered bed, with her hand between her legs, an expression of pure joy on her face.

Fran looked at Carla then at the photo in front of her. "They are all you."

"Yes, and that's sort of my menu. My customers, I prefer to call them my friends, can look through the album and select what they want without ever telling me directly what their desires are. It's often difficult for a cultured man to say that he wants to fuck my ass, or have me smack him with a Ping-Pong paddle. I'll play Maid Marion or a virginal bride. They can rape me, or tie me up. I've been to parties where the object was to make it with as many men as possible, and I've been on a cruise during which I belonged to a man who lent me out to his friends."

"Have you done everything that's in these pictures?"

"Just about." Carla sipped her wine, while Fran digested everything. "Listen, this must be a bit much for you all at once. Why don't you take some time to think about everything while I make a pit stop?"

Carla disappeared and Fran lay her head back against the sofa cushions. It was mind-boggling. She had always thought that because she wrote the kind of stories she did, she knew a lot about sex. She was just a baby. This woman was not only varied in her activities, she was comfortable with all of it. Fran thought over the stories she had written, including the sexual encounters in *The Love Flower*. All were heterosexual. Very steamy, with the lovers making love in every conceivable position and location, but they were all so conventional. These photos created some of the most erotic images in her head. She closed her eyes. Nicki could write so many stories . . .

But could she write them without first-hand knowledge? Could she write about a woman in bondage without having been tied up? How about a woman controlling a man or being controlled? She sighed. Of course she could, but she had to admit that she was titillated more than as a writer. She was just plain curious. Nicki would have done all these things. Nicki, world traveler, experienced with princes and maharajas. So far Nicki was all a figment of Fran's imagination. But what if . . .

She heard the whisper of Carla's footsteps in the deep pile carpet and opened her eyes.

"I thought you were asleep. I assumed that the jet lag had gotten to you."

"No. I was just thinking about me and about Nicki." She paused and sighed.

"And . . ."

"And . . . well . . . I was thinking that Nicki has probably done many of the things you illustrate in your album. And if I want to be like Nicki, maybe I have to experience some of the things that Nicki has. Maybe I have to be comfortable inside of Nicki's skin."

"I gather that you've led a pretty sheltered life," Carla said. "This is sort of like moving from a life of TV dinners to lobster and champagne."

"I guess you're right. It's like moving from Omaha to New York. There's no one here I know, so if anything really embarrassing happens I can crawl back home with no one the wiser."

Carla and Fran looked at each other for a few moments. Then

Carla said, "If that's what you want, I can certainly introduce you to the world of off-center sex. Or rather I have friends who would be only too happy to."

Fran snapped back to reality. She sat up straight, looked down at herself and shook her head.

"Don't do that," Carla said quickly. "I can see the wheels turning. You're thinking, 'I can't. I'm not beautiful enough.' Bullshit, if you'll pardon me for being blunt. You can be whatever you want to be."

"Oh please," Fran said, now feeling defeated. "I'm five foot nothing and flat-chested. I've always wanted to be tall and built. But I'm not. You can't make a silk purse . . ."

"Out of a sow's ear," Carla finished for her. "But I'm not trying to make silk purses and you are certainly not a sow's ear. I have several friends who, although they enjoy my body, wish I were petite." Carla stood up. "Me—petite? Never. Not a chance. But you . . ."

"Hmm. I must admit that I like the term petite better than short."

"Men would want to cherish you. Or be dominated by you. Yes. Certainly. Imagine a man who's always wanted to feel powerless. Picture his delight when he's rendered powerless by someone who's as tiny as you are." She giggled. "How delightfully wicked."

"Do you really think so?" Fran hesitated. "Not the domination part. I don't know about that. But do you think a man would really want a tiny busted woman like me?"

"No sweat. I would like to have your hair redone. And you need help with your makeup. And your choice of clothes is all wrong for someone of your size." She paused. "You know, I've always wanted to be able to wear five-inch heels. I've seen them in the foot fetish magazines. But with most men, I like to be shorter than they are and I'm already almost five-five. But you could pull it off so well."

Fran cupped her almost nonexistent breasts. "What about these?"

"You're obsessing about your bosom, but I guess I can understand. Men think big breasts are great. We'll get you a Wonderbra and create some cleavage. But once a man's hooked, the size of the fisherwoman really doesn't matter. It's her talent with the bait that got him and her skill with her equipment that will please him."

Fran laughed. "You really think I can pull this off, don't you. Not just pretend to be Nicki but actually lead her life, men and all."

"I think you're curious about good sex and that you've had an itch for years that never got scratched. I think that you're intrigued and titillated and yes, I think you want to do this. But I also want to give you some time to digest. We don't have much time since the dinner is only three weeks away." Carla looked at the small gold watch she wore. "It's almost time for Eileen to pick you up. Have dinner with her and get settled in the apartment. I've got kid duty tomorrow. Let's see, two to soccer practice, one to the mall, then later one to a friend's house and one home for several hours then to the mall as well. Phew."

"It sounds exhausting."

"It is, but great. They are such good kids that I would bust my butt for them. I'll call you sometime late tomorrow and we'll figure out next week."

As if on cue, the doorbell rang. As Carla rose, Fran said, "Eileen mentioned that your brownstone has some unique things about it. Beside you and your album . . . well I was just curious about what else is here."

As Carla left, she said, over her shoulder, "Soon I promise I'll play show and tell."

Chapter
3

Fran enjoyed dinner with Eileen tremendously. It was as though the two women had been friends for years. She felt as if she knew Eileen's husband Don, her two daughters, her friends, her business and in many ways Fran felt she had missed a lot. She hadn't meant to wall herself off from people, but now she realized that she had. She worked, she wrote, she talked to her mother and sister, but in reality, she had few friends. Oh, she went to a movie or to dinner occasionally with someone she recently met, but it never seemed to blossom into anything more. With Eileen, she felt a kinship that went deeper than anything she had felt in years. And, she thought, she felt that way with Carla, although they had only met that day.

Across the small table, Eileen was sipping her coffee. "What did you think of Carla? And it's really all right to be honest. If you didn't like her or her . . . shall we say, lifestyle, we can try to put everything together ourselves. She really is Nicki in some ways and that's why I thought of her. But I don't want you to feel coerced in any way."

Fran smiled. "I like Carla a lot. It's like some kind of immediate bond."

"I feel a 'but' at the end of that sentence. You don't approve of her?"

"There really was no 'but' on that sentence, except for me and what I want to do. And what I *can* do."

"What did she propose?"

"She didn't suggest, I did and she agreed. She thinks I can become some kind of sexual sophisticate, like Nicki is. A woman of the world. I thought when I got off the plane that I was just going to learn how to talk a good game. But she said that I could actually do it."

"I thought she might. From our phone conversations I thought you wouldn't be too put off. But it's not a necessary thing. However, it might just be good for you."

"That's pretty much what Carla said. And I will admit I'm curious and more than a little aroused by the prospect. But I'm still a little woman who grew up in a farming community. This is a bit much for me."

"Your choice, babe," Eileen said. "Definitely your choice." She signaled for the check. "And only you know what you want to do. So let's get out of here and I'll show you the apartment. It's only a block from here. Then I'll get home to my family and you can do some serious thinking."

Toting Fran's suitcases and backpack, the two women walked through the cold March wind to a multistoried building on Fifty-second between First and Second avenues. Eileen showed her how to open the heavy front door and introduced her to the man on the night security desk. They took the elevator to the eighteenth floor and Eileen used a key to open the door to 18C. She handed the key to Fran, then walked into the tiled entranceway and flipped on the light. Fran could only gasp.

The hallway opened into a large living room warmly decorated in shades of soft blues and greens, with a nubby tan carpet and two large sofas upholstered in soft oatmeal fabric. Eileen flipped on another light and Fran stared at the bronze statue that was now carefully lit with a wall of beige drapes as a backdrop. The life-size statue was of a man, and what a man he was. He was dressed only in a pair of jeans, standing wiping his face as if after some great exertion. His upper body was absolutely gorgeous, not in the Greek god mold, but very, very human. Fran thought of the Coke commercial that had been so popular a while before. A construction worker taking a break from his sidewalk smashing to have a drink, and all the women in the surrounding offices taking time to look at him. God, he was a sexy man and it was almost as though the artist had taken him and dipped him in bronze. Although there was nothing indecent about the statue at all, Fran's body tingled.

"AnneMarie is really quite famous for her work," Eileen said. "Actually that's why she and her husband are in Europe. She's been commissioned to create a statue for the front of some museum in Amsterdam. Her work isn't all this erotic. Most is just of people, going about their jobs. This one is actually of her husband and it's only for private consumption."

"AnneMarie. You mean AnneMarie Devlin? I'm borrowing an apartment from AnneMarie Devlin? I saw a big article about her in my Sunday paper. She's world famous." She reached down and picked up the backpack she had just set down.

"She's a peach and a really nice woman and she's an old and dear friend. Actually we went to high school together, and, if the truth be known, I introduced her to Barry." She pointed to the statue. "AnneMarie and I were both at NYU and we had remained good friends despite AnneMarie's art major and my major in English Lit. I had just met Don, and I sort of gave Barry to AnneMarie. I called it a double date but I invited both guys. Tacky of me, but it worked." She chuckled. "Actually we each got the best of that deal. We each married the man and have been happy for almost ten years."

"Phew," Fran said, now standing with her backpack in her hand. "What if I break something? I expected a small apartment, not a museum."

"Come on. Let me show you the rest." Eileen led Fran to the master bedroom, a much more normal room all done in country motifs with blue and white print covering one chair and the bedclothes. The bathroom was all done in ducks. Towels, bath mats, soap, everything was soft blue with dozens of little yellow ducks.

"This is certainly different from the living room."

"About as different as the two sides of AnneMarie. The front room, the dining room and the guest bath are for show. This end of the apartment is for AnneMarie and Barry. Come with me." Eileen led Fran further down a hallway and opened another door. "This is the guest room. Don and I stayed here for a week while I was having my apartment painted. It's comfortable and shouldn't be too intimidating." She turned on the light.

The room was tastefully simple. It was done in shades of brown, from the lightest eggshell to the deep chocolate of the bed covers. The dresser and bed frame were light ash, as was the exposed frame of the love seat that filled one corner. Eileen pulled open a drawer. "These are all empty, as is the closet. Feel free to use whatever you want. I stopped by yesterday afternoon and made sure you were well stocked. There's soap and toothpaste in the bathroom, as well as some bath goodies and such. Oh, and wait till you see the tub." She pulled Fran toward the bathroom door and again turned on the light.

"Good Lord, it's big enough for a party," Fran said.

"AnneMarie had a small maid's room ripped out and combined with the existing bath to create this. I've spent many happy hours in that tub." The tub was black, with what Fran assumed were air and water jets in the sides. There was an elaborate panel of controls on the wall at one side. The shower was glass enclosed and the double sink and toilet were also black. The tile, which covered the lower half of the walls, was white and the upper half was wallpapered in a slick-surfaced paper patterned in white, red and black. There were towels everywhere, white and thick. It should be almost sterile, but instead it looked like something out of an erotic story. She could see a couple playing some very kinky games in this room. She thought about the laptop in her backpack. What a story she could write about this room.

"Yes," Eileen said, "Don and I played in here several times. We were actually sorry to leave."

Fran looked at her friend and watched her face flush. "You're blushing."

"Not blushing actually. It's just that a few of those memories are very special. I think I'll have to remind Don about that week when I get home later."

Suddenly content, Fran walked back into the bedroom and dropped onto the love seat. "Listen, I've kept you too long already. You go home. I'll be fine." And she knew now that she would, whatever she decided to do.

"You're not intimidated by the apartment anymore?"

She grinned. "I think I could get used to this place." She would stay in only this room and be really careful of everything. She also sensed that the bathroom had brought back memories that Eileen wanted to share with her husband. "Go home."

"There's a kitchen at the other side of the entranceway and I put a few munchables in the fridge. The cupboards are well stocked and please just use anything you want. We can restock together before you leave. The phone's got unlimited local service so you can use it whenever you like. Actually it's Barry's modem and fax line so there is no danger of any of their calls coming in on it. They have a different number for themselves and they've got a service monitoring that one so all those phones are unplugged." Eileen pointed to the small black box on the bed table. "I even lent you an answering machine. You can put in whatever message you like. Right now it just says the phone number and, 'I can't come to the phone so leave a message,' in my voice."

Fran stood up and wrapped her arms around Eileen. "It seems you've thought of everything. You're a wonderful friend," she said. "And I suspect that this is going to be one hell of a few weeks."

Eileen kissed her on her cheek. "You and Nicki are going to have quite a time." Then she left.

Fran retrieved her suitcases from the front hallway, wandered into the living room and gazed at the still-lit statue. He's the sex-

iest thing I've seen in a long time, she thought. She couldn't resist the temptation to stand beside the lifesize man and touch his
hairless chest. The bronze was cool to the touch, but almost felt
alive. She placed her hand flat against his pectoral muscles, so
carefully defined by the artist, and caressed him. It must be Carla
and all this, she thought as she felt herself getting excited.

As she usually did when she was sexually aroused, she wanted
to write. She turned off all the lights and retired to the guest bedroom. She quickly plugged in and opened her laptop and placed
it on the bed. As it booted up, she kicked off her shoes, pulled off
her jeans and settled cross-legged. She thought about her story
and then, when the word processing program was ready, she
began to type furiously.

Terry stood in the museum and stared at the statue.
Apollo, the sign said and he was, in fact, a Greek god. Although carved from a block of cold marble, his body looked
warm, almost alive. His arms were strong and beautifully
muscled, his legs were long, an athlete's legs. His groin was
covered by a leaf, but she knew that he was well endowed.
She walked around to his back and gazed at his buttocks
and the muscle definition in his back and shoulders. Slowly,
she circled the statue, eyes gazing where her fingers itched
to touch. It was as if she knew that, had he been alive, they
would be together forever.

The statue was illuminated by a shaft of sunlight that fil-
tered through a dusty window and Terry settled herself on a
bench and watched the changing light alter and reform the
marble. It was late summer and it was already early evening
by the time the light left her god. Finally she sighed, rose
and, before the long ride home, stepped into the ladies'
room.

When she came out the museum was silent. She thought
she could make out a single set of footsteps, a measured,
leisurely pace. She looked at her watch and understood. It
was past closing time. She looked around and noticed that

the lights had been dimmed. How would her god look in this soft glow? She walked back to the gallery and gazed at the statue. The low light made him seem all the more real. His skin glowed like real skin. His eyes were warm and invited her to move closer.

Incapable of resisting the attraction of his eyes, she walked to the pedestal and touched the statue's calf. It was warm beneath her fingers. How was that? It might appear warm, but it was, after all, just stone.

"Not just stone, Lovely," a voice said.

Thinking she had been caught touching a valuable work of art she whirled, an apology leaping to her lips. "I'm so sorry. I just . . ." But the gallery was empty.

Okay, she thought. I'm losing it. Let me get home. I'm sure I can find someone to let me out of here.

"Don't go yet, Lovely," the voice said again.

"What's going on?" she asked, her voice quavering. "Is this some sort of bad acoustical joke?"

"No," the voice said again. "It's just my time now. Look up."

Terry tipped her chin and looked at the statue's face. The eyes were looking at her and appeared almost alive. The mouth didn't move, yet the statue said, "Step on my pedestal and kiss my lips."

"You're kidding," she said aloud. "I'll bet you guards have a lot of fun with this. It's like one of those large rooms where you can whisper in one place and, although no one in between can hear, the voice is clear as a bell somewhere across the room."

"It's not a joke or a trick," the voice said. "Please. Do it for me, for us."

Again Terry's eyes took in the entire room, every shadowed corner, everywhere where someone could hide and trick her. There was no loudspeaker for an audio system, no one lurking with camera in hand, waiting to snap an embarrassing photo. Nothing but her and Apollo.

"Please," the voice whispered.

Hell, she said to herself. So I look like a fool. She stepped onto the pedestal and touched her lips to the lips of the statue. Funny, she thought, they feel like warm flesh. Then there were arms around her. His arms. How was this possible? But she didn't care. Standing on the pedestal, she deepened the kiss and his mouth opened. A hand grabbed her hair and pulled her head back. His mouth devoured her throat, kissing and licking at the pulse that pounded in her neck. "Oh God," she moaned.

She felt herself lifted and carried down off the raised block, toward a bench at the side of the gallery. Hands quickly pulled off her blouse and bra and a mouth fastened onto her already tightly erect nipple. His mouth suckled and pulled at her. She reached around and grasped his well-developed shoulders, holding him against her. Her hands stroked his back, then the fronts of his thighs.

He was moving, always moving. His mouth was on her neck, her breast, her belly, her palm. His hands were in her hair, on her ribs, on her hips. He pulled off the rest of her clothes, spread her legs and knelt on the floor beside the bench, his mouth finding her most intimate places. His tongue lashed and licked, driving her wild. Never had she been so hot so fast. Two fingers were inside of her and his mouth pulled gently on her clit. When a third finger joined the first two and filled her, she came, hard and hot. She screamed out as the waves of orgasm crashed over and over her.

When she had caught her breath, she opened her eyes. It was too dim to see the man before her, but it was certainly no statue and the fig leaf was gone. Then his hard cock touched her pussy lips and slowly, so slowly slipped inside her soaked, slippery channel. The contrast between their previous wild movements and this slow filling of her passage drove Terry up again. Then, without a word, he slammed into her, pulled out and slammed again. The passion, the heat, the frantic movements. She came again, and a moment later he groaned and came inside of her.

She must have passed out for a few moments. When she awoke, she was still lying on the bench, naked. The statue was back on its pedestal, white marble gleaming in the dim light.

Not knowing what had really happened, she slowly picked up her clothes. As she pulled on her panties, the wetness between her legs was unmistakable and her bra covered the still-erect nipples. When she was fully dressed, she gazed at the statue, then walked over and touched Apollo's leg. "Come another evening," the voice whispered. "Come every evening."

Knowing she would be back, she left the gallery to look for someone to let her out of the museum.

Fran took a deep breath. She realized she had written the entire story in only an hour and now she was exhausted and breathless. She moved to the top of the document and typed, *Apollo* by Nichole St. Michelle. She would proofread it and run the story through the spellcheck program another time. She turned off her laptop, undressed and, wearing an oversized tee shirt with a picture of Garfield on the front, walked back into the living room. She flipped on the light over the statue. She walked up to it, ran her hands over its hairless chest, then gave it a friendly pat on the buttocks. Then she turned off the lights and climbed into bed.

When the phone rang at about ten the following morning, Fran was sitting in the kitchen drinking a cup of herb tea and wondering about how to spend her first full day in New York. "Hello," she said.

"Hi Fran, it's Eileen. Did you settle in okay?"

"Sure did," Fran said. "I did some writing and then roamed the cable TV. It's got more channels than I've ever seen. And I finally got to watch the Playboy channel. Holy cow. It's like Sesame Street for grown-ups."

Eileen laughed. "How do you mean that? Have you been thinking of doing kinky things with the cookie monster?"

"Not like that. But the Playboy channel is all short takes, bright colors, dancing popcorn bags and quick, very hot shots of beautiful women. Nothing lasts for more than thirty seconds. It's like they don't think the audience has the attention span of a gnat."

Eileen's laugh echoed through the phone line. "Or a three-year-old."

"But it certainly was educational."

"So have you thought about what you want to do today?"

"Not really. I'm a tourist so I guess I should do touristy things."

"Like?"

Fran hesitated then grinned. "Like Bloomingdales?"

"Ah, it's shopping time. Ready to get into the New York mode?"

"I think I'm ready for a lot of things."

"Whatever you decide is fine with me. Only you can decide. But for today, Don's off with the kids and his brother and so we can shop till we drop. We can create Nicki from the ground up."

And they did. By the time the two women returned to Fran's apartment, late that afternoon, Fran had happily put a major dent in her charge card. The two women, their arms loaded with boxes and bags, hurried into the bedroom and quickly unwrapped items and spread them out on the bed. There was a long black velvet skirt slit almost to the thigh that went with either of two revealing sequined tops for the various evening functions. There were two skirts that were so short that Fran thought they were indecent. But Nicki, the two women had concluded, would wear clothes like that. There were a few sheer blouses and a tight-fitting black leather vest. There were several pair of opera pumps and two pocketbooks. "Nicki can't wander around New York with a backpack," Eileen had said. Together they opened the remainder of the boxes, but the purchase that amazed Fran the most was in the last one.

"I can't imagine why you bought these," she said to Eileen as she opened the box. "They're so tight that they are almost in-decent."

"I want you to have them. And eventually, you will feel com-fortable enough to wear them," Eileen said. "Or at least Nicki will."

Fran reached into the box and pulled out a pair of buttery-soft black leather pants. She laid them on the bed beside the black leather vest that matched perfectly. Will I ever have the courage to wear them?

As they put their treasures in the closet the phone rang. "Fran, it's Carla. I just have a minute before dinner and I thought I'd give you a call. How are you doing?"

"I'm just great. Eileen and I spent the day creating a clothing persona for Nicki. I'm not sure about all of it, but I guess I'm willing to give some of it a try."

"I have a phone client tomorrow around eleven. Maybe we could get together before that, say around ten? I could drive in after I drop BJ at school. He'd rather *die* than take the bus these days. God bless teenaged boys."

A phone client? Fran wondered. She mentally shrugged. "I'd love to. Shall I meet you at your place?"

"Let me pick you up. That way if I get stuck in traffic I'm not leaving you on a street corner. Is ten good for you?"

"It's just great."

Fran heard shouting in the background. "Sounds like the Knicks just tied the game," Carla said. "I just get over football season when the boys move to basketball and hockey." Fran could hear the other woman's sigh. "But they have fun. I actually took them to a Knicks game a few months ago. We had a blast, al-though I'm not a sports fan at all." There was another cheer and Carla said, "Gotta run. See you in the morning."

"Sounds wonderful," Fran said and hung up.

"So you're getting together with Carla tomorrow?"

"She'll be here around ten. She's got a phone client at eleven, whatever that is."

"You know all about Carla now, don't you?"

"I know what she does for a living if that's what you mean."

Eileen raised an eyebrow. "Phone client. Phone sex."

"Of course," Fran said, shaking her head. "I'm still thinking Omaha."

"Don't be like that. I'm sure there are Carla-equivalents in Omaha, too. Sex is big business. It's everywhere from truck stops to the Internet. Why do you think your book sells so well? It's wonderful, don't get me wrong, but lots of women, and probably men too, read it for the erotica."

Fran took a deep breath. "You're right, of course." She looked at her watch. "Hey, it's almost six. Aren't you due home?"

"Holy shit, I didn't realize how late it's gotten. I do have to run. Will you be okay fending for yourself tonight?"

"Of course. The pantry's well stocked and I've got about a hundred TV channels to choose from."

"Okay," Eileen said, grabbing her coat, "I'll call you tomorrow. If you're not around, I'll leave a message."

"It's been a great day. Thanks." The two women hugged and, with her usual long stride, Eileen headed for the door. "Say hello to your husband for me," Fran called.

"I sure will." And she was gone.

After a dinner of peanut butter sandwiches and herb tea, Fran decided that she needed to broaden her outlook a little bit, learn more about the kinky side of sex. Her Internet service provider had a local number so, knowing that she wouldn't be incurring any charges for the Devlins, she spent several hours looking at Internet sites devoted to everything from foot worship to hypnosis. She read several stories about unusual activities, most of which were poorly written, filled with typos and misplaced punctuation. Some were so offbeat that she couldn't believe that people actually got pleasure from the described activities. Some, though, were so riveting that she could overlook all the editing problems the stupid story lines and, in a few cases, the non-consentuality. Those excited her so much that when she finally logged off she was really aroused.

She wandered into the living room and turned on the spotlight over the statue. Then she took off all of her clothes, spread a towel on the sofa and stretched out on it. With her head on the arm of the couch, she could gaze at the incredibly sexy body of the man in the statue. She positioned herself so that he seemed to be watching her. Then she slid her hands over her ribs and belly, slowly moving her fingers to her already-erect nipples. She pinched, enjoying the tightening in her groin.

"Are you watching me?" she asked the bronze man.

Oh yes, she imagined him saying. Show me.

She caressed her belly, worked her fingers slowly toward her sopping pussy. Pinching her nipple with one hand, she rubbed her clit with the other. She shifted so the statue could have the best view of her hands as she rubbed and stroked. "Watch me when I come," she whispered.

Oh yes, he said in her mind. Come for me, baby.

And she did. Her orgasm was tight, hot and very powerful. When she calmed, she blew the statue a kiss, then returned the towel to the bathroom and went to bed.

At ten o'clock the following morning, the doorbell rang. Carla, dressed in perfectly fitting designer jeans and a silk blouse with a paisley scarf inside the neck greeted Fran with a kiss on each cheek. "Multiple cheek kissing's very European," she said, "and something Nicki should learn to do."

The two women walked into the living room and Carla was captivated by the statue. She put her purse and shopping bag down and said, "God, he's gorgeous. How can someone make bronze look like that?"

"AnneMarie Devlin's a very talented woman."

"I'll say. I want to meet him," Carla said, running a finger lightly over the statue's chest.

"Eileen said that it's her husband."

"I'll bet they have some sex life." Carla put her pocketbook on a table.

"Coffee? Herb tea?"

"Coffee sounds wonderful. I had breakfast with the kids around seven and I really need a pick-me-up."

The two women puttered around in the kitchen and talked about unimportant things. Finally, cups in hand, they returned to the living room. Carla settled on the sofa and tucked her legs underneath her. "Fran, tell me about Nicki."

"What do you want to know?"

"If we're going to create her, we need to know everything there is about her."

"There's not much."

"Where did the name come from?"

Fran's grin was immediate. "I had just finished my first erotic short story and I was feeling brave enough to submit it to a magazine. But I couldn't have *Pussy Willow* written by Fran Caputo, and I certainly couldn't let anyone know that I was the writer."

Carla laughed. *"Pussy Willow?"*

"Yeah. It was about a couple who made it in a field on a blanket. Actually I reread it recently. It isn't half bad. Anyway, I had to find a pseudonym. I wanted it to sound exotic, but not like a stripper or the actresses in those XXX-rated movies. You know, Sally Sweet or Melinda Love. I was at the video store shelving some new travel videos and there was one about France. The picture on the cover was of Mont St. Michelle. The St. Michelle stuck so I added a French sounding first name and Nichole St. Michelle was born."

"Okay, what has been written about her? What do we have to be sure that Nicki knows, or does?"

"Eileen put out a few press releases when the book first came out. Nicki's a divorcée, who travels a lot, which is why she can't do interviews. Somehow it just snowballed into a mysterious temptress who has dazzled crowned heads and refused marriage proposals so she could remain on the prowl."

"That's it?"

"That's about all. When I think about it, physically this shouldn't be too hard. Since there's never been a description of her in any of the press releases, no one knows what Nicki looks like."

Carla sipped her tea. "That's great. So our main task is to teach you to think like a wild, free-thinking woman. Then we'll brush you up on some of the things you might need to know. I don't know a lot about Europe, unfortunately."

"Before I left, I watched every travel video the store had. I think I know as much about Europe as Nicki does. Except, of course, that I've never been there." Fran lifted her chin and looked down her nose at Carla. Lowering the pitch of her voice, she said, "But of course, I only travel to and from France on the Concorde." She grinned and returned her voice to its normal pitch. "There was a bit about it at the front of one of the films I watched."

"You know I love that voice. Can you do it so you won't slip?"

Again lowering her voice's pitch, Fran said, "I'll try to get into the habit of doing it all the time. If I slip, let me know."

"You know there's one more piece to this puzzle. We have to make you look like Nicki."

"But no one knows how she looks," Fran said, a bit confused.

"I know that, but she'd look more . . ." Carla shifted in her seat.

"Okay, I understand." Fran reflexively tightened the scrunchy on her ponytail. "I need a new face and stuff."

"The face you have is just lovely. You just need some help with how to enhance the good points and play down the bad." Carla looked at Fran closely, then cupped her hand beneath Fran's chin and moved her face left and right. "Great eyes. We need to make your chin come forward a bit. Good cheekbones but you need a bit of under eye coverup. And some properly applied lipstick will make your mouth just a bit larger. I've taken several makeup courses and I can certainly help you with that. But we do need to get you to a really good hair stylist. Any objections to going the whole way?"

Fran sighed and pulled on her ponytail. "I guess not."

"Good girl, and I've got just the man to do it."

"Do you really think you can do something with me?"

"I remember saying almost the same thing to Ronnie when we

first met. I had always thought of myself as medium brown and average, average, average."

Fran gazed at Carla's face and perfectly cut and styled auburn hair. "But you're really gorgeous. Me? I think of myself as oatmeal and short."

"Without makeup and a bit of help with my hair color," Carla said, running her fingers through her reddish bob, "I'd still be medium brown and average." Carla leaned forward and looked at Fran. "So much of how you look is attitude. If you think mousey, you'll look mousey. If you think smashing, you'll be smashing. By the way, 'smashing.' That's a Nicki word. She'd probably use it a lot." Carla glanced at her watch. "It's almost eleven and I need to make a phone call. I'll be a while."

Fran took a deep breath. What better time to begin her lessons. "Eileen told me that this is a client."

"It's a writer friend of mine who claims I'm his inspiration. When he's reached an impasse in something he's written, he leaves a message on my answering machine and I call him at a pre-arranged time. He says it gets his juices flowing in more ways than one."

The two women laughed and then Carla continued, "He left me a message on Friday asking me to call him this morning at eleven."

"Does he write erotica? Maybe I know his name."

"He writes horror. Very bloody stuff. I don't know why he wants an obscene phone call, but he said once that it celebrates life when his writing gets too much into death."

"Has he had books published?"

"If you want to know his name, I won't tell you. I never give out the names of any of my friends without their permission."

"I'm sorry. Of course not. I didn't think. So what will you say?"

Carla put her hand on Fran's arm and spoke seriously. "Why don't you listen? It won't embarrass me and he'll never know. Actually, if I told him he'd probably find it hot."

"No. I couldn't." But she wanted to.

"Of course you could. Nicki certainly would. It can be your first lesson in being a free spirit."

Having second and third thoughts, Fran sat silently on the sofa.

Carla pulled a cell phone from her pocketbook, checked her watch, then dialed a number. There was a pause, then Carla's warm laugh. "Good morning, lover. . . . I'm fine . . . Yes, very nice, thanks. How was yours? . . . Great." She settled back onto the sofa and pulled her legs more tightly beneath her. "What's the theme for today's scene?"

There was a long pause. "You mean you and two women? How interesting. Do you want to watch them play with each other, or just with you." Carla winked at Fran. "Okay. Tell me how things look? What's happening? . . . All right. Let's see."

As Fran watched, Carla stretched her long legs out and propped her feet on the coffee table. She rested her head on the back of the sofa and closed her eyes. "Your name is Ramash and you're in a large room. It's dimly lit with candles in wall niches and torches in holders on the walls. The light flickers making moving shadows everywhere. There's no furniture, just large soft pillows on a multicolored carpet that covers much of the floor. You're standing, dressed in loose-legged soft black pants, leather slippers and nothing else. It's warm and inviting there and you are totally comfortable, knowing what is to come. Do you have the picture, lover?"

She paused. "Good. You stand there for a while, waiting patiently. The air is perfumed with incense and there's soft music coming from somewhere far away." Carla's laugh was warm. "Yes, lover, that's wonderful. You probably should take off your clothes while you listen. In the room, you wait and then you hear rustling. Two women walk in, dressed in harem outfits, with sheer pants and tiny bolero jackets. Close your eyes, lover, and tell me how they look."

As Carla listened, Fran pictured the way the women would look if she were writing the story. Tall, one blond and one raven-black, voluptuous, shapely. Beautiful, with red lips and long slender fingers.

"Oh yes," Carla said. "I can see them. That's so good." She almost purrs, Fran thought. "They are so lovely. The tall one approaches and bows. 'What would you have of me,' she says. The shorter one hangs back. She's tiny and shy, I think. So you wait for a moment, then ask the bold woman her name. 'My name is Elana,' she says. 'And your friend?' you ask, pointing to the tiny woman almost devoured by the shadows. 'Her name is Tyra and this is her first time here.'

"You smile. What could be more wonderful than a tiny female just on the verge of discovering carnal pleasure. Without moving your feet, you stretch out your arm toward Tyra. She's reluctant to come to you. 'Don't be afraid,' you say. 'It will be such joy. Come to me.' Slowly she approaches and tentatively takes your outstretched hand.

"Her eyes are on the floor so, when she's close enough you cup her chin and lift her head so she's looking into your eyes. You see how beautiful she is. Tiny, like a precious doll. Her hand is only half the size of yours. You feel you could engulf her, overpower her without trouble but you want her to give herself to you.

" 'Undress her, Elana,' you say and slowly, deliberately, Elana removes Tyra's jacket. Beneath she is naked, her tiny breasts almost nonexistent. Her nipples are large, though, and tightly erect. From excitement or fear? You don't know and it doesn't matter. She will get her pleasure soon. You want to suck those tight nipples, but you also enjoy denying yourself the immediate pleasure." Carla paused. "Lover, are you hot? Tell me." She listened, then purred, a low sensuous sound. "Good. But don't be in a hurry. No touching your cock. Not yet. . . . Sorry. You know the rules. You have to wait until our hero gets his."

Fran sat, realizing that she was getting excited by the sound of Carla's voice and by the story she was constructing.

"Now where were we?" Carla said. "Oh yes. Elana is removing Tyra's pants. You can see the dark triangle of soft hair at the junction of her thighs. You know it hides a great treasure that you will

explore. But first, you tell Elana to remove all of her own clothing. She's tall, with large full breasts and soft blond fur between
her legs. 'Show Tyra how to please me,' you tell Elana. She
quickly removes your pants until you are standing naked in the
middle of the warm room. She puts a cushion at your feet, kneels
and wraps her long fingers around your cock, which is hard and
full."

Carla's deep throaty laugh startled Fran from the scene in the
large room. "I'm sure you are, lover, but have patience. It won't
be long now." Fran shook her head. Amazing, she thought. This
woman's just fantastic at creating a mood.

"She's holding your cock in her hand and she licks her lips.
Then her long pink tongue reaches out and licks the drop of fluid
that's leaking from the tip of your big hard penis. God, that feels
so good that you almost want to come right then, but you don't.
No lover, I'm not going to let you off the hook so fast. You may
not come. Now Ramash is standing with this beautiful woman at
his feet, but he wants to explore Tyra too so he tells Elana to
stop. He moves to a large pile of cushions and spreads them out
on the carpet. He stretches out and tells Tyra to lie beside him.
She does, her movements tentative. 'Relax, my little flower,' he
tells her, so she closes her eyes and just waits.

"Slowly he runs his large hand over Tyra's tiny body. He
strokes her arms, her shoulders, her belly, her legs. He can tell
that she's getting excited so he lets the pleasure build, deliberately not touching her in the places that he knows she wants to
be touched. When he knows she's becoming aroused, he flicks
his tongue over her nipple and smiles as she gasps with pleasure.
'Yes, dove,' he says, 'It's wonderful, isn't it?'

" 'Oh yes,' she moans. 'I didn't know how good it could feel.'
You suckle at her tiny breast, feeling her begin to writhe beneath
your mouth. Slowly you slide your fingers down her belly and
bury them in her soft cleft. You find her clit and it's hard and
swollen. You rub it and feel her hips buck, reaching for you.

"All right, lover, how shall Ramash climax? He has to decide.
Elana can use her mouth, or would he rather deflower Tyra? . . .

All right. Ramash tells Elana his idea and she nods her understanding. Then he kneels between Tyra's spread thighs and slides his hands beneath her buttocks, lifting her off the cushion, positioning her for his mouth. Then he gently spreads her cunt lips with his thumbs and uses the tip of his tongue to tease the tip of her erect clit. 'You are like nectar,' he says, dipping his tongue into her opening and tasting her juices, which flow freely.

"As he bends over, Elana settles behind him, reaches between his legs and cups his balls. Slowly she massages them while running her index finger up and down his shaft. He's getting so hot now that it's becoming increasingly difficult not to come. Tyra's ready for him, so he allows her body to drop back onto the cushions and positions his painfully hard cock at her entrance. With Elana's hand on his balls, he drives his cock to the hilt inside of Tyra. One small bit of resistance is passed easily and soon Tyra is moving with him as though she's been making love all her life. She's so small that his cock feels like it's tightly encased in the warmest, wettest velvet. Elana positions herself on the cushions with her legs wide so he can see her entire pussy spread before him as he drives into Tyra. 'Do it for me,' he whispers and then watches as Elana's hand moves between her legs."

As Fran listened, it was all she could do not to reach between her own legs to satisfy the hunger there. She was as hot as she often got writing her own stories.

"Ramash is about to come, buried deep inside of Tyra. He can feel the orgasm boiling in his belly. Can you feel it, lover?" Again she laughed. "That's good. You may touch it. But try to wait for Ramash. He's close now, watching Tyra's eyes as she learns of pleasure, watching Elana's hand as she pleasures herself. He reaches between his body and Tyra's and rubs her clit. He watches as her orgasm overwhelms her, then he holds still for an instant, feeling the waves of pleasure as Tyra's body clutches at his. Then he can hold back no longer and he lets the waves overtake him. He feels his jism spurt deep inside this wonderfully tight pussy. As he watches Elana's fingers fly over her skin, spurred on by his growls of ecstasy. Then she screams as an orgasm overtakes her as well."

Carla was silent for a few moments, listening. Then she said. "I'm glad that was so good. I may just have to satisfy myself, too. You're not the only one who's gotten hot here."

And you two aren't the only ones either, Fran thought, shifting position and rubbing her thighs together. She looked at Carla, who seemed to have forgotten her presence. If I could only be that free about sex. . . .

"Okay, lover," Carla said. "Call me soon." She pressed a button on the phone and slowly sat up and looked at Fran. "Phew. Doing that always makes me hot."

"You're terrific at it," Fran said.

"I've been doing it a long time and I know what my friends like. Exciting, isn't it? And I enjoy it so much."

"And you get paid?"

"I'll charge my friend's credit card $300 for that little interlude."

Fran swallowed hard. "Three hundred dollars? I'm in the wrong business."

"Anytime you want to give it a try, I have plenty of friends who get off on phone sex. And they are always interested in something, or someone, new."

Fran took a deep breath, dragging herself down from the sexual peak. "I think I'd be too embarrassed to do what you just did."

"But would Nicki?" When Fran hesitated, Carla continued. "Never mind. Let me take some time and play with your makeup. I'll also make an appointment for you with Jean-Claude tomorrow sometime. He's the miracle worker who did wonders for me when I first decided to do this. I'll tell him what we're going for and then you two can figure something out."

"Great," Fran said.

"There's still the bigger question here, though," Carla said, sitting forward and looking at Fran. "We've said that Nicki's a woman of the world. How far do you want to go?"

Fran wanted to pretend that she didn't understand the question, but she did. How far did she want to go? She remained

silent for a few moments while shards of thought formed and re-
formed in her mind. She wanted it all, she realized. She wanted
to learn, to become Nicki, to understand the more unusual
things. "You know," she said finally, "all my stories, hot as they
are, involve straight, heterosexual, one on one sex. Although *The
Love Flower* is really erotic, there's nothing out of the ordinary
boy-girl things."

"And why do you think that is?"

"Because that's all I know about. I've got a vivid imagination,
but an imagination can only take you so far." She looked at Carla.
She had only known her for two days and she felt like she could
tell her anything. "I want to experience it all." Phew. She'd said
it. She'd agreed to let this super-experienced woman teach her
about sex. "Did I really say that?"

"Yes, you did. If that's what you want, then there are several
ways to go about it. I have a friend. Actually he's an ex-customer.
He's urbane, very suave, and sexy as hell. He's not gorgeous but
he sure as hell turns me on. If you like, I can set you two up one
evening this week."

A slow smile spread across Fran's face. "You can tell him about
Fran, but set him up with a woman named Nicki. Let's begin her
real life there."

Carla took Fran's hand. "Done. And it's going to be wonderful.
You know, I almost envy you. I remember my beginnings. The
discovery is such a fantastic trip."

Fran lifted her teacup in a toast. "To discovery."

Carla touched the lip of her cup to Fran's. "To discovery."

Chapter

4

The two women spent several hours on Fran's 'look.' The shopping bag that Carla had brought with her contained what seemed to Fran to be an entire cosmetic counter. To begin, the two women gave themselves facials and organic cleansings. Between bites of peanut butter sandwiches from the Devlins' kitchen, using Fran's face as a canvas, they experimented with foundation and concealer, contouring powder, eye shadows and liners, mascara, blush, and finally lipstick and lip liner.

"Not bad," Carla said at about two P.M., gazing at her friend in the mirror. "Not bad at all."

Fran was totally boggled. She looked really good. Whatever Carla had done had accentuated her deep blue eyes, made her small nose more prominent and widened her lips so they looked inviting, almost kissable. Carla had also made an appointment with Jean-Claude for the following morning. If makeup could do what it had done with her face, how much further could Jean-Claude take her. "Wow. That's fabulous."

"Yes, if I do say so myself, you look terrific. We'll have to wait until after Jean-Claude does your hair to figure out wardrobe colors, earrings and such. It will depend on what color and style you end up with. And you need a scent. Go to Saks, sniff around and find Nicki's signature scent. Use it sparingly, but use it all the time so it becomes you and Nicki. And have your nails done."

Fran looked down at her short, utilitarian fingernails and sighed. "I guess."

"Did you know that in ancient Japan it was a status thing for a man to have a long pinky nail that was never cut? It was a mark of someone who never had to work. And Nicki never has her hands in dishwater." Carla reached out and felt Fran's hands. "Good. I guess you don't often either."

Fran's laugh was spontaneous. "I don't cook or do dishes. And I don't do windows either."

"I'm for ice cream," Carla blurted out, staring at Fran's face in the mirror. "This fantastic job we've done calls for ice cream in large quantities. Got some?"

"I've got just the half-gallon for us. I'm sorry, no chocolate though. Even chocolate ice cream is too much caffeine for me."

"No problem."

Giggling like schoolgirls, the two women scrambled into the kitchen and were soon sitting at the small table, spoons and bowls in hand. "I just love this," Carla said as she plunged her spoon in a large bowl of cherry vanilla cheesecake swirl.

"I've got a question about this morning," Fran said, licking her spoon. "I've just got to ask. Did you make one character small on my account? Were you trying to make a point?" Fran was surprised that the question hit a raw nerve.

"Not at all. I asked my friend to describe the two women and he did. One tall and statuesque, the other petite and trim." Carla put down her spoon. "Listen, Fran, that call this morning was business. He's paying good money for his own personal fantasy. I wouldn't do something like that just to make you feel better."

Fran grinned. "Thanks for that. I guess I wondered whether I was being had." She plunged her spoon into the red and white goo in her bowl.

"Not at all," Carla said. "And anytime you want to call this off, just say so."

"No." Fran's answer was so quick that it surprised even her.

"Okay then. Are you still up for a date with my friend?"

Caught off guard a bit, Fran blurted out, "I'm excited at the prospect. I'll probably be a nervous wreck in actuality."

"Nervous isn't all bad. Let me give him a call later and I'll call you this evening. Any night this week off limits?"

"I've got nothing planned." She giggled. "You know, I had a whole list of places to go and things to see. Now it all seems a bit pale."

"I know exactly what you mean. Let's take one evening at a time, but I have a few ideas for later in the week and the weekend."

"I'll just bet you do. What are your plans for the rest of the week? Will you be in town?"

"I've got some school stuff for BJ and Mike tomorrow, but I'll be back in town on Wednesday. Maybe we can do some more clothes shopping. I need a few things and by then we'll have a better idea of what kind of jewelry will go with your new haircut. Maybe we can get Eileen to play hookey from work and the three of us can see whether we can injure a few credit cards." Carla got up, put her dish in the sink, wandered back into the bedroom and got her coat.

"What about all this stuff?" Fran said, pointing to all the make-up and skin care products.

"It's yours. Consider it a late Christmas present. I've got lots more where that came from. I love shopping for makeup of all kinds and I can afford to indulge myself. And," she said leaning closer, "I deduct it all from my income tax as a cost of doing business."

"You pay taxes as a prostitute?"

"Not as a prostitute but as an escort. We always go to dinner first, and I decided when I started this that I couldn't worry about the IRS looking over my shoulder."

"But don't they get suspicious? You make a lot of money for an 'escort.' "

"That's not really their concern. I probably could slip some of it under the rug, but it's just not worth the Maalox to me." Carla slipped her camel wool trench coat on and neatly tied the belt. "Give my love to Jean-Claude."

"I will." As they walked toward the front door, Fran said, "How do you do it? You're wearing jeans and you really look wonderful."

"Smashing. That's Nicki's word."

"Right. You look simply smashing, so, oh I don't know, put together," Fran said.

"That's because I take some time to select my clothes and, even more important, the accessories. Like this scarf," she said, fingering the square of paisley silk inside the neck of her shirt. "And jewelry, too." Fran now noticed the large silver hoops in her ears and the silver bracelet that hung low on her hand. "I also stand straight. I actually took a few modeling lessons to learn how to carry myself. You've got no problem there," she added. "You carry yourself wonderfully. You stand tall and walk like a confident lady. I'm really glad of it, too, because Nicki would and that's a hard thing to teach in just a week or so."

"Do I really? I can't really stand tall, since I'm not tall."

"Tall is as much being proud of the way you look as it is stature. But you'll learn that. But from now on, think about what you said about me. Try to *put yourself together*. Use a pin or a belt. Wear jewelry, and junky is fine. Scarves are great. I have an article I cut out of a woman's magazine about scarves and how to tie them. I'll bring it on Wednesday. How about same time, same place?"

"Sure. Sounds great. I'll talk to Eileen, too."

The two women walked to the front door. In passing, Carla blew a kiss to the statue. "Remember, Nicki's a kisser. And she always touches any man she's with."

"Touches?"

"Touches. Try to lay your hand on a man's arm, or brush his shoulder as you pass his chair in a restaurant. Just lightly and it can even seem accidental. A woman never touches a man accidentally, but he doesn't have to know that."

Fran laid a hand on Carla's arm and kissed her on each cheek.

"It's been a great day." She strode to the elevator and pressed the button.

"Yes, it really has. And thanks for everything."

The elevator doors slid open and Carla winked. "Right on, baby." And with that, like a statuesque whirlwind, she was gone.

Fran walked around the apartment, tidying up after herself. Then she went into the bedroom and put all the cosmetics on the dresser. Every time she passed a mirror she was startled to see the nice-looking woman who looked back at her.

The following morning at eleven Fran arrived at Jean-Claude's midtown beauty salon which was known only as The Studio. Carla had told her that Jean-Claude was the hottest thing in town, but nothing had prepared her for this. The Studio was all done in off white with touches of dusty-blue. The female operators all wore tightly fitted, charcoal-blue smocks with beige leggings and the men were all in skin-tight blue tee shirts and beige slacks. Jean-Claude kept her waiting almost a half an hour, and when he arrived, she was astonished.

Jean-Claude was only five feet five, with a shock of yellow hair that stood out from his head in random spikes surrounding his round, well-tanned face. He looks like a black-eyed susan, she thought.

As Jean-Claude took Fran's hand a woman bustled out of the back of the studio and kissed him on both cheeks. "You're a genius, Jean-Claude. A miracle worker."

"Jean-Claude is delighted that you are pleased," he said, referring to himself in the third person in a thick French accent. It was all that Fran could do to contain her laughter.

"Well, I am most definitely pleased." She fluffed out a haze of fine black curls around her moon-shaped face. If anything the hairstyle made her look even rounder. I'm supposed to trust this man?

He blew her a kiss as she hustled out the front door. He leaned over and whispered into Fran's ear. "Isn't that just awful? She came in with a picture of some fourteen-year-old ingenue and insisted that I create the look for her. Jean-Claude couldn't talk her out of it. And she thinks I'm a genius." He grinned and shook his head. "And she paid a fortune." He held Fran's hand. "Come into the back and let's discuss the new you."

They walked through the organized chaos of sixteen stations for haircuts and comb-outs, twelve sinks and more than two dozen hair dryers, most in use by dusty-blue-covered women with their faces buried in fashion magazines. Jean-Claude opened the door to his office and led Fran inside. As they settled on overstuffed beige tweed chairs, Jean-Claude said, with a very New York accent, "How is Carla? She's such a fabulous woman."

"She's wonderful and she has such wonderful things to say about the work you do." Without meaning to, Fran's gaze rose to his hair.

His grin was infectious. "This is for appearances. It's Vaseline and washable dye. Someone said I had to create an image, and that it can't stay the same for long, so I do something outrageous every week."

"How do you think of new things to do?"

"I have a supply of pictures from trendy magazines and hairstyle journals. I pick women's styles mostly and then just have fun. Except when I'm showing a client her new self in a mirror I don't have to look at me."

"Your accent has slipped a little," Fran said.

"Actually I'm from the Bronx," he said in unaccented English. "Kingsbridge to be specific. This is all a front. Everyone knows I'm American, but I've got cachet and for as long as it lasts I'll play along. And, in truth, I'm very good at what I do." He studied Fran's face. "Carla tells me you want a new look. Something European and very sexy."

"I guess. It's for a party I have to attend."

Jean-Claude cupped Fran's chin and turned her face toward the light. "You have great skin and your makeup's really well done. Did you have someone do it this morning?"

"Carla and I spent all of yesterday working on it and I spent quite a while this morning practicing."

"Well, you did a first-rate job." He ran his fingers through her hair. "You need some body here, and this gray just has to go. This light brown will highlight beautifully with lots of blond streaks instead of the gray. I would leave it shoulder length so you can blow it dry in a fluff, slick it back or wear it up. Your hair has to make a statement every time you are seen."

"A statement," Fran said dryly.

"Listen, that's not just hairdresser talk. You're short. If your hair is ordinary, you can enter a room and no one will notice. But if your hair says, 'Notice me,' then your entrance will be dramatic. That's what you want, isn't it?"

A smile spread over Fran's face. Jean-Claude had her pegged and so, why not let him just do it. "It's exactly what I want. Go for it. And can someone do my nails, too?"

"You've got the entire day, of course?"

"Of course."

By two o'clock Fran had luxury-length nails polished in a deep wine. Every time she looked down she was startled by the look. But they were certainly sexy. She could imagine one of the characters in her stories raking those nails down the back of some naked man.

It was almost three when Fran got a first look at her new lighter, body-waved hair and the love affair began immediately. She looked years younger, airier, brighter. He hadn't blown it dry yet, but just the color was a lift. "Now," Jean-Claude said, walking up behind her chair in the main studio, "let Jean-Claude show you how to arrange it."

For the next two hours, Jean-Claude combed and styled. He slicked her hair back in a dramatic French twist, then restyled it into a soft French braid from which soft curls artfully escaped. He combed it close to her face, curling against her jaw, piled it on top of her head with three dozen pins, and finally blew it dry in soft waves around her ears. "For evening, you can even add combs or wind some pearls through it."

Almost speechless, she murmured, "It's wonderful."

"Didn't Jean-Claude promise you?" he said, his French accent thick. "But there's something more that you need." He bent over and licked a slow path up Fran's neck to just behind her ear. Then he sucked her earlobe into his mouth and nipped at it slightly. "You need to look like a sexy woman, and now you do."

Totally bemused, Fran looked into the mirror. Her gaze was slightly hazy and her eyelids were lowered. "That's the look," Jean-Claude said. "Keep that one." He grinned and squeezed Fran's shoulder. "Now refresh your makeup and you're ready for anything." He cocked his head to one side, gazing at her in the mirror. "You know, I see you and I think, 'If only I had met you. . . .' "

Fran giggled. "I'm sure that line gets you the biggest tips."

Jean-Claude leaned over and whispered into her ear in clear English, "It sure does, lady. But in your case I actually mean it."

Remembering Carla's comment about touching, she placed her hand on top of the one Jean-Claude rested on her shoulder. "Thanks, Jean-Claude. That's so good for the soul."

Half an hour later, and several hundred dollars poorer, a new Fran Caputo walked out of Jean-Claude's studio. Or was it now Nichole St. Michelle? Yes, Fran thought, I'm certainly closer to being Nicki.

The weather had suddenly become mild as New York will in the early spring and, enjoying the air, she started to walk the ten blocks to her apartment. On a whim, she wandered into a small restaurant and was seated at a tiny table just inside the large plate-glass window. She glanced at the menu, ordered a plate of cheese and fruit and a glass of Chardonnay. She had a book in her new purse but, although she usually read while she ate, tonight she was content to gaze out of the window and watch the passersby.

"Excuse me," a voice said.

Fran's head snapped up and she gazed at a moderately attractive man with owlish eyes who stood beside the table. He was wearing the midtown New York uniform, charcoal-gray pinstriped suit with a white shirt, and his conservative gray tie had a small white and red figure on it. Clean shaven, he had shoulder-length hair the color of milk chocolate that curled over his collar. His eyes were deep brown and his smile was warm and friendly.

"Yes?" Fran said.

"I've never seen you here before. Are you waiting for someone?"

"No," she said. "Can I help you?"

"I don't usually accost women," he said, "and I'm sorry if I'm interrupting, but I'm feeling kind of down today and . . ."

He was trying to pick her up. Holy mackerel. Her new look? Her new attitude? Her good luck? She wasn't going to let him, of course, but it was nice to be asked. Startled, she remained silent.

"I'm so sorry." He turned and headed back to the small bar area.

This was too good to pass up. She could indulge herself for just a moment. "Did you have a bad day?"

He turned but didn't close the distance he had created. "Listen. I'm really sorry." He looked genuinely miserable. "You looked a bit lonely so I thought I'd give it a try. I'm not very good at this."

"You're just fine at *this*," Fran said. "I'm not waiting for anyone so if you'd like to sit for a few minutes, I'm sure we could find something to talk about."

He looked at her, then a slow smile lightened his face. "If you're sure it's okay." He grabbed his glass of red wine from the bar, walked back to the table and sat across from her. "My name's Clark, and no, I don't rip open my shirt to reveal the large S on my chest. Clark Rothstone."

"Hi," Fran said and, after a heartbeat, she added, "I'm Nicki. Nicki St. Michelle."

Clark put his wineglass down and stretched his hand across the table. "Nice to meet you, Nicki. What do you do for a living?"

"Actually I'm here on vacation. From the Midwest."

"Really? You look so New York chic."

Fran thought about the few extra minutes she had spent that morning finding a soft gray scarf and tying it, ascot-style inside the neck of her white blouse the way Carla had the day before. She'd also stopped in a little boutique and bought a large pin for the lapel of her jacket. "Thanks. That's a wonderful compliment."

Over their wine, the two discussed movies and television, two passions they shared, his interest in sports, families and friends. Fran learned that Clark was the controller of a medium-sized corporation and was divorced with three children who all lived in suburbia with his ex-wife. He also had a wonderful, spontaneous sense of humor and a quick smile. An hour later, they ordered dinner and continued to find things they had in common over veal chops, rice pilaf and mixed vegetables. Dessert consisted of the sweetest rice pudding she had ever tasted. "You know," Fran said, "this pudding is so sweet it curls my teeth. The rest of the meal is really good, but this . . ."

"I know. It's like they doubled the amount of sugar. Maybe they think I'm not sweet enough already."

Fran looked at her watch, startled to see that it was after nine. She put her spoon down and sipped her tea. "This has been fun, but it's getting late."

She could see him hesitate, then make some internal decision and plunge forward. "I would really like to see you again. This has been such an enjoyable evening. Could I call you?" When she paused, he said, "I'm sorry. This is probably too sudden."

"No, it's not that at all," Fran said, putting her cup down. "It's just that I've heard so many horror stories about New Yorkers that I'm a bit reluctant to give out my phone number. And it's not my phone anyway." When Clark looked crestfallen, Fran said, "Let's do this. Why don't you give me your phone number and I'll call you?"

Clark's face lit up. "Really? That would be fine." He took out a business card and scribbled something on the back. "Here's my office number, my beeper, my cell phone and my e-mail address. I've put my home number on the back."

"Phew. Technology." She took the card and put it carefully in her wallet. Whether or not she'd use it was another matter. As Clark signaled for the check, Fran looked again at his tie. "You know, I've been admiring your tie. But I can't quite make out that tiny design."

His laugh was rich and full. He held out the end of the tie so she could look at it more closely. "I don't believe it," Fran said, a grin spreading across her face. "It's a tiny white dog peeing on a red fire hydrant."

"Very few get to know that. It's me thumbing my nose at this corporate thing." When the waiter arrived with the check, Clark put down his credit card before Fran could even take a breath.

She decided to be honest. "I'm a bit uncomfortable with you buying dinner. I'd prefer to pay my share."

"I've enjoyed this so much that I'd like to treat." He hesitated and looked at her carefully. "Okay. If it makes you uncomfortable . . ."

"It does."

Clark picked up the check and glanced at the total. "If you give me about thirty dollars that should do it."

Grateful that he understood, she handed him the money. "Thanks for not arguing."

They chatted while the waiter took care of the bill and gave Clark the receipt to sign. When he left, Fran sipped the last of her tea and stood up. "This has been a delightful evening," she said. She glanced again at his tie. "You know, that tie might just have earned you a phone call within the next few days."

Clark took her hand and gave it a firm squeeze. "I hope so."

They walked two blocks side by side, then said good night and parted company as Clark walked west and Fran turned east. As she walked through the brightly lit streets of the east Fifties, she thought about the evening. Clark was clearly lonely, and in a city this size and this impersonal, she could relate. Hell, she thought, you can be lonely in Omaha. She thought about the business card, now safely lodged in her wallet. She might actually call him unless life got too complicated.

When she arrived back at her apartment, the light was blink-blink-blinking on the answering machine beside her bed. She sat down and pressed play. "You have three messages." The first was from Eileen. "I've got to make this fast, but I talked with Carla and tomorrow's great. Can't wait to see how you look. Make plans for time and stuff and I'll meet you. Ciao. Isn't that sooo Nicki?" The machine said, "Four-oh-five P.M."

The second was Carla. "Hi Fran, it's Carla. I hope Jean-Claude took good care of you. I can't wait to see your new look. I talked to Eileen and we're on for tomorrow. I'll be at your place at about ten, and we'll call her and decide when and where.

"Also, I talked to my friend. His name's O'Malley. He has a first name but no one ever uses it. Anyway, he'll call and you two can have dinner or something. I've got a PTA thing tonight so I'll be out. See you in the morning. And have coffee ready." Then the mechanical voice added, "Six-fourteen P.M."

The final message began with a warm, friendly male voice. "Hello Nicki, this is O'Malley." A flash of panic ran through Fran's body. This was the man who was going to seduce her, teach her about sex. No. She couldn't. She'd have a dinner with Clark and to hell with this all.

"Carla Barrett suggested that I call. She told me a lot about you and I must admit that I'm intrigued. She says you are bright, witty and utterly charming. If you're not, please don't tell me yet. She also told me that you want to become . . ." There was a short silence. "Oh, how can I put this without risking your wrath. You want to become a woman of the world. I know that you can't see it but I'm smiling. It sounds so delicious.

"I'd love to take you to dinner tomorrow evening. We can meet in a public place and there's no pressure. None at all. But, my love, I am looking forward to the wonderful things we can do together." There was a slightly longer silence, then the voice said, "Now I've done it. I'll bet I've scared you off and I can't go back and change what I've already said." Fran could hear a heavy sigh. "Please, I'm a really nice guy. Call me." He finished with his phone number. "I'll be up for at least two hours so, if you get in early, do call."

"Eight-fifty-two P.M.," the machine said. Fran looked at her watch. Nine-forty. She reached for the phone, then jerked her hand back. She could call Clark. He should be home by now. She could suggest that they meet somewhere and have a drink tomorrow night. She didn't have to call O'Malley.

But she trusted Carla and she *was* interested. I'm a grown woman and I'm entitled to some fun. She had a sudden vision of O'Malley, looking like the quintessential New York cop, with ruddy cheeks, red hair and bushy eyebrows. They'd have dinner and go to some hotel room. He'd have large, workman's hands and he'd touch her and lick her and make her want, just like the characters in her stories. But would she be able to do the same for him?

She grabbed a slip of paper, replayed the last message and jotted down O'Malley's phone number. Then she pulled the business card from her wallet and placed it on the table beside the phone.

She dialed. "Hello?" a voice said.

"Is this O'Malley?"

She could hear a long exhalation. "This must be Nicki. I'm so glad you decided to call. You know I'm starting to understand what it must be like to be a high school girl, waiting for the phone to ring, hoping he'll ask you to the prom." He cleared his throat. "There I go again, talking too much."

"Not at all and I have spent lots of hours just as you describe. Sweaty palms, swinging back and forth from, 'He'll never call,' to 'I know he'll call because he really likes me.' "

"I'm so glad you did. Really." They talked about inconsequentials for several minutes. Then O'Malley said, "You really should see some of the great landmark New York restaurants. How about Cafe des Artistes? Tomorrow evening at seven?" He gave her the address of the restaurant.

The moment of truth. Do it, you chickenheart! You know you want to! "I think that would be lovely. No strings?"

"Of course not. Just a leisurely dinner between friends. Is it a date?"

"Yes, it is. How will I recognize you?"

"I'll get there a bit early and I'll have a table ready. What do you look like?"

"Carla didn't tell you?"

"No."

"I'm only about five feet tall, and I now have streaky blond hair."

"Now?"

She stood up, crossed the room and looked into a mirror. "New look as of this afternoon."

"I'll look forward to tomorrow, Nicki."

Truthfully, Fran said, "Me too."

Fran hung up but her hand remained on the phone. She'd done it. She had a date with . . . She decided to think of the entire evening as a date with a nice man. The rest? Who knew, and it was safer to just let that part rest. She thought about calling Clark, but decided to wait a day or two. But she *would* call.

Although it was after ten, Fran wasn't tired at all, so she pulled out her laptop, booted up her word processor and began to type.

Liza had borrowed the condominium from a friend. It was on the north shore of the island of Puerto Rico with direct access to a long stretch of beach. She had taken quite a bit of convincing, but her friend Lynn had finally explained that if someone didn't inhabit her parents' condo, everything would rust shut and get covered with mildew. Trying to recover from a bad relationship and having a week off from work, Liza finally allowed Lynn to press the condo keys into her hand.

Now she had been there for six days and the following morning she was packing and returning to the cold of January in Illinois. So, for a final evening, she put on her two piece bathing suit, grabbed a towel and let herself out through the gate with her key and walked onto the condo's beach. Lynn had warned her about the beach at night, but for several nights Liza had swum in the ocean in the dark and there had been no trouble. There had been no one else around.

She had been in the warm Caribbean water for about twenty minutes and, with the condo in plain sight she relaxed and bobbed in the sizable full-moon-driven waves.

"*Mi querida.*" The melodious, crooning voice whispered in her ear, as though someone were swimming beside her. As she started to turn to see who was talking to her, hands touched her shoulders, keeping her back to her mysterious visitor. "*Mi querida.* I have seen you here every night and I have yearned to be here with you."

Liza was unable to speak. She reached for the rocky bottom with her toes and was just barely able to stand. Saying anything, she reasoned, would only encourage whoever it was, so she started toward the shore. But the hands prevented her, holding lightly, yet firmly to her shoulders.

"*Mi querida*, I would never hurt you. Don't go."

She continued to try to make her way to the strand, but was unable to get a firm purchase on the rocky shelf beneath her feet. The hands and the waves combined to keep her from making any progress. She tried to turn but she was held fast. Each time a swell forced her to float, she lost her foothold.

"Please," she said, breathlessly. "Please leave me alone."

The mouth was on the tender spot below her right ear. As they floated together, he licked her there, the spot that Ray, the jerk, had always told her was her "hot button." Almost reflexively, she tipped her head to give him better access. Then she caught herself and straightened. "Please. No."

"If you really mean no, I will leave," the voice said, releasing the hold on her shoulders. The voice had a sweet Spanish lilt and somehow she really believed that, if she said so, he would leave. "But I hope you don't really mean it." He licked again at the spot below her ear.

She sighed and trembled, and said nothing.

"Ah, *mi querida,* you are an honest woman." Hands. His hands were on her breasts, holding her through the top of her two piece swimsuit. "So full and soft." His fingers found her nipples, already erect. "Yes," he purred. "Oh yes."

Part of Liza's brain was still functioning. He wanted her. Of that there was little doubt. But he was a stranger. She didn't know who he was or whether he was some rapist or murderer. But as he sighed in her ear, and nibbled her lobe, she didn't believe that he meant her any harm. They bobbed together in the moonlit swells, his hands kneading her breasts, his lips now on the tendon at the side of her neck.

She drifted, losing control over her mind. She couldn't think anymore. She wanted to feel wanted, needed, hungered for. Suddenly she burned for this anonymous stranger. She covered his hands with hers, cupping her breasts.

"Ah, *mi amore.*" The hands untied the back of her bikini top and allowed it to float held only by the strap around her neck. He cupped her now-bare breasts, pinching and pulling at her nipples, all the time nipping at the top of her shoulder.

She admitted to herself that she wanted terribly. She was a grown woman and she could do as she pleased. He wasn't going to harm her. How and why she was so sure of that, she didn't know, but she was.

She wanted his mouth so she took his hands from her breasts and held them as she turned in his embrace. Still without a foothold on the bottom, she kicked to keep herself afloat and used her hands to caress his face. She wanted to see him, to know what he looked like, but despite the full moon, she couldn't make out his features, just dark shadows and light planes. She could see that he was dark, his hair and his eyes, coal black in the moonlight. She knew his cheeks were clean shaven and he had a mustache. As she moved her fingers to his mouth she found it bristly against soft, warm flesh. She pressed her hot mouth against his, telling him with her kiss that, for this moment, she was his.

With her hands on his shoulders, she felt him tremble. He was as caught up in this moment as she was. Tomorrow she would be back in Chicago, and the following morning she would be back at her desk, but for tonight, this was where she belonged.

He was obviously taller than she was since he now held her and was able to walk toward the shore. As they got into shallower water Liza looked up and down the beach, but there was no one in sight. The man carried her toward a blanket she assumed he had spread before going into the water. Gently, he set her down on the soft material, and she lay down feeling the hard-packed sand against her back.

"You are so beautiful in the moonlight," he whispered, his Spanish accent romantic and enticing. He pulled her bathing suit top off over the top of her head, baring her white breasts to the cool light. He was quickly on his knees beside her, covering her flesh in kisses. He cupped her breasts and kissed the nipples, while constantly whispering to her in Spanish. She didn't know what he was saying, but it was no less erotic for the lack of understanding.

When his mouth found her nipple again, he brushed his coarse mustache against her hot breast. The slight burning added to the myriad of sensations racing through her. She combed her fingers through his wet hair and held his head against her. Need was consuming her. She couldn't keep her hips still and his warm lips, now on her cool belly, made it impossible to control her hunger. "Love me," she moaned.

"Oh yes, *querida,*" he said, pulling off first her suit-bottom, then his.

Liza could see that he was huge and rampantly erect. He wanted her and she would have him. She spread her legs, reveling in the slippery feeling of her pussy, wet from her juices as well as the water of the warm Atlantic. She had a flash of worry about protection but, ever the gentleman, the man picked up a foil package and quickly unrolled a condom over his cock.

Then he was on top of her, the weight of his body enfolding her in his warmth. She felt the tip of his cock nudging at the center of her need so she wrapped her legs around his waist and pressed her hips upward.

His laugh was warm. "So anxious. So hungry. Such a needy woman." With one quick thrust he drove into her. Then he moved slightly and his fingers found her hardened clit. He stroked and rubbed until she was unable to keep the waves of pleasure at bay anymore and she came. She tightened her legs around him and bucked to bring him still more deeply inside of her.

He thrust and together they rolled over. He pushed her to a sitting position and, still climaxing, she rode him like a wild thing riding an untamed stallion. And then he came, his hips driving into her again and again.

She collapsed on top of him, exhausted, panting, her heart pounding. *"Mi querida,"* he whispered over and over. "So beautiful. So hot."

Liza must have dozed, for how long she had no idea. When she awoke, she was alone, lying on her own towel on the hard-packed sand. He had gone, as she had suspected he would, as silently as he had appeared. But it was no dream, she thought, slowly getting up and wrapping her towel around her. She located the two parts of her swimsuit, let herself in through the gate and slowly walked up the path toward the elevator. Tomorrow she would be back home, with a most wonderful memory to warm her when the snow fell.

Fran sighed and pressed the save key. Another time, she told herself, she'd think of a title and proofread the story. For now, she was content and more relaxed. She had worked out some of the tension she had felt earlier.

Despite the usually calming effect of writing, Fran slept fitfully, dreams of men and sweating palms swirling through her head. She awoke the following morning tangled in the sheets, with a bad-dream hangover. She stood beneath a hot shower for quite a while, then brewed herself a cup of cinnamon apple herb tea. She also prepared a pot of coffee for Carla. She had found a radio in the kitchen and as she drank her tea she listened to a radio psychologist who advised one long-divorced woman to relax and enjoy her new dating life. "It's a different world from the one you left when you married and many of the rules are different," the melodious voice on the radio said. "Take a bit of time to learn the new patterns of behavior and go with the flow."

Okay, Fran, she said to herself, that woman's absolutely right.

As the program broke for the on-the-hour news the doorbell rang.

She greeted Carla with, "When you say ten o'clock, you mean exactly ten o'clock." Carla was wearing a multicolored floral-print skirt with a coordinated blouse and a three-quarter length black wool jacket.

The two women embraced, then Carla held Fran at arm's length. "Nicki, my love," she said, "you look fabulous. I knew you were one gorgeous woman and Jean-Claude did wonders. Your makeup is fabulous."

"Thanks to you." Fran grinned, glad she had again taken time to do her makeup and dress more New York chic, as Clark had put it. This time she wore a soft pink turtleneck with a brown wool calf-length skirt and a pair of cowboy boots that added a few inches to her height. She had topped it with a caramel-colored jacket with a pin on the lapel in the shape of a cluster of green grapes. Each grape was a smoothly polished bit of jade. "I love that pin," Carla said.

"I found it yesterday morning as I walked to Jean-Claude's. I'm taking what you said to heart." She looked at the toes of her boots. "Actually someone commented on it, told me I looked New York chic."

"Trust Jean-Claude to notice."

"I wasn't talking about Jean-Claude."

"Oh?" Carla took Fran's arm and led her into the living room, then gave her a small shove until she landed, sitting on the sofa.

Carla sat down beside her and stared at her new friend. "Something's up. Tell me, woman."

Fran looked up and couldn't suppress a grin. "I got picked up last evening. I stopped for something to eat after I left Jean-Claude's and, as I sat, a very nice man sat down at my table and we talked, then shared dinner." Fran filled Carla in on the conversation. "He's long divorced and he's really nice."

"So?"

"So what?"

"Is he going to call you? Did you make a date?"

"I wasn't comfortable giving him this number, but I have his. I'm going to call him in the next day or two. I don't want to sound too anxious." Carla silently raised an eyebrow. "I am going to call him," Fran said. "Honest. But, more important, O'Malley called. You know, I feel so silly calling a grown man O'Malley. Does he have a first name?"

"Michael, of course. Michael John Patrick O'Malley. But no one ever calls him anything but O'Malley. Don't change the subject. He called and . . . ?"

"And I'm seeing him for dinner tonight."

Carla shrieked. "Bravo, my dear. Scared?"

"Petrified. But if I'm going to become Nicki, I have to begin somewhere."

"And there's no one nicer or better for the job than O'Malley. I know you both and I'm sure you'll love him and he'll be taken with you." Carla cocked her head to one side. "Where are you going?"

"We're meeting at Cafe des Artistes."

Carla whistled. "Very 'in,' very intimate and very pricey."

"Can I ask you a silly question? Do I let him pay for dinner? I'm used to paying my own way."

"What did you do last evening?"

"We went dutch. I told him I wasn't comfortable letting him grab the check, so he let me pay my half."

"How civilized," Carla said dryly. "Listen, Fran, or should I start calling you Nicki all the time. Do whatever makes you most comfortable, but O'Malley makes more in a year than any of us will make in ten. He works hard, plays hard and can more-than-afford a dinner for two at Cafe des Artistes."

"What does he do for a living?"

"He's a commodity trader. Actually he buys and sells money. Ask him about it. It's really fascinating. So what are you going to wear tonight?"

"I was thinking about that. Maybe I should get something new."

Carla stood up and dragged Fran to her feet. "Get me some coffee and we'll sort through your wardrobe."

By ten-thirty, the two women had been through all of Fran's clothes. "I would suggest that wonderful black miniskirt with the cranberry silk shirt and that sexy leather vest. Have you got black shoes with high heels?" When Fran nodded Carla continued, "And you need a wide leather belt to show off that tiny waist of yours. And earrings. What have you got?"

After another fifteen minutes the two women had agreed that nothing in Fran's limited jewelry wardrobe would do. "You've got to graduate from these studs," Carla said, pulling off her earrings. "Put these on."

The earrings Carla handed Fran were large, thick gold hoops, that looked to Fran more like something a gypsy would wear than a girl from Omaha. She put them on and stared at herself in the mirror, amazed at how light they were.

"They look gorgeous on you," Carla said, running her hands through Fran's hair, fluffing it away from her face. "Why don't you borrow them for luck?"

Fran looked. She was someone else. Her hair was streaky-blond and full around her face and the earrings highlighted her slender neck. "I don't know whether I could get used to something this big. They're the size of coasters."

"And what's wrong with that?"

"They're so ostentatious. They're great on you, of course, but on someone my size they're so obvious."

"And?"

"I'm not used to looking so, I don't know, overt."

"So what's your point? What's wrong with being proud of the way you look? I think you look great."

Fran had to admit that if she had seen an actress in a movie who looked like she did she would have admired her style. And what was wrong with it? "Yeah," she sighed.

"Wear them for the day and let's see what Eileen says. One more thing before we call her. What about underwear for tonight?"

"Underwear?"

"Sure. You want something lacy and seductive."

"O'Malley will probably never see it," Fran said.

"And it's not for him. It's for you. Sexy lingerie is meant to make a woman feel soft and warm and sexy. And you wanted something to give you a little cleavage. Oh, and no panty hose."

"Why not?"

"Nothing slows down good sex like panty hose. I think they were invented by some secret chastity activists. Victoria's Secret, here we come."

They called Eileen and arranged to meet her at her office at noon. The two women walked through the brisk morning, chattering like the oldest and dearest friends they were rapidly becoming. The Harcourt Agency occupied a small, unassuming three-story townhouse in the east Fifties. Carla rang the bell and quickly Eileen opened the door.

"Holy mackerel," she said, staring at Fran. "Nicki, you look fabulous." She quick-kissed each woman. "I've told everyone that the famous Nicki St. Michelle was arriving for a brief visit this morning and they are all anxious to meet you. Ready?" Eileen grinned and pulled the two women inside.

"Do they know who I really am?" Fran asked softly.

"Most do, of course, but this can be your first test."

All right, Fran thought. I'm Nicki. She looked at Eileen, who was wearing a deep blue suit with a soft blue and white striped blouse. "It's so good to see you again," Nicki said, lowering the pitch of her voice. "You look smashing."

Eileen winked. "Piece of cake."

Nicki met everyone with a handshake and a smile. The staff in the office consisted of several twentysomething women who did everything from magazine rights to publicity and a crusty accountant who, when interrupted from his work on several royalty statements, actually flirted with her. "You're a hit," Eileen said, leading the two women toward the door. "Bill's a tough sell and he's quite taken with you."

"But he knows I'm not Nicki, doesn't he?"

"Of course. He's the one who sends you your checks twice a year. And speaking of that, how's the new book. Any progress?"

"Some," Fran said, bluffing. "This whole experience will really add to the ideas I already have."

"You should really strike while the iron's hot. If you can put together something while you're here, I can get Sandy to give it a quick read."

Carla said, "How about my life story? You can call it House-wife to Hooker in Thirty Days."

Fran stared at Carla. "That's not a bad idea at all." Carla would make a wonderful character for a book, she thought. And what an opportunity for sexy scenes. "I do have a few ideas that might work out."

Eileen grabbed her coat. "Let's eat, I'm starving."

The three women had lunch at a little Italian restaurant near Eileen's office. At Carla's insistence, Fran told Eileen all about both Clark and O'Malley. "Way to go," Eileen said, toasting Fran with a glass of club soda.

Raising her glass, Fran said, "Yeah. Way to go."

When Eileen returned to work, Carla and Fran headed for a Victoria's Secret on Second Avenue. The items in the window display walked a thin line between overtly sexy and practical. Inside, Carla made a beeline for the bras. "What size?" When Fran told her, she grabbed several off the rack. "Try these on," she snapped. When Fran hesitated, she all but dragged her to a fitting room. "Do it."

Fran pulled off her top and tried on something called a Wonder-bra in a shade of deep rose. "Wow," she sighed. The bra pushed her breasts up and together so, for the first time in her life she had cleavage. Real cleavage. "Wow."

Carla's voice came from right outside the door. "Can I come in?"

"I guess," Fran said. "But I don't believe it."

Carla burst into the tiny fitting room, several more colorful garments in her hands. "Shit, woman, you look really sexy."

Fran's eyes were wide. "I do, don't I?"

"Okay, that's only a beginning. Here's more."

For almost an hour Carla shuttled between the racks and the fitting room while Fran tried on bras, panties, garter belts and camisoles. When Carla arrived with a black satin teddy, Fran giggled. "Nah. I'm really not the slinky black type."

"You never know till you try. You don't have to buy it, but put it on. I want to see how it looks."

Now totally unself-conscious about undressing and dressing in front of Carla, Fran put on the black teddy. From behind her, Carla drove her fingers into Fran's hair and pushed it forward and up, until it was a wild golden mane. Then she took a black stocking and wrapped it around Fran's neck like a wide choker collar. "Oh baby," Carla said. "I have a customer who would love this look."

"You think so?"

"All you need is a small whip and he'd love you. Then he'd kneel at your feet and be your slave for life, if you'd let him." Fran could see Carla's gaze drop to her bush, now outlined by the black satin. "God, he'd go crazy. And he's got the most talented mouth. . . ."

Fran was amazed to feel her nipples harden and her pussy moisten. The idea actually appealed to her. She shook her head and quickly dressed in her street clothes. She bought three bras, several pairs of panties, a slip and a camisole, a garter belt with half a dozen pair of hose in assorted colors and, of course, the teddy.

The two women emerged from the store, and Carla kissed Fran on the cheek. "Nicki," she said, "have a wonderful evening.

Wear the earrings, and the underwear, and have fun. You're a consenting adult and I know you're ready for this."

Fran took in and released a deep breath. "You know, I really think I am."

"I'm running home," Carla said. "BJ's got a hot date and, for the moment, Mom has to drive him and the lucky girl to the mall."

"Have a nice evening," Fran said.

"Not as nice as yours," Carla said. Then she looked both ways then crossed the street in the middle of the block.

Fran looked at her watch. Four-thirty. She was meeting O'Malley at seven. Two and a half hours to get ready. Two and a half hours to get Nicki ready. At a brisk pace, Fran walked back to her apartment.

By six-thirty she was bathed, dressed and made up. She had on the outfit she and Carla had agreed on, with a wide belt she had picked up in a little store near Victoria's Secret. And she was wearing the wonderful rose bra that made the soft cranberry blouse look ever so much better. There was actually a shadow between her breasts. She reached down and slid her hands up the silky black hose which were held up by a black garter belt. She looked at herself again and, as she reached for her coat, she unbuttoned one extra button of her blouse, then tapped one gold hoop earring and watched it swing.

A few minutes stalling in front of the building, and a fifteen minute crosstown cab ride, and she arrived at Cafe des Artistes at exactly seven. She climbed out of the cab, straightened her back and pulled the door to the restaurant open.

She looked around at the sizable but strangely intimate restaurant. The walls were covered with paintings of nudes and nymphs. Vases and potted plants were cleverly placed to create smaller, more intimate areas in the several larger rooms.

"Madame?"

"Yes," Fran said to the tuxedoed maitre d', "I'm meeting Mr. O'Malley."

"Of course, madame. This way." He weaved between closely

packed chairs and tables. As she crossed the room she looked over the men sitting alone. Where was he? she wondered. As she approached a table in the quiet rear of the restaurant a man stood up and smiled at her. She panicked. That was all you could call it, panic. What the hell was she doing here? And what would that gorgeous man want with her? A friend of Carla's? He'd never had to pay for sex in his life.

She stared. He was tall, although everyone looked tall to her, even in her high heels. On closer inspection, he was probably only about five eight or nine, well built with broad shoulders that filled out his jacket without any padding. His hair was midnight brown, cut in a soft wave and obviously carefully blown dry. He had a kind of rugged good looks, not handsome but entirely masculine, with an angular chin with a deep Kirk Douglas cleft. His eyes were the deepest blue she had ever seen, surrounded by long, extremely dark curling eyelashes that women would kill for. His smile was broad and his hands—his hands were soft with long fingers. Fran flashed on a quick picture of his hands on her breasts. She felt the color rise in her cheeks.

Aware that she had been standing, rooted to the spot while the maitre d' held her chair, she mentally shook herself and took the final step toward the table. "You must be O'Malley," she said, trying to keep her voice level.

"I'm delighted to finally meet you," the man said, extending his hand.

Fran took it, held it momentarily, then sat down. She suddenly became aware that he had been staring at her almost as intently as she had been gazing at him. Suddenly she found the entire situation funny and laughed out loud.

O'Malley sat down and joined her laughter. When they finally quieted, he poured her a glass of deep ruby wine and said, "I'm so sorry for staring. You're not what I expected at all."

"Neither are you," Fran said. "You go first. What did you expect?"

"It's not too flattering, I'm afraid."

"That's fine. Go for it."

"When Carla explained that you were a writer from the Midwest who needed a bit of education on the ways of the 'worldly wise' I expected someone plain, glasses, sensible shoes. You know."

"I expected a cop-type. Big man with flaming red hair, gigantic mustache, a bit of a beer belly and big hands."

"And what did you find?" he asked softly.

"You're gorgeous," she blurted out, then almost choked. "I mean . . ."

"Leave it at that and I'll just sit here and bask. Actually I was thinking the same about you."

Not used to being totally flustered, Fran picked up her wine, being careful to hold the glass by the stem. She recalled having seen a video on wine appreciation so she carefully tipped the glass and held it over the white tablecloth as the film had shown. She looked down through the wine, then put the glass to her nose and inhaled.

"It's very young," O'Malley said. "It's light and very fruity. I thought you'd have very unsophisticated tastes so I picked something simple. I can see you're more well educated than I expected."

Unable to continue the fraud, she laughed again. "I have no real clue what I'm doing. Carla taught me how to hold the glass and I watched a video on wine appreciation. I remember the images, but not anything about the reason for all this rigamaroll."

"Ah. An honest woman. I think I'm in love."

Fran felt herself blushing again. "I'll bet you say that to all the women."

"Only the ones I like. Let me tell you about the wine. You look through it to appreciate its color. If it's quite purple, like this one is, it's very young. If it looks almost orange or brown, like the color of bricks, it's past its prime and might not taste good at all."

"Oh," Fran said, looking at the wine in her glass. It was purple, almost like watery grape juice.

"You smell it because it smells good and because most of what we think of as taste is really smell. Take a small sip."

When she did, he said, "Now try to inhale through your nose while you sip."

She inhaled and noticed that the wine tasted . . . she didn't know exactly how to describe it. It tasted more. "That's amazing. Despite the film, I never understood all the smelling and tasting."

His eyes softened and he looked into hers. "It seems there's quite a bit I can teach you."

The double entendre wasn't lost on Fran and she felt herself flush yet again.

"I'm sorry," O'Malley said, "I didn't mean to embarrass you."

"Actually I find this entire situation embarrassing."

"And as intriguing as I find it, I hope." When she hesitated, he continued, "Don't answer that. Let's think about dinner."

Yes. Dinner. A splendid idea.

Chapter
5

Dinner went surprisingly well. Over a delicious salad of mixed greens, a chicken breast in a sauce of dill and capers, rice and broccoli with slivered almonds, they chatted like new friends. They shared an interest in old western movies, Indian food and TV cop shows and disagreed on the facts surrounding the Cuban Missile Crisis. They had different tastes in music—he liking country and she soft jazz—but they agreed on Frank Sinatra and big bands. He explained the rudiments of buying and selling foreign currency, and complimented her when he called her a good listener. Fran also learned a bit about O'Malley's two daughters, who were the same ages as her niece and nephew, and they discussed how children now weren't as social as children had been when they were young.

"It's all those computer games and the inevitable head phones," Fran said over a raspberry tart. "Kids don't have to interact with the world anymore."

"And school? My ex-wife is forever going to the principal, complaining about some teacher who picked on Denise or Michelle. There's no discipline anymore. I'm big on discipline. Not beating kids up, but insisting on some kind of standards."

"I know just what you mean. If I came home and told my

mother that I had been yelled at, her reaction was, 'What did you do, you bum?' "

They shared more laughter. "You know, here we sit, sounding like old married folks arguing about the upbringing of their children." O'Malley reached out and took Fran's hand. "That's not how I want this evening to progress at all."

Fran was suddenly speechless. "How do you want the evening to progress?"

"I want to seduce you. I want to introduce you to new and different ways to make love."

Fran pulled her hand back. She had almost forgotten the reason for the dinner. "O'Malley, I don't know exactly what Carla told you . . ."

"Carla has nothing to do with this. You're a beautiful sexy woman who's only going to be in town a few weeks and I don't want to waste time."

"Come on, don't tell me that Carla didn't tell you that wine wasn't the only thing I needed education about."

O'Malley's grin was infectious. "Busted. She knows how much I enjoy introducing women to the varied pleasures of the bedroom and she mentioned that you might be a willing student."

Fran cleared her throat. "I don't think so. But thanks for the offer."

O'Malley retook her hand and held it tightly against the snowy white tablecloth. She should probably have snatched it back, but since she didn't want to cause a scene, she allowed it to remain. "Do you know what I'd like to do? I'd like to take you back to my apartment and light several candles. I know you'd look wonderful in candlelight. Then I'd take off that blouse, slowly opening one button at a time, brushing my fingers over your skin. I know how soft it will be." Without releasing her hand, he reached across the table with the other and ran the tip of his index finger from the hollow of her throat down to the valley between her breasts.

He continued, "Then I'll kiss you. You will be a bit afraid, but eventually you will open your mouth and let my tongue explore.

We will taste each other, getting to know one of the more intimate parts of our bodies." He paused, then said, "I think I will hold one of your hands behind your back so you will feel powerless to resist me. I will like that, and I'm pretty sure you will, too. I'm very good at ascertaining the naughty things that will give unexpected pleasure."

Fran took a shuddering breath. His words and the feel of his hand lightly restraining hers was filling her with an incredible heat. She felt his thumb slide under her hand and scratch her palm and it made her tingle between her legs. She stared at his hot, sexy mouth, the words 'naughty things' echoing through her head.

Without releasing her hand, O'Malley moved to the chair beside her. "You excite me." He released her hand and, in a lightning-fast move, slipped one hand between her thighs and found the crotch of her panties. Then the hand was gone.

"Your heat is enormous." When she started to protest, he placed one finger against her lips. "That's a pro forma protest and you want to make it because you think you should. You're a nice woman and nice women don't do the things I'm suggesting, the ones you're thinking about, picturing in your mind even now." Her lips moved against his finger but he didn't allow her to speak. "But they do. And you want them. You're curious and excited. You're a grown woman, free to do anything you choose. And you *do* choose. You just don't know how to agree and still be the woman you'd like to think you are."

He released her hand and moved back to his seat. "It's the age old war between what you think you should be and what you want. Now's your opportunity. You're under no obligation to me, but maybe you are to yourself. You deserve this, but it's your choice."

O'Malley signaled for the check, then stood. "I'm going to excuse myself for a moment. Think about what I said. And think about the unusual things you've read about, maybe even written about, that you're dying to try, but never thought you'd have the nerve."

Fran watched his back as he walked toward the men's room. He was graceful and moved like a dancer. He was right about the war inside of her and he was also right about what she deserved. She was free, over twenty-one and capable of making her own decisions. And, as she sorted out all the pros and cons, it was really a no-brainer. She allowed a small smile to lift the corner of her mouth and sipped her herb tea.

And what unusual things did she want to try? Almost everything, she admitted.

O'Malley returned as the waiter put the check on the table. He glanced at it, then dropped his credit card on top. As the waiter hustled away, he lay his hand on the table, palm up, inviting Fran to take it. She looked at the proffered hand, then looked into his eyes. She smiled and placed her tiny hand into his large one. "Oh yes," he sighed, his index finger dancing over her palm. "Now, can you tell me what leaped into your mind when I said I wanted to play naughty games?"

Fran took a deep breath and trembled. "I can't," she admitted. "I can read and enjoy stories about just about everything, but the thought of actually doing any of them is terrifying."

"Some of the things you've read about would be fun to do, some only fun to fantasize about. I love to 'force myself' on willing women and I often pretend that I'm actually raping them. But committing real rape? Never."

Being forced. She tried to still the shaking in her knees.

"You know, you're very easy to read, my love. Very easy." He squeezed her hand tightly. Silently they sat that way until the waiter returned with the charge slip. O'Malley signed it and they rose. He placed his palm against Fran's back and guided her to the check room where they got their wraps. He helped her on with her coat and, as he settled the garment on her shoulders, he placed a light kiss on the nape of her neck. Without giving her time to react to the rush of warmth that invaded her body, O'Malley placed his hand in the small of her back and guided her through the outside door. The evening was frosty, but even through her heavy coat, Fran could still feel the heat of his hand.

On the sidewalk, O'Malley caught her hand and drew it beneath his arm and held it against his forearm. "My apartment is only a few blocks. Are you cold?"

Fran exhaled and watched her steamy breath. "I'm not cold at all," she said truthfully.

"Then it's faster to walk," he said, striding toward the corner.

She pulled on her imprisoned arm. "Remember, I have very short legs," she said.

Chuckling, he immediately shortened his pace. "I'm really sorry. I guess I'm suffering from a certain urgency." He sighed, his breath making a cloud of vapor around his face. "I want you very much."

"We have time," Fran said, amazed at her boldness. But it felt good. She wasn't going to be a wimpy follower. She had made a decision and she was going to be a participant. "We have all night."

He looked at her and smiled. "Wonderful," he said, his breath making frosty clouds in front of his face. They walked the few blocks in silence.

O'Malley's building was a high-rise with terraces on the upper levels. They crossed the patrolled lobby and took the elevator to the seventeenth floor. Fran expected him to make a move in the small confined space, but he merely kept her arm beneath his. They crossed a small hallway and he used his key to open the apartment door and they stepped inside.

The entranceway was small, and they quickly made their way past the living room. "I've turned one of the bedrooms into a sort of sitting room. It's my favorite place to relax so I leave the living room pretty much unused." He guided her toward a small, homey room with overstuffed colonial-style furniture in shades of dark blue and cranberry with lots of light wood. "I wouldn't have expected this from you," Fran said.

"I know. Actually most of the furniture was from the house my wife and I vacated after the divorce, but I liked it and kept it. It's comfortable in both look and feel and that's what I always considered most important in a room for just me."

O'Malley put Fran's coat and his on a side chair, then, true to his promise, lit five slender white candles. Then he flipped off the light and turned on a CD player. Soft music filled the room and he opened his arms and willingly Fran stepped into them. He reached around and clasped his hands at the small of her back and just held her. She tipped her head back and his lips found hers. His mouth was soft and warm. It didn't possess, as she had expected, but shared, giving as much as it took.

The kiss was totally involving, leaving her no room for thoughts of any kind. She parted her lips and his tongue delved into her mouth, tasting and reaching, joining with hers in a primal rhythm. She slid her arms up his chest and around his neck, one hand coming to rest on his hair and one against his cheek. His skin was warm and she could feel his muscles moving as his mouth moved against hers.

His lips moved to her jaw and he placed long slow kisses down her throat. As he lightly bit down a shudder shook her entire body. "Oh God," he murmured against her neck, "you're so responsive."

So responsive? After sex her husband had always asked her whether she had enjoyed herself. "I can never tell whether you're enjoying yourself," he would say. She tipped her head back to give O'Malley better access to her neck and he took full advantage, kissing and nipping at her tender flesh. She felt his hand move up her back and his fingers comb through her hair, massaging her scalp. His lips traced a damp path down her breastbone and into the valley between her breasts.

Suddenly Fran didn't want to be a passive participant, she wanted to feel him. She backed up slightly and slid her hands beneath his jacket, sliding her palms over the hard planes of his chest through his shirt. She was Nichole, free, independent, able to do everything that she had written about in her stories. She slid her hands up to his shoulders and tugged at his lapels. "Take this off," she said, not recognizing her hoarse voice.

O'Malley slipped his jacket off and unbuttoned Fran's blouse. Suddenly they were all hands and clothing, pulling, dragging, stripping until both stood naked in the middle of the living room. He was even more masculine without clothes, she realized, and it was very obvious that he was very excited. His cock stood out from his groin, hard and needy. Nicki had done that, Fran thought. Nicki, the attractive, the anxious, the wanton. In the split second in which each gazed at the other, she wondered about her own body.

"Oh Lord, you're beautiful," he growled.

"You're looking at me the way the wolf must have looked at Little Red Riding Hood," she said. Where had this lightness come from?

"The wolf was thinking about devouring Red Riding Hood." He grabbed her wrist and pulled her against his heated body. "And I'm going to devour you." His mouth found hers and it was as though he was devouring her entire being. One moment she was almost kidding with him, the next she was enveloped in his carnal embrace. She felt his erection pressing against her belly and all thought was extinguished.

"Right here, right now," he moaned against her mouth, and he picked her up and lay her down on the sofa. He knelt beside her and took one erect nipple in his mouth. The feeling was electric, waves of heat and tiny sparks traveled in a direct path from her breast to her already-sopping pussy. Her back arched and she scraped her nails up his back and heard him groan.

Then his hand found her. Unable to get a breath, her body moved of its own accord, reaching for his fingers until he inserted one into her channel. She heard moans, screams and realized that they came from her. "Oh God, don't stop" she cried, reaching, needing, driving upward.

His mouth moved to her other nipple and his fingers moved between her legs. He rubbed her clit, then pushed two fingers into her again, stretching and forcing her to feel. "Yes," she yelled, "oh, yes."

Unable and unwilling to control her actions, she raised her hips and, as O'Malley drove two fingers into her cunt, she came. Spasms overtook her and filled her. She cried as she felt his fingers leave her. She dimly heard him take a condom from his pocket and then he was on top of her, his hard cock probing between her thighs. She opened to him and wound her legs around his waist.

Then he was deep inside her body. He drove, and relaxed, then drove again. She was unable to breathe, unable to think about everything she was feeling. There was just her pussy and his cock and nothing else in the world.

It was only a moment before he roared, arched his back and poured himself into her, then collapsed, panting. They lay silently in the aftermath of the whirlwind they had just experienced. Finally his mouth found hers and he kissed her long and slow. "I'm sorry. I'm really embarrassed," he said eventually.

Puzzled, she held him and said, "Why?"

"I acted like a fifteen-year-old, all hunger and hormones and no sense of your pleasure. I never do that. I just got carried away."

"I'm flattered," she said, feeling wonderful.

"You should be. I knew that you wanted me to go slowly, show you everything, and I will, but this time . . ."

"Who says I wanted you to go slowly," she said, grinning. "I wanted just what I got. You."

"But there's so much more."

"And there's lots of time."

He rolled off, stood up and disposed of the condom. Then he picked her up and carried her into the bedroom. He placed her on the bed, then asked, "Are you cold?" Without waiting for an answer he grabbed an afghan from a chair in the corner and, lying beside her, covered them both. He cradled her head in the crook of his arm and kissed the top of her head. "You are the sexiest woman I've been with in a long time."

Unbelievably flattered, she said, "Thank you. That means a lot to me."

"It's not just talk, you know," he said, taking her hand. He placed it on his penis, already getting hard again. "I'm no kid, yet I'm hungry for you already."

Beneath his hand, she wrapped her fingers around his hardening cock. He's getting excited again, and it's just because of me, she realized. She squeezed slightly and felt him react. Her grin was uncontrollable. She was like a child who'd discovered Christmas. She had always wanted to touch Eric but he had always been in too much of a hurry. Now she allowed her hands to explore. She tangled her fingers in his pubic hair, felt his testicles, ran the tip of one nail up the under surface of his cock. Everything she did seemed to give O'Malley pleasure. She stroked the inside of his thigh and his belly, feeling the muscles tense.

"I'm supposed to be the teacher," he whispered, "but you don't seem to need any lessons." He grabbed her hand. "But you'd better stop unless you want a quickie like we just had."

"And what's wrong with that?" she said, pulling her hand away and scratching her nails up his thigh.

He playfully slapped her hand. "I want more this time, for both of us."

He grabbed her wrists and rolled on top of her, pulling her arms until they were stretched high over her head. "You know what happens to naughty teases, don't you?"

"No," Fran said, suddenly breathless.

He paused, as if considering, then said, "They get theirs back." His eyes locked with hers. "I told you that I like to play." His grip tightened on her wrists. "Do you want to play with me? If not, tell me and I'll stop."

Fran wanted to play. She wanted to experience all the things she had read about. But she couldn't ask.

"I'll take your silence as an agreement." He jumped off the bed and rummaged in the bottom drawer of his dresser, dumping a handful of fabric onto the floor beside the bed. Then he captured both of Fran's wrists, again stretching them tightly above her head. "I think you want this, but if I'm wrong, you have only to say daffodil and I'll stop. Do you understand?"

He was playing yet he was entirely serious. "Daffodil?" she said. A safe word like couples agreed to in the bondage stories she'd read. Her breathing quickened and she could feel the moisture flow from her pussy.

"And I'll stop. I promise. Promise me in return that you'll say daffodil even if you merely think you want to. I can't share this pleasure with you unless you agree." He took one wrist in each hand and spread her arms wide, pressing his chest against hers so she could feel his weight, the power of his body. "Trust is an overused word these days but I need you to trust me. If you don't we will stop right now."

Her entire body trembling, Fran said, "I do trust you."

"Do you agree? You will say daffodil at any time? Promise?"

"Yes," she whispered. Her heart pounded and the sound was a rushing in her ears. "Do it."

In only moments her wrists were fastened to the headboard with the soft strips of velvet that O'Malley had found in the drawer. Then her ankles were stretched wide and tied to the footboard. He seemed to know just how hard to pull the ropes so she was stretched to the edge of discomfort but not over it.

"Has anyone ever done anything like this to you before?" he asked.

She stared up at him, feeling both totally vulnerable and totally trusting. "No," she said softly.

"How does it feel? Tell me."

Fran swallowed, then said, honestly, "It is incredibly exciting. I don't have to think, just feel."

His grin lit up his face. "Exactly. Just feel." He returned to the drawer and Fran could hear the sounds of things being pushed and pulled around inside. Then he was beside her, a furry mitten on his hand. "Are you ticklish?"

"I don't think so."

He rubbed the soft fur over her belly and all her muscles tightened. He stroked her stomach, ribs, thighs, but not any of the places she longed for. Her breasts and her pussy remained untouched. Then he took a piece of rough canvas and rubbed, making her skin tingle. Then he used his tongue, licking and lapping at her flesh, always avoiding her nipples and her groin. "Please," she moaned, moving as much as the ropes would allow. But as she moved, he reacted, staying just out of reach of the aching. "Please," she groaned again.

"You want me to touch you?"

"Oh yes," she said.

Then he bit her left nipple, hard. Pleasure and a small amount of pain knifed through her. "That hurts," she whined.

"I know. And you know what to do if you want me to stop. The word is daffodil."

"But you're hurting me," she said, begging him with her lack of use of the word daffodil, not to stop. His teeth fastened on her nipple and the pleasure almost made her climax. And when his teeth moved to the other nipple and bit down hard, she felt little ripples of pleasure flow through her pussy.

As if he knew how close she was, he moved away. "Not yet, my love" he said. "Not yet. I want to play, to show you all sorts of sensations. I want to see how high you can go without coming."

Fran groaned as O'Malley took a three-inch-wide strip of elastic from the foot of the bed, slipped it beneath the small of her back and fastened it tightly around her waist. The feeling of both entrapment and further loss of control was explosive. Grinning, he fastened another strip over her breasts, pressing it tightly against her erect nipples.

Fran didn't think it was possible to feel more excited yet not climax, but he seemed to know exactly how to drive her higher. He encased her thighs in more wide elastic strips until most of her body from her armpits to her knees was tightly encased. But not her pussy, which was wide open and devoid of any sensation.

Then, while she watched, he crouched between her knees. "You'll come now," he said, "and I won't even have to touch you. I control your body and I know exactly what will give you pleasure." He leaned over and blew a thin stream of cool air onto her clit and she came. Unable to move, all her senses were concentrated on the hard spasms. "Oh my God," she screamed. "Yes."

"And I can fill you, make it go on and on," he said, driving three fingers into her steaming cunt.

He was right. It seemed as though the orgasm lasted for hours. Her hips writhed and drove upward but his fingers never left her. She came and came, wave after wave of pure ecstasy washed over her. Even when his fingers left her for a moment, the orgasm continued.

He turned and stretched out on the bed beside her, his head against her thigh, his penis level with her mouth. She turned her head and, experimentally reached out her tongue and touched his erect cock. She had never had her mouth on a man's penis before but that didn't seem to matter. His cock still tasted from his previous orgasm, a bit tangy and sticky, but wonderful. "Oh baby," he groaned. "You're perfect."

She panicked for a moment, worrying about whether there was something she was supposed to know about licking a man's cock, then she thought, I'll just do what I want. I'm not in control anyway. He's calling the shots. She ran the tip of her tongue up and down the underside of his shaft, unable to move to reach anything more.

With one hand, he stroked her thighs as she came down, and with the other he reached down and held his cock, rubbing the tip over her lips. Then he crouched over Fran's face and again rubbed his cock over her lips. "Have you ever sucked a man's cock before?"

"No," Fran said with the small part of her that could think. "My husband just wanted to fuck."

"Will you take me into your mouth?" he asked.

"Oh yes." And she wanted to. Not for her own pleasure. She had come so hard that she was totally used up. But she wanted to give him as much pleasure as he had given her. She wanted to take his cock in her hand and slide it into her mouth, but she couldn't with her wrists tied. "Do it for me," she growled.

O'Malley straddled her and grabbed the headboard, his cock suspended over her open mouth. Slowly he lowered it until she could wrap her lips around the tip. Make it feel like he's fucking me, she thought, like the women do in all the stories I've written. She created a vacuum in her mouth and drew his cock in. Her tongue surrounded the head and she felt him pump into her as if her mouth were a pussy. She watched him, his head thrown back, his elbows and shoulders straining, his hips driving into her mouth. Her joy was no less because it was his, not hers. It was impossible to tell where his pleasure ended and hers began.

She wondered whether she was ready for him to come in her mouth, but she needn't have worried. He suddenly pulled out and she watched as he held his cock while semen spurted onto her neck. He quickly and silently unbound her and curled against her. Together they dozed for a while.

Later there was little conversation while they dressed. At one point he whispered, "So good. I never imagined you'd be so wonderful."

"It was amazing," she said.

As he held her in the cab that took them back to her apartment, he said, "I have a business dinner tomorrow evening that I can't get out of and it will probably last quite late. Can we make it the following evening? Dinner somewhere? Maybe Le Cirque?"

"Yes," she said, wondering whether she would enjoy spending time with him when it was just a prelude to what they both wanted, good hot sex.

"You're chuckling," he said. "What are you thinking?"

"I'm wondering how difficult it's going to be spending time with you outside the bedroom."

She felt him sigh. "Me too," he said. "All I want to do right now is ravish your body. To hell with dinner."

"Why don't you call me and we'll see whether we can talk on the phone without being able to grab each other."

He laughed. "There's more than one way to skin a cat. I'll call you late afternoon on Thursday and we'll make plans." He walked her to her door and then kissed her good night. "You know," he said, "if I weren't so exhausted, I'd push you inside and do you right on the floor."

"And if I weren't so exhausted, I'd let you. Call me."

He kissed her again. "You know I will."

Fran walked through the apartment and into her bedroom, dragged off her clothes and fell into bed. She wanted to sleep, yet her mind was whirling. After half an hour of tossing and turning, she got up, turned on her laptop and, with the evening's events swirling through her head, she wrote.

THE CHAIR

by Nichole St. Michelle

Anne was sitting on a straight kitchen chair in the middle of the living room, wondering what her boyfriend Tony was up to. All he had said was, "You know I'd never hurt you and I can guarantee that even a prude like you will eventually get into what I have planned for this evening."

"Prude!" she had yelled. "I am not a prude." Was she?

Now she sat wondering whether maybe she really was a bit of a prude. She had never really enjoyed sex that much. At twenty-seven she had had her share of boyfriends and of sexual experiences, but they had always been ordinary sex. Missionary position, some oral sex, but nothing earth shattering. Usually she was in a bit of a hurry to get it all finished. And as long as the guy climaxed, that was fine with her.

As she sat, waiting for Tony to return from something he was doing in the bedroom, she realized that she had always wanted the earth to shatter. She had read books in which the heroine got so carried away with passion that she 'burst apart.' "I never even broke a sweat," Anne muttered.

Tony was different from her previous boyfriends. He loved to experiment. Although they had only been together a few months they had already done things that she had never thought about. One evening he had painted her entire crotch with maple syrup and licked it all off, very slowly. She had really been hot that evening. But eventually he had entered her and she had urged him on until he came. It was wonderfully pleasurable, but no shattering for her that night. Another evening, Tony had used a vibrator on her lips and then inserted it into her channel. That was nice too, but still, no shattering. Not even a crack.

And she wanted it really badly.

"Did I keep you waiting too long?" Tony asked, striding from the bedroom with a canvas bag in his hands.

"I'm just really curious. What's going through your little brain?" Anne asked.

"Just this," Tony said. "I know that, despite all your protests and the obvious pleasure you get out of sex, you've never climaxed. And I want it for you. And I want it for me too and I think I know just how to get it."

"That's not really a problem," Anne said. "I love making love with you. Is orgasm what this is all about?"

"Partly. I want to have some fun this evening and I know just what I want to do. You trust me, don't you?"

"Of course."

"Not of course. Think about it. Do you trust me?"

"That's a silly question."

"But an important one." He paused and looked at her seriously. Carefully enunciating each word, he asked again, "Do you trust me?"

Anne hadn't ever seen him in this mood. What's he up to? she wondered. "Yes," she said softly.

"You know I love you, don't you?"

"Of course, silly."

"Sometimes I think you think too much. For tonight, will you just let loose and not think about orgasms and stuff?"

"Whatever you say." She loved him and had since soon after they met. But recently the feelings had intensified, deepened. She had been down with the flu a few weeks earlier and he had been helpful and kind, taking care of her when she needed him and leaving her alone when that was what she wanted. "I love you."

He leaned over and kissed her deeply. "And I love you. Remember that whatever happens."

What's going on? she wondered. This is obviously leading up to something big.

"Stand up," he said, his voice now taking on a commanding quality Anne had never heard before. "And take off all your clothes."

"Oh baby," Anne said, standing up. "I like it when you undress me."

"But I'm not going to undress you. You're going to do that like a good girl. Now strip."

Anne shuddered. He sounded almost cold. Demanding. Without much thought she removed her clothing, hesitating when she was down to her bra and panties. "Everything," Tony snapped. She unhooked her bra and pulled it off, along with her underpants.

"Good girl," Tony said. "Now turn around."

Trembling with a combination of fear and excitement, she turned her back to Tony. Suddenly he grabbed her wrists and pulled them behind her. She felt cold metal and heard a loud snap. Her wrists were now pinned behind her back. "Handcuffs?" she said. "Tony, this is silly."

"I don't really care what you think. Tonight this is what I want. Now sit."

Quickly Anne sat on the wooden chair, feeling the cold seat against her bare thighs and ass. "Okay. I'm sitting."

Tony reached into the canvas bag and pulled out a roll of silver duct tape. He pulled her bottom forward on the chair until she was perched on the edge of the seat, knees spread, then taped her ankles to the legs of the chair. He slid several small pillows behind her back until she was leaning back, then ran a length of tape around her waist, the pillows, the chair and her handcuffed arms. Then he used another length of tape to fasten her shoulders to the chair. "There now," he said. "I hope you're not too uncomfortable."

"It's not too bad," Anne said, a frisson of fear tickling the pit of her stomach. "But what's this all about?"

"I want to play."

"Play? Is this playing?"

"Oh yes, my love, it most certainly is." Tony reached into the canvas bag and pulled out two small alligator clips held together with a thin chain. "Do you know what these are?"

"Not really," Anne said.

"They're nipple clamps. Here's my theory about you and sex. I don't think you've ever let go. At least every time we've been together you've always been thinking, worrying, wondering what you're feeling. Well, not tonight. I'm going to occupy your body so that you won't be able to think." Tony knelt beside the chair and licked the tip of Anne's right breast. Quickly the nipple tightened and he nipped at the darkened flesh. Then he sucked the entire nipple into his mouth, pulling hard.

Anne loved having her nipples suckled just the way he was doing it. She sighed and thought about the wetness beginning between her legs. "Mmm," she purred. "That's nice."

He bit down, not so hard as to cause real pain, but enough to make her jump. Then, before she could react, he fastened the metal clip to her breast. "I tested all the clamps they had at the Pleasure Palace and these were the mildest I could find."

The pain flashed through her, but somehow it wasn't really serious pain, just little lightning bolts jarring her entire body. "That hurts," she protested.

"Oh it doesn't hurt too badly," Tony said. "I tried them out myself." He rounded the chair and started to lave Anne's left breast. When the nipple was hard and erect, he clipped a second clamp on it. "Tell me how badly it really hurts," he purred, his mouth against her ear.

"They hurt," she whined. "Take them off."

"Nope. That will keep your agile mind occupied while I play."

Play? Anne couldn't concentrate on anything but her nipples. The riot of sensation made her pussy tingle and her entire body flush.

"Now I can do things I've always wanted to do." Tony settled between Anne's spread knees, his face level with her crotch. He reached out his tongue and flicked the end over her hot wet flesh.

She jolted as the heat of his mouth flashed through her. "Oh," she groaned. "Just do it, baby."

"Not so fast," Tony said, tugging lightly on the chain that connected the two nipple clamps. "Every time you're in a hurry, I'll just remind you to slow down. This one will be at my pace."

The small jerk on the chain caused shards of pain/ pleasure to knife through her, yanking her mind from Tony's mouth between her legs. Now he alternated between sucking on her hardening clit and playing with the chain that connected the clips. It was driving Anne crazy.

Tony sat back, his eyes on Anne's face. "Now," he said, we'll add something new." He reached into the bag and pulled out a large dildo. "You remember this, don't you?"

"Yes." And she did. Once he had inserted that large plastic penis into her and licked her clit. It was really exciting. Slowly, he rubbed the cold, hard plastic over her slippery lips, then, with one firm thrust, he drove it into her. He left it inside of her, then got a vibrator and placed it on the chair, the tip against the dildo. When he turned it on, Anne felt herself climb. The persistent hum of the vibrator echoed all the way into her belly through the hard plastic dildo. As she climbed, Tony grabbed the chain and pulled.

"This is going to be the ride of your life," Tony said. "You've never climaxed before because you've never had the patience or the concentration to. Now you have no choice. And I'm going to take you there." He stood, pulled open his jeans and Anne watched his hard cock spring free.

Standing, his erection was just at the level of her mouth. "Open for me, baby," Tony said.

Anne's mouth opened without any thought on her part. It was quickly full of his flesh. Tony tangled his hands in her hair and drove his hips, fucking her mouth. Occasionally he let go with one hand and pulled on the nipple chain.

It was strange, but the pull on her nipples had become immensely pleasurable, bolts of pure heat flowing from her painful peaks to her pussy.

So many sensations. Her mouth filled with Tony's cock, the pain in her breasts, the hum in her pussy. Even the feel of the duct tape giving her no choice about how to move was pure heat.

Tony's fucking of Anne's mouth was becoming more intense. "I'm going to come in your beautiful mouth. Take it all like a good girl and I'll show you what it's like to come."

Anne created suction in her mouth and licked the underside of Tony's cock with her rough tongue. "Oh baby," he roared and her mouth was suddenly filled with his tangy semen. She swallowed, gagged slightly, and let the final spurts dribble from her lips.

Anne was almost incoherent with the need to climb higher. "Baby," she begged. "Help me."

"Yes, love," Tony said, settling back between her knees. He moved the vibrator, and slid the dildo in and out of her pussy. He moved the vibrating tip around, watching Anne's face. Her moans tried to tell him what she wanted and he knew. He found a special spot that Anne had never known she had and rubbed the humming vibrator there.

She felt the dildo fucking her. When he suddenly pulled hard on the nipple chain, flipping the clamps from her sore breasts, she felt the spasms start in her lower belly and crash like waves over her entire body. "Oh God," she screamed as the orgasm kept her at a peak for long moments. "Oh God."

Later, when Tony had released her and gently guided her

to the bed, they lay entwined, half dozing. "That was incredible," Anne whispered.

Tony giggled. "Yeah. It certainly was."

"What ever led you to do that?"

"I just wanted you to know what you were missing. It's so wonderful and I knew you were settling for less than the best."

"Oh Lord, I certainly was." She turned and stretched her naked body against his. "How long does it take to recover. My toes are still tingling."

Tony reached over and pinched one very sore nipple. "Do you really want to recover?"

Chapter
6

The following morning Fran awoke with a start. She saw herself as she had been the previous evening, tied to the bed, writhing in ecstasy. She pictured herself on O'Malley's bed, in his bedroom, a bedroom she had barely noticed while they were together. It was as though she were above herself, watching O'Malley's buttocks clench and release as he pressed his cock into her mouth. It was incredibly erotic and she felt her body responding. It was also humiliating. She had done things in the heat of sexual excitement that she hadn't dreamed that real people did or at least not nice, calm, Fran Caputo from Omaha, Nebraska.

It must have been Nicki. Fran stopped herself. I'm starting to sound schizoid. Nicki isn't a separate person, she's me. Was what Nicki did last evening, what I did last evening, so bad?

"Was it?" she asked aloud. She ran the palms of her hands over her belly, resisting the temptation to caress her breasts which tingled and tightened. And it *had* been wonderful. Oh yes, it had.

She spent the next two hours in a daze, vacillating between, "I couldn't have," and, "Oh, God, it felt so good." Just after eleven, the doorbell rang and she let Carla into the apartment.

"Morning, love," Carla said. "How's tricks, as they say?"

"Tricks are fine," Fran said, leading Carla into the kitchen where she had a pot of coffee brewing, along with hot water for tea.

Carla poured herself a cup of coffee and, as Fran made tea, she could feel her friend's eyes boring into her back. They walked into the living room and, with the statue watching, sat on the sofa. "Okay," Carla said, "out with it. What's bothering you?"

After a few denials, Fran finally said, "My date with O'Malley last evening was sensational."

"Hooray. He's a bit of a character, but he's a sexy beast, isn't he? And what a hunk."

"I guess."

"What's going on, Fran? Anyone who doesn't admit that O'Malley's the sexiest guy on the planet is either blind, lying or seriously deluded."

"Have you ever, you know, been with him?"

"Yes. We've been together."

"Oh Lord," Fran groaned, then buried her face in her hands. "That's just the point."

"What is? That he's free with his sexual activities? That he isn't your concept of a date, husband material, yours forever after?"

Fran looked up. "That sounds so conniving and it's not what I mean. It's just that he was with me for sex, because you asked him to."

Carla's eyes flashed. "Not a chance. He enjoys entertaining women but he's not a whore."

"I didn't mean it like that," Fran said.

"So exactly what did you mean?"

"I have always thought of sex as being part of love. This was sex for the sake of sex."

"And . . . ?"

"And everything." Fran burst into tears. "And I enjoyed it."

Carla started to laugh. "I get it. You're allowed to have good sex with someone who's a date, who you might eventually love, but with someone who enjoys hot rolls in the hay for their own sake, it's just not done. Right?"

Fran sniffled and grabbed a tissue from her leans pocket. "It sounds silly when you say it like that."

"Babe, it is silly. You and O'Malley had a wonderful evening together, and you ended up in bed. Right?"

"Right," Fran said, feeling her face flush at the memory of what "in bed together" had actually entailed. "But it was a bit . . ." She hesitated. ". . . unusual."

"Okay, let me guess. He tied you to the bed."

Fran's face snapped up. "How . . . ?"

"He loves to do that, and I remember loving it when he did it to me. You didn't like it? I'm sorry. I guess sometimes he does get carried away and I should have warned you. I'm really sorry if you didn't like that part."

Softly, Fran said, "But I did like it. That's the problem."

"Ahh," Carla said, nodding. "I get it. You aren't supposed to like the more adventurous stuff."

"Maybe Nicki does, but not me. But I'm Nicki. It's degrading somehow."

"But you write stories about control games, don't you?"

"Not really, until last evening." Her body tingled as the image of the woman taped to the chair flashed through her mind. "This morning I thought about the stories I had written before I came to New York and all of them have been comfortable, heterosexual and, well 'normal.' Nothing really kinky."

Carla giggled. "You think that's kinky? You should only know."

"But I've always been taught that it's wrong."

"Why should something that harms no one be wrong?"

"It just is."

"And why is it that way? Why is it all right for people to have fun in bed one way and not others? Who decides?"

Fran thought about it for a few minutes. Who did decide? She had read about all kinds of perversions in her recent wanderings around the Internet. But were they perversions or just kinky fun? Were they all wrong? "I guess I'm really confused. How do you decide what's kinky and what's wrong?"

Carla got serious. "I have to make a lot of such decisions in my business so I developed a simple rule. If what I do with a man gives us both pleasure and harms no one, then it's okay. If either of us is doing something that we aren't sure of, aren't completely comfortable with, and we are just doing it because someone else wants to or for any reason other than pleasure, then it's not okay."

Fran considered what Carla had said. "Then you think that it's okay to, I don't know, to hurt each other, urinate on each other, like that, as long as you both want to?"

"Absolutely. I personally don't get into water sports and heavy pain, although a few swats on the ass at the right moment can be delicious. However, I've been at parties where people inflict real pain on each other. And it's all totally voluntary and they both get off on it. Actually, I've slapped the occasional person around when he really begged for it and it gave the recipient a great deal of pleasure. There were times I really enjoyed the control part of that, and I love giving pleasure in any form. I don't understand the really painful stuff, and some of the other things that give sexual pleasure, but I don't judge. If everyone's getting their jollies, then so be it. Who am I to decide anyone else's limits, or anyone else's hot buttons?"

Carla continued, "You and O'Malley are grown-ups and certainly able to do what pleases without worrying about what 'society' says is good or bad." She leaned forward and rested her hand on Fran's arm. "And it was good, wasn't it."

Fran took a deep breath and let it out slowly. "Oh yes. It was wonderful. It's just looking back on it is embarrassing. I blush at the thought of some of the things we did."

"How delightful. I'm thrilled for you. It's kind of like having discovered a new game." She remembered when her friend Ronnie had introduced her to a man named Bryce, a man she still dated intermittently. "I envy you in a way. The newness is so exciting."

Fran ran her fingers through her hair, then said softly, "Yes. It is."

"Bravo. Are you going to see him again?"

Fran rubbed the back of her neck, shook her head, then smiled. "Yes. He's busy tonight, but he'll call me tomorrow."

"Did you call that man you met the other evening?"

"Phew. You really know how to push. I thought I should concentrate on one thing at a time."

"Why?"

Fran sipped her tea. "Why indeed? Maybe I'll call him later."

"I want to ask you a very personal question and I need an honest answer, or no answer at all. Are you interested in experiencing some of the more unusual things you've read about? This isn't for Nicki, although she'd love everything. This is for you, for Fran Caputo."

"Honest answer, I don't know. It intrigues me, titillates, but I don't know exactly what I want to experience in person."

"Good answer. Listen. I'm going to a party next weekend down in the Village. It's being held in a loft owned by a friend of mine named CJ. Actually I'll be CJ's date and this is for fun, not business. You'd be more than welcome to join us. You wouldn't have to participate in anything you didn't want to, but you'd be able to experience some of the control aspects of sex, at a distance or up close and personal. Think about it. You don't have to give me an answer. Lots of people go without partners and there are always a few who just watch. Nonparticipation is accepted and respected. Just consider it and let me know."

"I'll think about it, but I don't know. . . ."

Carla patted Fran's hand. "Okay. Today it's museums. Nicki probably doesn't go to them often, but she knows about European art and that sort of thing. We'll just wander and you can pick up some names to drop. We'll start at the Metropolitan Museum of Art, then go to the Museum of Modern Art. And we'll talk about theater, and books, which you probably know more about than I do since you told me that you're a voracious reader. We'll cover as much as we can. My kids are with my folks until tomorrow so we can have cocktails at Windows on the World at the top of the World Trade Center, then dinner, if you don't have anything else to do. Some kind of exotic foreign food, I think."

"Food. That's where this whole thing can fall apart. I've watched videos about some of the bigger cities in Europe, I've taken photographic tours of the wine country of France, the Rhine, Ireland. They always talk about the food, but the exotic restaurants I've been in have been either Italian, Chinese or Mexican. And most of that was in small restaurants and fast food. Taco Bell, Domino's Pizza and The Golden Wok hardly prepare you for haute cuisine. You know, it's hard to go into some weird restaurant alone and there wasn't much in my neighborhood even if I had been feeling brave."

"Well, for today you're not alone. How about sushi tonight?"

It was difficult not to make a face. "Raw fish?"

"We'll go someplace where they have cooked food too, but if I know you like I think I do, you'll really like it. Are you up for it?"

"I guess I'm up for anything," Fran said, really meaning it.

"And then, after dinner I'll show you a few things about my house that you haven't already seen."

"Okay," Fran said, a bit mystified.

The day passed in a whirl and Fran learned a great deal. She absorbed information about paintings and theater and she and Carla discussed everything from Shakespeare to Danielle Steele. She learned about Indian food at lunch and actually found that she liked raw fish and rice at dinner. But there was much more than that. She watched Carla, the way she moved, the way she interacted with people, the way she gestured with her hands, the way she accidentally-yet-quite-deliberately touched people, particularly men, while she talked. She began to try to emulate Carla's easy way of dealing with cab drivers and waiters, museum guards and coat checkers. There was a relaxed sensuality about everything Carla did. With some careful observation, Fran was able to adopt some of her small, flirtatious movements. Nicki was emerging and Fran loved the way it made her feel.

After dinner, the two women took a cab back to Carla's brownstone. They settled in the living room with glasses of Sauvignon

Blanc. "Are you going to call that man you met the other night?" Carla asked.

"I guess."

"Well, why don't you just use this phone," Carla said, handing Fran a cordless handset, "while I go to the little girls' room. Holler when you're done."

"But . . ."

"Do it, Nicki. It's your time now. Just enjoy." And with that, Carla walked away.

Fran thought for a few moments, then pulled out the business card Clark had given her, found his home phone number and dialed.

"Hello?" The voice was deep-toned and friendly.

"Clark, it's Nicki," she said, suddenly wondering whether he'd even remember who she was. Maybe she was making a fool out of herself.

"Nicki. Wow." He sounded shocked. "I didn't think you'd call."

Fran heaved a large sigh. "Well," she said, "here I am."

"I'm so glad. I must admit that I played our goodbye over and over and I was sure I'd come on a bit strong. You know, sounded desperate."

Men have all the same fears women do, Fran thought, shaking her head. It's amazing. "Don't be silly. I had a wonderful evening."

His voice softened. "I did too. I was wondering whether you might be interested in getting together. Maybe tomorrow evening?"

Tomorrow. O'Malley. "Actually, tomorrow's not good for me."

"Oh." His voice sounded dead. Fran was delighted.

"How about Saturday?" she asked, shifting the phone to the other ear. "Does that work for you?"

"Sure. That would be great. I know a small Indonesian restaurant. Do you like Indonesian food?"

Could Nicki say that she'd never had Indonesian food and still sound worldly? "Actually I don't think I've ever had it."

"Great. Then I can introduce you to something new. Can I pick you up? You were kind of reluctant to give me any information about yourself when we last met."

"That would be wonderful." She gave him her address and they agreed on seven o'clock.

"And this one's my treat," Clark said. "I guess I'm just old fashioned enough to want to pay since this is a date."

Fran grinned. It was a date, with a nice, comfortable man and the evening would probably not involve the erotic tension that had flared between herself and O'Malley. "Yes," she said softly, "it is and I'll see you at seven on Saturday." As she hung up, she wondered whether Fran or Nicki would be at the door Saturday evening when Clark arrived. As she thought about it, the line between the two women blurred. She really was becoming the best of both.

Several minutes later, Carla returned. "Did you make a date?"

Fran grinned. "Yeah, I did. He was afraid I wouldn't call."

"Of course he was."

"He wants to introduce me to Indonesian food. I told him that I, Nicki, had never had it."

"It makes a man feel wonderful to be able to show someone he cares about something he enjoys. It's not too different from O'Malley and sex."

"I never really thought about it that way."

"Maybe it's time for me to show you the upstairs of this joint." With Carla leading, the two women climbed the thickly carpeted stairs and walked into a large bedroom, all done in shades of soft pink and greens. There were ferns and pots of trailing ivy in the corners and a heavy oriental carpet on the floor. "I want to show you my closet. Actually it was Ronnie's first, and now we share it."

Carla opened the doors to a large walk-in closet filled with colorful garments. At first glance, there wasn't anything unusual about it. Suits, conservative blouses and tailored dresses filled part of one rod. The clothing that filled the rest of that side and all of the other was more unusual. When Carla pulled out a few items, Fran gasped. One section was filled with costumes, everything from a red vinyl minidress to a maid's outfit, from the Egyptian outfit that Fran had noticed when she looked through Carla's album to a sheer pair of harem pants and a matching bolero jacket.

"This is where I create the fantasies that my customers want to act out," Carla said. "And on each hanger is a bag with any special accessories, like wigs, special jewelry, or particular underwear that goes with each." She pointed to several shoe racks on the floor. "And the proper footwear, of course."

Fran pulled out a short, fluffy, pink chiffon dress with a white collar and puffed sleeves. "What's this?"

Carla held the dress against her body, then put her index finger in her mouth. Her voice became that of a little girl. "This is my dress," she said in a singsong. "I love to be with men who like to play with my bottom. I've got a wig with long braids, white socks and even a real pair of Mary Janes."

"You're kidding."

Carla's voice returned to normal "Not at all. Lots of men really like the idea of deflowering a little girl but would never dream of actually doing it. This is the next best thing." In the child's voice she said, "You'd be surprised at what I'd do for a candy bar."

"I never imagined real people would like to live out their fantasies."

"Some dreams are wonderful to live out and my friends and I can do it in complete safety. Other fantasies are never meant to be acted out, just to dream about. And we do that sometimes by telling stories in the dark."

Carla hung the dress back on the hanger. "And here are some entertaining clothes." She turned and showed Fran dozens of satin lounging outfits, peignoirs, nightgowns, pairs of babydoll pajamas, both on hangers and in the drawers of a small chest at the back of the closet. "And in the bottom drawer are old sets of underwear that are ready for the garbage."

"Okay, I give up," Fran said, totally puzzled. "Why do you keep them?"

"Some men like to rip the clothes off a woman's body so Ronnie and I have our 'disposables.' " She walked out of the closet and closed the door. "Luckily Ronnie and I are the same size. Actually, some of this stuff is stretchy one-size-fits-all, or is two piece and very flexible. If you ever want to borrow an outfit, I'm sure we could create something for any occasion."

"I don't think so."

"I wouldn't be so sure. Just keep an open mind."

"You really do create fantasies for your customers."

"And for men I date, too. I think every man has a fantasy and if you can find out what it is, you and he can have the most wonderful fun."

"You really believe that every man has a fantasy?"

"Absolutely."

Carla opened the door to a smaller closet on the other side of the room. "And for the evening out . . ." Inside were evening dresses in every color of the rainbow, sequins, laces, full, slinky, everything anyone could dream about for formal or semi-formal occasions.

"Wow," Fran whispered.

"Again, the offer's open. Just say the word and we can rummage through and find something. Maybe for that party next weekend."

"I'm still thinking about that one."

"Hey, no pressure." Carla paused, then said, "Are you interested in seeing the other room up here? It's a bit bizarre. If you hadn't had an unusual evening with O'Malley last night, I wouldn't show you this, but maybe now you'll understand."

Carla led Fran down the short hall to what had originally been a second bedroom. She opened the door and stood back so Fran could precede her. Fran stepped inside and Carla flipped on the light. The room resembled a cave, with dark wood paneling and heavy drapes that completely covered the windows. The walls were festooned with eyelets and chains, straps and buckles, and there were several hooks in the mirrored ceiling. There were two odd-shaped wooden benches with attached hooks and leather straps and three large cabinets. Carla opened the door of one and Fran saw paddles and whips of all kinds. "Ronnie's a dominatrix and many of her special clients spend time in this room. Ronnie's incredibly adept and seems to know exactly what will excite a man beyond his ability to control his own body."

"Oh," Fran said. "Do you use this room, too?"

"I have a number of clients who like to tie me down, but I don't let anyone hit me. I'm actually learning a lot from Ronnie. Originally I was really passive. I loved being tied up or made to feel powerless in other ways, but now I can occasionally wield a paddle with the best of them. CJ is really into having his bottom spanked and I will probably be doing that next weekend."

"I don't think I ever could do that."

"Neither did I, but it's amazing how your horizons expand as time passes."

"I guess."

"Well, now you know my secrets." She laughed. "As if I ever had any."

"I think you're the most genuinely honest person I've ever met," Fran said, embracing her friend. "And you've given me a lot to think about."

"I'm glad. That's what I like to do, expand people's notions of what is just good fun."

Together they walked downstairs and Fran got her coat. "I have a bit of a time problem for the next few days," Carla said, frowning. "I'm afraid that between the kids and my social life, I won't be able to get together with you until Monday. Will you be able to entertain yourself until then?"

"Of course. This is New York and I've got a lot more to explore. And I'm probably seeing O'Malley tomorrow evening and Clark on Saturday. What could be better?"

"What indeed? I'll call you though, so you can give me all the juicy details."

"Great," Fran said as she opened the front door. "Have a great weekend."

Carla winked. "I certainly will."

*   *   *

O'Malley called later that evening. Without preamble, he said, "I had a great evening last night and I'd really like to see you tomorrow."

"I'd love to."

"Unfortunately I have a business meeting that just came up and it will run through dinner. Can I ask you to meet me at my place at, say, nine? I'm really sorry about not picking you up or inviting you to dinner."

Fran was a bit let down. She was looking forward to spending some time getting to know the man better. "It's fine. But would another evening work better?"

"I really don't want to wait. Unless you'd prefer."

"Of course not," Fran said. "I'll be at your place at nine."

Fran had lunch with Eileen the following day. Once again, Eileen suggested that the time was right to give her editor the proposal for another book. And again Fran promised to think about it. After lunch, the two women parted, and for a few minutes Fran was tempted to return to the apartment and bury herself in the TV and her writing and bide her time until her date with O'Malley. Be brave, she told herself. Be Nicki.

So, gathering her courage, she decided to get to know New York. For a few hours she wandered the crowded streets of midtown Manhattan. It was a magnificent day, as only April in New York can be, bright blue skies and a gentle, warm breeze. She browsed in several boutiques and bought a few things that she thought Nicki would want. Later in the afternoon she took a taxi to Chinatown and, when her feet were finally too sore to walk anymore, she stopped in a tiny restaurant that boasted something called dim sum. As she was guided to a table, she watched waiters push small carts covered with small plates of Chinese specialties.

When a young Oriental man in a white jacket arrived with a pot of tea and a glass of water, he asked her, "Have you ever been here before?"

"No," she said, waiting for a menu.

"Well, there's no menu. just pick anything you like from the carts. Eat as much as you like, and when you're done, signal me and we'll figure out what you owe."

Mystified, she asked, "How do you know what I've eaten?"

The waiter smiled indulgently. "Of course I count the empty plates."

So Fran took plates from many of the carts. She tasted a dozen different concoctions, from dumplings filled with meat to small rolls of pastry stuffed with mushrooms and some sort of fish. With each item she selected she asked the person pushing the cart what the delicacy was, but many of them weren't very good at English so she ate several unidentified items. But everything was delicious.

After dinner, she looked at her watch and discovered it was only six-thirty so she walked through still-busy streets and found herself in Little Italy. She stopped at a small coffee shop and had a cup of tea and a super-caloric, whipped cream dessert. Finally, satiated, she found a taxi and returned to the apartment to get ready for her date. She showered, used a blow dryer on her hair and gazed into her closet trying to decide what to wear. As she stared, she thought about the closets at Carla's. Feeling brave, she pulled out the leather pants and vest that she and Carla had bought. She paired them with a white satin shirt and a pair of black leather boots. She pictured O'Malley slowly unwrapping her like a Christmas present. She carefully applied her makeup and sprayed just a touch of Nicki's now-signature scent, Opium, between her breasts.

At eight-thirty she went downstairs and, with the doorman's help, found a cab. She arrived at O'Malley's just after nine. "You're late," he said, throwing open the door. "I was afraid you'd changed your mind."

Fran gazed at him. He was wearing a soft yellow tennis sweater, brown slacks and loafers. "Of course not."

He all but pulled her into the apartment and wrapped his arms around her, trapping her arms at her sides. He kissed her soundly. "You smell good," he growled. "Makes me crazy."

"I'm glad," Fran said, wishing he would notice how nice she looked as well. But his kisses were dizzying and almost immediately her body was humming with excitement.

"I'm glad you found our games Wednesday evening as delicious as I did." He pressed his groin against her so she could feel how excited he was. "I'm so hot for you already that I could explode." He reached into the crotch of her pants and felt her heat. "And you're hot for me, too. I love that about you."

O'Malley cupped her face and used his thumbs to push her head up. He quickly found her throat and placed deep wet kisses there. "You do such wonderful things to me. Come, darling, let me love you."

He led her into the bedroom and quickly removed her clothes. Before she could think, she was again tied to the bed, her heart pounding, her breathing rapid. "Now, my sweet, let me appreciate my newest toy." He stood beside the bed and stared down at her. "Wonderful. Hair spread on the pillow, red lips, a bit swollen and so ready for my cock, small breasts with large erect nipples, aching for my mouth, legs spread wide so I can play with your wonderful pussy."

His words excited her still more and she ground her hips into the bedspread in what she knew was a useless effort to ease her need.

"Look how excited you are, how needy. I love to watch you wanting me. Let's see whether we can watch together." O'Malley crossed to a closet and, from inside, said, "Have you ever been on TV?"

"What?" Fran asked.

"TV. Have you ever seen yourself on TV?"

Puzzled she replied, "I've seen demos in the local Radio Shack."

His chuckle was warm and filled with genuine good humor. "That's not what I mean at all." He emerged from the closet, then fussed behind the TV set that sat on the bureau. Finally he stood up. "We're ready."

He was holding a video camera. He pushed a button and suddenly Fran's body filled the screen of the TV. Her eyes widened, but she said nothing.

"Look at yourself, and how helpless you are. Look at your arms, tied to the head of the bed, unable to get free." The picture zoomed in on the strips of soft velvet that imprisoned her wrists. "Look at how powerless you are, love."

Fran just stared, unable to tear her eyes from the screen. As the camera slowly panned down, Fran gazed at her breasts, then her belly and her cunt. Slowly, the picture traveled down her legs and zoomed in on the bindings that held them widely spread.

O'Malley placed the camera on a bracket on the wall at one side of the bed and aimed it at Fran's chest. The view of her breasts, with their erect nipples, filled the screen. "Now, I'm free to play with your luscious body." He opened the bottom drawer of the dresser and pulled out a box, which he opened very slowly. Inside were two odd-shaped pieces of flexible flesh-colored plastic. "I'm sure you have no idea what these are, so I'll explain. Contrary to the stories I've read, I've never found a pair of nipple clamps that don't *really* hurt, and I don't think pain adds anything to this experience for you, yet. I did, however, find these in a small store in the Village. They're suckers."

He bent down and licked Fran's nipple, wetting the entire dusky area. Then he squeezed one of the plastic devices and pressed it against Fran's tit. The sensation was like a pulling, a sucking, a constant awareness of her breast.

"You see why they are called that, I'm sure. Maddening little devils, aren't they?"

Fran remained silent as he laved her other nipple and attached a sucker to it. "Look at them on the TV," he said, picking up the camera and moving it to her face. "See how your face gets flushed? They really make you hot, don't they?"

"Yes," she said softly.

"Actually this entire situation makes you hotter than you've ever been, doesn't it?"

She had to admit that it did. "Yes."

His laugh was powerful and deeply erotic. "It's difficult for you to admit that you're so, excited by being tied up, completely helpless, with suckers on your tits and a camera recording every expression. But it makes you crazy, doesn't it?" When Fran remained silent, he lifted one of the suckers so it pulled more firmly on her nipple. "Admit it. You're really enjoying this. Be honest with yourself."

He was right. "Oh yes. I am enjoying it."

Again the camera roamed her body, zooming in and panning back. Then O'Malley placed the camera on another bracket so it was aimed at her pussy, so visible between her widely spread legs. He got another box from the drawer and from it he lifted a pencil-thin dildo. "This will do nicely for our next step," he said. "You know what this is, of course."

Fran's gaze darted between the dildo and the view of her wide-open cunt on the TV. "And it excites you still more. Look at how your pussy is getting wet," O'Malley said. "As you think about this little beauty sliding into your beautiful cunt, you can't help but get wetter." He walked to the camera and pressed the zoom button. Now Fran's pussy filled the screen, the lips swollen, wet and glistening.

"Oh my God," she moaned.

O'Malley sat on the side of the bed and, as Fran watched the TV screen, he moved the dildo closer to her pussy. She saw him touch her hot flesh as she felt the cold plastic almost sizzle against her. The feeling was doubled as she both watched and felt the dildo. "Now, my love, watch it slide into your beautiful pussy."

He slipped just the end of the flesh-colored plastic penis into her. She couldn't stop her hips from reaching for more of it. "Anxious little girl, aren't you?" He slid it in another half inch. "Is this what you want?"

"More," she whispered.

"Ask me."

"Please."

"Please what?"

"Oh God," she said, "please fill me with that."

"You ask so nicely." He slid it in another half inch, leaving half of the dildo still outside of her hungry pussy.

"Don't tease," she begged, gazing into his eyes.

"Tease?" he said with mock innocence.

"Please."

With one quick stroke he rammed it home. "Watch me fuck you," he said, and Fran's eyes returned to the TV screen. She saw his hand driving the dildo into her, then pulling it back. Her hips bucked and her back arched, but, even with the suckers on her breasts and the dildo fucking her, somehow it wasn't enough.

"I know," he crooned. "You want something more."

"I want your cock."

"No, actually you want any cock. You want to be filled." He left the dildo inside her channel, and reached into the drawer again. He pulled out a ten-inch-long dildo, as thick around as Fran's wrist. "You want my monster."

"That won't fit," Fran protested.

"Oh, but it will," O'Malley said. "You'd be amazed. And you'll eagerly watch as all of it disappears into you."

Fran threw her head back and closed her eyes.

"No. Don't do that. Watch your pussy on TV. Watch what I'm doing."

Fran opened her eyes and looked at the screen. She saw and felt him remove the slender dildo and push the larger one against her opening. She knew it would never fit but relentlessly he pushed and slowly it stretched her wet channel. It pressed against all of her, touching everywhere at once. She trembled with the need of it, the fullness, the hunger, the possession of her body by this enormous cock.

"Now watch as you come," O'Malley said. He withdrew the cock, then inserted it again. Over and over, more and more rapidly he fucked her with the dildo, then he placed his fingertip on her clit and rubbed. "Come for me, baby," he said. She screamed as she came, spasms stabbing through her entire body. She writhed as much as her bindings would permit, driving her hips upward to meet the thrusts of the dildo. She was out of control, unable and unwilling to stop the waves crashing over her.

It was long minutes before O'Malley removed the dildo and the suckers, and untied her. He quickly undressed and lay on the bed beside her, then slowly unrolled a condom over his cock, which stood straight up from his groin. "Ride me." He had positioned his body so the camera was now directed at his cock as Fran straddled him and slowly lowered her wide-open dripping cunt onto his rigid erection.

He grabbed her waist and, using his hands and hips, found his rhythm and drove into her. Only a few thrusts were needed for him to climax and throughout they both watched the scene on the TV.

When he was calm, he lazily sat up and switched off the camera, then covered them both. Fran must have slept because the next thing she remembered was looking at the clock and seeing that it was 1 A.M.

"Mmm," O'Malley purred. "That was as wonderful as I knew it would be."

"It was amazing," Fran admitted.

"May I confess something to you, Nicki?" he asked.

"Of course," Fran said.

"I didn't have a business dinner this evening. I just didn't want to spend several frustrating hours in a restaurant. All I could think about was being in here with you."

"Why so late? I could have been here at seven."

"But I needed to let you think I had plans and anyway, I enjoyed just sitting here and imagining what it would be like. And it turned out to be better than any of my imaginings."

Fran wasn't sure that she liked being manipulated, but the sex had been explosive. "I've really got to be getting home," she said, for want of other conversation.

"Of course," he said, rising and handing her her clothes. "I'll take you."

"No need."

"No need, but I want to."

They dressed in silence and, when they were ready to leave, he ejected the tape from the VCR. "This is a record of this evening. I know it would upset you if you realized that there was a visual record lying around, and I thought you might be brave some evening, and watch it."

Fran took the tape, holding it as though it might explode at any minute. Would she ever watch it?

As the taxi pulled to a stop in front of her building, he kissed her. "I'll call you," he said.

Fran nodded, then got out of the cab and entered her building.

Fran undressed and put on an old tee shirt and leggings. Keyed up from the evening and rested from her nap, she turned on her laptop.

Power, she thought. It was a seductive tool. She began to type.

POWER

by Nichole St. Michelle

I don't know when I discovered I had this quirky power but I do remember using it on my second grade teacher. Okay, let me explain. You know how some people can wiggle their ears? Well I can't and I've no clue what muscles to use to try to do it. Well, I can send these pulses that seem to force the person at whom the pulse is directed to tell the truth. I can't control anyone or make someone do stuff, although you can be sure I've tried.

I remember my second grade teacher. Miss Gilbert was her name and she was a thoroughly nasty woman with a pinched face and a sour expression. One day she yelled at me for not being able to do some arithmetic problem or other on the board. Arithmetic was always my Achilles' heel. So she screamed at me, called me a moron who would never learn anything, and read me out in front of the whole class.

Well I was a mess. I wanted to run home, hide under my

bed and never come out. But several of my friends told me just forget it. That she was a flaming bitch and didn't deserve to triumph by driving me out. They were right, so I stayed.

A few days later there was a fire drill and we all lined up outside. Miss Gilbert suddenly remembered that she had left her roll book inside, a cardinal sin since without it, if the fire were real, she wouldn't know which students were actually present that day and who might need to be rescued. So she told one of the other boys to sneak inside and get it. She had it in her hand when the principal arrived to check out the results of the drill.

"Glad to see you're prepared," he said to her as we all stood around in the cold.

"Oh, yes sir," she said, brandishing her book. Well, I sent this pulse. She stuttered and said, "W-w-well, actually I left it on my desk. I sent Carlos back inside to get it. And truthfully these fire drills are a gigantic waste of time." I remember how puzzled she was that she had actually said that, but I knew the reason, and I giggled.

That was the first time I remember using it, but I've pulsed folks many times since. It really helps in the business world and I've made lots of lucrative deals based on just pulsing the other guy so he tells the truth.

But it works best with women. Now, I'm not a particularly attractive man. I'm twenty-seven, with sharp features and hair that kind of looks like used packing twine—you know, kind of light brownish and frazzley. But I'm charming, and modest, and I have several girlfriends at present. And this ability I have makes me a very desirable person, since I'm a very talented lover, with the help of my power. I'm not being egotistical when I say that after an evening with me, women are spoiled for other men.

Let me tell you about last evening. I had met this woman at work several weeks ago and we had been having lunch once or twice a week ever since. Amanda is pretty, I guess, with soft brown eyes and long straight brown hair, but being pretty doesn't really impress me much. What I like about her was that she is a wonderful person, warm, interested in most of the things I enjoy, and she has a great sense of humor.

So finally I asked her out for a real date. We had dinner and talked, then went to a movie. I held her hand in the theater and then, as we walked home, I smiled at her delightful shyness. She kept looking at her feet as we walked, stuttering each time I asked something the least bit personal. I didn't pulse her, though. Everything in its own time.

On the elevator in her building I put my hands on her shoulders and kissed her. It was a wonderful kiss, with my lips moving over hers. She tasted delicious. I held her and reveled in her trembling. My cock was swelling. I wanted her. Very much. I wanted to slowly remove all her clothes and kiss and lick her all over. I wanted . . . Actually I wanted to know what *she* wanted so I could give her the best sex she'd ever had.

"I'd like to come in for a little while," I said when we got to her door.

She blushed. "Well, I have to get up early tomorrow morning. You know, work and stuff."

"But I don't want the evening to end so soon." I kissed her again. It was a warm evening so neither of us were wearing jackets, so I could easily slide my hands along her ribs until I could just brush the underside of her full breasts. She shivered and I could feel her nipples hardening against my chest.

"But, you know, this is only our first date," she said.

As I nibbled on her left ear I pulsed her.

"I guess I'd really like it if you came inside," she said.

I kissed her again so she wouldn't be too confused at having told the truth. In the throes of passion most women have no clue what they're saying anyway.

I knew from our conversations that she lived alone, with

only a cat and a parakeet for company. With any luck at all, I would keep her company that night. We wandered into her kitchen and, with trembling hands, she poured us each a soft drink. Alcohol confuses my abilities.

Back in the living room, we sat side by side on the sofa. I turned her to me and brushed her lips with mine, teasing, tasting, nibbling. I placed a line of tiny kisses from her mouth along her jaw to that wonderfully sensitive spot beneath her ear. Then I nipped at the tendon and worked down to the place where her neck joined her shoulder.

Her hands had been resting passively on my chest so I took her wrists and drew her arms around me. I tangled my fingers in her long hair and pulled her head back so I could continue kissing her throat. Then my lips traveled down to the wonderfully mysterious shadow between her breasts. When my face was buried deeply in her cleavage, she started to push me away.

"This is a bit too fast for me," she said, breathless and flushed.

I pulsed her.

"But it feels so good. I don't really want you to stop."

I didn't. My hands slid to the front of her ribs and then upwards until I was cupping her breasts. Her arms became limp and she almost swooned against the back of the couch. I gazed at her and my heart pounded. Suddenly my head was filled with images of me ravishing her, dragging her clothes off and plunging my now-throbbing dick into her pussy. I shook my head. No. Slowly. I had to move slowly. Control yourself, I told my aching body.

I caressed her breasts, then rubbed her nipples. Again she grabbed my forearms. "We really shouldn't," she moaned.

I pulsed her and asked, "Are you a virgin?" I would have to really be careful if she was.

"Oh no," she said. "I've made love before."

"Do you like it when I touch you?" I asked, continuing the pulse.

"Oh God, your hands feel so good. Please don't stop what you're doing."

I didn't. As I kneaded her cloth-covered breasts I had the mental picture of my hands ripping off her blouse and bra so I could feel the softness of her skin. Exerting all the mental control I could, I slowly unbuttoned her shirt and removed it and her bra. Her breasts were magnificent, full and round, with pink nipples that begged for my mouth. I suckled, feeling the tips swell still more under the ministrations of my tongue. I moved from one to another, licking, sucking and then blowing on her wet skin. Soon she grabbed my shoulders, holding me close.

Still laving her nipples, I placed one hand on her nylon-covered thigh and slid it upward toward her heat. I was anticipating having to deal with panty hose, but I found a stocking top and inches of bare skin above. The picture of my fingers plunging into her cunt formed in my mind but I forced myself to be patient. I caressed the soaked crotch of her panties, then worked my fingers beneath the side elastic. She was so wet that, as I rubbed, it was almost impossible to keep from sliding into her.

Naked. We had to be naked. Now! I quickly pulled off my shirt, slacks, shoes, socks and underwear. When I looked back at Amanda her shyness seemed to have vanished and she was also undressed. God, she was so gorgeous. So hot. So magnetic. She almost drew me to her. I knelt beside the sofa and spread her thighs. I buried my face in her hot, wet pussy and licked. I wanted her to enjoy it all. I flicked my tongue over her clit. "Does that feel good?" I asked, pulsing her at the same time.

"Oh yes. Lick just like that. And put your fingers into me too."

I did as she wanted, driving first two then three fingers deep into her channel. I finger-fucked her hard while my tongue did its work. Soon I felt her spasms begin, but she pushed me away. I pulsed her. "I want you inside of me when I come," she said.

I had to be inside of her. My cock was so hard it almost hurt and only her pussy could relieve the pain. I climbed onto the sofa and knelt between her spread thighs. "Would you touch me?" I asked, not knowing exactly where that request had come from.

She wrapped her hand around my marble-hard dick and squeezed. Then she placed the tip of my cock against her opening and I rammed it home. I wanted to be patient, to make it last for her, but I was incoherent with lust. I pounded my cock into her slick passage over and over. I reached between us and rubbed her clit until I felt the spasms return to her pussy. The clenching of her internal muscles was too much and, with two more deep thrusts, I came. As I did, she screamed, her orgasm joining mine in a frenzy of lust.

It was several minutes before I was sane enough to speak. "I hope that was as good for you as it was for me," I said.

"Oh yes, it was." She was silent for a moment, then said, softly, "It always is."

"Always is what?" I asked.

"It always is good. I make it that way."

I was a bit taken aback. I was used to gushing praise for my prowess as a lover. She seemed to take it all for granted. "What do you mean by that?"

"Well, I seem to be able to put lustful thoughts into a guy's mind. It's like I can push thoughts of fucking and need into a man. Like when you asked me to hold your cock. I put that thought there. Once I've put in a few ideas, I just let nature take its course and it's always great."

"But you said no? I thought you didn't want to at first."

"I always do that, but I know I don't have to worry about the guy leaving. I just push such lustful thoughts into his mind that he wouldn't even consider going home."

"You push thoughts?"

"It's hard for someone who can't do it to understand. Actually you were more difficult to urge on. You wanted to go slowly even when I was in a hurry. But don't get me wrong, it was great."

I was flabbergasted. She had been pushing thoughts into my mind as I had been pulsing hers. I thought about her responses. Her body was in a hurry but her mind was enjoying the slightly slower trip. "I was pulsing you, too," I admitted. "I was making you tell me exactly how you wanted to proceed."

"You were? Is that why I told you I wanted you to finger-fuck me?"

"Yes."

She snuggled more deeply into my arms. "Wow. Wow."

I wanted to think more about the implications of all this, but I was too sleepy. So together we fell asleep on the sofa. As I dropped off, all I could think about was what I wanted to do with Amanda when I awoke.

Fran closed her laptop and climbed into bed. She was asleep almost instantly.

Chapter
7

Saturday morning Fran lay in bed for a long time, thinking over the events of the past week. She had arrived in New York as Fran Caputo, sexually unsophisticated, Midwestern writer. Now she felt like she was mostly Nicki St. Michelle, sexual free spirit. And it was fantastic.

She realized that she was a bit disappointed with O'Malley. On their first date he had been charming, interested in everything and a great dinner companion. Last evening he had just wanted to fuck. And that was what it had been, no love involved, just hot sweaty sex. And it had been sensational, but it was one-dimensional.

Tonight she had a second date with Clark. She thought about his slight shyness, his boyish good looks and the adorable dimples that appeared in his cheeks when he smiled. He's so cute, she thought. Since he wasn't due to pick her up until seven, she had the entire day to herself.

She finally climbed out of bed after nine, showered and dressed in a pair of well-worn jeans and a mint-green man-tailored shirt. She flipped on the radio and listened to the weather report. It was to be a mild afternoon so she added a sleeveless camel-colored sweater vest and pulled on her trench coat.

She found a trendy little restaurant on the east Fifties, had a sumptuous brunch of eggs Benedict, and eyeball flirted with a man at a nearby table. Although they never spoke, it was obvious that he found her attractive. Her. Fran Caputo. She blossomed. After brunch, she wandered through midtown, peering into the windows of all the trendy shops. Since most of them had no prices on the items in the windows, she knew she couldn't afford them, but Nicki might have been given some trinket by some Middle Eastern sheik so she looked carefully. She wandered into a few stores and looked over their jewelry with an eye toward her new hairdo and Nicki's lifestyle. The collection of little bags and receipts in her large purse grew as the day progressed.

Midafternoon, after a genuine New York bagel with cream cheese, onions and lox, she found a large bookstore and spent over an hour roaming, checking out the shelves. She found several copies of *The Love Flower* on the romance shelf and carried them to the manager, as Eileen had suggested she do. "I'm Nichole St. Michelle," she told the amazed woman, "and I wondered whether you'd like me to autograph them." The manager, whose name tag said Tiffany and who looked about fifteen, was delighted and, after Fran signed *Nichole St. Michelle* with a flourish, she put stickers on the covers stating, *Personally Autographed*. Nicki then wandered through the Romance Novel section, then browsed through the General Fiction area, looking at covers and titles, hoping for the germ of an idea for another book. Nothing jelled.

It was almost five when she arrived back at the apartment. There was a message from Carla, hoping that she had had a wonderful day and saying that she would call the following afternoon, just to check in. There was a similar message from Eileen. Nice to have friends, Fran thought, who were worried about her being lonely. Lonely, indeed. She was blissful.

By seven she was dressed in a rose silk blouse, a short black skirt, and her black leather vest. She wore chunky gold earrings, a heavy gold necklace and a pearl ring she had picked up that afternoon in a tiny boutique. Admitting that she hoped the evening would end up in bed, she put a few condoms she had bought at a neighborhood drugstore in her pocketbook, shaking her head at her bravery as she did so. She had just finished spraying on a bit of Opium when the doorbell rang.

Clark looked wonderful in a gray tweed sports jacket and navy slacks, with a white turtleneck. He stood in the hallway, staring at her. "You look fabulous," he said. "Very New York." She stepped back and let him walk in. As he passed he said, "I love that scent. Opium, isn't it?"

"You've got a great nose," Fran said, taking his coat.

"It's a classic and it was my mother's scent. It brings back wonderful memories."

"Thanks," Fran said a bit dubiously.

Clark looked chagrined. "I didn't mean it that way. It's wonderful. Really."

She placed her hand on his sleeve. "Relax and don't worry about it. You're right, it is a classic and it's the only scent I wear." Together they walked into the living room.

When Clark saw the statue, he gasped. "That could really give a guy an inferiority complex." He walked over to the half-clothed man and looked him over. "That looks like some of AnneMarie Devlin's work. Don't tell me this is the famous secret statue of her husband."

"You're wonderfully knowledgeable. It certainly is. I'm borrowing her apartment for a few weeks while she's in Europe."

"I'm a bit of an art buff. I haunt the museums and I've taken several courses. I've always wanted to go back to school and become a fine-arts major."

"Do you paint?"

"Actually I sculpt, but I'm really just a dabbler." He continued to stare at the statue. "Nothing like her. I love it but I get almost no time."

"So why don't you do more of it?"

"I guess I'm just part of the corporate rat race and I'm stuck."

"No you're not. That's your choice. I've been thinking a lot about choices lately and I'm becoming a believer in, 'If not now, when?' You're not married anymore and you told me that your children were well provided for, so what the hell."

"If not now, when? An interesting philosophy for a girl from Omaha."

"More interesting than you might imagine."

Clark wandered around the living room gazing at the smaller bits of bronze on the shelves of the wall unit. Fran realized that she hadn't even taken the time to explore. Together they gazed at several beautiful pieces and three sketches of larger works, framed on the wall.

"How do you know her?" Clark asked.

"She's the friend of a friend."

"Well, you have some very famous and talented friends." He sat on the sofa. "I never expected anything like this from the way you talked about yourself when we first met. You sounded so, I don't know, so small town. Not like you weren't sophisticated, but more like you didn't think of yourself that way."

Fran sat beside Clark and tucked her leg beneath her. "You know that's how I felt then. I was fresh off the plane and I felt really out of place. Now I guess I feel more like I belong here." She remembered her manners. "I've got a bottle of white wine chilling. Can I get you a glass?"

"That would be lovely. Let me help."

Together they walked into the kitchen and Fran retrieved a bottle of Sauvignon Blanc from the refrigerator. "You know," she said, remembering some of what Carla had told her. "Americans think that Chardonnay is the only white wine, but I really prefer something crisper."

"I couldn't agree with you more." He took the corkscrew from her and deftly removed the cork from the bottle, then poured two glasses. He touched the rim of his glass to Fran's. "To a wonderful evening," he said.

"To a wonderful evening."

They sipped two glasses of wine, then traveled across town to Bali Nusa Indah. They shared a wonderful assortment of tiny spicy dishes called a rijstaffel, then, since the restaurant wasn't full, they sat for a long time over tea. "So how did you manage to get three weeks off from your job?" Clark asked.

"I had lots of vacation saved up and I just decided to do it."

"The offer of Ms. Devlin's apartment must have made it easier."

"It did, but there's another reason I'm here, actually."

"Oh?"

"Well, what you don't know about me is that I'm also a writer."

"Really?" Clark's eyes widened appreciatively. "What do you write?"

"I've written a romance novel and it's up for an award."

"Congratulations," he said seeming genuinely pleased. "That's sensational. I know very little about writing romance novels. Tell me all about it."

Fran talked for a while about the book and about the Madison Writers' Conference and Prize.

"I'm sure you'll win," Clark said, squeezing her hand across the table.

"Actually I'm just as sure I won't."

"Why in heavens not? If you write half as well as you speak, the book must be very good."

"There's more to it than that." Fran dropped her voice and said, "It's not really just a romance novel and it's related to the rest of the things I write." She lowered her eyes and stared at her hands.

"Hmm. More hidden qualities about this woman. Layers beneath layers. Tell me, mystery woman."

"I write erotic short stories. I've had quite a few published and *The Love Flower*, the book that got the nomination, is really much more explicit than the average romance. That's why I'm really sure it won't win."

"You write erotica?" Clark looked stunned.

"I do."

Fran watched Clark's face as he considered her revelation. "Well. That's very interesting."

Shit, Fran thought. That's it. This is a really conservative guy. He's shocked. So now he's going to get up, pay the check and take me home. I knew I shouldn't have told him. Me and my big goddamn mouth. "I'm afraid I've shocked you."

"It's not shock. If I can be frank, I was thinking of our next date or the one after that, you know, the one where you invite me into your place and we end up in the bedroom. It's kind of like being in a sculpture class with AnneMarie Devlin."

Fran burst out laughing. "You have no idea." She spent the next few minutes giving Clark an expurgated version of what she had been like until her arrival in New York. "I've had some experiences this week that have opened my eyes. But until last Saturday I was little Fran Caputo, divorced and all but celibate."

"I thought your name was Nicki. It's Fran?"

Fran explained her need to become Nicki, at least for the conference and the award ceremony. "I'm sure you can't possibly understand."

"I can, but it sounds like something out of a novel itself. You know, innocent little Fran Caputo gets big city education from various men."

Holy shit. That's just what Carla said and they're both right. The pieces suddenly jelled. It *is* a novel. Nichole St. Michelle's next novel. "You're brilliant. It certainly is." She leaned across the table and kissed him.

"I must come up with brilliant ideas more often."

Fran looked at her watch. "It's almost eleven. How about coming back to my apartment and we can work on the rest of the Sauvignon Blanc?"

"Me and the famous erotic writer? Despite all you've told me, you've still got me a bit intimidated."

"I didn't mean to. I'm enjoying the evening so much and I don't want it to end. But these chairs aren't meant to spend hours beneath my behind."

Laughing, Clark paid the check and together they returned to Fran's apartment. Again sitting in the living room with glasses of wine, Clark looked at the statue wistfully. "I find him just as intimidating as I find sitting here with a writer of erotic fiction."

"You really needn't be. What I write are fantasies." She pointed to the statue. "And even if he's based on her husband, he's a fantasy too, a sexy idea of what turns women on."

"And, of course, fantasies aren't reality."

"I'm not sure where fantasy ends and reality begins, certainly not after what I've been through this week," Fran said. "I have a friend who says that everyone has a fantasy. Do you?"

Clark looked a bit nervous. "Am I to be grist for the writer's mill?"

"Maybe. You told me that my experience should be a book and I think you're right. I'm just thinking about my characters. You might even be the hero."

Clark spoke in an exaggerated southern accent. "Shucks, Miss Scarlett, I'm not the hero type."

"Maybe you are more than you know. But you haven't answered my question. Do you think that every man has a fantasy?"

Clark considered the question. "Yes, I guess most men do."

"What's yours?"

"Ouch. A really personal question from the writer?"

Fran answered quickly, "I'm really sorry. You're right, it is a very personal question and I do apologize."

"No need. Do you have one?"

"I have dozens, and I've written most of them down. Actually several are in print in magazines even now."

"You really write from your own fantasies?"

"Until this week I had no other basis for my writing."

"I'll bet it's been some week."

Fran raised one eyebrow. "It's been an education."

Clark sipped his wine and Fran remained silent, sensing that he was making a decision. "Actually I do have a fantasy, but it's really difficult to talk about."

"I can understand that. I can write about mine in the privacy of my bedroom-office, but to say it out loud?" She made a face.

Clark turned and stared off into space. "I've always wanted to seduce a virgin."

"I've read lots of stories about that. Can you explain why that excites you?"

"Wow, you sure do ask difficult questions."

"Sorry again. They just slip out. I guess I've had a bit too much wine." She put her glass on the side table. "Let's change the subject."

"No. It's an honest question so let me try to give you an honest answer." Clark leaned back, let his head rest on the back of the sofa, and stared at the ceiling. "I want a girl who's never had anyone else, someone who I can watch enjoy sex for the first time. And, of course, someone who has no one to compare me to."

"Interesting." She thought about Carla's little pink dress with the black Mary Janes. "Would she be a child?"

"I guess she'd be about fourteen, with a small body just becoming a woman." He turned and stared at her. "I would never actually do that, you understand."

Fran spoke immediately. "Of course not. We're talking about fantasies." She understood her own dreams, but she was now really interested in what illusions men created so she pressed on. "In the fantasy she's in school, I guess."

"Right. And she's wearing a uniform, green and blue plaid skirt, and a white blouse."

As Clark returned his gaze to the ceiling, Fran rested her head beside his and reached out to take his hand. Then she let her mind float. "And how did you meet her?"

"She walks home from school every day, just as I'm getting home from work. We say hello and I ask her about her schoolwork and she asks me about my office work. It's become something of a joke." He let out a long breath. "I don't believe I'm telling you this."

"And why not? It's not unlike fantasies of mine."

"Really?"

"Don't ever think you're the only one." Fran wanted to explore more, so she encouraged him to continue by picking up the story. "If I were writing this, one afternoon, she would tell you that her parents aren't going to be home until very late and she's really upset that she's forgotten her key. She's not sure she can get into the house."

"Right," Clark said, his grip on her hand tightening.

"You could invite her into *your* house," Fran suggested.

"I could. Should I?"

"Why not?" Fran said. Sharing erotic stories was so much better than writing them alone in her room.

"Phew. This is really getting into scary things."

"They aren't scary if they're just stories and this is just a dream. We both know that you'd never act on it. But it's really hot to think about, isn't it?"

"You have no idea."

"So let's say in the story you invite her in. She's so happy that she won't have to sit on the front porch all afternoon. You give her a soda and make sandwiches. It's sort of like a party. Tell me what she looks like."

"She's got blond hair, kind of like yours, but she wears it down around her shoulders."

Fran ran her fingers through her hair, undoing all the blow drying so it flowed softly. She pulled off her earrings and removed her necklace and ring.

"She's got blue eyes like yours," Clark said.

"And she's very grateful for your help."

"Yes, she is."

Although Fran wanted to continue the story, Clark seemed reluctant to go further. So Fran said, "Maybe she had gym class that afternoon and she's feeling all sweaty and dirty. Maybe she asks if she can use your shower. She always showers when she gets home after gym class." Fran felt Clark's fingers tighten still further around her hand. "Is that all right? Can she use your bathroom?"

"Yes," Clark said, his voice hoarse.

"She takes a long time in the shower and you just sit in the living room, thinking about what she must be doing, rubbing her soapy hands all over that young body. And when she comes out, she's wrapped in a towel, rubbing her wet hair. 'Thanks,' she says. 'That feels so much better.' "

"I'm sure it does," Clark says, slipping into the role of the man in the story.

"The towel is slipping," Fran said, "and she can't quite manage to hold it up and dry her hair. Suddenly it slips all the way to the floor and she is standing in the middle of the living room, naked. How does she look?"

"She's smooth and soft. Her breasts are small but the nipples are erect from the cool air. Her mound is covered with soft hair. It's blond like the hair on her head."

Could Fran do it? He could have fantasized about Dolly Parton, but he didn't. His fantasy involved someone with a boyish shape, like hers. Well, nothing ventured, she thought. She opened the buttons on her silk shirt, unhooked the front clasp on her bra and bared her breasts. She took Clark's hand and placed it on her flesh.

"Oh God," Clark said. "This isn't happening."

"Do you want to stop?"

"God, no."

"Well then, maybe you reach out from your seat near the girl and touch her naked body. Is she afraid?"

"No," Clark said, his hand resting on Fran's breast. "She's curious really."

"So she says, 'Would you show me?' And you agree. What should she do now?"

" 'Come over here, sweetheart,' he says and she slowly walks over so he can touch all of her. She's so soft."

Fran pulled off her blouse and bra and knelt at his feet. "Does he want to kiss her?"

"Oh yes." Clark sat up and stared down at Fran, his eyes clouded. His mouth enveloped hers, the kiss hungry.

" 'Oh, mister, that's such a big kiss for such a little me,' she says."

"Right," Clark said. Then he kissed her softly, his hands stroking her hair. He kissed her eyes and her cheeks gently, like the first kiss of a new lover. "I want to touch all of you," he said, and Fran didn't know whether he was talking to her or to the girl in the story. It didn't matter.

She stood up and slowly peeled off the rest of her clothes until she was naked, standing between his knees. His hands were almost reverent as they caressed her. He leaned forward and placed a small kiss on her belly. "So beautiful," he whispered.

"I like the way your fingers feel on me," she said.

"Would you undress me?" Clark asked tentatively.

"Yes," Fran said and unbuttoned his shirt. Quickly he was naked. "How would you make love to this little girl?"

"I would put her on my lap," he said.

Fran took a condom from her purse and unrolled it on Clark's erection. Then, with her knees on either side of his hips on the couch, she held her body above his. She adjusted the pitch of her voice upward. " 'Is this how I'm supposed to do this?' the little girl asks."

"Oh baby, yes," Clark said, grabbing Fran's waist and driving her down onto his rock-hard cock. The two rocked together, and quickly Fran felt the now-familiar heat blazing in her belly. She clenched her vaginal muscles and felt Clark's body tense. With a groan, he came and only moments later, Fran's orgasm joined his. She collapsed in his arms.

Later, when they had both cleaned up, Clark said, "I don't believe that. Are you sure you're not a professional at getting men to discuss their deepest desires? I never imagined I could tell you the things I told you much less act them out."

"I have a wonderful friend who has taught me a lot about sexual freedom and the joy of living your dreams in every way. You really must meet her sometime."

"If she's the one responsible for this evening I love her already." When Clark realized that it was after midnight, he got his coat. "I'm not sure of my schedule for next week. Can I call you?"

"I hope you will," Fran said at the front door. "It was wonderful." She looked at his face and thought she saw doubts, like the ones she had had after her evening with O'Malley. "And damn the second thoughts."

Clark grinned and kissed her on the cheek. "Yes, damn the second thoughts."

Over the next week Fran had one date each with Clark and O'Malley. With Clark there was lots of conversation, but after the initial fantasy evening, the sex was satisfying but ordinary, despite her efforts to improve things. On the other hand, with O'Malley, it was all hot sex with very little personal interaction.

On the Friday afternoon of her second week in New York, Fran got to sit and visit with Carla, who had been really busy with her children and her business. She discussed her relationships with each of the men and the two women agreed each man gave Fran only half of what she needed. Each man was fun in his own way, but neither was complete. But there was nothing wrong with fun, and neither was troublesome enough to give up.

"Don't you ever want a long-term relationship?" Fran asked.

Carla gave it almost no thought. "Not really. I had a very unsatisfying marriage and right now I'm happy. I like my life, strange though it might seem to an outsider, and I'm not about to change it. Do you know what you want?"

"I thought I did. The Fran Caputo who lived in Omaha wanted a husband and children, but she was also happy just being a writer and an employee. Now, I'm not really sure what I want."

"Well, if you ever decide to move to New York, you could join me. I know you and Ronnie would hit it off and we've got more business than we can handle, pardon the double entendre."

Fran's laugh was immediate. "You know, stranger things have been known to happen." She studied Carla's face. "You really are happy doing what you do."

"I really am."

"Tell me what it's like, doing what you do," Fran said.

"I love it. I make people happy and I get my pleasure, too. What could be better?"

"Are most of the men horny guys who just need to get their kicks, or do they want really unusual stuff?"

"A lot of them are out-of-town businessmen who know someone who's been with either Ronnie or me before and know that we're discreet and, let's say, flexible."

"I'm dying of curiosity. Tell me about your most recent experience, if it's not too personal."

"Oh, I have no problem telling you about my friends. It's just that most of them are pretty ordinary. A hotel room, a bottle of champagne and some time spent on the bed." Fran watched as Carla's eyes glazed over. "A few stand out in my mind."

"Like?"

"Oh, a man named Alex a few months ago. He called me up and we talked on the phone for a while. It seemed that the guys at work were making fun of his lack of success with women. He had a record of one-date then strike-out and he wanted to show them that he was more than just that. We met for a drink and, as we talked, I wondered why he was having any problem with women. It certainly wasn't his looks. He was in his early thirties yet boyishly attractive with sandy hair that flopped over his brow, green eyes and an inviting smile. I guessed that it was his defeatist attitude that turned women off.

"At one point he said, 'I have no clue why I'm on this losing streak, but the guys at the office are getting to be a real pain in the ass. I get jokes on my desk, silly innuendos in my e-mail and remarks, even dares, from my friends. It's humiliating. So I've come up with a plan.' He spent quite a while telling me what he wanted and we discussed and refined his idea until it sounded like it might work. He paid me in advance and we set a meeting for the following evening at five-thirty at a local watering hole."

As Carla talked, the picture was so clear in Fran's mind, that she could see it.

* * *

Carla sat at the bar, sipping a white wine until Alex arrived with three of his office buddies. The four men sat in a booth across the room, but if Carla listened closely she could make out the conversation. As the jokes began, Carla pointedly looked at her watch, then at the door, as if waiting for someone to arrive. She crossed her legs so that a goodly length of shapely thigh showed beneath her conservative suit-skirt.

Drinks arrived at Alex's table and voices rose. Carla again looked at her watch, and recrossed her legs, allowing the skirt to ride higher. Then she stood and removed her jacket to reveal a very tailored print blouse that was a size too tight and spanned across her ample breasts. Again she sat and ordered another glass of wine.

Over the next few minutes, she checked and rechecked her watch, then got up and walked toward the ladies' room. Her path took her past Alex's table. When she returned, she caught Alex's eye and smiled softly.

"Hey guy, there's your date for the evening," one of his buddies, a flaming redhead with a face full of faded freckles said as she passed the table.

"Yeah," another, a Latin-looking man said. "She's hot for you. And wouldn't you like to get your hands on those tits?" Carla winced as she returned to her seat at the bar, still able to hear the ribald conversation from Alex's table.

"Go over," the third, an older man with a dark brown crew cut said. "Grab her. She's yours for the taking. And God, she's quite a woman. Those legs . . ."

"Okay guys," Alex said. "Cut it out."

"I dare you," the redhead said. "I double dare you."

"I stopped taking dares when I was twelve," Alex said, looking at Carla and catching her eye. "But I think I could get somewhere with her. She really did give me the eye."

Carla looked over at the booth and smiled at Alex, who smiled back.

"Come on, guy. Let's see you try. Unless you don't think you can do it."

Feigning reluctance, Alex slowly rose and crossed the room. He took the bar stool next to Carla. Softly, he said, "It's working great so far. They are panting. Let's just sit here talking for a few minutes then I'll invite you over."

About five minutes later the two rose and walked to the table where the three other men waited. He pointed as he introduced them. "Carla, this is Kelly, Ricardo and Mack. Guys, this is Carla." All three men stared at her wide-eyed.

"Good evening," Carla said softly. "I hope I'm not spoiling your get-together."

"Not at all," the Latin-looking man who had been introduced as Ricardo said, sliding over and patting the seat beside him. "Please, join us."

Carla pointedly looked at the seat beside Ricardo, then, after Alex slid in, she slid in beside him. "Looks like you were stood up," the redhead, whose name was Kelly, said.

"It seems so," Carla said. "This is the last time he'll do something like this to me, the shit. We're through."

"How about another round?" Mack, the third of Alex's friends, said.

"Sure," Carla agreed. "White wine for me."

The five talked through a round of drinks. Fortunately Carla had already given the bartender twenty dollars to cut her drinks half and half with water so, although she played at being a bit tipsy, she was cold sober.

As they finished their round, Carla felt Alex's hand on her thigh, slowly sliding her skirt up. Making it obvious, she playfully slapped his hand away with a wink and a giggle. Then he draped his arm around her shoulder and played with her earlobe.

"Hey," she said, "we've got an audience, lover." She turned to face him.

"Does that matter?" He placed a soft kiss on her lips.

After a moment, she deepened the kiss, turning her head so his mouth pressed even more firmly against hers.

As they kissed, with the men watching, Alex reached up and flipped open the top two buttons on Carla's blouse. His hand slipped inside, cupping her bra-covered breast. Carla enjoyed the kiss, and enjoyed the gasping sounds coming from the other three men.

When they broke the kiss, his hand remained. She batted it away, but Alex kept his fingers deep inside of her blouse. She could feel her skin flush and she quickened her breathing.

Carla looked around at the faces of the three observers. "He's really fresh, isn't he?" she said, giggling.

"I guess," Mack said.

"Not usually," Ricardo said.

Carla again glanced at her watch. "I really should be going." The protest was obviously halfhearted.

"You don't really want to leave, do you?" Alex asked. He bent his head and kissed and licked her ear.

Carla allowed her eyes to close as though in the throes of passion. She felt Alex's hand on her knee, then between her thighs. "You know," she said to Alex, "since that shit ex-boyfriend of mine is a no-show, how about we have some dinner somewhere and see where it all takes us."

Four men said, "Great," simultaneously.

"Oh," Carla said, a bit surprised. "I guess I didn't make myself clear. I just meant Alex."

"Sounds wonderful," Alex said. "Let's get our coats."

Fran watched Carla's smile widen. "You know," Carla said, "although he hadn't planned it that way, we ended up in his apartment and he was really great in bed. I told him so and I think it boosted his confidence."

"So you are really more than just a sex object."

"And what's wrong with being a sex object?"

"Nothing. Nothing at all."

"By the way," Carla said, "have you given any thought to the party tomorrow evening? I think you'd enjoy it."

"I have, and I think maybe I'll give it a try. Just to see what goes on, not to participate, of course."

"Wonderful. It will be very educational, if nothing else. And I

will certainly give you lots of ideas for stories. And frankly, I
think you'll have a blast."

"What should I wear?" Fran asked.

"Just pick something that makes you feel good. Many people
will be dressed for the occasion . . ." Her eyes twinkled. ". . . and,
of course, some will be undressed for the occasion. And some will
be in street clothes. Just feel good about yourself and let it all
flow. Why don't you meet me at my place at about six?"

"Will you be paid for the evening?"

"This one's for fun. CJ and I have known each other for quite
a while and I'm going to be with him."

"So you do this for fun, too."

"I always do it for fun. Sometimes I'm lucky enough to get
paid, too."

Later that evening, Fran sat at her laptop and again wandered
the Internet, reading stories from several different web sites, trying to get an idea about what the party would be like. She read
several stories about group sex, several men with one woman,
several women with one man. Energized and open to new experiences, she brought up her word processor and began to put
down some of the ideas that had been swirling in her mind.

Lord, it's dark, Hank thought. With all these clouds, there's
no moonlight, no nothing yet here I am, traipsing through
the woods, looking for that damn dog. "Okay, okay," he
muttered, "the dog will probably find his way back to the
cabin but, well, maybe he won't."

He had been house sitting, or rather cabin sitting for an
old friend for almost a week and Renfrew had, in fact, found
his way out and back a few times. Why Hank was so worried
about him this night in particular he didn't know but here
he was, flashlight in hand, wandering deeper and deeper
into the woods behind the cabin. He had walked much of
this area during the previous days, but now he realized that

he had gone farther than he had on any of his previous wanderings.

He sighed and aimed his light at the ground to prevent
himself from falling on the tree roots and small shrubs that
littered the area. What the fuck are you doing? he wondered.
You're going to kill yourself. But who'd notice. Certainly not
Jennifer, his ex-girlfriend. She'd left the apartment they
had shared one afternoon three months earlier. One minute
she'd been there and then, poof. He'd returned from walking Renfrew and she had disappeared, lock, stock and mois-
turizer. And he had really loved her.

"Renfrew, you lousy dog, get over here!" he yelled for
the hundredth time. "It's late. Time for your biscuit." That
was the usual magic word. "Biscuit," he called again, but
when he listened, he heard nothing.

I'm not such a bad guy, he mused, Jennifer and I had it
pretty good. We laughed, partied, had great sex. Well, he
admitted, maybe good sex. Adequate sex? But we could
have talked about it. I wanted it to be great. They had
talked about it but Hank had been unable to understand
what Jennifer was saying. Affection, loving, playing, experi-
menting. "All you want is to stick it in, wiggle it around
until it comes, then sleep. Not my idea of good sex."

I won't think about that. "Renfrew!" He stopped and listened. He heard a rustling in the leaves and headed in that
direction, crashing through underbrush in the pitch darkness. God, I'm a nut case.

"Where are you?" He listened again and this time he
thought he heard a low moaning, almost a chant. Get a grip,
Hank, he told himself. As he walked forward more slowly,
the moaning became a soft song. No words but a melody, so
sweet and low that it was almost as though it came from inside his head. Shining the beam of the flashlight ahead of
him, he continued through the now-thinning vegetation.

Suddenly the woods opened onto a small lake, no more

than thirty feet across. And just as suddenly, the clouds parted and the moonlight spilled over the water making silver pathways across the still water. The sound still filled his head and he moved, trying to home in on its location. He turned and saw something white on the far side of the tiny lake. Shapes in pale floaty dresses slowly emerged from the darkness. Not wanting to startle whoever was there, Hank flicked off the flashlight and walked quietly around the water toward the far side. When he finally pushed some branches aside, he saw them. Four women, holding hands, formed a ring around a large, flat rock. Their humming reverberated through his entire body.

As he watched, the women slowly circled the rock, moving gracefully in something that resembled an old pagan dance. How did I know that? he wondered. A pagan dance indeed.

But there was something totally sensuous about the entire scene. The four women were dressed in flowing white gowns that brushed their limbs as they circled. Their hair was long, flowing almost to their backs, but different in color, one flaming red, one soft russet brown, one soft golden blond and one almost white. He found his eyes drawn to their bodies, outlined as the fabric of their gowns undulated. All were voluptuous, with shapely breasts, slender waists and graceful thighs.

And above those thighs? Hank, he chided himself, stop that!

"Are you ready to join us, Hank?" a voice asked.

"Are you talking to me?" he asked, totally startled to realize that they knew of his presence. "Hey, how do you know my name?"

"We know a lot about you," the voice continued. Then the circle broke and the blonde walked toward him. He noticed that her feet were bare, but she seemed unconcerned about the leaves, branches and debris beneath them. She

held out a graceful hand to him and said, "We've been waiting for you."

He stared at the graceful fingers that beckoned him, then
at the lovely face, the eyes, the soft lips, and fought the almost irresistible urge to take the hand she offered. "Just
who the hell are you? And what are you up to?"

"We appear here once a month," the blonde said. "And
this time we were waiting for you."

"That doesn't answer my question," Hank said, stuffing
his hand into his pocket to resist reaching for the woman's
hand.

The blonde sighed. "I am called Summer and these are
my sisters, Autumn, Spring and Winter."

Hank almost giggled. This was too weird. Summer indeed. Probably escaped from the local looney bin. But as he
gazed into her deep blue eyes, he softened. There was an
honesty there, an affection for him, as if she felt a genuine
pleasure at looking at him, as he felt pleasure looking at her.

"I know, it seems weird but we are what we appear to be.
We didn't escape from a looney bin, as you put it."

Had he said that out loud? Certainly not. But then how
did she know?

"Take my hand," Summer said. "We won't hurt you.
Come."

He pulled his hand out of his pocket. What did he have
to lose? He would just play along. He reached out and took
the hand that was offered. As he touched the incredibly soft
skin a rush of warmth flowed through him, easing his mind
and tightening his groin. Suddenly all he wanted was to caress her to find out whether her skin was as smooth all over,
her breasts, her thighs, her belly.

"Soon enough," she whispered. "All in good time." She
led him toward her sisters and the four women surrounded
him, hands joined, bodies swaying. As they moved around
him, their breasts brushed against his arms, his back, his

chest. Breasts with hard, pointed nipples swayed against him, mouths brushed his neck, his cheeks, his ears.

He wanted to reach out and touch what was being so freely offered, but his hands remained at his sides. He closed his eyes and breathed in the fresh scents, listened to the women's soft keening, felt the soft flesh pressing closer and closer.

Now their hands were everywhere, stroking his shoulders, rubbing his back. Fingers ran through his hair and traced the outline of his ears. He wanted to grab, to invade, to thrust, to take, but still his hands remained immobile, as if unable or unwilling to move. His senses were filled with them but he remained still.

Hands removed his clothing until he stood naked, his cock sticking out hard and hungry from his groin. Then the women backed away, smiling and moving their bodies, allowing only their dresses to brush against his body. Enough, he told himself. Enough teasing. Time to get to it. But as he tried to turn, something held him fast. He tried to raise his arms but he was totally unable to move. Walking, kneeling, moving his hands, nothing worked. It wasn't uncomfortable actually, he realized, it just was.

"The more you relax and just accept what is given, the more you will be able to move," Summer said. "Are you cold?"

"No," he said, realizing that, although the night air was chilly and he had been wearing a jacket when he started into the woods, he was now warm and comfortable. Well, as comfortable as he could be with the crying need in his cock.

"Soon," the redhead whispered. "Soon." He watched as first one and then another removed her gown, revealing naked bodies so perfect that it made him ache. Breasts were tipped with rosy nipples, pubic hair matched the varied hues of their hair. Now their hands stroked their own bodies as he watched. Long fingers stroked their ribs, bellies, then cupped their breasts. "Would you like to touch?" the brunette asked.

"Yes," he said. Touch. He wanted to ravish.

"Only touch. There's joy in just touching. If you move very slowly you can reach out and caress us."

Restraining his need to grab was one of the most difficult things Hank had ever done, but, since he had no choice, he slowly raised one arm and extended his fingers. The woman with the white hair moved close. "I'm called Winter," she said, and my skin is cold as stone yet warm to your touch." She moved so her breast brushed his hand. Surprised, Hank found that she was right. The surface of her breast was cool yet as he pressed slightly, warmth filled him. He caressed the breast in his hand, swirling his fingers over her skin, not touching the darker center. "Yes," she purred, allowing her head to drop back as he rubbed. Finally he touched her nipple and watched her gasp. "Lovely," she whispered.

"I'm Autumn," the redhead said, taking his other hand and placing it on her breast.

Hank cupped one breast in each hand, feeling the differences in texture and temperature in the two women's flesh.

"I'm Spring," a voice said from behind him, and then nipples were rubbing sensuously against his back. Then the breasts slid down his spine and rubbed against his buttocks. His cock was so hard it hurt and his head was filled with images of driving it into a soft, warm pussy.

"You're rushing," Summer said, her hands cupping his face. "Slowly. There's too much pleasure to rush." She turned his face and pressed her lips against his. "Slowly," she purred against his mouth. She licked around his mouth, dampening his lips, then blowing on the cool skin. Then she covered his mouth with hers and kissed him deeply, allowing her tongue to explore the damp cavern.

Hank was unable to sort out all the sensations. A mouth on his, kissing him more expertly than he had been kissed before, breasts in his hands and rubbing against the backs of his thighs. The smell of the women, the taste. It all filled him, tantalized him, yet satisfied him too.

Minutes later, Summer backed off. "Come," she said, taking his hand and leading him to the large rock around which they had been dancing when he first saw them. She guided him until he lay on the rock. It should be cold against my back, he told himself, but it's warm and almost soft.

"Now," Winter said, "would you like to touch us?"

"Oh yes," Hank said. "Very much."

"Then you may, but you can't do anything quickly. Do you understand?"

"Yes," he moaned.

The blonde, Spring, crawled onto the rock and straddled his chest. "Touch me," she said. Hank slowly explored her breasts and belly. As the other women told him what to do, he caressed her shoulders and arms, then explored her face with the tips of his fingers. "How does she feel?"

He had never really thought about how a woman felt before and he marveled at the different textures he experienced. Smooth skin, rough nipples, wet mouth, silky hair. Warm places and cool places. It was wonderful, a joy in itself without wondering when he was going to get to the "main event."

He then used his mouth to sample all the different temperatures and textures of her body. Then, as he cupped her breasts, Winter put her nipple into his mouth. "Suckle softly, gently." And he did, flicking his tongue over her erect bud.

Summer spoke in his ear. "Only when her nipple is hard and pointed is she really excited."

Hank felt Winter pull back and his mouth was filled with another nipple, this one small and flat. "Feel Autumn's nipple harden between your lips. You do that to her. You have the power to please her."

He paid attention to the reaction of Autumn's breast in his mouth and marveled at the changes as it hardened and swelled. For a long time he sucked, kissed, licked as different breasts were placed in his mouth and hands. Then his mouth and hands were empty. Spring, no longer straddling his chest, but now kneeling beside him, took his hand. "Now touch here," she said, guiding his hand to the junction of her thighs.

"Not until a woman is very wet is she ready for your hands," Summer whispered. "Is she ready?"

He touched and felt slick lips. "Yes," he whispered.

"Then touch, slowly. Explore. Get to know her and what makes her shudder."

He used only his index finger and rubbed her outer lips and the creases and folds of her outer flesh. He found her clit. "Is it swollen?" Summer asked. "if it isn't, then she needs more time."

Her clit was hard, rising from the surrounding wet skin.

"Now this," Autumn said. She climbed onto the rock on the side opposite Spring, took his other hand and placed it between her thighs. She was only slightly wet and her clit was difficult to find. She parted her legs to give him free access and again he explored, finding that different places excited her and made her wetter. While Spring liked his fingers to rub on either side of her clit, Autumn liked light touches on the head of the clit itself. Hank found himself wondering what the other two women would like.

"Yes," Summer purred and she and Winter climbed onto the rock, sat beside him and he touched each in turn. And each was different, reacting to slightly different combinations of rubbing, stroking and probing. Winter even liked to have her flesh pinched. Then he pushed one finger into Autumn's channel. "More," she said and he pressed a second and a third inside of her. Again he experienced the four women, watching in wonder as they writhed under his ministrations. He had his fingers inside of Spring's body when she reached down and touched her clit with her own fingertips. He felt the clench of her body and then the spasms of her channel.

"My God," he said in wonder. "I never felt anything like that." He moved his hands trying to find ways to prolong her climax.

When she finally calmed, he said, "That was amazing."

Autumn smiled. "Yes, it was."

Summer climbed across his body and held her sopping opening just above the tip of his cock. "Are you ready?"

He was, and yet he found that he was regretting the end of the exploration. "Yes," he said.

"It's not the end by any means," Summer said. "Feel." She placed the tip of his cock against the slippery opening of her body and lowered herself. Slowly Hank's cock entered her. "Feel," she said again. And he found that he could feel. He could hold his excitement tightly in check as he experienced the wet, tight pussy slowly enveloping him. She filled herself with him, then remained quite still, using her muscles to massage him. He could feel her and, although he wanted to throw her onto her back and pound into her, he found he was enjoying the sensations she was causing.

She lay on his chest and rubbed her breasts against it. She kissed his mouth, his cock still deeply embedding inside of her. Then fingers were on his balls, caressing the orbs and rubbing the skin between the back of his sac and his anus. "See, you don't even have to move," Summer whispered.

And he didn't, yet he came. Without moving his hips spasms wracked his body and semen erupted into Summer's body. He climaxed for longer than he had believed possible and it was long minutes later before he was coherent again.

"But now you've left me unsatisfied," Summer said, allowing his now-flaccid cock to fall from her body. The other women had left the rock and she lay beside Hank and said, "Now help me the way I helped you."

Hank climbed onto his knees and crouched between Summer's spread thighs. He explored her folds with his fingers, remembering what she liked, then he placed his mouth on her clit. He quickly discovered that she liked to have her clit sucked hard while his tongue flicked over the tip. When he felt she was ready, he invaded her channel with his fingers, and felt her come, her hips bucking, almost dislodging his mouth from her body.

As he enjoyed her climax, Hank became aware that Spring and Winter were pleasuring each other, mouths on pussies, fingers probing, bodies straining. Soon the two who hadn't already come, did, screaming their pleasure.

For almost an hour, Hank just lay on the rock, between sleep and waking, his hands idly touching whatever part of whatever woman he could reach.

Then Summer sat up. "It's time for you to go now," she said.

"Can I visit again?" he asked.

"No," Spring said. "It's not possible. But you will remember everything we've done and everything you've learned here. And there are so many other women who will enjoy your newfound talents."

"You will find your dog on your back porch," Autumn said. "He's waiting for you."

"I forgot all about him," Hank admitted.

"We knew you would," Autumn said. "But we knew he'd get you here and that's what we wanted."

"This was all a setup?"

"In a way," Summer explained. "We saw you this afternoon and knew you would be wonderful once you learned. So we took the liberty of using your dog to lure you here. Are you angry?"

Hank grinned. "Of course not." Winter handed him his clothes and he dressed quickly. "It was great."

"Yes," Spring said, "it was."

Quickly Hank hurried back to the cabin and found Renfrew sleeping on the back porch. He went inside and spent the rest of the night reliving his amazing experience. At about nine the next morning, he climbed out of bed, made some coffee and sat beside the phone. With a sigh, he picked up the receiver and dialed.

"McMillan and Son," a familiar voice said.

"Jennifer?"

"Hank," she said, her voice suddenly wary.

"Listen, I'm sorry about everything. I think a lot of our troubles were my fault. Maybe you'd like to have dinner with me one evening. No strings. I'd just like to spend some time with you. I've missed you more than I realized."

Hank could hear a heavy sigh. "I don't know."

"I can give you time to think about it if you want. I can call back tomorrow."

"No. It's okay. Maybe this weekend?"

"Sure," Hank said, suddenly lighthearted. "Yeah. Great. Saturday? That little Italian place you always loved?"

"That would be nice," Jennifer said.

"I'll call you Saturday afternoon and we can agree on a time. Okay?"

"Sure," Jennifer said. "You sound different."

"You'd be amazed at how different. Maybe we'll find out together."

"Yeah. Maybe."

"You've grown, Nicki," Fran said aloud, typing *The Pagans* by Nichole St. Michelle at the top, then closing her laptop. She thought about the calm, one-on-one sexuality of her earlier stories and smiled. "You've come a long way, baby."

Chapter

8

The following evening, Fran arrived at the brownstone at six. Carla greeted her at the door, wearing a full-length, cranberry velour robe. Fran had debated for hours about what to wear, what she wanted her clothes to say. She finally selected a fitted, light blue knit dress with a deep scooped neck. Beneath it she wore a bra that enhanced her shape so the dress clung to her new curves and showed a bit of cleavage. She wore black pumps with modest two-inch heels, little jewelry and light makeup. She had pulled her hair back into a French twist. "You look terrific," Carla said as she ushered Fran inside.

The two women sat in the living room sipping white wine. "This party will be very unusual and I need to explain the ground rules so you can make a serious decision." Carla sat back. "CJ's last name is Winterman and no one really knows what the CJ stands for. Like OJ Simpson before the troubles. He's an unusual man. He's a teller of erotic tales, and he records tapes of his stories which he sells in his store."

Carla grinned. "And what a store it is. It's called *A Private Place* and it's downtown. He sells more kinds of erotic toys and games than I have ever seen, and he specializes in bondage and discipline equipment. He also works leather like no one else I've ever met and he made a few of my best outfits."

"Anyway, this party is for several of his friends, all into the dominant-submissive lifestyle. At this party they will trade slaves, or bottoms as they're usually called, play games together and do some things you've probably never seen before, even on the Playboy channel. There is only one rule. There's a back room for those into whipping and heavy pain. None of that will go on in the main room so you, or anyone else, won't see things that might disturb you, except by choice."

Fran tried to take it all in. Two weeks ago she had been in Omaha, dreaming about anonymous lovers and soft, warm sex. Now, here she was in a New York brownstone owned by a high-priced hooker seriously thinking about going to a dominant-submissive party. She imperceptibly shook her head in amazement.

"There are always people, brought by friends, who are interested in learning about this lifestyle but aren't into it just yet. They dress in street clothes, but they each wear a green ribbon around their neck as a sign that they aren't players."

"I'm intrigued. And what stories that would trigger."

"You understand that this is very personal. Nothing factual goes outside that loft."

Fran laughed. "Of course. I understand that it's all private."

"Sorry. Of course you do. I'm almost dressed under this robe so I just have to finish up. I'll be down in just a few minutes."

While she was gone, Fran let her mind wander over the stories she could write, maybe even parts of her next book. But it was difficult to write about situations she'd never been in so this was really for research. Wasn't it? She snorted. *Right.*

When Carla reappeared, Fran could only stare. She was dressed all in red. A tight, red leather teddy, with black laces up the front. The bra cups were missing so Carla's full breasts were displayed for all to see. Long red garters hung from the bottom of the corset and held up long red stockings. On her feet she wore knee-high red patent leather boots and her red leather gloves came up high enough to cover her elbows. Her hair was wild, her makeup severe. Her jewelry was all silver, with heavy-looking earrings, bracelets and a necklace with a large, irregularly shaped, pendant that hung between her breasts.

"Oh my," Fran gasped. "If I didn't know it was you, I'm not sure I would recognize you."

The grin was pure Carla. "Thanks. It's taken me quite a while to perfect this look, and longer to feel comfortable with it."

"Comfortable? You look totally relaxed."

"When Ronnie and I first got together, and I played power games for the first time, I was a submissive. I loved taking orders, being told what to do. It's really much more difficult, I think, to be the one in charge. You always have to consider not only your own pleasure but that of the person you control. In stories it always seems like the boss gets to do anything he or she wants, but it's not like that at all. To be a really good dominatrix, you've got to be thinking all the time."

"I never considered that."

"You like it when O'Malley ties you up, don't you?"

"Yes." Fran was startled at how easily she discussed the most intimate details of her sex life with someone she had only met two weeks before.

"He's wonderful and considerate. Think about what it would be like if the person in control didn't care as much about your pleasure as his own. It wouldn't be satisfying for you."

"But I'm sure there must be people who aren't like O'Malley."

"Sure but, for me and my friends, that's not what the dominant-submissive lifestyle is all about." Carla took the black cape she had over her arm and draped it around her shoulders. "There's a hired car coming to pick us up assuming that you're still interested in coming along?"

Fran stood up and got her coat. "I wouldn't miss it for anything."

There was a chilled bottle of champagne waiting in the limo and Fran and Carla sipped as the car wove downtown through Saturday evening traffic. It pulled to a stop in front of an ordinary storefront with the words *A Private Place* in gold lettering on the darkened window. "His loft is upstairs," Carla said. "Ready?"

Fran squared her shoulders. "I'm more than ready."

Carla pulled a narrow green ribbon out of her pocket. "Here, tie this around your neck. And if, at sometime during the evening you decide you want to play, just take it off. Then just assume some persona that feels right and someone will get the message."

Fran tied the ribbon around her neck. Together the two women entered the shop and walked to an elevator in the rear.

When they arrived at the upper floor, the elevator doors opened and Fran's eyes widened and her muscles tensed. There were about three dozen people of all ethnicities in the room. About half were standing, or sitting, talking animatedly. "The ones with the freedom to move around, talk, drink, are the dominants, the tops," Carla explained. Then she indicated the remainder of the partygoers, who were crouched on the floor or sitting alone, silent. "Those are the slaves, the bottoms. They can only eat, or drink, or speak when they are given permission." The contrast was remarkable.

Fran stared at two men who stood talking, dressed identically in tight leather pants, vests and boots. Each had a woman at his feet, one a brunette with long flowing hair and one with steel-gray hair cut very short. Both women were naked and the men idly stroked their heads. There was a woman dressed in a tight green sheath dress with five-inch spike heels holding a man wearing a leather jock strap by a collar and leash. She was walking along a buffet table with the man awkwardly crawling behind.

A man and a woman stood near the bar, talking softly. The man was large, with long sandy hair pulled back in a ponytail, a beige suede western-style shirt, matching skintight pants and brown boots. A dark-skinned woman, dressed in a light blue teddy which bared her breasts, stood behind him as he chatted with a small Asian woman.

Of the male and female bottoms, many wore nothing but collars. Others wore tiny garments with openings in strategic places. Naked breasts, cunts and penises went unnoticed by everyone. A man stood in the corner, facing the wall wearing an all-over garment of skin-tight leather, with sleeves that attached in the back like a straightjacket. "Some form of punishment," Carla whispered as she followed Fran's gaze. "Just remember there's no whipping or paddling in here and everything is consensual."

As Fran put her coat on a chair, she noticed a few men and women with green ribbons like hers. Although the situation was totally bizarre, she forced herself not to stare. But despite her efforts, she found herself again gazing at the man with the beige ponytail and this time he caught her glance. He just stared at her with eyes the color of sherry, until Fran was forced to look away.

With a flourish, Carla removed her cape. Her red outfit stood out like a flame in a forest. "Oh my dear," one man in a one piece leather outfit, which allowed his large, semierect penis to stick out through an opening, said, "you look wonderful." He then stared at Fran, his eyes almost black. "Who's your friend?"

"Everyone, this is Nicki. She's an old friend and she's visiting tonight. I told her she was in for an eye-opening evening." Carla took the hand of one man who had crawled over to sit at her feet. "Nicki, this is CJ. It's his party and he's my party for tonight." She reached down and took the leash he handed her. She noisily clipped it to a large ring on his collar.

Slightly tongue-tied, Fran stammered, "It's nice to meet you."

Crouched as CJ was, Fran couldn't tell how tall he was, but his face was almost angelic, topped with a cap of soft brown curly hair. He appeared so innocent, yet here he was rubbing his shoulder against Carla's calves. CJ looked at Carla as if for permission and she nodded. "It's a pleasure. I'm delighted you could be here." He pointed to the bar at one side of the room. "There are drinks, hard and soft, and lots of food on the table over there." He motioned. "Please help yourself. Or let someone serve you."

Carla jumped in. "I don't think she's ready for that just yet. Maybe later."

"Of course," CJ said. He looked at Carla. "May I serve you, Mistress?"

"I'd like a white wine. Fran?"

"Sure."

"Yes, Mistress." CJ rose to his feet and hurried off.

Softly, Fran said, "Wow. Are there any rules I should know about?"

"I don't think so. Just understand that everything here is for fun. Other than that, just watch and listen. These people aren't shy. At least not most of them."

"Okay," Fran said.

"And if something is going on that bothers you, move away. And if the entire scene turns you off, feel free to cut out and head home. I'll call you tomorrow. And if someone approaches you in a way you don't want, just touch your green ribbon. It's an absolute rule that no one will violate your position as a nonparticipant."

"I understand." CJ returned with two glasses of white wine and Fran took hers, happy to have something to do with her hands.

"Do you want to stay with me or circulate?"

"I think I'll wander around for a while." As she moved around the room she realized that, other than the bizarre dress and the positions of the submissives, the party was like lots of others she had attended. The conversations were really rather ordinary, ranging from television shows to politics. She chatted with a few of the dominants and, although she would have liked to hear how the submissives felt about their situation, she didn't want to speak to any of them without permission and she didn't yet feel comfortable enough to ask.

Soon, however, much of the conversation turned to discussions of recent events in the lives of the couples. Training was a frequently discussed subject and many of the tops discussed different methods of introducing new bottoms to their situation.

Fran was standing with two slender, leather-clad men when the elevator doors opened again. A tall, well-built man walked into the room, greeted by several tops. "Walt, I haven't seen you in quite a while," one said. As Fran watched, his gaze turned to the woman now crawling off the elevator.

Fran looked at her. She was wearing a tight leather corset that cinched her waist in so it appeared that she could hardly breathe.

She had a thin gold collar and gold wristbands all connected with long chains. As the woman emerged, Fran could see that her ankles were joined by a foot long length of gold chain.

"Oh, Walt. How wonderful. Is she new?"

"Yes. She's only been with me for about a month but her training's going wonderfully." He unzipped his tight leather pants and took out his cock. Immediately the woman knelt at his feet, his cock in her hands, her tongue flicking over the tip. Carelessly, he pushed her head away. "Not yet."

She crouched at his feet. "Of course, sir," she whispered.

CJ knelt at Carla's side in the center of the room. Carla tapped on her wineglass with a long fingernail and soon everyone was silent. "CJ tells me that everyone's here so who would like to begin the fun and games," she said. "A few of you are here with new bottoms, I see. Does anyone want to play? As you know, my CJ is still the champ at over eleven minutes. Anyone want to challenge him?"

Fran had no idea what was going on, but she took a seat on one side of the room to watch.

"I'll play," one man said.

"I'll bet on my Laura," another voice said.

Several others volunteered people for the game, whatever that was going to be.

Soon, CJ was standing along one wall with a woman at his feet. Three other men were beside him, each with someone sitting beside him. Two were women and one was a man.

"You're new here. Do you know about the game?" a voice said in her ear.

Fran turned. It was the man she had stared at earlier with the magnetic eyes and beige ponytail. Since he was now sitting so close, she could see that he was enormous, muscular, with wide shoulders, forearms as thick around as her thighs and tremendous hands. He sat stroking the thigh of his soft suede pants. Fran could feel the heat rise to her face. "No," she whispered.

"It's a 'don't come' contest. Pretty simple. Each bottom will try to make his or her target climax by doing whatever he or she wants. It will, of course, be mostly cock sucking but you get the idea. CJ lasted eleven minutes at our last party."

"Go," someone called and the four contestants began to stroke and fondle their targets. Fran had never seen a man caress another man so her gaze was riveted on the couple at one end.

"You can't imagine the feeling of being so hot, with a hungry mouth on your cock, yet trying with all your concentration to think of anything else. The bottoms will do lots of things to try to break their target's concentration. That's the way the bottom wins, by making her target come quickly."

Although the man beside her didn't touch her, he kept up a running erotic commentary, his huge hand rubbing up and down his thigh. "I'm Steven but my bottoms call me Sir Steve. That's my slave, Deirdre," he said in Fran's ear, indicating the woman in the light blue teddy and skin the color of milk chocolate. "Second from the left. She's got a very talented mouth indeed. See how she's scratching Bart's thigh? She's trying to get him to focus on what her mouth is doing."

Fran could feel the lips of her cunt swell. Any minute she was going to have to go to the ladies' room and masturbate to relieve the pressure. "Please don't," the man said.

"Excuse me?"

"You're moving your hands as though you're stroking yourself."

Fran looked at her hand, then made a fist in her lap.

The man's chuckle caused his warm breath to tickle her ear. "This atmosphere is almost guaranteed to make one very hungry. But it's so much better to let one of us satisfy that hunger." He ran his finger along the ribbon around Fran's neck. "Want to take that off?"

Fran realized that she did, but she said, "Not right now."

"Ah yes. Well, maybe later. I would like to be the one to introduce you to all this." He ran one finger down Fran's upper arm. Even through her dress, she could feel the heat. "I will be right here when you change your mind." Fran noticed that he had said "when," not if.

The contest continued. Suddenly Deirdre's target arched his back and, as the audience watched, a thick stream arched from his cock to cover her face. There was a burst of applause and she smiled. Steve stood up and walked to her. "Is that pride I see, my dear?" he asked.

Her face changed instantly as if she had realized her mistake. "No, Master."

"That's good. Pride is a sin."

"Yes, Master."

Steve snapped his fingers and Deirdre rushed to his side and sat beside him. He spoke to her in a low voice and she disappeared into what Fran assumed was the bathroom.

Fran returned her attention to the three remaining contestants. The man on his knees had his hand buried between his target's legs. "He's probably fondling the man's heavy balls," Steve whispered, returning to his seat beside her, his breath tickling Fran's ear. "Or maybe she's rubbing his asshole. Have you ever had anyone play with you from behind?"

There was a commanding quality to Steve's voice so, without thinking, Fran answered, "No."

"Oh how wonderful. I would love to be the one to take that virginity from you." Again he stroked her ribbon. "Tell me to stop if you want me to, or give me hope that you will take this off later by your silence."

Fran said nothing and Steve's warm laugh warmed her ear. "You give me such wonderful expectations for this evening. I never dreamed . . ."

"I never did either," Fran said breathlessly.

Together they watched the contest continue, Steve's comments heating Fran's body. "Until you are mine," he said, "I will ask permission. May I touch you, just once?"

Fran remained silent, and Steve's hand slid up her stockinged thigh and rubbed the crotch of her panties. "So wet. You want this. You want to belong to me. Here. In public. You're titillated, aroused and so curious. I could satisfy everything and show you so much."

Fran looked at Carla, who was watching CJ's attempt to win the contest intently. Fran shook her head. She could almost admit that she wanted to play, but it was so public. She might be able to do it in front of strangers, but not in front of her friend. She sighed.

Steve leaned over and bit Fran's earlobe. "Carla will be going into the other room with CJ later. He likes his games a bit more painful and Carla will more than satisfy him."

"I thought she didn't really like the pain stuff," Fran blurted out.

"Here, tonight, she will do it to please CJ. She always does. And she'll enjoy it too, of course."

"But . . ."

"She forgets how wonderful it is to give a slave the pain he craves. I've been in the back room with her and she wields a paddle as well as anyone. I'll let her tell you about it if she wants to. But you needn't worry about Carla watching, if that's what is bothering you."

Steve sat beside Fran until the final target, CJ spurted into the mouth of the woman at his feet. "Only nine minutes," someone yelled. "You can do better than that."

"And he will," Carla said loudly. "Later."

"You see?" Steve said.

A few minutes later, Carla sought Fran out. "CJ wants to go into the other room to play and I really want to go with him. But I won't if you're uncomfortable. Will you be all right out here alone?"

"She won't be alone," Steve said.

Carla's look was filled with understanding. She squeezed Fran's arm. "It's okay, Nicki. I'll be quite a while." She paused. "Listen. There's a back entrance and I'll leave that way so you can be assured that I won't come through here again. Do whatever you want." She squeezed again. "Whatever you want, and no more. Yes?"

Fran looked at her friend seriously. "I don't want to force you to sneak out the back."

"Please. Let me do this for you. I want you to experience everything."

Fran hesitated. "Are you sure?"

"I'll tell you all about it tomorrow over brunch. I'll call you."

Fran placed her hand on Carla's arm. "Thanks for understanding."

Cape in hand, Carla winked and walked off, with CJ crawling behind, his leash in his mouth.

"She's quite a woman," Steve said. "And obviously a good friend."

"Yes." Fran's knees shook with the reality of what she was considering.

"Do you trust me?" Steve asked.

She nodded. She trusted Carla, and through her, she trusted Steve and all the people in the room. She knew that Carla wouldn't play with anyone who wasn't completely dependable. But that wasn't the issue. Could she trust herself? Did she have to?

"It's all right. Tell me how far you've gone into this kind of play. Have you ever been tied up?"

"Yes," Fran said, her eyes on her hands which rested nervously in her lap.

"Did you enjoy being helpless?"

"Yes."

"But with me you wouldn't be tied. You'd be helpless because you want to belong to me. Because you want the ecstasy that you know I can give you. Do you understand that?"

"Yes."

"You will do what I say, behave the way I tell you to, here, in public. You will answer all my questions, calling me Sir Steve at all times and you will speak only when I tell you to. And you will do it all because it will be the greatest pleasure you can imagine. Do you understand?"

"Yes," Fran said, "but tell me one thing. Why?"

"Why for me?"

"Yes."

Steve stared at her, his eyes boring into her very soul. "Oh

God, you can't imagine how excited I am at the prospect of introducing you to all the things we can experience here tonight." Steve took Fran's hand and placed it in the crotch of his buttery-soft leather pants. He was erect, hard, hot. "That's why."

Fran looked at this man who was asking for her complete trust and surrender. He was strong, powerful, commanding, yet there was a softness, an understanding in his eyes. She reached up and untied the ribbon from around her neck. As she did so, she watched Steve's eyes. He was almost glazed with lust. She put the ribbon into his hand and listened to his breath catch in his throat. "I don't know what to do," she said, then added, "Sir Steve."

He cleared his throat and snapped, "Stand up."

Fran stood, trembling but incredibly hungry. "Take that dress off," he ordered.

Fran reached down, grabbed the hem of her dress and pulled it over her head in one smooth move. She watched Steve's eyes roam over her body, now clad in a white lace bra with matching panties, and white thigh-high hose. "Take off your jewelry. All of it. It makes you proud and that's not allowed."

Fran removed her earrings and watch, the only jewelry she was wearing and dropped them into her purse.

"Your hair. I want it loose."

Her fumbling fingers pulled the comb and pins from her French knot and then she slid them through the newly released blond strands. She stood, watching his eyes possess her body. "So tiny," he moaned. "Take the bra off."

Fran felt a moment of panic about her small breasts. In for a penny, she thought, unhooking the clasp.

"Beautiful," he whispered. She knew he was saying those things for her benefit. No top, she reasoned, would say complimentary things to a new bottom, and she was glad he was helping her.

She watched him take a deep breath. "Take off the panties," he said, rising, "but leave the stockings. And wearing high heels is usually a privilege reserved for special women but I like the way they make your legs look so you may continue to wear them for the moment. Say thank you."

As Fran pulled off her panties, she whispered, "Thank you."

"You made two mistakes. First, you always call me Sir. Second, you never whisper. You thank me in a loud voice for whatever I do to you."

Loudly, she said, "Thank you, Sir Steven."

"Deirdre," he called, "come here."

The woman she had seen only from a distance walked over. She was barefoot, and Fran now saw that the blue teddy was a size too small, forcing her large breasts to spill over the top. "This is Nicki. She's mine for this evening. Welcome her."

With no warning, the woman put her arms around Fran and kissed her full on the lips, her breasts rubbing against Fran's. It was all Fran could do not to push her away, and her reluctance must have showed.

"So, that's how it is," Steve mused aloud. "Good. It pleases me to use the things a woman doesn't yet like." He walked toward the center of the room. "Follow me."

Fran walked behind Steve, with Deirdre behind her.

Steve moved a few chairs around until there were several grouped around a large wooden coffee table. "Sit," he said to Fran, pointing to the table. "And the rest of you, gather round." Several men and women settled into the chairs and Deirdre sat at Steve's feet.

"Nicki has consented to remove her ribbon for me and she's mine for tonight. She's never done anything like this before so I want anyone who enjoys initiations to join me. But only to watch unless I say otherwise." Tops talked eagerly while their bottoms, both male and female, settled into obviously accustomed positions. "Now, Nicki, sit on the table. We first have to clean you up."

Fran sat demurely on the edge of the table. "No." Steve pushed her back into the center of the table, then grabbed her ankles and put her feet onto the table with her knees spread, her cunt clearly visible to all. She supported herself straight-arm with her hands on the table behind her and her heels hooked into some carving in the edge of the table. Steve slid his finger through her slit and leered at her. "She's soaking wet." As if on cue, a man arrived with a pan, a towel and several other items which he handed to Steve.

"Wonderful," someone said.

"Can I have Gerry do it?" one man asked, patting the head of the slender black man who rested his face on the man's thigh. "He's got the softest touch." He stroked his cleanly shaven face, then rubbed his crotch suggestively.

"All right," Steve said, "but if he hurts her in any way, both you and Gerry will answer to me. And you know what that means."

"Of course, Steve." The man motioned to Gerry, who stood up. "Shave her."

Shave her? Fran gulped. Did she really want to have her pussy shaved? She could, of course, say no, but then Steve would be disappointed and it just wouldn't be the same from then on. She wanted to please Steve and prove herself worthy of his time and energy. And it sounded kinky.

"And," Steve said to two of the men in the audience, "maybe you'd better distract her while Gerry works."

Fran watched as Gerry picked up a pair of scissors and clipped all her pubic hairs very short. As he reached for a can of shaving foam, she felt men approach her from both sides, fastening mouths on her erect nipples. The sucking and biting filled her mind, so she barely felt Gerry soap and quickly dispose of all her pussy hair. "She's getting really juicy," Gerry said, laughing from between her legs. "It's difficult not to slip."

There was the sound of a slap and someone barked, "You forget your place."

"I'm so sorry, Master," Gerry said, and Fran felt the soap wiped from her skin while the mouths remained fastened on her breasts. Warm water trickled over her cunt. "Lick it dry, Gerry," a voice said, and Fran felt a tongue on her *now*-hairless mound.

She should be humiliated, with men sucking and licking at her while others watched, a few making ribald comments. Yet the

pleasure was overwhelming, leaving no room for negative feelings.

"All right, everyone," Steve said. "I don't want her to come
yet, so you'd better stop."

The mouths were gone.

"Get the mirror so she can see what a shameless slut she is,"
he said. Someone positioned a full-length mirror so Fran could
see herself. The sight that greeted her made her gasp. Her pussy,
framed by her white stockings, was naked, pink and glistening
with her own wetness. Her breasts were swollen, the nipples
damp and erect. Her hair was wild around her face. She was a
bitch in heat, startled at the obvious extent of her own hunger.

"Stand up, slut."

She stood.

"Let's see just how much of a slut you are." He opened the
front of his leather pants and pulled out his erect cock. "I'm too
hot to have the necessary patience so get on your knees and suck
me off."

She quickly knelt down and took his cock into her mouth. She
fondled his balls and used her nails on the underside of his shaft.
Almost immediately she felt his ass muscles tighten. She reached
around and cupped his cheeks as she created a strong vacuum
and pulled back, holding his cock in her mouth with the force of
her sucking.

With her nails digging into his ass cheeks, he came in her
mouth with a roar. Only a few drops of his come escaped her lips.

"You're losing your stamina," a voice called.

"Yeah, Steve. You wouldn't have lasted two minutes in the
contest."

"Not with a talented little cocksucker like this working on my
dick," he said, laughing. "Now I'll be able to wait until later to
fuck her brains out." He tucked his now-flaccid cock back into
his pants.

"Test her submission," someone said.

"Yes, test her."

"I can test her, Master." The voice was Deirdre's.

"Did you speak without my permission?" Steve said to her.

Deirdre's gaze dropped to the carpet. "I'm sincerely sorry, Sir Steve," she said, kneeling at his feet and hugging his legs. He pushed her away and she sat on the floor beside him.

"Slips like that usually merit punishment, but I'm feeling lenient," Steve said, reaching down and pinching Deirdre's nipple. "And just remember that she's not anyone for you to worry about." He stroked her cheek. "You will always be mine. She's only a diversion for this evening." He tipped her face up and kissed her on the lips. "Always mine, my love."

Fran watched Deirdre's face light up. It must be difficult, Fran thought, to be as obviously in love as Deirdre was, yet watch Steve play with another woman. But she was also delighted at his consideration of Deirdre's feelings.

"Have you ever been with a woman, Nicki?" Steve asked.

Fran swallowed hard. "No, Sir Steve."

"Then that's a good test. Stand up." He motioned to Deirdre. "You too."

The two women stood, facing each other. "Now hold each other, and rub your tits together. Deirdre, you know what I like to see." He reached over and cupped the woman's breasts, lifting them out of the cups of the teddy. Her large almost-purple nipples were fully erect.

Deirdre wrapped her arms around Fran's waist. Since she was several inches taller, her large breasts rubbed the tops of Fran's naked tits. Fran inhaled Deirdre's soft fragrance and smelled the scent of their combined lust. She placed her face close to the other woman's neck and whispered, "This is only for tonight. I promise I'll never see him again." She paused, then added, "He's obviously in love with you."

Deirdre leaned down and pressed her lips to Fran's. "Truly?" she purred within the embrace. "You really think so?"

"Yes," Fran said truthfully.

Deirdre smiled as her tongue licked along the joining of Fran's lips, inviting them to part. The kiss was gentle, almost loving and, when Fran's lips parted the kiss deepened. She was kissing a woman like a lover, Fran realized. It was very confusing.

"Nicki, I want you to lick Deirdre's tits so we all can watch."

"But Sir Steve," Fran said, "I don't know how."

"Of course you do. You like it when men suck your tits, so just do what you enjoy. Does it embarrass you?"

Fran looked at the floor. "Yes, Sir Steve, it does."

His grin was wide and genuine. "Good. Do as you're told."

Fran took a deep breath, then lowered her mouth to one of Deirdre's large breasts. Tentatively, she licked the erect nipple. Deirdre must have put scent between her breasts because when Fran inhaled she smelled a soft, flowery aroma.

"Come on, Nicki. You must enjoy having your tits sucked better than that. Stop. Let Deirdre show you." Steve pulled out an overstuffed chair. "Sit down, Nicki."

Fran walked to the chair, marveling at the slutty feeling of her shaved pussy. She sat on the chair. "Now lean back and spread your legs." She obeyed. "Now, Deirdre, show her how to suck titty."

Deirdre knelt between Fran's spread thighs and fondled her breasts. She pinched her nipples and Fran was surprised at how easily she became more aroused. She watched Deirdre's long red fingernails flick over her buds and knead the flesh of her tiny breasts. Then Deirdre's mouth fastened on her right nipple.

Somewhere in her mind, Fran accepted that this was a woman laving, sucking, biting her, and it felt wonderful. It was a hot, hungry mouth and whether it was a man or woman mattered less and less as excitement coursed through her. The mouth moved to her other nipple and, while the mouth sucked, fingers pinched and pulled. Fran moved her hips trying to ease the ache between her legs. Touch me, rub me, she thought, but she knew enough about Sir Steve to say nothing.

"Oh that's so hot to watch," a voice said. "I love to see two lezzies sucking tit."

Not lesbians, Fran thought. Just seekers of pleasure. She

cupped the back of Deirdre's head and held the woman's face against her.

"Now switch places and let's see what Nicki's learned."

Quickly Deirdre settled in the chair and Fran knelt between her knees. The breasts she gazed at were full and so much larger than hers. She touched, lifted and held the flesh, so soft and full in her hands. She leaned over and tentatively licked one brown nipple and, as she blew on the wet skin, she watched the bud contract and tighten. With increasing confidence she sucked the turgid tip into her mouth and flicked her tongue over it.

As she felt Deirdre move beneath her mouth, she bit down on the tip, holding it with her teeth and pulling backward. She heard the woman groan so she bit just a little harder. Nails scratched down her back and held her shoulders. She moved to the other nipple and repeated her actions. God, she thought as Deirdre moaned, it was good to be able to give this much pleasure, to a man or a woman.

"I would love to watch this more," Steve said, "but I have other plans." He grabbed Fran's shoulder and pulled her back onto her haunches.

"But it's so lovely to watch," someone said. Fran looked over and saw a small man with thick glasses, with a woman openly fondling his cock.

"Paul," Steve said, "will you lend me Maddy so she can tend to Deirdre's pleasure? That way you all can continue to watch and I can play with my little toy."

Paul chuckled and gave Maddy, his slave, some hasty instructions. While the two women made themselves comfortable in the chair, Steve told Fran to kneel on the table. She complied, placing her knees and elbows on the pillows a tall man provided.

"Gentlemen," he said to the audience, "you might be interested in helping me. This little lovely has never had her ass penetrated and I intend to take that particular cherry this evening. I want her really hot."

"I'll donate Jose," a woman said. "Use him as you want."

"And I'll give you Bill."

Steve quickly told the two men what he wanted and the two moved to opposite sides of the table. Each man placed his head beneath Fran's chest and took a tightly hanging breast in his mouth. Two mouths. It was heaven. Then a hand was playing with her pussy, rubbing over the now-smooth skin. "She's very wet and slippery, but not hot enough yet. Maybe she needs a mouth on her cunt."

"Oh let me," a female voice said. Fran shuddered as a talented mouth found her clit. Now she had three mouths sucking, licking, playing with her body, driving her higher. Her thighs trembled and she could barely keep her balance on her knees.

"Is she close?" Steve asked.

"A few more moments," the female voice said, then her tongue thrust into Fran's channel. In and out, the tongue fucked her.

"She's really hot," the woman said again, "and I can keep her just at the edge of climax until you're ready."

"Good. Do that. But there will be hell to pay if you make her come."

A female chuckle. "No problem."

"Nicki, raise your head and watch what I'm doing." Fran looked up and saw that Steve was covering his cock with a condom, then adding a large handful of lubricant. "I'm going to fuck your ass. I will be gentle, but it's going to hurt momentarily." His voice softened and dropped. "Trust me."

She nodded almost imperceptibly. Then Steve moved behind her, the three mouths still working on her body. She felt something cold and slippery being rubbed on her ass. How was he doing that while the woman's mouth still sucked on her clit?

Then a finger began to invade her ass. It wasn't an unpleasant feeling just a fullness and a stretching. "Oh," Steve groaned, "so tight."

The finger slowly massaged her rear passage, reaching deep into her, then withdrawing. Again and again the finger invaded, then it was joined by a second one. She was stretched and it hurt, but somehow the pain wasn't spoiling her pleasure. Rather it was adding to it, dividing her brain between her breasts, her clit and her ass.

"It's time, my dear. What you're going to feel now is my cock."

The fingers were removed and replaced with a larger force pressing against her ass. Never, she thought. It will never fit.

Slowly the tip slid in and held still just inside her rear passage. It hurt a lot, but then suddenly something in her body released and the pain eased. She was filled. So filled. The invading cock slowly penetrated more deeply.

"Oh God," Steve moaned. "Such a tight, hot ass." He pumped a few times, then held still deep inside her. "I want to feel her come," he said.

The mouth moved from her pussy and fingers lightly pinched her clit. Then several fingers, Fran had no idea whose, filled her cunt. She could hold back no longer. With several fingers fucking her cunt and her ass filled with Steve's cock, she came, wave after wave of orgasm rocking her. "God, oh God," Steve cried. With a few sudden thrusts he came as well.

The men at her breasts moved away and she collapsed onto the table and curled into a ball, trying to recover from the most violent orgasm of her life. Someone covered her with a light blanket and she drifted for a long time.

"I would love for you to stay with me, but I think you might be ready to go home," Steve whispered in her ear sometime later.

What had happened had left her drained and she had really, for what might be the first time in her life, had enough sex. "Yes," she admitted, "It's time for me to leave."

Steve helped her dress, then got their coats, called a car service and silently rode back with her to her building. As the limo pulled to a stop, he said, "I hope it was as wonderful for you as it was for me. I would love to get together again."

Fran looked at him. This had been fun for an evening, but that was all. This lifestyle wasn't for her. "It was wonderful. I enjoyed every minute of it. But this was a one time thing. At least for right now."

"I was afraid so. I was just hoping."

"And anyway, Deirdre's the woman you want."

"I know. But diversion is fun occasionally, and if you ever change your mind, Carla knows how to reach me."

Without asking, she cupped his chin and kissed him firmly on the mouth, an indication of the fact that she was no longer his slave. "Good night, Sir Steve."

"Good night, Nicki."

Finally in her apartment Fran undressed and fell into bed. Although stories were whirling in her head, she fell asleep immediately.

As Fran partied, on Long Island, Zack Barklay lay beside his wife Diane. While Zack finished the last few pages of the book he was reading, she'd been editing a chapter of her next novel. As Zack finally closed the paperback, Diane put her pages aside. "Well?" she said. "That's the last of them, isn't it?"

Zack sighed. "Yup. That's the last."

"So?"

"So what? I'm not an editor or a critic and I haven't read many romance novels, besides yours of course." This was the conversation he'd been avoiding for a while.

"But you have a right to an opinion. What did you think of them? Be honest."

Zack rolled his eyes. "*Addie's Travels* should win easily. The others aren't in the same league."

"You're just saying that because it's what I want to hear. Come on, tell me. Really. Let's do them one by one."

Zack let out a long breath and gritted his teeth. "Okay. Virginia Cortez. Hasn't she written lots of these books?"

"She's got nearly forty in print. She turns them out in litters. And they're always trilogies or tetralogies or lotsologies. And always the same theme. Three sisters who need husbands. Or a family of brothers and sisters, all really nice people. I could gag."

"But *Come to Papa* wasn't part of anything, was it?"

"No. It was one of her few stand-alones. What did you think of it?"

Zack sighed again. "It was good, but I thought the characters weren't as strong as yours." That should dispose of her.

Diane smiled. "You know you're right. I think she was nominated for her body of work, not for this book. But they can't give the prize to someone for lots of books. It's the book that's nominated, not the author." She adjusted the pillow behind her. "And what about *Joys of Paris?*"

"It was a bit too cerebral for me," Zack said, remembering the slower pace of the book about lovers in Paris after World War I. "The characters spent all their time thinking. I like a book in which something happens."

"So do the judges, I hope. And *Miranda?*"

Zack reached over to the stack on his bed table and picked up one volume. "Ms. Allonzo's got a really fine book here," Zack felt he had to admit, patting the cover. "A good character and an unusual location. I found all the information about life in Alaska at the turn of the century really interesting."

"Didn't you find it a bit much? I felt like she'd researched so much that she had to tell us everything she'd learned."

"Yeah," said Zack quickly. "I did too."

"And you just finished *The Love Flower*. Isn't that a piece of trash?"

Zack put *Miranda* aside and picked up *The Love Flower*. He shifted his position beneath the covers and tried to conceal the remains of his raging erection. "It was really trashy," he said, knowing what Diane wanted to hear.

"It's a joke. It's not a real book, just a collection of steamy scenes strung together like beads. No real plot."

Zack's sense of justice forced him to say, "I don't think it's really that bad. There's a traditional plot, boy meets girl, complications occur, then boy and girl get together in the end."

"Come on. It's smut and you know it. And you just admitted that you don't read many of these things so you wouldn't know. It's cliché, hackneyed."

It might be cliché, Zack thought, remembering a scene he'd reread three times, but it's really hot. God. He sighed and twisted under the covers. Rhona and that sailor, Flint. The night he seduced her.

Chapter
9

Rhona knew that Flint was there even before he revealed himself to her. She knew because her body flushed, her neck tingled, her breasts swelled. She wanted him and she knew she didn't hide it very well. But she also knew that it was forbidden. He was a stranger, and the laws of her people forbade any interaction. And anyway, she told herself, in a few weeks he would sail away and she'd have nothing.

But he was there, and her body knew it. "Good evening, Miss Rhona," he said, his low voice penetrating the sweet night air.

She turned toward the sound. "Good evening, Mr. Flint." He was standing at the edge of the beach, partially hidden by the line of palms. She turned and walked onward, hoping that he wouldn't follow, yet knowing that he would.

He walked softly, barely disturbing the air, yet she heard every footfall as his shoes crunched over the sand. The moon was almost full as they emerged from the shade of the palms onto a strip of brightly lit beach. The sand glowed cool and white, small threads of spume washing back and forth by small wavelets at the waterline. She tried to concentrate on the waves' whoosh, whoosh and she kept walking.

"It won't help," he said softly. "You know it won't help."

"Help?" she said, barely able to keep the trembling from showing in her voice. "I don't know what you're talking about." A warm, callused hand touched her shoulder and she froze. Her back stiffened and her shoulders tightened.

"Oh, but you do. You feel it, like an irresistible pull, drawing us together." His breath was hot on the back of her neck as he grasped her other shoulder. He took a small step so his body was pressed against her back, his hardness pressing against her spine. "I can feel you trembling. You know, don't you?" When she remained silent, immobile, he whispered again, "Tell me that you feel it."

Unable to control her body, she shuddered. "Yes," she moaned.

He turned her around and his firm lips devoured hers. She was no stranger to loving but this was all consuming as nothing else had ever been. She wanted to resist but it was like trying not to look at a beautiful sunrise, or trying not to eat when you're starving. She attempted to keep her mouth closed but when he sucked on her lower lip and then nipped at it, she was lost.

Her mouth opened and his tongue plundered, tasting, delving, reaching, demanding. And she could not resist. Her tongue dueled with his as he probed her mouth. He was a fire, and suddenly she would do anything to feed the flames. She had no idea how her arms ended up around his neck, but she hung on, pressing him tightly against her. She stood on tiptoes to better fit against his large body.

Flint held on and rode the waves of passion. As he had suspected, she was incredibly hot. Once he cut through her silly taboos, she was one sexy broad. She flattened her breasts against his chest, and pressed her pelvis against his cock. Yes, he thought, she's mine now. All he could think about was sinking his engorged member into her, but, like gentling any small animal, he'd have to go slowly.

And he knew she had her sexual tricks. All the women had been initiated into their sex cult and he wasn't going to rush. This little piece was going to give him the best loving of his life. He tangled his fingers in her long straight black hair and dragged her face back. He planted small kisses on her eyelids, her cheeks. He tightened his grip, not to hold her but to keep his hands off her tits. Not yet, he warned himself. Don't screw this up.

Rhona sighed as he used her hair to pull her head back and his lips found her throat. A soft warm breeze brushed over the wet trail he left, making her shiver. She flattened her hands on his chest, feeling his heavy breathing and the pounding of his heart. But it wasn't enough. She needed to feel his skin so she quickly unbuttoned his shirt and slid her palms against his furred chest. So hard, so hard. She tangled her fingers in the thick pelt, so different from the other men she had known.

His lips were on her collarbones now but she needed more. She opened the top of her sarong and let it fall to the sand. She smiled when she heard him gasp. "You are so lovely," he purred, and she watched his eyes ravish her flesh. Where his gaze traveled, his hands followed. Rough palms cupped her breasts, rasping the surface in what should have been a painful movement. But the slight burning just added to the sensations that overwhelmed her.

He pinched one nipple and it was all she could do to remain standing. As if sensing that, Flint spread the single layer of cloth she had been wearing on the sand and lowered her onto it.

God, she's spectacular, Flint thought. Her body is perfect, small waist, large tits, and curly, dark hair hiding her secrets, which wouldn't be secrets much longer. How long I waited for this juicy little piece. The other women of the village he'd fucked had been pale imitations. She was the real thing.

He quickly pulled off his clothes and stood in the moonlight as she looked at him. He was proud of his lean body, hard and muscular from months of back-breaking work on the ship. He watched her eyes as she tried not to stare at his rampant sex, but he wanted her to look. Slowly he raised his hands to his belly, then slid them down the hairy surface until he held his swollen cock.

Rhona just stared, allowing her eyes to fill with him. His thighs were heavily muscled and she wondered how they would feel against her. His belly was flat, with a thick arrow of hair pointing, drawing her eyes to his cock. His huge hands held his raging erection, offering it proudly to her. He was built like an animal, huge cock and large, swaying balls. Her animal.

She spread her legs, inviting him, urging him. When she raised her arms to him, he knelt on the sand at her feet, cupping her buttocks in those rough palms. He lifted her hips and lowered his mouth so he could worship her. She had never felt anything so wonderful as his mouth on her. Others had played with her this way, but no one had made her feel what she felt with Flint. His mouth was both loving and demanding, his tongue dancing over her wet skin then plunging into her channel. It was as though he knew how to drive her upwards, yet stop just before she reached the pinnacle.

Flint licked and sucked in a frenzy. She tasted of woman, and salt, and heat. He found her with his thumbs and opened her lips so he could lick her clit. He pushed the tip of his tongue into her and listened to her gasp and cry. He wanted her so hungry she would do anything, show him all her tricks. He took charge of her arousal, pushing her up, then stopping, listening to her tiny protests.

He knew she was ready to do anything for him. He lowered her hips to the cloth, then crawled around to her head.

He held his cock in one hand and stroked her lips with the other. When she opened her mouth, he pushed his engorged member inside.

Rhona instinctively used her lips and tongue to give him pleasure, as she had been taught. She flicked over the small hole at the tip of his penis, tasting the salty fluid that oozed from it. She reached up and cupped his heavy sac, gently squeezing his testicles. She used her index finger to scratch the sensitive skin between his balls and his anus and, as she did so, she felt him buck. She was giving him pleasure and this made her proud.

Flint was in heaven, and now had to concentrate on not shooting into her mouth. No, he wanted to shoot into her tight little pussy. Reluctantly he pulled back, slowly withdrawing his cock from her lips. He crawled between her legs and rubbed the swollen purple head of cock against her sopping cunt. Although he wanted to drive into her, he knew that he would defeat his purpose. He didn't want to come yet. He just wanted her hot as a firecracker. These women could do things with their cunt muscles that could drive a man insane.

She was so tight that at first he pushed into her just a bit and gave her time to adjust to his size. Then a bit further. It was sweet torture for him, but he knew the reward for patience. These native women knew things that would put a London doxie to shame.

Inexorably his cock filled her and he reached down to rub her clit, a trick he'd learned from another woman of the village. That had been the first time he'd felt that clenching that they did and he wanted it again. He held perfectly still and he rubbed.

Rhona lay still and just sailed. She was filled, so full that it was as though every wonderful feeling was centered in her belly. She felt his cock, held torturously still as his fingers urged her upward. Gently, she squeezed her vaginal muscles, testing the fullness of her channel. No man had ever given her what Flint was giving her, had joined with her so completely so that she couldn't tell where her pleasure ended and his began.

She squeezed again, and felt Flint's back arch. And then she could hold back no longer. His fingers drew her climax from her, sharp spasms clutching at his great cock. And she knew when he could hold still no longer as well and suddenly he pushed into her, pounding her against the sand. Again and again he thrust into her as shards of color enveloped her. Then, with a roar, he poured himself into her and the brilliant colors of her climax were as nothing she had ever experienced.

He rolled onto his back, carrying her with him so she lay, pillowed on his large body. Together they rested, with his cock still inside of her.

Zack remembered that scene so well he could play it like a movie in his head. "It's just smut," Diane continued. "And Mort and I have been spreading the word."

Zack pulled himself back from the beach and Rhona. "Spreading what word?"

"Mort and I have been making it plain to anyone who will listen, that it will really demean the image of The Madison Prize if it goes to a piece of trash like *The Love Flower*."

A snapshot of Mort Lieberman, Diane's editor at Romance Classics, flashed through his mind. He was a small man with rimless glasses, a bow tie, and an expression that always looked like he had just smelled something rotten. Zack had taken an instant dislike to him at the one dinner they had attended together, but he had kept his feelings to himself. And, Zack thought, he was a fine editor and it was Mort's careful work that helped push Diane's books onto the romance bestseller lists. "Who will listen?"

"We've been heating up controversy on the various Internet writers' lists. You'd be amazed at who reads those messages." As Diane sat up to put the pages she had been working on on the bedside table, the sheet fell to her waist, revealing her lush breasts beneath the filmy lavender nightgown she wore.

Zack tossed *The Love Flower* onto the floor beside his bed and turned toward his wife. As she reached over to turn out the bedside light, he placed a light kiss between her shoulder blades. She stilled and he continued to kiss her spine, down to the line of her nightgown. "How about taking that thing off?" he said.

Obligingly, Diane turned toward him and drew her nightgown off over her head.

Sunday morning, Carla called Fran and they agreed to meet for brunch at a trendy local restaurant called Eat At Joe's. The two women ordered and when they were finally alone, sipping champagne and orange juice, Carla asked Fran about the previous evening.

"It was fan-flipping-tastic. Bone-jarring, tooth-rattling, body-satisfying wonderful. I'm really sorry about pushing you off into the back room."

"Why? I told you I'd end up back there with CJ."

"I know, but I feel I chased you."

"And if I retired to give you some privacy, is that so bad?"

"I guess not. Privacy. That's a funny word for what went on with so many people watching."

"Yes, but you didn't know any of those people. It's anonymous and that's a different kind of privacy. That's why so many men enjoy sex with prostitutes."

"You're probably right. How was your time with CJ? It's hard to imagine him involved with kinky sex. He looks so angelic."

"I know. And he's anything but. He can play the dominant, but he particularly enjoys it when I spank him like a naughty boy. Last evening he was anxious to give me a new leather paddle he made. Very springy, and noisy. The sound, as much as the pain, turns him on."

At Fran's raised eyebrow, Carla continued. "I spend a few minutes calling him a bad boy and forcing him to tell me all the really naughty things he's done all week. Each one gets ten slaps. That way he can tell me how much he wants, without really telling me. When he thinks the count's high enough, he runs out of bad deeds."

"Clever."

"It was Ronnie's idea. She's so good at this, gauging just where the line is between pleasure and pain. Anyway, he was up to fifty when he finally stopped."

"And he enjoys this?"

"Tremendously. I don't understand it, but I accept it. And I do enjoy his pleasure."

"So did you paddle him?"

"I make him volunteer for it, forcing him to admit that he really wants it. That admission makes him even hotter. So I have him lay across my lap, very slowly, and then I make him count each swat and thank me for doing it. And the new paddle was wonderful. It made a loud smacking sound as I reddened first one asscheek, then the other. Then I moved to the backs of his thighs. By the time I got to forty he was crying like a baby."

Fran just shook her head. "I don't understand it. If he's crying, isn't that torture?"

"Not to him. He can stop any time by saying the safe word or just by standing up. But he doesn't. He cried and counted, his cock getting harder and harder, trapped against my thighs. When I'm finished, he has to walk across the room and get a special soothing lotion."

"Weren't other people there? What did they think?"

"There were a few, into whippings and such, but they were involved in doing their own thing so they paid little attention. I put him back across my lap with his cock between my thighs. I love to wiggle just enough to make his cock harder. I rubbed the lotion on his butt, working it into the crack in his ass."

The waiter arrived with two orders of eggs Benedict, coffee for Carla and herb tea for Fran. When he was gone, Carla continued, "When I knew he couldn't hold out much longer I made him stand and masturbate while I watched. While he did, I kept telling him that only bad boys jerk off with someone watching."

"And the orgasm he had had earlier didn't slow him down?"

"Actually, I've learned that unless he's already climaxed once, we can't play for long. He gets too excited too quickly. But eventually he came and then he took me home."

"So you never really had an orgasm?"

"It doesn't matter to me anymore. I love CJ's pleasure and it makes me happy to watch him."

During the rest of the meal, they talked about sex a lot, Fran completely comfortable sharing all the delicious details with her best friend. Her best friend. She had been in New York only two weeks, and was only going to be here one more. How was she going to go back to Omaha? She wondered that on and off for the rest of the wonderful day the two women spent together.

Monday morning, Fran dressed carefully for her lunch with Sandy and Eileen. It was to be the first time that Nicki had met her editor and, although Sandy knew that Nicki wasn't quite as she had been portrayed, she didn't know any of the details.

The sun was shining and the temperature was predicted to be in the sixties, so Fran selected a floral print wool skirt in shades of teal and deep red with a matching deep red silk blouse and a long purple jacket that hung to the hemline of the skirt. She'd forgo a coat and hope that she'd be warm enough. She added Carla's hoop earrings for luck, with several gold bracelets. Purple panty hose and black pumps completed the outfit.

She walked the few blocks to the restaurant and as she entered, she spotted Eileen sitting with a slightly older woman, who quickly stood up and beckoned her over. "Nichole," the woman said. "I'm so delighted to finally meet you in person. We've talked so much over the phone that I think I would have recognized you anywhere."

Sandy was about five foot four, with very short iron-gray hair and sparkling deep blue eyes. She grasped Fran's hand warmly, then leaned over and kissed her on the cheek. Remembering that she was Nicki, Fran quickly moved to kiss the other cheek.

"And I'm so happy to meet you, too," Fran said, sitting down in an unoccupied chair. "I've had such a mental picture of you from our chats on the phone, that it's really strange to see you in person."

"Do I look the way you pictured me?"

Fran wasn't sure how to answer, since Sandy didn't look at all as she'd expected, but Sandy jumped in. "Don't say a thing," she said. "You didn't expect the gray." She combed her fingers through her short hair. "I've been this color since I was in my early twenties, and I kind of like it."

"And you should. It looks," she paused, "smashing." And she smiled to show that she really meant it.

During lunch, the three women talked about books in general and they agreed on some of their favorites and disagreed on others. Eileen was a mystery reader, while Sandy preferred science fiction. They discussed the publishing business and all admitted that no one really understood it.

When dessert and beverage arrived at the table, Sandy asked, "Nicki, have you got any ideas about your next book? I'd love to give my boss a proposal for the next Nichole St. Michelle goodie."

As Eileen started to answer, Nicki said, "Actually I've been working on an idea."

"Do you want to give us the gist or is it too early yet?"

"It's about a thirtyish woman who's never known much of the big world, who comes to New York to spend the summer with an old school friend. In New York, she not only meets a wonderful man, but she learns about sex and life and finally understands that there's more to life than Milwaukee."

"That sounds wonderful," Sandy said. "Have you got a title?"

"I want to call it *Pleasures.*"

"Great title," Sandy said. "Will it be as explicit as *The Love Flower?*"

"I think more so, if you think the powers that be won't object to some serious sex."

"Not at all. As a smaller house, we can pretty much do as we please. And Phil Spencer likes good hot sex." She giggled. "In books, that is. I have no clue about his personal life." She leaned forward and looked at Fran. "And will it be a romance? I mean will the girl get the guy in the end?"

"You know, I'm not really sure. But for me, the most important part of the plot will be that the girl grows up."

"Sounds wonderful. I can't wait to read a full proposal."

Eileen had been silent throughout the discussion. "About next weekend," she now said to Sandy. "What's the schedule?"

"Friday evening Majestic will have a suite with hors d'oeuvres and drinks. Very Tahitian motif. You know, really good plastic palm trees, girls in grass skirts, guys with little strips of cloth around their waist and nothing much more. All very sexy." She leaned forward. "I was wondering. Could you dress like Rhona? You know, a sarong?"

Fran thought about it. Nicki could. She could. "Sure," she said. "I'll come up with something."

"I've got the names of several costumers," Sandy said, handing Fran a piece of paper from her purse. She looked down and grinned. "I was hoping . . ."

"Of course," Fran said. "I will be there with bells on. Or rather, with Tahiti on."

"Are you planning to go to any of the workshops during the day?"

"I hadn't planned on it. Should I?"

"It's not really necessary. But Saturday I'll have a table set up for you in the main hall, with lots of copies of *The Love Flower* for visitors to buy and for you to autograph. All the other nominated authors will be there too, of course."

"I'm looking forward to meeting them. Especially Virginia Cortex. I've been a fan of hers for years. And Diane Barklay too. I just loved *Addle's Travels*."

Eileen laughed. "Don't be so generous about the competition."

"Why not?" Fran asked honestly. "They're good books."

"This isn't tea and cakes," Sandy said, lowering her voice. "This is important stuff. There's lots of money riding on this award. And the others are playing hardball."

"Hardball? I don't understand."

Sandy's expression became serious. "Let me be blunt. I don't expect *The Love Flower* to win."

Fran's face fell. Not that she had really expected to win, but . . . "Why?" she said.

"Because there's a serious campaign against it."

Eileen remained silent, obviously already knowing what Sandy was saying. Fran was mystified. "I don't get it."

"Oh my dear, you're so naive. There are letters all over the Internet calling the book smut and trash and saying that the integrity of The Madison Prize will be compromised if they award it to a novel as clearly erotic as yours. I assume at least one of the publishers is behind it, or maybe just one of the other authors. Actually you should be complimented. Someone must think your book is stiff competition."

Fran sat, immobile. She hadn't realized any of this.

Sandy sipped her coffee and continued. "We've gotten a lot of really good press from all of this. It's kind of like being on the church's banned list. Lots of people are buying and reading *The Love Flower* because it's being called names and we'll cry all the way to the bank. So we're getting what we want out of all this. I just don't want you to wander through all this thinking that all books have an equal shot. They don't."

"But it's not fair. *The Love Flower* is a really good book." Fran blushed at her flatly immodest remark.

"We know it is, but it's also explicit and, in some places, downright kinky. I love it and keep a copy beside my bed. Every now and then I read a section to Josh before we go to sleep. It's like a sleeping pill."

"I think I'm insulted," Fran said.

"Not at all. Good hot sex is a great soporific."

The three women laughed heartily. "So just have your eyes wide open," Sandy said. "By the way, is there anyone you would like to invite as your guest to the dinner and festivities Saturday evening?"

Fran thought about O'Malley and Clark. No. She didn't feel

that way about either of them. She knew who she'd really like to invite. "Do you think Carla would come with us?" she asked Eileen.

"I certainly think you should ask her and I think she'd be delighted. I have no clue about her schedule, however."

"Okay," Sandy said, "let me know and if you need any extra tickets I'll be sure to have them for you."

Carla called Fran midmorning on Wednesday. After some pleasantries, Fran said, "I'd love for you to come to the award dinner Saturday evening, that is if you don't have other plans, or have to be home with the kids."

"That's great. I'd love to. I kept the evening free and if you hadn't invited me I think I might have crashed the party. And I've got an invitation for you, too. If you hadn't told me how much you enjoyed the party Saturday evening, I wouldn't think of asking this, but here goes. I got a call from a friend of mine named Jason. He enjoys entertaining and being entertained by two women at the same time. He's got some unusual tastes in fantasies, but he likes his sex pretty straight. I have several female friends who have played with us, and they've always enjoyed the evening. I wondered whether you'd be interested in joining us tomorrow evening." Before Fran could answer, Carla added, "Please understand that I won't be insulted if you say no and we'll see each other Saturday night anyway, but I just thought I'd ask."

"Sounds interesting."

"Really?" Carla sounded startled.

"I don't know what I'm ready for, but last Saturday evening really whetted my appetite for the unusual."

"I'm so happy. Oh, and he pays us each seven hundred dollars for the evening."

Fran almost choked. "You're kidding."

Carla's laugh was warm and caring. "Amazing, isn't it? We get paid for doing what we did Saturday evening for nothing."

"It is amazing. But what if I can't do something he wants to do? If he's paying, then he has certain rights."

"I have the same arrangement with him that I have with all my friends. If it doesn't go the way we planned and if he's not satisfied, he doesn't pay. No strings. It's so much better that way. He always knows that we're both enjoying everything."

"But that way don't you sometimes do things for the money? If you don't do it, you don't get paid, after all."

"I don't need the money. Somehow, taking money under those circumstances *would* make me a whore."

"Okay. It sounds like something Nicki would do, and, after all, I'm Nicki now, through and through. Fran is dead and buried."

"No, she's not really. You're still the nice, educated, interesting woman you've always been. You just have lots of Nicki's adventurousness too."

They talked about the evening for a while. Then Fran asked, "What should I wear?"

"We'll be going out to dinner first. He likes La Cote Basque, Rain, Cafe des Artistes, like that. I know he hopes that he'll run into friends or business associates so that he can show off his good taste in dinner companions. I've met some of his friends that way in the past. As for what you should wear, as I remember it, you have a long black skirt, slit up to the thigh. Bring a very dressy top, but I have a blouse that would go with it perfectly, one that I know Jason would particularly love."

"Sounds easy enough."

"And wear your highest heels. He loves sexy shoes and since Jason's not too tall, wearing very high heels isn't an option for me."

When Fran arrived at Carla's house at six, Carla flipped through several tops in her closet, then pulled out a soft top made of some sort of clingy fabric in shimmering gold. "Try this on," she said.

Fran took off the top she was wearing and pulled on the one Carla handed her. It was cut so that it draped almost to the waist both in front and in back, with a string tie across the back of the shoulders to hold it on. "Bra off," Carla said as it became obvious that the undergarment showed both front and back.

"After all the trouble I went to to get this bra that gives me cleavage, now I take it off and lose it all."

"Just watch," Carla said, as Fran removed her bra from beneath the top. It looked fabulous. It gave her almost a model's figure, with just a hint of swelling on either side of the neckline. And her large nipples made tents at the front. "I bought that and I really thought I could wear it, but I've got too much bosom. You look sensational."

Fran gazed into the mirror. "It does look good," she admitted. "Have you got earrings?"

Carla found her a pair of rhinestone earrings, long enough that they brushed her collarbones, calling further attention to the neckline of the blouse. "And those shoes are perfect. He'll drool all through dinner."

Fran had selected a pair of three and a half inch gold strappy pumps and gotten a small gold purse to match. She might as well do this in style. And seven hundred dollars? She had calculated how many stories she'd have to write to earn that much and her mind boggled. It was all she could do not to giggle. But what if he's a troll? she thought. If he had to pay, maybe he's got bad breath or body odor.

"What's Jason like?" she asked tentatively.

"He's about fifty, kind of ordinary looking with thick glasses. It took me a while to get used to him, naked, but with his glasses on. When I suggested that he might be more comfortable without them, he said, 'And miss something? Not on your life.'"

"So why does he have to pay? I mean he sounds okay."

"Not every man has a woman to date, and most men want sex. If you remember it took Clark quite a bit of courage to pick you up. Me, I'm a sure thing, as Julia Roberts said in *Pretty Woman*."

"I guess I've just got stereotypes in my brain."

"Well, just wait until you meet him."

When Jason arrived, Carla kissed him warmly. "This is . . ." she said but Fran interrupted. "Fran," she said.

Carla looked puzzled, then smiled in understanding.

"It's wonderful to meet you, Fran," Jason said, taking her hand and kissing the back. "I thought we'd go to Le Cirque this evening," he said.

Fran had heard of the world-famous restaurant but with prices in the stratosphere, she'd never expected to dine there. An unexpected bonus. Inwardly she giggled. And she was being paid, too. She slipped on a velvet jacket that Carla had lent her and with Jason in the middle the three walked out into the New York evening.

Fran found Jason delightful company as they sipped champagne in the limo on the short drive to Le Cirque. He was a wonderfully intelligent man, in his late fifties, overweight, with marshmallow-white hair and a tightly clipped white beard. As they rode, Fran frequently found Jason's gaze on her breastbone and almost as often on her ankles.

During a fantastic French meal, during which Fran spotted several famous faces at nearby tables, she and Jason did most of the talking with Carla obviously content to listen. Jason was an architect with an exciting new project that he discussed at length. Fran found it fascinating. She asked what she thought were intelligent questions and got involved and excited answers. They discussed some of the books that Fran had read over the years, and movies they had seen. He was well traveled and Fran quickly decided not to try to discuss Europe as though she had been there as Nicki might have done, but rather to listen to Jason's opinions.

"This is quite some friend you have, Carla," Jason said at one point. "Not only good looks, but intelligent and such a good listener." He patted her hand. "Remember that woman you brought one evening? Louise, I think her name was."

Carla laughed. "How could I forget. She was a friend of a friend and I hadn't met her before that night. She had the IQ of a houseplant and the figure of a Playboy bunny."

"I don't usually complain, and the evening ended on, shall we say, a high note, but dinner was stultifying. But this wonderful woman is just what an old man needs."

As they sipped coffee and tea, Carla asked, "What are you in the mood for this evening, Jason? Shall we go back to my place and wander through my album?"

"I'm sure whatever we do together will be delightful. What about you, Fran, what do you enjoy?"

"It's funny. Three weeks ago, I would have had a very limited answer. Recently, however, I've widened my horizons. I find that I'm really up for most sports."

"I read a story about a threesome in a bathtub. How's the tub at your place, Carla?"

"It's a bit small for the three of us, I'm afraid."

Could I? Fran wondered. Could I invite an almost perfect stranger to the Devlins' for sex games? He'll know the address. But if Carla thinks he's okay, then he must be. And I think he's adorable. "I have a bathtub that's large enough to land a small plane in, if you'd like to come over to the apartment I'm borrowing from a friend."

Carla nodded. "What a wonderful idea. I've wanted to try out that bathtub since I first saw it. Jason?"

"Sounds perfect." He signaled for the check and they were soon back in the limo, speeding through midtown Manhattan. In the elevator on the way up to Fran's apartment, Jason removed Fran's jacket and untied the strands of fabric that held the back of the blouse together. The shoulders slithered down her arms until she was bare to the waist.

As he kissed her neck and shoulder, she said, "What if someone comes?'

"Actually," Jason said with a chuckle, "if someone comes it will be me. You ladies make me so hot." He patted the crotch of his suit pants. "My little man is ready to go."

Fortunately, when the door opened at Fran's floor no one was around. She let them into the apartment and they walked quickly into the guest room. "I would like you two to undress me first," Jason said.

Slowly, caressing his body as they went, Carla and Fran removed Jason's clothes. Although he was quite pudgy, his body wasn't unattractive. "Now," he said, "may I return the favor?"

First he undressed Carla, and then she suggested that she'd fill the tub while he undressed Fran. While Fran listened to Carla putter around in the bathroom, Jason almost reverently slid his hands over Fran's still-bare breasts. "No one ever understands the beauty in small breasts. They seem to be obsessed with huge melons, like Louise had. Not that I'm averse to breasts in any size, but you, your body is so beautiful." He leaned over and kissed Fran's breast. "So beautiful." He kissed her belly. "Take off your shoes. I love how tiny you are."

She quickly complied. The feeling of his near-worship of her body filled Fran with feelings of tender heat. She allowed her head to fall back and placed her hands on Jason's naked hips while he caressed her. "You feel so good," she said. "I love it when you touch me."

"And I love it when you tell me that you are enjoying what I do. Tell me more."

"Your hands are strong and so soft. They seem to be able to play my body like an instrument. It makes my knees tremble and my lips are getting swollen and so wet."

"Oh, baby," he groaned. "Any more comments like that and I'll come right now."

"Would that be so bad?" Fran asked as Jason pulled her blouse and skirt down until the garments puddled at her feet. Then he quickly rolled down stockings and removed them and her panties.

"I never want to rush. That's why the hot bath. It will slow my body down." He took her hand and together they walked to the bathroom.

Carla had already filled the huge tub with steaming water, and added some bath salts. "Oh my," Jason said. "You are right. This tub is a dream come true." He took Carla's hand and, clasping fingers the three climbed into the warm water.

For almost half an hour they soaped each other, rubbing and caressing, playing and teasing. They added more hot water from time to time, but finally all three were starting to shrivel. Jason asked Fran to sit on the edge of the tub and spread her legs. For long minutes, while Carla rubbed his back and shoulders, he licked and sucked Fran's pussy. Then he urged Carla to sit on the tub and he lavished his affection on her cunt as well.

"I think it's time to get out," he said, standing and allowing water to sluice off of his body. They got three enormous white towels and began to dry each other. Fran knelt at Jason's feet, now eye level with his soft cock. "Using a towel seems like such a waste. Let me dry it this way." She took him in her hands, caressed his cock, then placed it into her mouth.

He gasped as Fran created a vacuum in her mouth and drew his cock further inside. "That's not getting it dry," he said. "But it sure feels wonderful."

His cock grew larger as Fran sucked. Soon he pushed her away. "Let's go inside." They spread towels on the bed and Jason stretched out. "This is every man's fantasy," he said, looking at the naked bodies of the two women. "You two are so beautiful. Carla, come here, and Fran, go back to what you were doing. You're so good at that."

Soon, he had his face buried in Carla's pussy, his hand rubbing her wet skin. His other hand was playing with Fran's cunt while she sucked his cock. "Oh yes, baby," he said, his cock growing firmer as the moments passed. "Did you bring everything?" he asked.

"Of course," Carla said.

"Then first I want to watch you, Carla my love."

"I would like that." While Fran lay with her cheek against Jason's belly, he watched as Carla rubbed her cunt and pulled at her breasts. After several minutes, she said, "Help me, Jason."

Jason leaned over and pulled a thick dildo from Carla's purse. Without hesitation, he rammed it home, then put his face between Carla's legs. In only a few moments, she screamed as she climaxed. "Now do it for me," he said, as Carla withdrew the dildo from her sopping pussy.

Carla got her purse, then unrolled a condom over Jason's now-hard cock. Then she put on a rubber glove. Jason lay on his back and grabbed Fran by the waist and lifted her until he could impale her on his member. Following his rhythm, she rose and dropped on his erection feeling him fill her pussy. "That feels wonderful," she panted. "Don't stop. Whatever you do don't stop."

Suddenly she felt Carla drive a well-lubricated finger into her ass. "Oh my God," she yelled.

"Oh shit," Jason cried, and Fran guessed that Carla had one finger in his ass as well.

Now the movements of cock and fingers were coordinated so that when Jason's cock filled her, the finger vanished and when she rose off of the cock, the finger thrust into her. The sensations were too much. "Oh God," she yelled. "Don't stop."

"Don't you dare stop," Jason screamed as she felt the first pulses of his climax. Hers was not far behind.

Together, the three rested then Jason rose and dressed. "That was incredible. Carla, my sincere gratitude for introducing me to your wonderful playmate." He took out a handful of bills and put them on the dresser. Fran wanted to tell him that she would have done this for nothing, but then again, this was Carla's business.

"It was truly wonderful," she said.

"Call me," Carla said.

"I will. And if you're in town, Fran, I'd love to have you join us again."

"If I'm in town, I would love to."

"Carla, I assume you'll get a cab later?"

"You go ahead. I'll talk to you soon."

It was a while later when Carla said, "You really have blossomed, Fran, or Nicki, or whoever you are."

"The name doesn't matter anymore. I'm only one person."

"I really wish you lived here. We could have such fun together. Wasn't this a gas?"

"It certainly was." She watched Carla rise and dress. Then Carla picked up the pile of bills and counted half for Fran.

"You could make a nice living here, if you ever decided to move," she said, putting the money on the bed table. "You could get a place, write and," she winked, "earn a bit extra from time to time. I know you'd love Ronnie and she'd love you as well."

"Me. Living here in New York."

"You could pull it off. And what's there for you in Omaha? A job in a video store?"

"How are they going to keep them in Omaha after they've seen New York?"

"How indeed? I'll see you Saturday evening."

"You know with all this excitement, I almost forgot what I'm doing here." She stretched. "Yes. Of course. See you Saturday. Cocktails begin at six."

Carla phoned a car service and, when the doorman buzzed that the car had arrived, she said, "You know, I will miss you like crazy when you go back to Omaha."

"God, I'll miss you too. But maybe not for too long."

Carla stood and held her hands out in front of her. Slowly, she crossed the fingers of both hands. Then, with a breezy, "Good night," she was gone.

Move to New York, Fran thought. What an idea.

Fran arrived at the Manhattan Sheraton at six-thirty Friday evening and made her way up to the suite that Majestic Books had rented. As she entered, the room was already filled with more than two dozen people. Many were dressed in street clothes, but a few men were bare chested and barefoot, wearing very little to cover their obvious assets. She removed her trench coat and placed it on a chair.

A man approached her. "You must be Nicki, and I'm to be your escort this evening." He looked her over. "Nice outfit," he said. She had to agree. She had rented a pink and green flowered sarong that draped seductively over one shoulder and across her breasts. It was cut to below the knee on one side and far up her hip on the other. She had arranged her hair so it was slicked back behind one ear, held there by several pins and a large blood-red orchid, exactly like the one on the cover of her book.

She looked at the man who had spoken. "You look very familiar," she said. "Do I know you?" He was very tall and bare to the waist with just a strip of bright red cloth around his loins. She had to admit that he had a gorgeous body, smooth and muscular, just the way she had described the island men in her book.

"In a way. I'm on the back cover of *The Love Flower*."

Fran burst out laughing. "Of course. You're the famous Marco. I've seen quite a number of your covers."

"Marco's a stage name. Actually mine's Brad. Brad Crajeski. And you're gorgeous. They should have used you in that shot."

"Yeah," Fran said, craning her neck despite her three-inch heels. "And I could have stood on a box for that kiss. How tall are you?"

"I'm actually six one, but I say I'm five eleven and a half. It gets me better jobs."

"Well, Brad, I think we're supposed to mingle."

And mingle they did. Eileen and Sandy were already there and they introduced Fran to their husbands, and then to several people with familiar names from the world of romance publishing. For more than two hours, she smiled, behaved slightly outrageously as Nicki would have and in general had a wonderful time.

When, for the hundredth time, someone said, "Wow, that was quite a book," she slipped out into the hall and took a few deep breaths.

"You must be Nicki," a woman's voice said. She was wearing worn jeans and a plaid shirt, a wide-brimmed western hat and boots with high heels.

"Yes," Fran said patiently, extending a sore hand. "I'm Nichole St. Michelle. Thank you for coming."

"I just came to see the woman who wrote that piece of trash." The woman's eyes slid down her body, then back up to her face. "I expected you to look like a slut, and you do." The smile was nasty and didn't reach her eyes. "I just thought I'd take a look at the least of my competitors."

"Competitors?" Fran sputtered.

"I'm Diane Barklay and I've got what I came for. I saw you and you look like someone who should have a nine-hundred exchange phone number tattooed on your chest with the words, 'For a good time, call me.' It's nice to know that you write like the whore you are." She glared at Fran. "Of course it does sell books to the perverted segment of our population. That's why there are no people on the cover, so the weirdos can read it without anyone thinking they're reading the pornography it really is." She turned on her heel and strode away.

Fran didn't want to admit how shaken she was. Slut. The woman had called her a whore. In her mind she repeated, over and over, "Sticks and stones." But the names had hurt her. She caught a glimpse of herself in the mirror across from the elevators. Who the hell was she? She was half dressed, here in a midtown hotel filled with tourists from the Midwest. And she was really a tourist from the Midwest and she did look like a whore. She had to admit that she had behaved like one for three weeks. She was seven kinds of fool. She brushed the moisture from her eyes. But she'd be back in Omaha where she belonged on Sunday afternoon and back at work the following day.

She hurried back to the suite to say her goodbyes. She wanted no part of this anymore. Maybe she wouldn't even show up for the damn awards ceremony. But no, she thought as she sought out Eileen and Sandy, each looking very conservative in spring suits, she owed it to them to at least show up. "Nicki, there you are," Sandy said. "I want you to meet someone."

Fran plastered a smile on her face and prepared for the standard greeting, after which she would run for the hills. "This is Ty Gardener," Sandy said. "He's the CEO of Aurora Books and one of the judges."

Swell, Fran thought. One of those traditional, old-school, stuffy pillars of the publishing world. She turned and looked into a pair of sea green eyes. "Ms. St. Michelle," the man said. "I'm delighted to meet you."

Fran took in the man's deep brown hair with the white wings at the temples. "Mr. Gardener. It's so nice to meet you."

"Let's eliminate this formal Mr. and Ms. stuff. I'm Ty."

Fran smiled in spite of herself. "I'm Nicki." His handshake was firm and she winced slightly.

"You know, I should learn not to do that, shake hands with authors at these things, that is. Your hand must be sore after shaking everyone's paw this evening. How many people do you figure you've greeted?"

She felt her shoulders relax a bit. "Several thousand, or at least it feels that way."

When they had been silent for a moment, Sandy jumped in. "Ty is one of the new stars in publishing. But don't let him sucker you in. Your next book is ours."

"Of course, Sandy," Ty said.

"Ty's on the judging committee because Aurora's *Heavenly Hosts* won last year."

"Do you have any of your books nominated this year?" Fran asked.

"No, or I would have declined to judge. And I've read all the books. I'm really very impressed with your talent, Nicki."

After what Diane had said, his remark struck her as hilarious so Nicki's laugh was immediate. "Thanks for the kind words." The wine she had been drinking and the fact that her emotions were so close to the surface made her add, "But I don't believe a word of it."

The startled expression on Ty's face was genuine. "Excuse me?"

"I'm really sorry. I just had someone tell me the truth about the book. My ears are still ringing."

When Ty took her hand, she realized that it was cold as ice in his warm one. He led Fran to a pair of chairs at the side of the room. "Why don't you tell me what *someone* told you."

Her voice shaking with a combination of embarrassment and deep sadness, Fran dutifully repeated Diane's words without revealing her identity. When she finished, she wondered why she was talking about this most difficult subject to a perfect stranger. She blinked rapidly to control the tears that threatened to spill over.

"Nice looking woman, maybe in her thirties, in a western outfit?"

When Fran nodded, Ty continued, "Listen, Nicki, you must have been talking to Diane Barklay. I recognize the vitriol. She's been stirring up trouble for weeks. She's a very frustrated woman who's been nominated for the second time and wants this award more than anything else. I talked with her for a while earlier and she all but offered me her body in exchange for my vote. I don't know why it's so important to her and we could play psycho babble all evening to try to figure it out, but why bother. Suffice it to say that she's not a disinterested party."

"But the book's still pornography."

"Let's define the terms here. What's pornography to you?"

"Trashy. Dirty. Kinky."

"And?"

"And the book's full of sex. I just thought I was adding a little spice to the story."

"You did. And that's just great. People enjoy reading your book. Look at the sales."

"Yes, but most of them are reading it to get turned on."

"So?"

Fran hesitated. What was so bad about a book that turned readers on? This was fiction and fiction was designed to rouse emotion. So what if hers aroused more than that.

Ty smiled and continued to hold Fran's hand. "I can see the wheels turning. Are there people who will take offense at your writing? Probably. Are there people who think Stephen King and Dean Koontz are too violent? Definitely. Are there people who want Jackie Collins' books banned. Of course. So what?"

Fran took a deep breath. He was right.

"And why do you think *The Love Flower* was nominated for The Madison Prize. It's a well-written, well-constructed romance novel. Is it more explicit than the ones we usually honor? Yes. But that didn't prevent us from considering it and considering it quite seriously."

Another sigh. "I guess."

"And I assume you write because you enjoy it, not to be nominated for some prize. Right?"

"Right."

"Well Nicki, then write. Because you want to. And I hope to see more books like this from you. As an author you've got a clear voice that says, 'Hot, enjoyable coupling is okay,' and that's an important message. For everyone." He winked, took her hand and, with a flourish, kissed it.

Fran blushed. Everything he said made sense. Nicki's existence made sense. And Nicki made her happy so what was wrong with that. She returned the squeeze of her hand. "Thanks. As they say in the cliché films, 'I needed that.' And what you say makes wonderful sense."

"I'm so glad. So whether your book wins or loses makes very little difference. And, by the way, I have no clue. We'll meet tomorrow afternoon to decide. But remember this. You've got a great voice and a valuable message. Don't stop writing."

Together they stood up and, feeling wonderfully refreshed, Fran returned to Sandy and Eileen. "What was that all about? Do you know who's going to win? Did he tell you anything?"

"He told me a lot, but it had nothing to do with who's going to win. We won't know that until tomorrow evening."

Back in the apartment that evening, Fran put in a call to her mother in Colorado. "Is something wrong?" her mother asked quickly. "You usually call on Sundays."

"I know, Mom, but I've got something I probably should have told you long ago."

"Oh my." Her mother's voice was suddenly filled with concern.

"I'm not just in New York on vacation. I wrote a romance

novel a while ago and it was nominated for a prize. The dinner is
tomorrow evening and I'll know then whether it won. I'm sure
that I didn't, but it's a great honor to be nominated."

"Oh darling, that's wonderful. Why haven't you told me this
before?"

"I was afraid you'd think less of me. The book's a bit racy."

"I don't understand. I read a lot of romances, but I never read
anything by you."

"I wrote it under a pseudonym. I guess I was a bit embarrassed."

"You're hedging. Come on, out with it. What's the name of the
book?"

"I wrote *The Love Flower* under the name Nichole St. Michelle."

There were several seconds of absolute silence on the other
end of the phone. "Oh my. I've got a copy of the book right
here," the older woman said. "I never imagined. Oh my." She
started to laugh. "I never imagined. . . ."

Fran lifted her chin and just waited for her mother's reaction.

"You know, I gave a section of it to your father to read. That
initiation scene where Rhona's introduced to sex by the priest.
Well, I don't know whether I should tell you this, but, let's just
say he enjoyed it as much as I did a few minutes later."

The picture of her parents rolling around the bed flashed
through Fran's mind. "Mother!"

"Wait until I tell your father. Oh my. Oh my."

The two women talked for another half an hour, her mother
anxious to hear the details of everything from getting the book
published to the prize nomination. Finally, when Fran had told
her mother everything she could, she finally said, "Listen, Mom,
it's been a really long day and I've got to sit and sign books all afternoon tomorrow."

"Of course, dear. I keep forgetting the time difference. Get
some sleep so you'll look wonderful tomorrow. What are you
wearing?"

After another few minutes of fashion tips, her mother finally
said, "I can't wait to tell your father. I just can't wait. Please call

me as soon as you know about the prize. I just can't wait to tell your father. This is so exciting. Can I call Susan and tell her?"

The thought of going through the entire thing again for her sister exhausted her so Fran said, "Of course, Mom. Call Susan and give her all the gory details. I'll call you both tomorrow evening late."

"Just one more thing. How long will you be in New York?"

"I'm scheduled to go back to Omaha on Sunday."

"Any thoughts of moving to *The Big Apple*?" her mother asked, giggling over the term. "To be closer to the publishing world and such?"

"Actually, I'm seriously considering it." She might just do that.

"I can't wait to hear about the prize."

Fran heard her mother cover the mouthpiece of the phone and yell, "Vince, get up here. I've got very exciting news from Fran." She uncovered the phone. "Darling, I'll let you go. We love you and miss you."

"I love you too, Mom. And give my love to Daddy."

The two women blew kisses into the phone and then the line went dead. Slowly Fran hung up the receiver. She lay on the bed for several minutes, then went to her laptop and began to type. "*Pleasures*. A book proposal by Nichole St. Michelle."

The following day whizzed by in a blur. Fran sat at the velvet-covered table in the main room of the conference and signed books for gushing women who were, "So honored to have an autographed copy." Many confided that they already had copies of the book but they wanted another one, signed to them personally. Several women whispered that they had had great sex with their husbands after reading a particular scene. And the questions soon became repetitive and she gave that same charming answer each time.

"Ms. Michelle, who makes better lovers, French men or Italians?"

"I love men, no matter where they're from," she would answer.

"Don't you just love the Louvre?"

"You know, I prefer being with people to being with great art."

"I've always wanted to write a book like yours, Ms. St. Michelle. How did you get started?"

"I just sat down at a word processor and began to type. I used both my life and my fantasies in the book."

"Have you done *everything* that Rhona did?"

She smiled. "And more."

It was the most exhilarating afternoon of her life.

As the afternoon wore down, she chuckled internally as she realized that she hadn't really needed all the "education" she'd worked so hard to get. She talked a good game and that was all that mattered. And with Jason, she'd been intelligent and witty, without pretense.

At five, she dashed back to her apartment to change for the dinner. She put on a black sequined top with a gold geometric design and her long black skirt. She fluffed her hair, put on shoulder-dusting gold earrings and carefully applied her makeup. She had a serious look at herself and realized that she was an amalgam of Nichole and Fran, and she liked it that way. She was herself and that was wonderful.

When she arrived at the door of the ballroom, there was a slight delay in finding her table assignment so she stood to one side, waiting. A woman's voice hissed from behind her. "Well. I'm surprised you even showed up."

Fran turned to see Diane Barklay. Her stomach clenched, but she forced her muscles to relax. She took a deep breath. "You know," Fran said, gently, "I hope you win."

"Excuse me?" Diane said.

"I just said that I hope you win. You obviously have so little that this is enormously important to you." She brushed some nonexistent lint from her shoulder. "I have so much that this is of little consequence. Obviously you need it more than I do."

Diane's mouth fell open as someone handed Fran her place card and she walked away.

She found her table and joined Sandy and Eileen and their

husbands, and Carla and several other editors from Majestic Books. The evening sped by. At one point, she slipped Eileen a fifteen-page proposal for her new book. "It's really good," Fran whispered. "I can't wait to get started on it."

"I have no doubt that it's wonderful. Sandy and I loved the idea when you told us about it so I'll read it and, unless there's some problem, I'll pass it along to Sandy."

Later, she and Carla again discussed the possibility of Fran's moving to New York. "It would be so great," Carla said. "I'm really down at the thought of never seeing you again. We've gotten so close. And, besides Ronnie, I don't have a lot of real friends."

Fran grinned. "Me too. I think you'll be hearing from me sooner than you might expect."

The lights dimmed and a man walked up to the podium. "That's Peter Hunt," Sandy whispered in Fran's ear.

"Who's he?"

Sandy turned to her. "Only the most influential literary agent in New York."

"Oh," Fran said.

After several stale jokes, Peter Hunt said, "Ladies and gentlemen, the time has come to announce this year's winner of The Madison Prize. Let me take a minute to congratulate all the nominees." He called the five names and each stood to loud applause. Fran's was the last name called and she rose, listened to the ovation, then quickly sat back down.

"Each of this year's novels had something a little different to offer and our choice was a difficult one. We had Alaska, World War I, we had passion and great writing."

He paused as the audience again applauded the nominees. "We discussed it all at great length and finally decided to give this year's Madison Prize to an author whose work has grown and expanded over the years, who has taken us from Barbara Cartland's fade-to-black-in-the-bedroom to Nichole St. Michelle's wonderfully erotic novel."

Fran realized that, although it was obvious that she hadn't won, she was being paid a great compliment.

"So I am proud to award the prize to Virginia Cortez."

Amid a tremendous round of applause, a large woman, clothed in lots of flowing rayon, rose and walked to the podium. Sandy squeezed Fran's hand. "I'm really sorry."

"You know," Fran whispered, "I'm disappointed, of course, but I'm going to write *Pleasures* and I'm going to enjoy doing it. I just love all of this."

"That's a great attitude."

After the presentation, the crowd quickly dispersed. Fran caught a glimpse of Diane on the arm of an attractive man. She looked dejected but Fran knew she would adjust and probably be nominated again.

As she stood up to leave, she gathered Carla, Eileen and Sandy around her. "You know what I've discovered?" Fran said to the three women who had become so important to her. "It took all this to help me understand what makes me happy. First, and most important, friends." She hugged each woman tightly. "And then my writing and living life to the fullest. If not now, when? So I'm going after it. I think I'm going to move here and do what I love." She winked at Carla, whose eyes sparkled with amusement.

"All I can say is that I'm thrilled and excited and I can't wait to begin."

GREAT BOOKS,
GREAT SAVINGS!

When You Visit Our Website:
www.kensingtonbooks.com
You Can Save Money Off The Retail Price
Of Any Book You Purchase!

- **All Your Favorite Kensington Authors**
- **New Releases & Timeless Classics**
- **Overnight Shipping Available**
- **eBooks Available For Many Titles**
- **All Major Credit Cards Accepted**

Visit Us Today To Start Saving!
www.kensingtonbooks.com

All Orders Are Subject To Availability.
Shipping and Handling Charges Apply.
Offers and Prices Subject To Change Without Notice.